"Give Hubscher's latest . . . to fans of enemies-to-lovers stories and those looking for humor in their romance."

—*Library Journal*

Praise for

IF YOU ASK ME

"A gracefully crafted tribute to searching for the right answer—and to finally realizing that sometimes it doesn't exist. *If You Ask Me* is a heart-mending tale about the importance of being our authentic selves, and the joys to be found in embracing our vulnerability. Equal parts funny and moving, Violet's messy, hopeful journey and her beautiful romance will resonate with everyone who struggles with the unexpected twists and turns of life. Libby Hubscher is a master at creating compelling, relatable characters and heartwarming, emotional stories. I cannot wait for her next book!"

—#1 *New York Times* bestselling author Ali Hazelwood

"I gasped, I ground my teeth, and I cheered along with Violet as she gathered the smashed pieces of her life and used them to build something better than before."

—*USA Today* bestselling author Jesse Q. Sutanto

"Full of Southern charm and self-discovery. Libby Hubscher brings a light touch to heavy emotions in this witty novel about starting over in life and in love."

—*New York Times* bestselling author Virginia Kantra

"A funny, feminist, feel-good novel about making mistakes, asking for advice, and writing your own happy ending. I laughed and I cried—this novel is an absolute joy!"

—Freya Sampson, *USA Today* bestselling author of
The Busybody Book Club

"*Meet Me in Paradise* will sweep you off your feet. Marin's leap into the unknown is full of love, romance, and adventure, and I felt like I was right there with her on the pristine beaches of Saba as she climbs mountains, dives for pearls, and learns how to open herself up to the possibilities of love."

—Sonya Lalli, author of *Jasmine and Jake Rock the Boat*

"Hubscher's debut novel is the perfect book for anyone longing for family, travel, and romance. Prepare for some tears mixed with the happy-ever-afters." —*Library Journal*

"A poignant, emotionally authentic story of sisterly bonds and unexpected love. . . . This is sure to tug at readers' heartstrings."

—*Publishers Weekly* (starred review)

"Debuting author Hubscher gently weaves in the more somber story lines, so readers aren't blindsided yet will still feel the full emotional impact. The romance blooms beautifully, and while there are several complex and endearing secondary characters, this is primarily Marin's story told mostly through her own captivating narrative. Tissues should be on hand." —*Booklist*

"Not simply a breezy romantic comedy, *Meet Me in Paradise* captures the duality of life's highs and lows. This romantic comedy offers tropical vacation mishaps, a burgeoning romance, and an undercurrent of heartbreak." —Shelf Awareness

TITLES BY LIBBY HUBSCHER

HEART
MARKS
the
SPOT

LIBBY HUBSCHER

BERKLEY ROMANCE
NEW YORK

BERKLEY ROMANCE
Published by Berkley
An imprint of Penguin Random House LLC
1745 Broadway, New York, NY 10019
penguinrandomhouse.com

Book design by Kristin del Rosario
Interior art: Heart compass by Vikki Chu;
Paper background © Mark Carrel/Shutterstock

Library of Congress Cataloging-in-Publication Data

Names: Hubscher, Libby, author.
Title: Heart marks the spot / Libby Hubscher.
Description: First edition. | New York : Berkley Romance, 2025.
Identifiers: LCCN 2024050605 | ISBN 9780593547243 (trade paperback) |
ISBN 9780593547250 (ebook)
Subjects: LCGFT: Romance fiction. | Novels.
Classification: LCC PS3608.U2524 H43 2025 | DDC 813/.6—dc23/eng/20241119
LC record available at https://lccn.loc.gov/2024050605

First Edition: July 2025

Printed in the United States of America
1st Printing

The authorized representative in the EU for product safety and compliance is
Penguin Random House Ireland, Morrison Chambers, 32 Nassau Street,
Dublin D02 YH68, Ireland, https://eu-contact.penguin.ie.

For everyone clinging to
that last little bit of hope

AUTHOR'S NOTE

Treasure hunting is a bit like reading a book for the first time. It's a leap of faith and bit of a risk for the potential promise of a great reward. While this adventure is full of romantic fun and ends in a happily ever after, there are some challenges and sensitive matters along the way. This book touches on themes of parental and romantic abandonment, verbal abuse, death of a parent in the past, and alcohol abuse. Brief minor violence, peril (including a serious life-endangering underwater event), and sea sickness are also present. If these topics are sensitive for you, please embark with care.

HEART
MARKS
the
SPOT

PART ONE

THE PAST

· · · · ·

Hunting for treasure isn't always daring
adventure
and markings on maps,
Sometimes it's the universe aligning
on a quiet night far from home
To bring you and the thing you're looking for
together in the same place.
I came to Iceland searching for something
And I found him.
If only we'd been ready
The first time we fell for each other.

*So, I love you because the entire universe
conspired to help me find you.*

—PAULO COELHO, *THE ALCHEMIST*

ONE

Stella

I've made a life out of searching for lost things. Not tonight, though. After nearly two weeks of trekking around the wilds of western Iceland in the hopes of unearthing the fabled Gunnarsson's treasure and coming up empty, my friends have forced me into a laid-back evening in a bar in Selfoss. I protested at first, but then Zoe presented her blistered feet, Gus muttered something about how this November trip was *supposed* to be a vacation, and Teddy fixed his deep blue eyes on mine, his expression half-pleading, half-dare. I caved like a bridge made of tissue paper.

Gus parked the camper van at the edge of a small gravel lot, and we pulled on our coats and headed into the damp cold toward the bar Teddy had heard about from a local while picking up groceries at Bónus. Hlýjar Nætur—Warm Nights, according to Zoe's pocket phrase book—was housed in a squat metal building next to an outdoor outfitter. The interior lived up to its name, with rich wood accents, fireplaces, and a variety of subdued, eclectic lights ranging from chandeliers to bare bulbs hanging from the ceilings. It was cozy. We found a dim nook in a corner and plunked down on soft vintage couches.

"Aren't you glad you listened to us, Stella?" Teddy asked, pulling off his hat and leaving his sandy blond hair in disarray. He tousled it back into submission. "This place is perfect."

A small group of women standing nearby eyed him. "I'll say," one with a distinctly Australian accent said before clapping a hand over her mouth. Her companions giggled and then migrated out of earshot.

Zoe pushed back her cloud of dark curls and scrunched her face. Over the years, we'd grown accustomed to having an audience when Teddy was around. The amalgamation of his James Dean looks and charming charisma often proved magnetic. He enjoyed the attention, and as a result he was never lonely, even if his admirers never stuck for long.

"What's everyone drinking?" I asked. "My treat."

"Beer," Gus said.

"Vodka on the rocks." Zoe tipped her head toward her feet. "For the pain."

"I'm sorry," I said. "I did warn you to break in your boots."

"She feels no remorse," Zoe said, a smile playing on her lips.

"If Stella's buying drinks she must feel pretty bad," Gus told her. "When was the last time she took us out?"

"Three seasons ago, Key West," Teddy said.

"Oh yeah." Zoe reached down to massage her socked foot. "It was so rough that day and we were in that tiny boat, the one we had before the *Lucky Strike*. Stell refused to go in because the metal detector we were towing had turned up something. Gus and I were both so sick. He threw up in the cooler."

The image of Gus's hulking figure hugging the Igloo to his chest had been impossible to forget, and that *something* had turned out to be nothing exciting, just some chain. I'd spent the rest of the trip trying to atone for the bad call.

"Stella's very focused," Teddy said, draping an arm around me. "And we love her for it. Without her leadership, we'd all have soft hands and no stories. C'mon, vicious leader. Let's fetch the refreshments."

"I do feel bad about Zoe's feet, and Gus having to throw up in a cooler," I confessed to Teddy once we were clear of our friends.

"Bad enough to call it quits on this trip?"

"Let's not get ahead of ourselves."

"I knew you'd say that. I also knew that the whole vacation thing was complete bullshit and you'd have us wandering near and far looking for the next clue to the location of the Stolen Treasure. Hence why I broke in my boots."

I glanced over at Teddy, trying to maintain a neutral expression.

He raised his eyebrows and stared me down comically. "Admit it. I'm right, aren't I? Gunnarsson's treasure is a clue, just a means to an end . . . if we ever find the damn thing, that is."

"You know me best," I admitted. He did. Me being so utterly fixated on treasure that I forgot we should also be having a good time was nothing new, but my reasons for searching were not the same as my friends'. They loved the exploring, the diving, the possibility of it. Not me. Treasure hunting was in my blood and I had something to prove. It was serendipity that the four of us had met in the Outer Banks of North Carolina ten years ago and found a Piece of Eight that we were convinced was part of Blackbeard's treasure. After that, they were hooked. Each summer, we'd come together for one month, just the four of us, in search of legendary riches based on clues from the past, my past, enjoying each other and the thrill of the hunt until we had to go back to the real world. Teddy still wore that Piece of Eight around his neck—matching the one my parents gave me on my eighth birthday that I'd never taken off. Anyway, for my friends, the enjoying part was especially important, since so far our trips had yielded plenty of memories, one gorgeous ruby pendant that Teddy's lawyers were in a legal battle with the Bahamian government over, a slew of antique coins, some small chips of emeralds, the infamous chain, and a lot of rusted-out trash. Nothing of any remarkable value that we could claim as our own. We had yet to find a major wreck, and my main objective—the Stolen Treasure of the Sea People and the rare red Elephant's Heart Diamond it was fabled to contain—was proving as elusive as whispered legends told. But this trip was different. It wasn't just the change of our usual timing or the location of the search. The aching sensation in my hands that started the moment we'd set foot in Iceland told me we were close to finally finding something big.

"How about tomorrow we do something fun and relaxing and I can make it up to them before they head back to the States?" I said. "Maybe we could head north and visit the Secret Lagoon in Flúðir?"

"Sounds great. And then afterward we can check out whatever bog is nearby and see if Gunnarsson's gold is hidden beneath it. There's probably one on the way to the airport, right? It's adorable that we've been friends as long as we have and you still think you can fool me." He laughed. "We all know what we're signing up for when we take these trips. I support you. Especially since I've invested half my trust fund in you by now. Honestly, at this point I have no option but to wait around for my payday."

I bumped Teddy with my shoulder. "I'm not sure which part of that is more ridiculous—the idea that you've spent half your money or that you're only here to cash in once we finally find our treasure."

"It's lucky for you that I am so loyal," he told me. "Those two would leave you for an all-inclusive spa in St. Thomas first chance they get. They're nowhere near as hard-core as us."

I glanced back to where Zoe and Gus were nestled on a love seat. "I don't know about that," I mumbled. "They were pretty hard-core last night."

"I think it's nice that they're taking it to the next level after all the years of pining."

"You wouldn't be saying that if they were bumping into you during their sleeping bag gymnastic routine while you were desperately trying to sleep, but where were you again . . . ? Sigrún, Helga; gosh, I don't know, Ted. It's getting hard to keep track of all your local sleepovers."

I wanted to be happy for my friends, but I did not think their hooking up was nice. I thought it was dangerous. Sure, it seems lovely at first, two old buddies taking it to the next level, but the higher you go, the harder you fall. I knew this well. I couldn't keep myself from exploring the possibility of what would happen if it didn't work out. There was a distinct chance that our friend group, this little family of ours, wouldn't survive the impact. Sure, the rest of them had fallback plans, jobs, and families, but they were it for me . . . except for my mission to find my own personal holy grail. Nope. Bringing romance into our mix was a terrible idea. Teddy's approach of pure promiscuous tourism seemed more advisable. But even that made me feel a bit irked. These trips were supposed to be about spending time together and finally finding major treasure after so many tries, getting closer to what the whole treasure hunting world thought unfindable, but this time around, it seemed like my pals were more focused on the wrong kind of getting lucky.

"Stop overthinking, Stella," Teddy said, using his thumbs to flatten my furrowed brow. "The only trouble with this situation is that we should've gotten two camper vans so you didn't have to be subjected to their amorous activities—since for some inexplicable reason you refuse to engage in any yourself." He handed me his credit card and I glared at him. "I'm going to hit the bathroom. Order me an Einstök white ale, will you? I'll help you carry everything back."

"I *engage*," I muttered to his back. "Sometimes." Which was true. I had been known to have a stint of amorous activity here and there, provided it stayed light and easy and I didn't get invested. Getting invested in treasure was one thing, but signing up for potential heartbreak—that was not something I did. At least Ted and I were in agreement that it was best to keep our extracurricular activities purely fun and casual. I flagged down a woman with pale hair behind the bar. "Can I get a vodka on the rocks and three white ales?"

"Have you tried the Icelandic Doppelbok?"

I turned to face the owner of the voice that was deep and so rich, it bordered on buttery. He was slouching on a barstool next to me, picking at the label of his beer. Dark hair, the jet-black of a volcanic sand beach, blocked the top half of his face from view.

"What's so great about the Dopplebok other than the fun name and the"—I leaned a bit closer to eye the label—"Rudolph the red-nosed Viking gracing the bottle?"

He turned slowly, lifting his face, using one hand to push his hair back and the other to slide the beer toward me. "See for yourself."

The stranger's irises were a striking, glacial blue. I followed the line of his nose down to full, unsmiling lips and a jaw that was as strong as it was sharp. At first glance, he was exactly the kind of man I might like to *engage* with for the evening, if it hadn't been for the defeated expression and shadowy half-moons beneath his eyes that screamed of sleeplessness. It was odd, but he almost looked like someone I'd seen before, I just couldn't think of where. I spent enough time trying to place him that the bartender cleared her throat. I picked up the bottle and lifted it to my lips. The beer he recommended tasted of malt and chocolate, with a smooth, rich finish . . . and I wasn't even much of a beer drinker.

"That is delicious," I said to the guy. "You are good."

He took the beer back from me. "Thanks. You might be alone in that particular sentiment, though. I can think of literally thousands of people who wouldn't agree, including several book reviewers."

"Can I get two Doppleboks as well?" I asked the bartender. I handed the extra beer to the man. "You look like you could use a refill. What's this about a book reviewer?" I asked.

"You heard that?" He cringed.

"Afraid so."

He was silent for a beat, his expression pensive. "I'm a novelist."

"Really?"

"Well, I'm not sure I still am, but I was once. Is that so unbelievable?" he asked.

I shrugged. "It just seems like the kind of career that everyone has in movies or books, but no one actually really does. What do you write?"

"Adventure fiction, mostly." He paused. "Currently, I'm doing everything *but* writing."

"Anything I might know?"

This stretch of silence was longer than the first. "The Casablanca Chronicles." He said the series title so nonchalantly that I almost missed it.

This guy could not be serious right now. Did I know it? It was only my favorite series of all time. When I found out that it was over and I'd never learn the fate of the main character, Clark Casablanca, I'd spent an evening drowning my sorrows in too many gin gimlets—Clark's drink of choice—and contemplating ways to compel the author to write one more book. *That's* why this guy looked familiar—I had seen him before, in his author photo on the back of his book jackets, but he'd had a beard and worn glasses in the picture.

"I've heard of it," I said. Then, playing it cool, I added, "What's your name again?"

"Huck Sullivan." *Huck Sullivan.* Frenetic energy filled me. I stretched out a trembling hand to shake his. I was sharing a beer with Huck-freaking-Sullivan. I was about to have actual human contact with Huck Sullivan. I resisted the urge to pinch myself.

"I'm Stella Moore." Huck wrapped his fingers around mine, and that strange longing I'd been feeling in my fingertips dissipated in an instant, replaced by a light tingle on my skin. His hand was warm and his grip strong, but not overly firm.

"So, Stella who thinks being an author is unbelievable, what do you do for work?"

I lifted my shoulders a fraction. "This and that," I said, which was true, but really I was trying to sound intriguing. The fact that I spent my off seasons doing property maintenance and moonlighting on fishing boats wasn't the first impression I wanted my favorite author to have of me. Besides, I'd learned that it was safer not to share too much of myself.

"Very mysterious. What brings you to Iceland, then?"

"You first," I challenged.

I expected him to counter, but instead, he pulled at the corner of the bottle label. "I guess you could say I'm searching for inspiration," he said. "I'm supposed to be working on a new book. Easier said than done after the way the last one went down."

I wanted to say something encouraging, but I didn't have any idea what. The final book in the Casablanca Chronicles had been beautiful, but the ending . . . it was like driving down a gorgeous, winding highway, wind blowing in your hair, warm salt breeze on your skin, and then suddenly the road is gone and the car simply plummets into the sea. I remembered buying a second copy because I was sure that mine had been a misprint and was missing the last fifty pages or so. The critics had hated it. Literary legend to epic letdown, the rise and demise of the Casablanca Chronicles. *It's like Huck Sullivan just gave up*, the *New York Times* had printed.

It seemed unnecessarily mean, but then, they hadn't been wrong. Ostensibly, he *had* given up. He hadn't had a book out in three years.

"Everything I've written since then is awful, trite bullshit. Or some knockoff of a classic, done worse, mind you. I can barely even look at my laptop, let alone open it. I guess I thought a change of scene to someplace wild and completely different would shake me out of my funk—well, my agent did. I'm not exactly here of my own volition . . ."

"How's that going?"

"Super. So far, all this trip has done is make me strongly consider switching my profession to sheep farming."

"The sheep are pretty cute."

That won a smile from him, and it was just as warm and inviting as I anticipated. "Right? I went over to the Westman Islands and I was standing in a field near this cliff, high above the ocean, contemplating my place in the world, and one waddled over to me and booped me on the leg with its nose."

"Sounds life-changing."

"Oh, it was. Didn't cure my writer's block, but I felt much less inclined to hurl myself into the sea, so there's that. Anyway, I've told you my story, Stella Moore. Now it's your turn."

I wondered if I should tell him. What the four of us do on our expeditions is something that we keep to ourselves—after all, treasure hunting has its dangers—but there was something about Huck Sullivan that made me want to spill my soul. Maybe it was because I'd read his books and that made me feel like I knew the kind of man he was . . . someone brave and trustworthy and authentic. Someone who had just been totally vulnerable with me.

Someone who would find my focus compelling instead of thinking I was a stupid dreamer.

I don't know why, but I didn't want to hold back the way I normally did.

I wanted to tell him.

Because the Huck Sullivan I knew from reading every word he'd ever written was going to eat this up. I hoped. And not just because I'd been fantasizing about him since book two, *The Einstein Endeavor.*

I took a breath and tried not to think about the number of times I'd pictured an innocent book signing event ending with us entangled in the back room of Barnes & Noble. I hoped the flush in my cheeks could pass for being alcohol related instead of a lustful fantasy fulfillment. "Believe it or not, I am also searching for something."

The corner of his mouth quirked. "Oh yeah, what's that?"

I pressed my lips together for a moment, preparing to be laughed at.

"I'm hunting for a treasure."

Understanding flashed in his eyes, an instant of lightning in the glacial pool, and it was as if my body forgot how to breathe. I had to force myself to take in air. He rotated toward me on his stool; in the process, his knee glanced my thigh and practically turned me into molten lava. "And how's *that* going?" he asked, his voice low and full of intrigue. "Are you also contemplating a life of sheep farming . . . or have you found it?"

I took a slow sip of my beer, a smile playing on my lips as I lowered the bottle between us. I waved him toward me until our faces were only a whisper apart and made my voice quiet. "So far the only thing I've found is you."

TWO

Huck

Back when I still did publicity for my books—when I still wrote books—an interviewer from NPR asked me how I got my ideas. It was a simple question on the surface. An interest I understood. After all, the creative process and the idiosyncratic nature of inspiration is intriguing. I owed people a glimpse behind the curtain even though a shred of me always worried that, like in *The Wizard of Oz*, they'd end up disappointed by the man with the microphone . . . Still, I should've been happy to share. The people watching bought my books, doled out stars to me like first-grade teachers—Good job, Huck, exclamation point, smiley face. Four and a half stars, rounded up. They paid my rent and fed my self-esteem. They made me forget that I was worthless; at least they did when they loved me, when they told me I was great. I owed them attention, access, answers to their questions. I'd waxed poetic about reaping the fields of my life for kernels of inspiration and the host had nodded along generously, feigning interest, before moving on to a cooking segment with some celebrity chef who didn't have allegations of impropriety yet.

I didn't have an answer for how I got my ideas.

If I knew, I wouldn't have been trying to find them at the

bottom of a bottle of ale in a bar set atop an active volcano. Months ago, my agent and longtime friend, Jim, had decided to get real with me. "Listen, Huck. I've held off the pressure as long as I can. You have to write something. What's it going to take for you to break out of this funk and get something new together?"

I didn't have an answer for that question either. I'd exhausted pretty much every other avenue of unblocking my writing and gotten so demoralized that Jim promptly hung up the phone, booked a trip to Iceland on his own dime, packed my duffel, and shoved me onto the tarmac. He knew me well enough to realize I'd never do it myself.

This trip felt like my last chance to make something, but I'd been failing so miserably that at this point, I figured I might need to move to Iceland permanently, change my name, and go full fucking hermit. No more books, no more questions. The fact that I didn't speak the language was a serious plus. And yet, a woman stood at a bar minding her own business, and for some incomprehensible reason, I found myself *wanting* to talk to her. Even before she'd acknowledged my presence. Even when she recognized my books, which shocked me to my core.

After my last book tanked, I punished myself by reading the posts on social media that called me a has-been, or worse. I got used to seeing my name intentionally mangled to Hack Sullivan and receiving emphatic messages telling me to give up, go underground, never write another thing. Worse things that I couldn't bring myself to talk about. Maybe I'd let those messages get to me. Most of them weren't anything I hadn't heard before. My own inadequacy had been hammered into me even before I put myself out there for public consumption. My aversion to writing had to be more than some form of horrible inertia. After years of trying and now coming up empty on this charity trip to Iceland, a place that could inspire poetry from stone, I was starting to believe that whatever my problem was, it might not be something that I'd ever overcome. And yet, we started talking and we hadn't stopped. I told her about the Casablanca Chronicles and she didn't throw her drink in my face. She somehow managed to make me feel comfortable. I went from telling her about my downfall, something that would normally have sent me to the bottom of a well of self-loathing, to laughing about sheep.

I racked my brain trying to remember the last time I'd laughed. Months? Years? No, had it actually been years? I had binge-watched *Brooklyn Nine-Nine* and *Young Sheldon* in that time, so no, I'd laughed in between, but not with another human. Until her. It was natural. So easy. And then she started telling me about herself and I was hooked. Her focus as she talked was utterly entrancing; I almost forgot about my problems.

"Can I get you another?" the bartender asked.

I shook my head. My beer was empty, but I was so riveted by the story Stella was telling about a Viking named Arnbjörg Gunnarsson who had amassed a fortune in English gold and silver that I was almost drunk on her words. I glanced over at her. There was something about the way she spoke with her hands, in smooth almost artistic arcs and fine gestures. I couldn't bring myself to stop watching her. She practically shimmered with enthusiasm as she described ancient texts and Icelandic legends. I was rapt. The combination of self-assuredness and excitement transformed a topic that could've been considered boring on the surface into one that I couldn't get enough of. Even though I didn't claim the title of writer anymore, I was sure that she had main character energy.

Stella was like a book I wouldn't want to put down. The kind that could keep a person up all night dying to know what happens next. How was it that this majestic ball of energy just happened to appear beside me at this random bar in the middle of Iceland a thousand miles from home? I wondered. I was not a lucky guy;

the past four years had confirmed that for me. But in this random place, she found me, and even though the bar was full of aesthetically pleasing people, who were probably way more interesting than a failed author, she stayed and kept talking with me.

I think I would've found her interesting even if she hadn't been beautiful. She was beautiful, though—hazel eyes, a kaleidoscope of green, gold, and brown; golden hair falling over her shoulders; smooth skin smattered with freckles. Her lips were rosy and vaguely chapped; I found myself staring at her mouth wishing I were the kind of guy who carried a ChapStick in my pocket so I could brandish it like some sort of hero saving the day just to watch her put it on.

"This Gunnarsson guy was a raider?" I asked, trying to get my mind off her lips. "*And* a poet? That's an interesting combination."

She nodded. "It is, isn't it? But yeah, he was supposedly. He's featured in Gunnar's Saga, which details his bloodline, conquests, and how he secretly stashed his treasure. Several epic poems are attributed to him. According to the saga, he took four of his servants out to a bog in the dead of night to hide his treasure, but the servants never returned. The saga mentions a few places in southern Iceland where it might have been stashed, but no one ever claimed to have discovered it."

"Maybe they secretly kept it?"

She shook her head. "I mean, I guess, but chests of ancient English silver, golden armbands, maybe even a massive axe made of precious metals and gems? It's not exactly the kind of thing a person could keep in their hut without anyone finding out. In the absence of any evidence to the contrary, we have to assume it's never been found."

"So, it's still out there somewhere."

She pulled up some pictures on her phone and pushed it toward me. Our fingertips made momentary contact as I took the phone from her, a spark of static electricity discharging between us in the dry air. "There are six cairns that mark important locations in the saga, but this one"—she tapped the table for emphasis—"near Þórsmörk, has a placard that says 'Hér liggur gull og silfur Gunnarsson.'"

I squinted at the image briefly before looking back. She was eyeing me intently, awaiting my reaction.

"Does that mean what it sounds like?" I asked. Even though I'd been in Iceland a few weeks and the many hours spent trying to learn the language had been an exercise in futility, some of the words sounded vaguely familiar.

She gifted me a conspiratorial grin and pushed her hair away from her face. The movement revealed a tattoo shaped like a compass rose, discreetly placed on the nape of her neck, small and special. I liked knowing it was there, this tiny secret treasure on her skin that in that moment in the crowd, only I knew about.

"'Here lies the gold and silver of Gunnarsson,'" she said. "There was no sign of it, though. Anyway, so far we've searched all over southern Iceland, where he lived, but didn't find anything there. Then I had this idea. The saga also says that Gunnarsson never told anyone the true location, and it got me thinking . . . maybe the locations suggested in the saga are wrong? The four men he sent never returned, which suggests to me that he didn't want the location revealed. Gunnarsson was a brilliant man, egotistical and proud. He loved his sons but wanted them to earn his treasure. I started to wonder if we'd missed something. It occurred to me that the only part of the saga that came directly from Gunnarsson were the poems that had been included."

"You're thinking that he left a clue somewhere in one of the poems for his sons to decipher?"

"Exactly. I've been studying the poems trying to see if anything in them reflects a landmark or something that could give us an idea of where the treasure might be hidden, but so far nothing's jumped out. There was a line about gold and giant's bones, so we searched near a peak that looks like the skeleton of an ogre but found nothing."

"Do you have the poems?" I asked.

She nodded and pulled up a document on her phone. "They're all here."

"Mind if I have a go?" I asked.

I pored over the words on the page. The language was beautiful, stark in places, but rife with meaning and imagery. "There's something about a massive tree here."

"Hopefully it wasn't buried beneath a tree," she said. "We'd never find it."

I remembered that Iceland was nearly devoid of trees, mostly as a result of Vikings like Gunnarsson razing the forests long ago, and felt like an idiot. Shit. I returned to the poems and scanned for anything that alluded to treasure or gold. I needed to redeem myself.

My gaze ran over a line. *Gold of my life, spoils of blood spilt and treasure taken, behind the constant storm, within the slice of earth, you wait in dark of night and rainbow of light.* I gulped.

"What? Have you got something?" Stella asked.

"Maybe." I showed her the line.

"'Behind the constant storm,'" she muttered, thinking. Her eyes widened and my heart started to pound. Loud, exciting percussion in my chest, in my ears. It beat the way it used to when I got a really good idea for a story. I wasn't sure exactly what was happening, but I knew what she was thinking. We were completely on the same page.

"Constant storm, like a roaring sound," I said.

"Dark, but with rainbows around in the sun . . . from flowing water." She looked at me, biting her lip.

"Did we just figure this out?" I asked.

She grinned, nodding, her eyes crinkling at their corners, and I felt more alive and inspired than I had in recent memory.

"It's behind a waterfall," we said almost in sync.

A puff of air escaped my lips. "Damn."

"I had a feeling about you when we met, Huck Sullivan. Not everyone can see it, but you do. I can tell about these things."

She was right, which was, frankly, a little freaking terrifying. Because I had a feeling about her too. And if she could tell that I could understand the mystery of the treasure hunt and the clue an ancient writer had left in a poem, she was probably keenly aware of the obsession I was developing with her mouth and the three freckles gracing her pouty bottom lip where I wanted to kiss her under the warm bar lights.

I saw the whole story about the treasure. I saw her.

How do I get my ideas? I imagined myself answering a crowded room with confidence. *Easy. They sidle up to me at a bar in Iceland and change my life.*

I had thought I would never write again, but I didn't think that was true anymore. Now, I had a different problem.

I'd never have an idea as good as her.

No one was that lucky.

THREE

Stella

As a rule, I generally avoided talking to people outside of Teddy, Zoe, and Gus about treasure hunting. We had to be extremely careful who we let inside our circle. In the treasure hunting world, nobody trusted anybody else. Letting the wrong person in could put an entire search at risk or even be dangerous, especially when you were holding on to valuable knowledge like I was. Not only did I now have an important clue about the true location of Gunnarsson's treasure, but beyond that I knew if we found it, we'd likely also discover an important piece of evidence. One that could provide the connection I'd been seeking between the entire treasure trove of the world's first pirates in the Mediterranean Sea off the coast of Africa—the Sea People—and England. It was the kind of find that my dad would've given up everything for, the kind that people killed for. I needed to be more careful than ever. But even if you didn't share anything that had the potential to compromise your search, just mentioning it as a profession didn't usually go well. The few times I'd brought it up in the past resulted in a mixed bag of responses. Some people would get super excited because they'd think I'm rich and maybe they could get in on the action. None of those people had seen my apartment. Others only wanted to hear about glittering gemstones and as soon as I uttered one word about history their eyes would glaze over. Then there was always my personal least favorite—the ones who'd dismiss it—and, honestly, they made up the vast majority. Even if they didn't say anything, I could still read their expressions. It's ludicrous, a waste of time and resources, the stuff of daydreams. It's never going to happen. Or it might happen, but not to me. Even my own father, who would have done absolutely anything to locate the Elephant's Heart, hadn't believed I could find it.

But not Huck Sullivan.

He was interested, watching me intently with those ice-blue eyes that I had to avoid so I could stay focused on what I was saying. Even that was proving to be a challenge. They were very nice eyes. The kind a girl could get lost in. My mind drifted back to those amorous activities I'd pondered earlier. I wondered if I should tell him that if we found this treasure, it was just the beginning.

"There's only one problem," Huck said. "There's so many waterfalls in Iceland. It seems like it could take years to search them all. Is it even possible? That's probably a dumb question. You have a plan already, I'm sure."

"That's the thing. The search area would be massive . . . there's not enough time in our lifetimes to cover it all. But, based on a couple of other lines from the saga, and what we know of Iceland at the time, it could really only be in a couple of zones, which limits our search to a reasonable number of falls."

"I don't believe it!" Teddy dipped his head over my shoulder to kiss my cheek in greeting and then reached one of his long arms over me to grab his beer. I turned to see what was so unbelievable. Had he heard that Huck and I had figured out a totally new angle on where the treasure might really be hidden?

"Of all the gin joints in all the towns in all the world," Teddy said.

Huck rose from his stool with a grin. "Theodore Preston the Third walks into mine. Holy shit, man. How long has it been? How are you, buddy?" They hugged over me, leaving me practically manwiched between them. Not that I felt like complaining. Huck even smelled good, fresh and clean—a nice soap, I guessed—with traces of ocean and woodsmoke.

"Hold on—you two know each other?" I asked.

"This guy?" Huck said, stepping back and nodding at Ted. "We're practically related. Wait, he's never talked about his old boarding school roommate?"

"He's literally never mentioned you," I admitted. Which was wild, considering that if they were rooming together in high school, then Teddy had known Huck longer than he'd known me.

"Theodore, I'm wounded. I covered for you missing curfew so many times, and you pretend I don't exist? Is this because we can never seem to work out that hiking trip we've been talking about since college?"

"I have no desire to hike and you know that. My physique is purely for show. I was, however, pretty chafed when you didn't take me along on your research trip to Amsterdam. What was that? I am made to be a traveling companion in Amsterdam and you know it. But you also know I could never hold anything against you, dude. I just don't like to brag about having famous friends," Teddy said with a laugh. "Then they get more attention than I do."

"Yeah right. You always were more popular than I was. Even now." Huck tipped his head toward me. Teddy winked.

"Stella, I guess I should officially introduce you to the very famous Sully. He's seen me in my underwear."

I choked on my beer at the mention of underwear and the

accompanying visual that flashed in my mind. Sully. Suddenly it all made sense. I pursed my lips. "I guess you can be unwounded. He has talked about you. A lot. I didn't make the connection between Sullivan and Sully because he never mentioned that you were a writer. I've only heard about your high school shenanigans and the very eventful reunion five years ago."

"Not the shenanigans, or god, the reunion—that's worse," Huck groaned. "I was hoping to make a good impression here."

"Of course I couldn't tell you, Stella. I'd never hear the end of it. Dude, she's obsessed with your books!"

My face heated, and I whacked Teddy on the stomach.

Huck's lips curved into a perfect crescent moon, mischief twinkling in his eyes. "I thought you'd only *heard* of my books."

This level of embarrassment called for a giant swig of beer. "I might've read one or two," I confessed.

"Or seven!" Teddy exclaimed, taking an inappropriate level of delight at my mortification. Fire flamed in my cheeks.

Despite his graciousness, Huck was not doing a good job hiding his amusement at the loss of my dignity. My face crept toward full-inferno territory. Freaking Teddy. I generally loved his trouble-making, but then, usually, it wasn't making trouble for me. Now he was just being a punk. I glared at my friend.

"I was just telling Huck about Gunnarsson."

"Jesus, Stell, I can't leave you alone for a minute. One bathroom run and you're spilling our secrets to anyone with ears," Teddy said, his expression full of mock judgment.

Huck mimed being shot with an arrow. "That hurts, man. Like I'm just some random dude with ears? What about all the deep conversations on the roof while we froze our asses off back at Monadnock? You once used my bike to streak the homecoming football game."

"Gross," I said.

"Guilty as charged. But, Stell, you of all people know that loose lips sink ships and big mouths get their treasure sites looted."

"Whatever, Teddy. You'll be wanting to celebrate me and my big mouth when I tell you what Huck and I just figured out," I told him.

He leaned over, resting his forearms on the bar, fully engaged. "Alright, kid, what've you got?"

"Remember that line in the poem—the one about the constant storm?"

"Yeah, we thought it referred to a sea battle he had with the English king at the time, where he supposedly lost some of his treasure."

"What if we were wrong? The timing in the saga didn't seem to fit any battles that we know of, right? Isn't that what Zoe and Gus thought? Anyway, it talks about life's gold and spoils of battles past, sleeping behind a constant storm."

Teddy nodded. "The ocean."

I shook my head slowly and cast a glance at Huck, who was smiling as he watched for Teddy's reaction. "It's a waterfall."

"No way!" Teddy shouted. "That was you, Sully? Working your magic with the words, yet again." He grabbed on to Huck's shoulder and shook him before he turned to me. "Turns out you were spot-on about me wanting to celebrate you and your big mouth. I could kiss that giant, blabbing mouth of yours right now." He pulled me in and squeezed me tight. "This is freaking amazing. Just like that, we are back in business."

"We've got to tell Zoe and Gus," I said.

"Not yet. Let them have their alone time . . . you already gave us the night off, boss lady. If we're right, the treasure's been behind a waterfall for hundreds of years . . . What's a few hours more so we can have some fun?"

I laughed in spite of myself and the implications of what my friends were using that alone time for in the dimly lit, secluded corner of the bar.

"Besides, we'll need time to figure out where to look," Teddy said, "given there's something like ten thousand waterfalls in Iceland."

"Yeah, but it's not likely that they'd be on the northeast coast, right? Isn't that what you were saying, Stella?" Huck said.

"Exactly. Probably not."

"Don't give her any ideas," Teddy said. "Stella is truly hardcore. Every summer we take a trip and spend the whole time hunting for this truly epic treasure motherlode and a possibly cursed red diamond."

I arched an eyebrow at him. "The *whole* time? I seem to remember you having ample opportunity for other activities."

"Well, maybe not the whole time. I mean we all have basic needs to meet. Anyway, she'd stay here and search every last possible site if she could. She'd probably drag the rest of us along too, if Zoe and Gus didn't have to go back to work."

Huck lifted an eyebrow. "Is that what's behind the waterfall? A cursed red diamond?"

I shook my head. "No, but I think Gunnarsson might be the missing link to finding that diamond. And it's not cursed. I don't think."

"So you and your friends have an even bigger goal? How many of you are there?" he asked. "Seems like you've got quite an entourage."

I wasn't sure if he was talking to me or Teddy. "Just the four of us," I answered.

"How long have you been searching for treasure together?" he asked.

Teddy ruffled my hair, grinning. "Since the day we met.

Actually, if I'm being totally honest, if it weren't for our shared interest in Blackbeard, we probably wouldn't be friends. Do you know the first time I met Stella, she robbed me?"

"It wasn't a robbery," I shot back, smoothing down my hair.

"You took my wallet! And our cooler."

"I was hungry. You're the one who was just speaking to the importance of basic human needs."

"We both know I was talking about *other* appetites, Stell. Anyway, you were like a tiny blond pirate. Looting up and down the beach in a bikini."

"Maybe you should've just pressed charges," I said, shrugging. We'd been over this story a million times.

"Yeah, well, I was seventeen. I probably thought you were hot." Teddy shrugged and took a drink.

"Probably?" Huck asked.

"I'm bored," Teddy announced. "Let's get some shots. It's not every day that my two oldest friends meet randomly thousands of miles from home. It's an occasion that should be marked with overindulgence."

He ordered a round and knocked his back before Huck and I even had a chance to pick ours up. Then he got another. "Sully," he said, "Stella has something she wants to ask you."

Huck looked intrigued and I turned to face Teddy wide-eyed. *What are you doing?* I mouthed.

Teddy leaned in close and rested on my shoulder. "Aren't you going to ask for your epilogue? *Casablanca.*" His breath was warm on my neck. The scent of alcohol stung my nostrils.

I picked up one of the shots and gulped it down. The liquid seared my throat. It was true, I was desperate for that epilogue. I'd pictured a thousand different ways that I could ask, but after Huck's confession about being shredded by critics and doubting himself, I had no intention of putting him on the spot. "First of all, you know you want that epilogue just as badly as I do. You love those books as much as me."

"Do it for both of us, then." Teddy handed me a fresh shot. "Another dose of liquid courage, my dear?"

I wrinkled my nose.

"Take your medicine," Teddy said. His features had already softened a little; there was a distance in his eyes like he was here but not completely. I was used to this when Teddy was tipsy. He downed the rest of his beer. We'd come to have a good time, I told myself. What was more fun than meeting your favorite author, discovering he's friends with your best friend, and getting a little bit drunk in Iceland? Nothing . . . except all of that plus being one step closer to the treasure of a lifetime. It did call for celebration. Not all of Teddy's notions were bad, often they led to an awesome time. I lifted the shot glass to my lips and drank.

"Good. Now quit being a baby and ask him." He grinned. I knew he wasn't going to let this lie.

"Ask me what?" Huck asked. "Why do I feel like you two are up to something?"

I stood, frozen between them. The room was cool, but the alcohol and the excitement kept me warm. My pulse thrummed. I panicked and took another shot. "Boxers or briefs?" I asked, wincing at the burn of the alcohol. "You have seen his underwear after all." A new song started, right on cue. It had a good beat. One I knew. I reached down and grabbed both their hands.

"Let's dance," I called, my voice loud over the music, knowing full well that Teddy could never resist an opportunity to cut loose on the dance floor. The lights were low; bright-colored spotlights zinged around the room. They swept over Teddy, his sharp jaw, his wild hair, and then Huck, illuminating his pale eyes, just for an instant, and we danced. Zoe and Gus joined us. We all rocked and twisted to the music; we should've probably been embarrassed by our moves or lack thereof, but we were too busy enjoying the bass beat reverberating through our bodies. Teddy kept us supplied with drinks and laughs and new friends as he showcased a multitude of embarrassing moves and the dance floor grew crowded. A familiar song came on, one that all of us loved to sing to as obnoxiously as possible when we were out on the boat, and I looked around to get their attention, but Zoe and Gus were busy grinding up against each other like a music video and Teddy was making out with one of the Australians who ogled him earlier. A strange surge of loneliness overwhelmed me in the crowd. I probably shouldn't have drunk so much; I stopped moving.

"Great song," Huck shouted. He held up two tiny bottles of Coke and stepped over. "Looks like our mutual friend is enjoying himself."

I took one of the bottles. "You know Ted."

"That I do. He's always prioritized fun. And what about you? Are you having a good time?"

The Coke sizzled sweetly on my tongue and the loneliness subsided. I nodded. The music shifted to something slower, something decidedly sexy. Around us, people coupled up. I took another sip of my drink.

Huck leaned toward me. "You wouldn't want to dance with me, would you, Stella?"

I gave him a smile and his hand drifted to the small of my back. We took a few measures to learn how to move with each other. He was a good dancer. I liked peering up at him, his scent, the way his grip tightened and pulled me closer. I pressed my hips to him.

We danced together for a long time. It got late. The music ended, and the dance floor cleared. I turned to him, breathless.

"I needed this," he said, before I could say anything.

He took my hand and even though it had only been a few

hours, most of which we'd spent intoxicated, not able to hear each other over the music, I wondered if *this* could mean me. And the wild thing was, I wanted it to, not in some huge way—we'd only met, I knew that—but it wasn't small, certainly not inconsequential. Normally, I would've already been thinking that whatever this chemistry was between us might be really fun to explore for a night or two before I slipped out for an early, emotionally risk-free exit. This was different. I'd known Huck Sullivan through his books for years. I couldn't help but feel the passage of every hour I spent in those pages with the characters he'd created and think that meant something. He was still holding on to my hand.

"I'm serious," he said, reaching up with his free hand to tuck a damp tendril of my hair behind my ear. "This is the best night I've had in a very long time."

I felt the same, that's why I didn't want it to end. Maybe it didn't have to. It occurred to me then that if Huck needed inspiration, then it was fortunate that we found each other here. He'd helped me figure out where to look next . . . I could definitely give him better material than some dancing in a bar.

I leaned close to him. "If you thought this was good, wait until you see what I've got in store for you next."

FOUR

Stella

The night out dancing had been exactly what we all needed. Huck was the first to say yes. And even though Zoe's feet still hurt and Teddy was buzzed and raw-faced from his Australian companion, my friends didn't need convincing to leave the dance floor and head out to see if the revelation I'd had with Huck about the waterfall was right.

We piled into the van, and Gus, who had been far more interested in making out with Zoe than drinking, climbed into the driver's seat. Zoe sat in the front with him, navigating toward the closest waterfall that fell within the plausible zone I'd mapped out at the bar, and I was wedged between Teddy and Huck, my whole body vibrating with anticipation.

"Do you usually go out in the middle of the night?" Huck asked.

"Not when we're hunting shipwrecks in the Florida Keys, but here . . . definitely. It's not the kind of activity you want to broadcast. The middle of the night is perfect. Just remember to watch your step."

Finally, the sign for Skógafoss came into view and Gus took a hard right into the empty gravel parking lot. After he parked, we hopped out and stood beside the van donning coats and double knotting our boots. Beyond the gravel lots, Skógafoss rose up several stories before us, slicing through the inky black night like a silver blade in the moonlight. I had to be near it. My hands started to tingle again as I ran toward the waterfall. Lanky Teddy, who also was blessed with the energy of a golden retriever puppy, got there first, skidding on the slick rocks beside the pool formed by the falling water. Even at this distance, mist washed over our faces and we reveled in it for a few moments before pressing on.

Huck stopped beside me. He didn't say anything, but from the expression on his face, I knew he was feeling the same thing I was—some mix of wonder and awe and excitement. I liked that he came along and that, unlike me and the rest of my friends, he didn't run. He wasn't rushing and he took things in.

"Are you writing this in your head right now?" I asked, extending my arms and slowly turning in a circle.

I felt his eyes on me. "I might be," he said. I was expecting a different response, something playful, a corner of his mouth turning up, a glint in his eye. But I wasn't disappointed by his words, even though they weren't exactly what I'd expected. His tone was thoughtful, colored with hope. As a person who charged into things, I didn't fully understand his reserve, but that didn't prevent me from being fascinated by it. By him. Already, he was more than I thought he would be.

"So how exactly does this all work?" he asked.

"We use metal detectors. The ones we have give off different tones depending on the type of metal. We work together to cover a pattern called a grid. It's pretty simple, just takes a bit of luck and a lot of patience."

"Sounds like publishing," he said.

"Really?"

He nodded.

"Interesting. So you should be set, then. You ready to check it out?" I asked. I shouldered the bag with our gear and took off toward the rushing water.

"Hell yeah!" Teddy shouted, and launched into motion. His unbridled enthusiasm was just one of my favorite things about him; it got us all fired up.

"Should someone keep an eye on our enthusiastic friend who, unlike the rest of us, appears to still be a little drunk?" Zoe asked, gesturing at Teddy.

"Good plan, babe," Gus said. "I'll babysit him and make sure he doesn't go for a swim." Gus followed Teddy, lugging the rest of the equipment easily. As the archaeology expert on our team, he had the important job of documenting and verifying anything that we found, but he was also the strongest and had useful training from his time in the military, which made him the perfect Teddy wrangler.

At the base, the roar of the waterfall was thunderous, just like a constant storm; we had to shout to be heard. I handed Huck a flashlight.

"I'm going to start scanning with my metal detector," I said. "It's set to pick up any precious metals. Can you light the way?"

"You got it," Huck said. His flashlight beam sliced over the damp earth, encrusted with rocks. We stepped carefully over the slippery terrain, mindful not to trample the plants dotting the landscape. I strained to hear the sound of the metal detector tones over the waterfall. It was painstaking work, mapping a site. We had four detectors and each of the team members knew to take an area, cover it methodically, ensure not a square foot was missed. It was the same thing we did on the ocean floor off the coast of Florida and around the islands in the Caribbean. The same thing we'd done every summer since Teddy, Gus, and Zoe vowed to help me find the treasure that was supposed to be my legacy. It was practically second nature at this point. We swept over every inch, pausing only to dig when the machines alerted us and being careful to always put things back as we found them. An excited yelp from Zoe got our adrenaline pumping, but the hit turned out to be modern material—a metal locket on a thin chain, precious to someone, surely, but not what we came here for.

After a time, Huck and I took a break on some high ground away from the falls where we were protected from the mist. The skin on my hands was wrinkled from moisture exposure, and I trembled from the cold. Around us, the sky was lightening, signaling the arrival of dawn. Soon the tourists would descend, and we'd need to leave, erasing any trace of our search. We would check to make sure that we'd completely filled in the handful of holes we'd dug during the night and drive away. Wash, rinse, repeat.

"Are you disappointed?" I asked Huck. I was used to this roller-coaster feeling—getting hyped up that this time might be *the* time only to find nothing is the nature of treasure hunting—but I recognized that I really sold this story to Huck in the bar, and to a first-timer, a whole night spent getting drenched only to come up empty-handed might be more than a tad anticlimactic.

"Not even close," he said. "It was exciting. I enjoyed watching you work. Speaking of which, you look cold."

"Freezing," I said. "I got all excited and totally forgot to put on my rain gear."

"You know what's good for warming up?" he asked, rubbing my arms gently, turning friction to heat.

I raised an eyebrow, acutely aware of the sensation of his hands against me and desperate to hear what he was going to say.

"Coffee."

"That sounds perfect," I laughed.

Huck pulled me to my feet, and I signaled to everyone to head back to the van.

"So no new hits? Did we cover the grid completely?" I asked them while we stripped out of our soaked clothes and into dry ones.

"Yeah, we got nothing," Zoe said. "I really thought this was it when I got that first hit."

"Me too."

"You were brutally rebuffed," Teddy said. "But you did better than I did, Z. I got a big fat nada."

Gus planted a kiss on top of Zoe's mass of curls gone even more wild from the moisture. "Unlike my charge, who had a temper tantrum and split his pants trying to climb a rock face after I told him not to, you took the disappointment like a champ," he told her.

My heart gave a little squeeze at the tenderness. Maybe this wasn't just a vacation hookup after all. I would've said it looked like love, but I didn't know much about that. People learn love from their parents. Not me. They gave me other things, like lessons in self-reliance and confusing maps. Quests I never seemed to be able to complete.

"What about it, first-timer?" Teddy asked. "Is this going to end up in your next book?"

Something unreadable passed over Huck's face, but he gave Ted a small smile. "You never know. I might need to embellish a few things."

"Like what?" Zoe asked, interested.

"Maybe that locket you found was actually a giant heart-shaped sapphire, worn by a Viking queen," Huck said. Teddy, Gus, and Zoe all glanced over at me. "Just as you pull it from the earth, an ancient society of Viking assassins crests over the waterfall, wielding silver axes and swords. They attack with vicious precision honed over hundreds of years of training. Unarmed, you fight back using the landscape and darkness to your advantage, but you're losing ground and blood as the—"

"Dang," Gus mumbled. "I'm so invested I'm not even worried about the historical accuracy."

"I die?" Zoe interjected, her tone a mix of incredulity and awe. "And here I was, starting to like you."

Huck took the opportunity to peel off his soaking-wet fleece, revealing a taut torso with defined musculature that showed he balanced his hours at the keyboard with time at the gym. He wasn't big like Gus, but I could tell that he was strong. I considered averting my eyes, but honestly, I was enjoying the sight, the lines of him, the smoothness of his skin over the muscles of his chest and abs. I had to give it to him—Huck Sullivan was incredibly sexy. Teddy handed him a sweater and he pulled it on over his head, shaking out his damp black hair. I turned my attention to making sure the equipment was properly stowed so I didn't get myself into trouble. "Death?" he said to Zoe. "Haven't got that far yet. Could be so, or maybe you step into a sink hole that is actually an entrance to an underground passageway, where you're able to narrowly escape."

"I would read that," Teddy said. "I would."

"Me too," Gus said.

"Same," Zoe added. "And not just because I want to ensure I make it."

The grin Huck displayed in response to this positive feedback was genuine. I could tell by the crinkles at the corners of his eyes, the lift in his shoulders, which was new. He met my gaze and I couldn't help but smile back at him.

We moved toward each other as if pulled by some invisible force.

The rest of the crew was busy stuffing the wet clothes into a bag—later we'd lay them out to dry in the sun—and Huck and I took advantage of the solitude to step to the side of the van. He reached up and pushed a damp curl away from my face.

"What about you, Stella?" he said. "Would you read it?"

I met his eyes. "Not sure I can wait for it to hit the shelves. What happens next?"

FIVE

Huck

I never imagined that I'd be standing in a gravel parking lot in the middle of Iceland wearing another man's sweater while I was torn in two. I was freaking desperate to get back to my laptop or, hell, even a piece of paper and a pen to write. I hadn't felt this inspired in . . . actually, I couldn't remember a time in recent history when I felt so desperate to pour the words from myself. I'd basically given up on ever being inspired again. Now that it was back, I didn't want to turn away from it. But I was fixed in this spot, in the gaze of Stella's hazel eyes. She smelled like fresh rain and wildflowers, and the way she was looking at me stirred up something else I hadn't felt in so long that I almost couldn't name the feeling.

Interest. Not just want. And I had a pulse, so yes, I wanted her. I was desperate to press my mouth to her chapped lips, trace along her fine collarbone and down her strong arms, slide my hands over her hips and reel her into me, but it was so much more than that. I wanted to captivate her. I had to hear her opinion and know that she thought what I was creating was worthwhile. That it was good.

What happens next?

I considered her question for a long moment, breathing the air she exhaled into the space between us. An entire universe of possibilities unfurled before me. I shook them off; after all, we'd only just met, and I knew better. I looked pretty good right now. I was still novel and interesting, and maybe even a little mysterious. She hadn't had a chance to see the cracks in my veneer, the web of flaws and weaknesses beneath . . . the stuff Dad and Vanessa had seen so clearly and made sure I could never forget. I hadn't ruined things yet, the way I always did. But it was only a matter of time.

"I'm going to need caffeine if you want me to keep plotting," I said, tucking my worries and painful memories away.

"I guess we better find a café, then. Someone told me that coffee is the perfect way to warm up." Her voice was solemn, unlike her playful expression. Was she flirting with me? I wanted her to be, even though this couldn't go anywhere.

"Let's go, friends," she called. "The writer needs caffeinated fuel, and I am desperate for one of those poppy seed pastries."

"Múnstykki!" Ted hollered. Of course Ted had already picked up the key vocabulary of Iceland. He hadn't changed much since our school days. He was still as charismatic as ever, the most fun guy in the room. The leader of every trip, with the most beautiful, interesting girl right next to him. After a day in any country, he probably knew all the important food-, alcohol-, and navigation-related words, along with the best pickup lines. The essentials. He gave Stella's shoulders a playful squeeze and bounded to the van.

We found a *bakari* a few miles down the road, and within minutes were scarfing down sweet dough swirls speckled with poppy seeds, sandwiches thick with egg, and lattes that were somehow better than anything back at home even though they came from a machine. It must've been the milk. Stella took big bites of her pastry, declaring it the best one she'd had so far. Then she drank two cappuccinos, leaving a tempting trail of foam on her top lip that she cleared with a tantalizing flick of her tongue. I pulled a notebook and pen out of my messenger bag and started working on a storyline based on the idea that I'd been playing around with in the parking lot with the gang but found it hard to concentrate. In between sips and bites, Stella pored over a map, marking things down with a pen, crossing other things out, and pulled my attention away from the fictional world I was trying to conjure.

"Will you go to another site today?" I asked.

Stella shook her head and disappointment settled into the pit of my stomach. "Zoe needs to fly home tomorrow for a case and Gus is going back too to finish a grant for his research," she explained. "We need to head to Reykjavík to take them to the airport."

"Are you leaving then as well?" I tried to sound nonchalant, but my voice was leaden. "You won't keep searching?"

Ted plopped another pastry down in front of me. "Eat up, buddy."

I watched as Stella pressed a soft thumbprint to her plate to collect the remaining poppy seeds and then sucked them off. "Nope. Teddy and I are more flexible. Our tickets are open-ended. I definitely want to check out some additional falls. This trip is high stakes. I'm not just looking for Gunnarsson's treasure. I'm also hoping to confirm the existence of a much bigger find we're also searching for that belonged to the Sea People—the earliest pirates. I won't stop searching. It will be more of a process, though. Covering the grids takes a lot longer with only two people." She glanced up at me, her eyes narrow with mischief.

"Unless . . ." She was about to proposition me somehow, I was certain. I was also sure that whatever she was about to ask me, I would agree to. I was in.

"Yes," I interrupted.

"You don't even know what I was going to ask," she teased.

"Maybe, but aren't you impressed by my level of investment?"

She tipped her head and looked at me, the heat in her hazel gaze saying more than an entire conversation would have.

"So how should we spend our last day in Iceland?" Gus asked, and took a sip of espresso. "Digging in the dirt, another hike, bicycle tour of Reykjavík?"

Zoe raised a hand. "It's not quite as thrilling as all of those things sound, and I know it's kind of touristy, but I was kind of hoping to visit the Blue Lagoon before we go. Get a little vacation on before my vacation is over, if you catch my drift?"

Teddy got on his phone and started investigating. "Looks like there are some spots left at one p.m.—that should be enough time to get there. What do you think, Stella?"

"I'll never say no to a lagoon, or Zoe."

Would it be strange to invite myself, pathetic even? I wondered. I didn't want breakfast to be the end of whatever this was.

Stella turned to me. "What about you, Huck? Have a bathing suit in that writer's satchel of yours?"

Something about the way she lifted her eyebrow made me swallow hard. "It fits a surprising number of important things," I said, "but I didn't think to pack my trunks in there."

Ted swung an arm around my neck. "Amateur," he said with a chuckle. "I would've thought I'd taught you better."

"I seem to remember you being more of a clothing-optional guy."

"Okay, yeah, but I've matured and am well-traveled now. So I'm keenly aware that one should always have a bathing suit handy in Iceland. You never know when you'll stumble upon some unofficial hot spring. That's why I harnessed my inner Boy Scout and packed three."

"Didn't you get kicked out of the Boy Scouts?" Zoe said.

"Wouldn't you like to know. Sully, I'll come to your rescue

and let you borrow one of my extras. It'll be just like when we were at Monadnock. You were always stealing my polo shirts among other things. Maybe that's why I was clothing-optional. You were wearing it."

I wanted to make sure this bathing suit was not some sort of Euro-style mankini before I committed, because Ted was the kind of guy who would have one solely to ensure he could fuck with some dude who found himself in need of some swim apparel—in this case, me—but Stella was still watching, waiting for an answer.

Honestly, who the hell am I kidding? I thought. I'd wear a Speedo if it meant getting to spend more time near her.

"I guess I'm in too," I said.

SIX

Huck

The air was sharply cool at the Blue Lagoon. Steam wafted up from the milky surface of the water, curling like smoke over the black rocks. This place wasn't exactly what I'd pictured—in the distance I made out the outline of the power plant that created these pools, but somehow it only added to the otherworldly quality and didn't detract from the beauty of the scene. My mind wandered. A lagoon like this, so ethereal and eerie, would be a good setting for some kind of murder. You'd never be able to see a body under the surface. Was there a body under the surface? I wondered, as I stepped into the waters.

The spare trunks Ted had lent me were not a mankini, thank god, but they did fit a bit more snugly than I would've liked, so I was relieved that Stella and Zoe hadn't emerged from the locker room yet. The heat of the water was a welcome change after the brisk walk through the frigid air from the building housing the locker rooms to the edge of the lagoon. I tried to push the curiosity about what might be hidden in the opaque liquid out of my mind as I made my way deeper into the pool. At least the lack of water clarity meant that no one outside of the men's changing room had any idea of the degree of nut hugging I was enduring with these borrowed shorts. The guys and I found a nook in the side of the pool, where I sunk into the warm water up to my neck.

A family drifted by us—mom, dad, a middle school–aged girl, and a younger boy—in a tight pack. "I saw a lot of butts," the boy said.

"Oh my gosh, same," the girl replied. "It was giving middle-aged nudist-colony reunion. Thank god Mom lent me her robe. No one's seeing my butt."

Ted laughed. "Those kids aren't wrong." The locker room had been decidedly uninhibited, and everyone seemed to take the naked, full-body soap-up requirement seriously.

"You were in your element," I said, chuckling.

"Both valid points," Gus added.

"Okay, I would fit in nicely in Europe."

"Or a nudist colony."

"Maybe that should be my next venture if we ever give up treasure hunting," Ted said. "Preston Plains, where you are free to let it all hang out. You want to invest, Huck? You've got that book money, right?"

"Hey, there they are," Gus said, saving me from answering. "Zoe, over here." He waved a hand over his head.

I followed his gaze to the racks where Stella and Zoe were removing their bathrobes and hanging them on hooks. Stella's blond hair was darker, slicked to her head and tied in a tight bun at the nape of her neck. Against the black fabric of her sport-cut two-piece, her bare skin was creamy. Zoe's skin was shades darker than Stella's, a rich light brown complemented by a shiny fuchsia string bikini. She waved back at Gus, and together the women strode toward the ramp into the water. Zoe took careful steps, but Stella raced in. There was something about the way that she simply forged ahead in every situation—no fear, no hesitation—that

I admired, even as the curves of her body disappeared beneath the milky teal water.

"So, Huck, how's your love life these days? Seeing anyone special?" Ted asked, diverting my attention.

"Not at the moment," I said. Not for a long time. Not since Vanessa had moved on to better things than a failed writer, leaving behind a closet full of empty hangers and the ring I'd given her on the bathroom counter.

"Weren't you dating that actress? What's her name . . . ?" Gus trailed off.

"Scarlett Johansson?" Ted filled in. "Most beautiful woman alive. What I'd give to go out with her."

"That was a rumor." One that was better than the quiet, sad truth. "To be honest, I don't date much." That was true. "I'm sort of a homebody—I think sometimes people have this idea of a writer's life as being glamorous, but I spend most of my days staring at my computer screen, thinking. Kind of a letdown for potential partners," I said.

Vanessa never let me forget the disappointment she'd felt when she realized how boring my life actually was. She'd signed up for a hero, like in my books, and the reality of me wasn't even close, and when I started to struggle . . . she couldn't get away from me fast enough.

"You weren't that boring in school," Teddy said with a laugh. "What happened? Did you go downhill and return to your former state once you stopped hanging out with me full-time?"

"Ouch," Gus said.

"What's a letdown?" Stella asked.

I flushed. I hadn't wanted her to hear that. In fact, I'm not sure why I admitted it in the first place. "Nothing," I said.

"Oh good, for a second there, I thought you were talking about this place, and if that was the case I was going to have to stop liking you since you clearly can't appreciate the divine." She swished her arms in the water like a washing machine agitator. She was enchanting.

I surveyed the lagoon again. "Not at all. It's ethereal," I told her. I considered whether I should share my thoughts of using it as a setting for an action scene.

"It is. You know, your eyes are the same color as this water."

My core tightened at these words, contracting at the implication, under the weight of her eye contact. I swallowed. "Oh yeah?"

She nodded, but then she was off again, moving.

"Let's get face masks, Zoe." She grabbed her friend's hand and waded toward the mask station at the water's edge on the left. There, a woman in a Blue Lagoon polo shirt doled out scoops of various mud masks. I couldn't help but follow them. Ted and Gus joined too. We smeared the white silica mud over our cheeks and foreheads, except for Gus, who applied a pale green algae mask to his dark skin. He flexed.

"Babe, does this make me look like the Incredible Hulk?" he asked.

Zoe eyed him. "Yeah, it's kind of doing it for me actually."

"She's clearly biased, Gus. You look ridiculous. Now, I make this shit look good," Teddy said. "They could put me on the brochure to advertise this stuff. Isn't it miraculous? I feel it working already. I'm going to swim over to the bar to get my complimentary drink while it works its magic. Stell, you coming?"

Stella had her eyes closed and was leaning back against a rocky outcropping. "I think I'm going to chill here."

"I'll stay with you," I said.

"I'm in for drinks," Zoe said, and she wrapped her arms around Gus's shoulders to hitch a ride. "C'mon, Bruce Banner, carry me across this lagoon."

Stella and I sat quietly against the rock wall as I tried and failed to not think about our proximity and the occasional brush of her bare thigh against mine.

"Would it be cliché if I asked what you were thinking about?" I said.

"Not at all. I've never understood why people are so anti-cliché, to be honest. I love them." She scooped a handful of water and let it trickle through her fingers. "I'm a simple girl. I'm thinking about treasure. I really was hopeful last night at the waterfall. I wanted the gang to finally see that I hadn't dragged them all over Iceland for nothing. They're good sports, and we have a great time together, but last night at the bar, Zoe and Gus had been expressing some mild irritation at the fact that we'd been hunting and nothing else, especially since I'd sort of framed this late-fall trip as a departure from our usual summer voyage and sunken-treasure-search routine. I may not have told them that the main reason I wanted to come to Iceland was to find Gunnarsson's gold and finally locate the missing connection that we need to figure out where to search for the red diamond Teddy mentioned to you. Zoe had been envisioning nightlife and lagoons, not hiking and being cold and soaking wet ninety-nine percent of the time. I rationalized it by thinking we'd definitely find it and all the work and missing the fun and hot springs would be worth it. I guess I feel like I've let them down since we didn't find it. Not that me failing to lead us to treasure is anything new. We started searching when we turned eighteen—ten summers—and we've turned up a few cool finds but nothing life-changing. I'm waiting for them to all realize one day that they've wasted a decade because of me."

"I doubt they see it that way," I said. I know I didn't. Last night was one of the most exciting nights of my life. "I can't imagine anyone feeling anything other than electric spending time with you."

She lifted her shoulders out of the water. "Really? I don't know about that."

"What's this legendary, probably-not-cursed diamond called?"

"The Elephant's Heart. It's a rare red diamond from Africa that is supposedly massive, hence the name. It was part of a stolen treasure from the world's first pirates."

"Sounds like it'll be worth the wait."

"I hope so. I just want to find it for them so bad. They've always been there for me, so I guess I want to return the favor with something equally monumental. I know I get obsessive sometimes."

I got the feeling that there was more to this than Stella was saying but didn't push. We took turns rinsing the masks from our faces at a freshwater tap. She reached up and smoothed her hand over my jaw. Her touch was gentle but it made me hungry for more.

"There's a bit of residue in your stubble," she said.

"Oh. These masks are persistent," I said, rubbing the last of the residue off. "You've got a little left too." I reached out to brush a small smear of white on her cheek. "There. Got it."

"Thanks. Teddy would've let me walk around with stuff on my face all day while giggling about it like a child. You're a rare gentleman."

"I guess you bring it out in me," I admitted. She bit her lip and gazed down at the water, where our legs were nearly intertwined below the surface. "Seriously, I'm really enjoying spending time with you, Stella."

We locked gazes for an instant, but something pulled her attention over my shoulder. "Shit, Zoe, don't get your hair in the water—"

I swiveled just in time to catch Zoe dipping her whole head below the surface. She must've missed the signs warning that the minerals in the water were great for the skin but would ruin a person's hair. When I looked back at Stella, the intensity of the moment between us was broken. But all I could think was how freaking cute she looked when she was trying not to laugh.

Stella

Zoe and I stood in the shower together in our bathing suits while I put a third coat of conditioner in her stiff hair.

"It won't be that bad," I assured her. "It's already starting to feel softer." This was not true. Her hair felt like straw and didn't look great, but I didn't want to dash her hopes just yet. Zoe caught my expression and touched her hair to confirm.

"This can't be happening," she groaned.

"I'm sure Gus won't care."

"Of course Gus won't mind. He claims he loves my intellect, but he is absolutely an ass man."

I snorted. "I did not need to know that. Though I am also a huge fan of your brain, and to be fair, your ass is objectively quite nice."

"He won't mind my hair situation, but *I* do. I have to be in court tomorrow. I can't afford to look like a dark-haired version of Albert Einstein during jury selection. Who would take me seriously?"

"Einstein was a brilliant man."

"I heard that he took credit for his wife's work."

"Things seem to be going pretty well with Gus," I said, switching topics. "Is it just a romantic vacation tryst between friends or something more long-term?"

Zoe grabbed a towel and wrapped it over her bathing suit. "If we're being technical, I'd have to say long-term. We sort of started up a while ago," she said.

First I'd been hit with the revelation that Teddy was old friends with my favorite author slash celebrity crush. Now my other best friends had been having a secret love affair? There were only so many revelations my brain could process in a twenty-four-hour period, and I was reaching that limit, fast. "How long is a while?"

"Last summer?" She grimaced.

"Wait—you hooked up while we were on the boat? I had no clue. Why didn't you tell me?"

"I think at first we did kind of think that maybe it was just a vacation fling between friends. And then when it was clear that it wasn't, we worried that it would mess up the group dynamic. I wanted to wait for the right time, and Gus had some wild idea that you and Teddy would hook up and we'd tell you at the double wedding."

I turned to Zoe, mouth agape. "Wait. Me and *Teddy*?"

"What? You two never thought about taking your friendship up a notch?"

I was horrified. Teddy was Teddy. He was family. He was practically my brother. And a full-fledged man-whore—not that I was judging, especially as a sex-positive commitment-phobe myself. I shivered as I pulled on my jeans.

"Fine, don't answer. It seems my line of questioning isn't relevant at this point given the appearance of the newest character in our Icelandic chapter, Mr. Huck Sullivan, author extraordinaire. Seems to me that you've taken a bit of a shine to him."

I tried to keep my face neutral, but I couldn't stop my lips from curving into a grin. "He's, um, very nice."

"He does seem nice. At least his face is nice and his body is *nice*. I saw you checking him out when he took his shirt off in the falls parking lot. Pervert." Zoe handed me some lip balm. "Seriously, though, I love this plot twist for you. Tell me you're loving my literary jokes."

"They're amazing."

"So . . ."

"What?"

"Do you like him?"

I shrugged, avoiding Zoe's gaze in the mirror. "I don't know."

"Are you blushing, Stella? The entire time I've known you, I don't think I've seen you blush."

"I like his books," I deflected.

"Yeah, his books are great. He's a super creative and smart guy. But I think you like the way he sets your body ablaze."

"Get real."

"I am getting real. I'm not the one who isn't being honest here. I'll tell you right now, the man is hot. If I weren't already with Gus, I would've been hoping to get into those trunks. Did you see how snug they were? Teddy is the perfect blend of generous and vicious by lending him those microscopic swim trunks instead of the board shorts, and I'm here for it," Zoe said. "Okay, it's hopeless." She rotated and gestured toward her hairbrush, which was fully lodged in her tangled hair. "Looks like Lawyer Einstein is going to have to have her day in court. Let's get dressed."

"You could wear a wig," I suggested. "That's what television actresses do."

"I don't know. Maybe I can use this to my advantage. It's distracting, that's for sure. Opposing counsel will think that I don't have my shit together. Then I can eviscerate them and enjoy extensive salon treatments while I celebrate. It feels like a real *Legally Blonde* moment."

"Legally Brunette," I said, and we laughed.

We met the guys in the lobby and took the short drive to the airport, where we bid Zoe and Gus goodbye.

"It was really nice to meet you finally," Zoe told Huck.

"You're good people for sure," Gus said. "Not that we're shocked. Teddy has good taste." He turned to me and picked me up off the ground in a bear hug. "Little Stella, it's been a pleasure tromping all over this freezing island with you, but please find this treasure so we can plan a vacation without metal detectors before I'm too old to enjoy it."

"I know. I get it. Sorry we didn't get lucky," I said. "Actually, you *did* get lucky, didn't you? Both of you," I teased. "And I hear that you've been getting lucky for months behind our backs, so maybe you and Zoe should be apologizing to me instead of the other way around."

"I ought to drop you in this parking lot," Gus said. "Good thing I'm feeling rather magnanimous given my current level of sexual fulfillment." Zoe fixed him with a courtroom look that made him clear his throat. "Deep, sublime emotional fulfillment, that is." She slid her hand into his.

"Get a room!" Teddy shouted before bursting into wild laughter.

"He's serious," I said. "Speaking for myself, I'm never sharing a van with you guys again. And when we're out on the boat next summer, I'm not rooming with you. I know way too much about your sexual repertoire."

Zoe threw her arms around my neck and gave me a big squeeze. "Find that treasure for us, Stella. I may not have a job after they see my hair and I'll need you to be my sugar mommy."

"I'm okay with sugar-mommy status. I do know your sexual repertoire, after all." I smoothed my hands affectionately over her tangled tresses. "Coconut oil. Leave it on all night."

She waggled her eyebrows at me.

"For your hair, sicko."

"You know, it is actually a very nice natural lubrican—"

I shook my head as my cheeks turned red. "Nope. Don't want to know."

"Alright, then. I'll just say, until next time." She turned back to Huck. "Listen, writer man, when you write a book about us, can you leave my little hair incident out of it? It's not how I want to be remembered."

"You got it," Huck said. "No hair."

"Well, maybe good hair. Bald is beautiful, but not really what I'm going for at the moment."

"Deal. But I'm keeping the part where Ted split his pants."

"I'm okay with that," Teddy said. "The funny guy is always everyone's favorite."

"We've got to go, babe," Gus said.

I gave them both one last hug, and then they headed inside, pulling their bags behind them.

Teddy stretched his arms wide, and I yawned reflexively.

"I guess the sleepless night has finally caught up to me," I said. "I'm a mess."

"Why don't we go back to my cabin?" Huck said. "It's not far from here, and I have a spare room and a hot shower . . . if we're lucky—the water heater is a bit temperamental. I haven't quite figured it out yet. Either way, we can get a fire going and get some rest."

"That sounds perfect," I said.

"Sleepover at Huck's place," Teddy announced, sliding into the van's driver's seat. "Just like old times."

After twenty minutes on the Ring Road, we turned off onto a gravel path that wound through an old lava field just as the sun dipped below the horizon. Teddy navigated several sharp turns, and finally a small building came into view amidst a shadowy backdrop of rocky outcroppings and moss and cotton candy–colored sky. Huck hopped out ahead of me and Teddy and switched on the lights around the deck and inside the house, creating a welcoming glow. The cabin was small and spartan, with a wall of windows and a modern wood stove.

"So, how come you never told me that your Sully was Huck Sullivan?" I asked as Teddy and I grabbed our backpacks. "You know how much I love his books. You could've been holding his friendship over my head for years."

As we walked toward the porch, I could make out Huck stooped in front of a stove, filling it with pieces of wood.

"Do you have any idea how annoying you would've been? Don't act like you don't know that you get majorly obsessed with things. You've spent the past ten years engaged in a relentless search for the world's most infamous and elusive lost treasure. I can't even imagine how many times you would've bugged me for a meeting or an early copy of a manuscript, and, anyway, Huck's super private."

"I don't get obsessed. Okay, maybe a little fixated, but I would not have misused the knowledge."

"Keep telling yourself that, Stella. Call it self-preservation on my part. I prefer to live my life in peace."

"Wanted to keep him all to yourself, huh?"

Teddy flipped my ponytail over my shoulder. "Something like that, kid."

"I get it," I said, and flushed at the blatantly dreamy quality of my voice. I might as well have had glowing red heart eyes broadcasting my crush across the Iceland night for all to see: *Here we have the Northern Lights, folks, and over there, well, that's an embarrassing amount of hero worship and sexual frustration emanating from an American lady.* I was very glad that full darkness had arrived so Teddy couldn't witness my mortification. I cleared my throat. "I mean, he seems really genuine and smart, but also nice." Zoe's words about all of Huck's nice qualities came to mind, and I shook them off.

"Yeah. He's great, a very lucky guy."

I was struck by this characterization. Most people would've thought Teddy was the luckiest guy they know. His dad invented a sensor that was in most modern boats, making his family so wealthy that I'd lost count of the number of mansions they owned and charitable foundations they'd founded. Teddy had always been surrounded by people and he'd never wanted for anything in his life. Not friends, or women, not cars or clothes or food.

"How so? I find it hard to believe his life is more charmed than Theodore Preston the Third's," I teased, jabbing him in the ribs as we stepped onto the porch. "Bestseller or no, can we take a moment to reflect on the size of this cabin? You have to admit it is objectively very small."

"Well, he hasn't had a book out in years. New York's an expensive city. No wonder he didn't want to invest in my nudist colony."

"I don't want to know."

The cabin door opened and Huck waved us inside. "Come get warm, you two."

"Teddy was just telling me how lucky you are."

"That's not what I said," Teddy countered.

Huck tucked Teddy under his arm roughly. I hadn't noticed before that he was several inches taller than him. "Oh yeah? I guess I am pretty lucky. Like that one time he stole that golf cart— have you heard this one, Stella? He crashed it into the pond on campus, knocking me out in the process."

"Why would I tell her that, dude? I almost got expelled!"

"If I recall, I almost drowned and you ended up with a few weeks' worth of detention. How'd you manage that anyway?"

"New library wing, courtesy of Pops, I think." Teddy pulled off his boots. "Good thing it was my dad getting that call and not yours, right, Sully?"

Huck didn't answer.

"Sounds like you two guys were trouble."

"Just enough to be interesting," Huck said. "He did almost do me in a few times with his antics, but he's also a big part of how I got where I am."

"What can I say?" Ted laughed. "I've got beauty and brains. I recognized his talent right away."

"It's extremely annoying that you're brilliant and that pretty, Ted," I said.

"Agreed," Huck chimed in.

"Do I have a special talent for bringing out the best in my friends? Yes. I admit it. It's one of my many skills. We won't discuss the others right now." Teddy winked at me. "Anyway, Sully just needed a bit of nurturing."

"That's you," Huck said with a chuckle. "So nurturing."

"A splash of fun, a couple of smidges of liquid courage, a few rooftop brainstorming sessions, one near-death experience, and more words of affirmation than I ever want to have to utter again . . . Sully's creative talents were like a very high-maintenance house-plant. He just needed the right conditions to blossom."

"Well, this is the cabin. I'd give you both a tour but this is basically it. The shower is right down the hall—as I mentioned, it's a little finicky. Stella, do you want to use it first?"

"I'm okay, actually. What about you, Ted?"

"Oh, hells yeah, I'll take the shower first." He motored off down the hall, whipping his sweatshirt over his head as he went. I plopped down in a soft chair beside the fire.

"Did Teddy really help your writing career? Or were you just tending to his fragile ego?"

"You *do* know him well." Huck laughed. "As much as I fear for the integrity of his self-esteem, it's true. I owe him a lot."

And I got it. I owed Teddy a lot too, though it wasn't something I felt comfortable sharing with Huck, or anyone really. There was the obvious bit—his financial support, which had started the day he got access to his trust fund and began underwriting our expeditions—but there was also the other part before that . . . our origin story, the day we met on the beach when I was at my absolute lowest. I didn't like to think about where I'd be now if Teddy hadn't come into my life, much less discuss it. What would have happened if I hadn't met him that day after my dad left me on the beach with a bit of cash and a false promise that he'd be back in a few hours so we could head out to hunt for the Heart together for the summer. I was finally going to be part of it. All these years later, I could almost see myself standing on that beach, slurping a sweet tea and scarfing down fries in the baking sun, full of hope and anticipation, completely ignorant of the fact that my dad was never coming back.

There were stories about how some treasure hunters were cursed by the bounties they searched for or found, and that certainly rang true for my family. Treasure had torn us apart. My mom had loved searching shipwrecks for fun. Her job as a pilot took her all over the coast of the Southeastern U.S., where she'd charted hundreds of potential sites to search for shipwrecks. But my father was obsessed with finding one thing: the Elephant's Heart—the centerpiece of the Stolen Treasure. The Heart was a massive and brilliant red diamond, the rarest of all diamonds in the world. A priceless treasure. He'd told me about it every night like a bedtime story when I was little. He was a true believer.

My mother argued that salving the wrecks she'd located would make us richer than we ever imagined, buy us a good life; the Elephant's Heart was something we should leave alone. It was an impossible find. But Dad wouldn't listen. He was determined and spellbound; we had to find it before someone else did. That was why he was always running some scheme in pursuit of the Heart and we never had enough money. He gambled her salary away trying to pay for a boat, double-mortgaged and lost our house. When all his plans didn't work out, he drowned his failure in alcohol. They fought. And then just as I was starting high school, he had this idea to sell my mother's maps. I think that was the last straw. She went silent and one day she took off, leaving me and the maps behind. She said she was done searching, but somehow . . . she was done with us too.

Dad sometimes told me tales when he'd had a few beers and hadn't gotten weepy or belligerent yet, about better times when they were young and happy and would spend their days searching for treasure down the Carolina seashore and along Treasure Coast in Florida while I ran around in my bathing suit, a small, freckly girl, asking questions about storms and pirates and chasing the seabirds. They'd taught me diving and navigation and I had a knack for both. I was a good researcher too, but even with all that I hadn't been enough to keep them around. By the time I was graduating high school, he'd disappeared from my life as well. My throat tightened. Not having answers, all these years later, still made me feel like I was choking. The fresh intensity of the pain was surprising, even though I'd always carried it with me, just like my mother's maps, which I managed to save. The pain was what drove me to be so relentless in my own pursuit of treasure and the Elephant's Heart. I would show my parents, wherever they were, that I could do what they couldn't.

A high-pitched screech reverberated from down the hall, snapping me back to the present; apparently the hot water had failed again. I was thankful for the distraction.

"I'm kind of glad I didn't volunteer to go first," I said. "Poor

Teddy. He thought I was being magnanimous but, really, I was strategically avoiding being a guinea pig."

Ted emerged in a bathrobe moments later and thrust himself directly in front of the fire. "This Lilliputian cabin has a vendetta! The temperature of that water went from tepid to unspeakable in mere moments. I'm not sure my nuts will ever emerge."

Huck stifled a laugh. "That's unfortunate."

"And unnecessarily graphic," I added. "As much as I love you, Teddy, I don't want to think too much about the well-being or location of your nether regions."

"That hurts, Stella, I thought we were close. Sully—please tell me that you care."

"Oh yes, *deeply*. Glad to see you've helped yourself to my robe."

"It's very cozy. I might sleep in it. I saw you've got a pretty nice bed in there with a down comforter."

"Help yourself."

"Don't mind if I do. You don't care, do you, Stell? And if you do, you can always join me." He wiggled his brows.

"Tempting," I teased back. "But I think I'll take the couch."

"There's a small guest bedroom," Huck said. "It's more of an alcove, but it has a door and a bed, so I'm sure it will be more comfortable for you. I can take the couch."

SEVEN

Huck

"Excited for today?" I asked Ted while I poured myself a coffee. Ted looked up from his breakfast of toast with an offensive amount of butter. "Absolutely," he said. "Being able to scuba dive between two continents is a once-in-a-lifetime experience."

"Sounds like a freezing experience." Ted left the informational website for the diving tour of the Silfra fissure open for me to look over last night, and while it had the makings of what seemed like a very cool adventure, according to the year-round water temperatures of two to four degrees Celsius, I wasn't feeling too sad that I didn't have a diving certification and was unable to take part.

"Worth it," he said. "Kind of like the time we hid in the walk-in after formal dinner so we could get all the ice cream for that epic winter blowout sophomore year?"

I thought back to that party. Like all of Ted's extravaganzas, it had been a night to remember, all the way from the sub-zero status of my nuts to the make-your-own-make-out-sundae game Ted had kicked off that culminated in me getting my very first girlfriend. I smiled in spite of myself.

"That was a good one. But I can't scuba, so I'm still out."

"You know, they do have snorkeling. You could still join if you want."

I shook my head. I planned to stay behind at the cabin, resolved to actually get some words in today. While we didn't find anything on our search the other night, I enjoyed the story I'd started. Mulling it over with my morning coffee, it felt promising.

"It's fine," I said. "This is supposed to be a working trip for me anyway. And writing is kind of a solo endeavor."

"So you're okay, then." It was part statement, part rhetorical, part loaded question. One that I didn't really want to delve into. He eyed me while he took a loud sip. Ted had always been good at this sort of thing, getting under your skin in such a way that something seemed like your own decision.

I shrugged. "Yeah, I'm good."

"Really? Because, holy shit, man. That was a lot. Losing a parent and a fiancée in the span of a few months and having your book tank—"

"Yeah, wasn't fantastic for a while, but I'm getting there."

"I mean, I know your relationship with your dad was not the best, but still."

Ted was putting it lightly out of kindness. He knew what my dad was really like and the kind of impact he'd had on me. My relationship with my father reminded me of brittle metal, forged in the flame of his rage, unbending in his constant disappointment in me, his words predictably sharp, efficiently cutting me down to the very last moment, but so fragile. It shattered with one blow a few winters back. Ted knew that too.

"I've moved on from the past," I said.

"Really? I'm stoked to hear that you're writing, but I look around and it kind of seems like you're wallowing. Why are you staying in this tiny little hut? The roof's not even big enough for both of us to sit on and relive our glory days."

"I'm not wallowing. Jim booked it. Anyway, I really *am* doing better. People say it gets easier with time."

"Is that what they say," Ted quipped.

"So I've heard." Too many times to count. But that was what humans did when someone was struggling, I supposed—they went for the tested comments that are so safe and repeated and vague that they are as meaningless as they are innocuous. Time heals all wounds. Something better is waiting for you. It's for the best.

"Hmm. Is it true, this thing they say?"

"Well, it's been a while and I haven't cried in months, so maybe they're onto something?" This was a lie. I'd cried two days earlier, when I'd tried all day to write something, anything, and failed, then went out to buy myself a sweet treat only to get back to the cabin and realize that I'd purchased licorice-flavored chocolate. I blamed the jet lag. It was not the jet lag. I'd been broken by licorice flavoring.

Ted seemed to see through my cover. I don't know why I thought I could fool him. "I still think you should come and get some adrenaline flowing through your rusty circuits, but I get it. You have better things to do, like stare at that screen all day."

"Actually, I stare out the window that's on the other side of the screen. Occasionally I type a few words before deciding that they're bad and deleting them."

"Sounds productive."

I rotated to face Stella, who was dressed in a sweater that was the exact shade of blue of a perfect day and grinning as she poured a cup of coffee. My face heated a bit at her presence.

"And that is what makes you a genius, I suppose. If you need any ideas, you'll have to wait to hit me up when we get back. Meet you at the van, Stell," Ted said. He snagged his coat from the hall tree and headed out the door.

Stella sipped her coffee. "Are you really planning to write today?"

I nodded. "I have to do something to pass the time until you get back." Maybe it was a bold thing for me to assume that they'd stay here, but fuck it, I wanted to see as much of her as possible, and what better way to do that than for her and Ted to stay with me instead of their cramped camper van?

Her eyes twinkled as she eyed me over her mug. "Are you sure that's not an imposition?"

"I mean, Ted's already made himself comfortable in my robe and my bed."

"Good point." She laughed.

"Besides, I've been enjoying getting to know you. I was hoping that we could spend more time together."

"I like the sound of that."

EIGHT

Stella

Teddy and I left Huck's cabin and drove to Thingvellir National Park, where the Silfra fissure and our diving guides were waiting. When we'd planned the trip, this was the one thing I had wanted to do, other than search for Gunnarsson's treasure. The fissure was the meeting place for the North American and Eurasian continental plates, so we would be able to touch two continents at once while we dove. There was something epic about the idea of placing our hands on something so ancient and to cross the divide between the place we were from and the one we were in. When I had found the tour website during my research, I immediately knew I needed this experience.

"You're awfully smiley this morning," Teddy observed.

I thought back to the admission Huck had made in the kitchen about wanting to spend more time with me and how I'd felt excited and completely aligned with him in that moment. "Oh, I'm just feeling renewed after finally experiencing a full night of sleep without being awakened by some sort of coitus taking place in my vicinity."

"Tell me about it. I slept like a baby in Sully's bed. I stretched out my arms and legs like a starfish in a luxury robe. But I don't know if I buy that as your answer . . . You're in a good mood because you slept well? Well-rested or not, you're generally borderline petulant after we go on a search and come up empty. You've been taking it suspiciously well."

I shrugged. "I guess it has been kind of neat getting to know Huck. Who gets to meet their favorite author and hang out at his place? And he said we could keep staying there."

"You're happy about that?"

"Aren't you?"

"Oh, I'm delighted. Did I just miss our turn?"

On site, we quickly joined the group and donned our dry suits while the guide shared the obligatory warnings—don't go off alone, respect the surroundings, don't underestimate Silfra, make sure we don't accidentally go out into the glacial lake, and, most importantly, don't pee in our dry suits. Then we made our way down the metal stairs in our flippers, into the clear, cold, glacial-spring-fed water. Beneath the surface, we could see for what felt like forever.

Teddy swam beside me. We'd been diving partners for so long that we easily anticipated each other's movements. Some of the other people around us twisted and writhed, making sure they could see their partners in the water, but we didn't have to do that. I glanced over and Teddy gave me an OK sign. The area we were diving was pretty shallow, nothing like some of the wrecks we'd been on, and we didn't need to worry about sharks, so we were able to relax and just enjoy ourselves.

Our first stop was Big Crack, which Teddy thought was absolutely hilarious. Despite the laughable moniker, this spot was where the two tectonic plates were nearest to each other and the water was the deepest, though we didn't approach full depth. We snapped pictures of each other touching both rocky walls before moving on to other parts of the fissure. I found myself thinking about Huck while we meandered between the rock walls, fingertips hovering just over the surface—wondering how he'd describe this, planning how I could put it into words for him. He'd stayed at the cabin, where he would be warmer than us, surely, but missing this incredible experience. And bigger than that, and more surprising, I found myself missing *him*.

I didn't do this.

I didn't get attached or miss people that I'd just met. Still, Teddy was filming with his underwater camera, memorializing the adventure as he always had, and instead of absorbing the walls of rock or the one hundred meters of visibility, I was worrying that the video wouldn't do this experience and the sights justice when we shared it with Huck later.

Teddy and I spent about forty minutes in the water, and then our tour leaders let us know that it was time to come out. Our guide Anna had hot chocolate prepared, and we sipped, relishing the heat and sweetness. While we drank to warm up, the other guide, Einar, gave us a brief geo-history lesson. We listened in silence. A light rain started to fall.

When Einar's presentation ended, Teddy leaned over and said, "Stell, send the picture of me in the fissure to Sully, will you? Let's caption it: I touched Big Crack and I liked it."

I made a face. "You're going to have to send that one yourself, bud. Hey, I meant to ask you, what were you and Huck talking about this morning when I came in the kitchen?"

Teddy lifted his shoulders. "Nothing major."

"It seemed important," I pressed.

"Since when are you so interested in non-treasure-related conversations?" Teddy teased. He took a long draw of his drink. "Anna, this cocoa is incredible. Is there more?"

She returned his grin and walked over to us with another cup. They had a moment of extended eye contact, in which I recognized all of Teddy's tells of an impending hookup—the slight lift of his eyebrows, the slow movement of his thumb tracing the rim of his cup—and her response, a slow flutter of her lashes, pale and rain-speckled, against her cheeks.

"I know a place nearby where there's better hot chocolate," she said.

Teddy nodded. "Sounds amazing."

Trying my best to be a good wing woman, I took my cue to step away and take a few pictures of the landscape before we had to leave. Einar was busy stowing the scuba gear and dry suits away in preparation of our departure. Teddy jogged over.

"So Anna invited me to join her and some of her friends for a bit of climbing and dinner after this. I guess she knows the chef at this restaurant in Reykjavík that I really wanted to try and she says she can get us in after."

"Sounds great."

"You don't mind if I ride back to the city with her? You know how to get back to the cabin, right?"

I nodded. "Sure. I'm pretty beat anyway. I'm good to head back on my own."

I was well accustomed to Teddy's desertions by now. He would meet someone intriguing and go off with them for a while, but he always came back. That was all that mattered. Sometimes his crow-like nature of being constantly attracted by shiny things irritated me, but I got it. He wanted to suck the marrow out of life, one climb or conquest at a time. His bailing had little impact on me today, though. I planned to make the most of my time alone on the drive back to think more about Gunnarsson's treasure—I knew there was something there that I just hadn't seen yet. And then back at the cabin . . . I'd be on my own with Huck.

Only the two of us.

And just the idea of it gave me a little thrill.

NINE

Stella

The sun started to break through the clouds just as I pulled up in front of Huck's rental cabin. I found him inside, tucked in a corner, tapping away on a laptop keyboard. I didn't want to disturb his writing, so I stood for a moment observing him before shutting the door behind me as quietly as possible. The electronic lock beeped, and he looked up.

"You're back. How was it?" Huck's voice was bright and he took off his glasses and shut his computer, giving me his full attention. He didn't seem to mind the interruption.

I settled onto the couch, tucking one leg under the other. "Transcendent. I've honestly never seen water that clear. We took a bunch of video and pictures— Shit, Teddy has the camera with him."

"Wait, he's not here?"

"He had what seemed like a date with the guide."

Huck shook his head, chuckling. "That guy. It's so funny to me that we haven't seen each other in years, but he hasn't changed a bit. Still, she must've been impressive if he chose to go off with her and send you back on your own."

"She was exquisite," I admitted. "And there was something

about her knowing the executive chef at this restaurant in the city that Ted had been dying to go to. You know how he is—determined to eat, drink, and sleep his way through every new place he visits." My stomach grumbled with envy at the mention of eating.

"Are you hungry?" Huck asked. He must've heard my stomach. I flushed. "Because I'm ravenous and all I have left around here is a licorice-flavored chocolate bar and strange bottle of some local liquor."

"I'm famished," I confessed.

"That settles it. We're going out. I'm sure there's someplace nearby that we can go for food," he said. He eyed his phone for a moment. "It looks like there's a pizza place a few miles south. They should be open. Pizza okay with you?"

"Pizza's perfect. I hate to admit this as I consider myself an adventurer, but I did not care for the Icelandic hot dog I had the day before yesterday."

"Was it the onions two ways, or the sauce?" he asked.

"It was the whole package. I wanted to love it. I tried. Teddy liked it—he ate four."

"I think we both know that he will eat anything. You know, back when we were in school, he was known for making weird concoctions in the dining hall and eating them purely for everyone's amusement. For a whole month, he got super into making a sandwich and pouring different liquids on it each day. He called it marinating his food and ate it with a spoon while everyone cheered him on." Huck chuckled at the memory.

"Sounds like Teddy."

"Meanwhile, I can't even handle the licorice in my chocolate bar. I bought it by accident."

"I never was a licorice girl." I flashed him a conspiratorial grin. "Give me peanut butter with my chocolate any day, but never licorice. Let's go."

The pizza place was still serving, thankfully. Huck opened the door for me and my stomach did a little flip; I couldn't be sure if it was a result of his gallantry or the enticing aroma of food. A waitress led us to a booth nestled in a dark corner at the back of the restaurant. We settled in with our menus.

"No pressure, but I'm expecting sparkling conversation given your literary chops."

"Oh, I'll take that challenge, Stella Moore. I have so many questions for you as soon as we order."

We fell into a comfortable silence while we examined the menus. I picked a specialty pizza that sounded intriguing, featuring an Icelandic cheese assortment in conjunction with jam; the description had me convinced that it would either be sublime or super revolting. Huck went with a standard Margherita-style pizza. We got Úlfrún beer in golden cans, which we clunked together too hard, sending a bit of foam spilling over.

"So you have some questions for me," I said when the waitress had departed.

Huck nodded. "I do. But I'll warn you, these aren't the standard what's-your-favorite-film and what's-your-family-like kind of questions."

"Fine by me." The last thing I wanted to do was spoil the evening by talking about my family.

Huck leaned forward a bit. "First question: If you could have dinner with anyone—besides your current dinner companion, of course—who would it be and why?"

"Okay, I was not expecting that."

"What were you expecting?"

"I don't know. Maybe something like *Why'd you order the pizza with the jam, especially after the hot dog let you down . . .*"

He grinned at me. "Oh, I know why you ordered that. You thrive on danger! You still owe me an answer, though."

I pondered his question while I laughed. I wanted to say something cool and light, but somehow this question had steered me to the one place I didn't want to go. There was only one person who I would've asked for . . . my dad. But I knew it wasn't possible. He was gone and had been since that day at the beach in Corolla. And I didn't have a habit of asking questions I probably couldn't handle the answers to, like, *Why did you leave me all alone when you'd promised that you'd be back and we'd go hunt together, when I* needed *you?* I fiddled with my napkin.

"This is hard!" At least that part was honest. "I gotta go with Amelia Earhart. I mean, one, she was amazing, way ahead of her time, totally brilliant and ballsy, right? And then two, I've always been desperate to know what exactly happened to her. It's like one of those great mysteries."

"Mmm, solid choice. You know, I actually wanted to write an Amelia Earhart book a while back. I had it all outlined, but there wasn't a lot of interest at my publisher for it. They're less hearty nonfiction and more heart-pounding adventure, I suppose. Definitely an easier sell."

"Their loss. Seriously. That would've been amazing. Just think, if I had dinner with her, I could tell you what happened and then you'd have a bestseller on your hands."

"Let me know if it works out, because I absolutely would take you up on that. *Stella and Amelia Have Dinner.*"

"Title might need some work."

Huck laughed. "Maybe so. I try not to get too invested in my titles since they often change."

"How so?" Though I'd been trying not to bring up his career too much, I was genuinely curious about the whole writing and publishing process with the same level of interest that he'd shown earlier when I was telling him about Gunnarsson.

"Well, not sure if all publishers do this, but mine changes a lot of my titles. I guess I'm not great at naming my books."

"Okay, well now I need an example."

Huck thought for a moment. "My third book in the Casablanca Chronicles was originally called *Everybody Loves Clark's Bar*."

"Like the candy?"

"I'll have you know that it's peanut butter and taffy combined then dipped in chocolate and has been around for over a hundred years, so clearly an epic candy choice for a title. Way better than licorice. You'd love it. But I didn't name it for the candy. In fact, I didn't even realize it at the time. It was supposed to be a reference to *Everybody Comes to Rick's*—the play that was adapted into *Casablanca*—though my editor said no one would get it and that the sales team found it boring."

"Your editor told you that?"

"No, he's way too kind to tell me that they thought it was boring. He said something a million times more tactful and sent a couple of suggestions."

I laughed. "That's interesting. Now I have to know who you'd pick to have dinner with. Is it Humphrey Bogart or Ingrid Bergman?"

"Honestly, my current dinner companion is tough to top. But since this is a hypothetical, I guess I'd have to say Tolstoy?" he said, like he was asking a question. "He's written some of the most amazing books of all time, at least in my humble opinion. I'd like to talk literature with him, and maybe ask him if he ever got writer's block and how he got over it."

"Good plan. Do you speak Russian?" I took a sip of my drink.

"Well, I figure in this magical world where a deceased writer can eat dinner with me, we wouldn't have a language barrier, but that is a good point. Maybe I should keep working on that one and have a backup plan just in case."

"Google translate? A guest interpreter, maybe?"

"I really didn't think through the stipulations of this question before I asked it. It's turning into a Schrödinger's cat situation."

"Ask me another one, then."

Huck took a leisurely sip of his beer, thinking. "Hmm . . . okay, how about this one? Do you ever get the feeling that you know how you're going to die?"

"Jesus!" I said. "You just go right for the emotional jugular. Not even a *what's your favorite sexual position*, just straight to death."

He choked on the sip he'd taken. "Sorry," he said, and cleared his throat. "A while back I read an article where they shared all these questions that would help you get to know someone on a deeper level. I can't claim ownership of these. I think I may have gotten the order wrong."

"It does make sense that a person might need a bit of an ice-breaker before discussing their eventual demise, but I'll give you a pass about your death question. Consider yourself saved by my generous nature." I tried to suppress my grin. "I don't have a sense, but I hope it's glorious. I want it to be doing something I love, like having some great adventure."

"'To die will be an awfully big adventure . . .'"

"*Peter Pan?*"

He nods. "I always loved that one, except for the racism, of course. Once upon a time I toyed with trying to write a modern version but didn't think I could do it justice."

And I smiled then because even as a teen I felt a kinship with those Lost Boys, all on their own, having to tend to themselves but never growing up. "Honestly, given the odds, it'll probably be something with the ocean. I spend most of my time there—

Iceland's kind of a one-off trip that I convinced everyone else to go on. All our other expeditions have been at sea, mostly around Florida and in the Caribbean."

"I think I'm going to go in my sleep when I'm extremely old. I'm a boring guy who eats a lot of vegetables."

The thought of Huck Sullivan calling himself boring was laughable, but also so incredibly endearing. "That doesn't sound half bad. What's the next question?"

"I'll give you two for balance," Huck said, shifting our drinks so the waitress could set down our pizzas more easily. "Thank you so much," he told her before continuing. "What's your greatest accomplishment, and what's your most embarrassing moment?"

"I don't have a greatest accomplishment yet. I'm working on it. For now, maybe my friendships? They're the most special part of my life, but I wouldn't be here if it weren't for them, so I guess, it's not really *my* accomplishment . . . I'm sort of theirs, and they have tons. I like to think I'm on the cusp of my greatest triumph."

"I believe that." Huck flashed such a genuine smile at me that I stopped breathing for a second.

"I've got way more material in the embarrassing department," I admitted, breaking the moment. "But I want to hear about your greatest accomplishment before I ruin myself for you."

"I don't think that's possible." He pulled a slice of pizza onto my plate and handed it to me before taking his own. "I have to confess, I'm skeptical about the jam, Stella."

"I thought you had faith in me." I took a bite and grinned at Huck while I groaned obnoxiously. It was fabulous. Rich and salty and sweet—the amalgamation of the diverse flavors creating the perfect bite. A little weird and utterly scrumptious. "It's amazing." I held it out for Huck and he guided my hand closer. An incandescent thrill ran down my spine as he took a bite of the slice.

"How is this good?" he asks. "My mind is blown."

"I hope it's not completely blown, because you still owe me an accomplishment," I said.

"Good point. It's probably an obvious choice, but I guess it would have to be publishing the Casablanca Chronicles. I always wanted to write—I was super into it even when I was at Monadnock. I got an agent with the first query letter I sent out my freshman year of college. I know how it sounds, but I stupidly thought I had it made. I was a dumb kid. I wrote six books that went nowhere before I thought to write a story with Clark as a main character, and I penned the first book in the Chronicles. I clocked so many rejections and it was like the only word anyone had for me was *no*. But I got better each time and kept pushing and didn't give up. It changed my whole life, but I worked for it. I guess that's what I'm proud of. Not the most exciting answer . . ."

"I can relate, though. I imagine that there were plenty of people telling you that it wouldn't happen, right? I hear that all the time. And it's brutal to keep trying to make something happen when the universe and everybody else keeps telling you no, or that you aren't good enough. It's up to you to block all that out and keep going."

"Exactly."

"That's what hunting treasure is like for me. We all have our own reasons for going out there and searching again and again when the odds are against us. Gus trained in underwater archaeology, so it's his passion and his fieldwork. Zoe loves diving and interacting with sea life more than just about anything."

"Interesting."

"Believe me, it's a very useful proclivity when there are sharks in the waters we're searching. She can redirect a shark away from us with the same mastery that she uses when she's cross-examining in the courtroom."

Huck swallowed. "You swim with sharks?"

"Zoe does. The rest of us just occupy the same vicinity and try not to pee in our wetsuits."

The humor transformed the anxious expression on Huck's face, and he joined me as I laughed at my own joke.

"What about you? What's your reason to keep at it?" he asked.

I ran through my mental Rolodex of memories, trying to select how much to share with Huck. It was so easy to talk to him. I could've told him about my father's obsession with the Elephant's Heart Diamond. That my mom was convinced it was cursed . . . And maybe it *was* in some sense since it had destroyed my family. There were things I could barely admit to myself, though, like the reason why I couldn't give up on searching for the diamond because somewhere deep inside I believed that if I discovered it eventually, maybe my parents would find out and realize what they'd lost by leaving me. I'd show them how wrong they'd been, about the curse, about not believing, about leaving. I took a deep breath.

"I guess you could say that I feel like I have something to prove."

"Same here. It makes perfect sense to me why you get what writing is like for me," Huck said. "Both are acts of faith."

"We're motivated and persistent. True believers. At least they can give that to us."

"I'll toast to that."

TEN

Huck

The cabin was empty when Stella and I returned from dinner. Ted must've been calling it a night with the guide he went off with. The knowledge that Stella and I were truly alone here had my heart thrumming faster than its normal pace. We'd had an amazing meal and an even better time together. The more I learned about Stella, the more fascinated I became. I was still getting used to the strange dichotomy of being around her, of my heart racing with anticipation and the rest of me feeling strangely comfortable at the same time.

The air temperature had dipped and the cabin was cool, so I turned my attention to building a small fire in the stove. I liked the idea of making sure Stella was warm enough. While I arranged wood, she toured the small living room, tracing the books on the bookshelves with her fingertips.

We had talked nonstop through the meal, and even though I had used questions I'd borrowed from a *New York Times* article to get the conversation started amidst my nerves, it had flowed naturally. My ex-fiancée, Vanessa, was the last person I'd dated, and after she left, I'd essentially gone full recluse. It'd been so long since I'd been on a date, I hadn't been sure that it was possible for me not to have some sort of stilted encounter, but Stella was easy to talk to. Now, the silence that settled between us wasn't the awkward kind. It was taut, electrically charged. Exciting. A little terrifying in how much I enjoyed it. A flame finally rose from the kindling, and I added another small log for good measure before closing the glass. I didn't want to have to go back to the stove again tonight. I brushed my hands together and joined her at the bookshelves.

"They don't have the Casablanca Chronicles," she said, her voice tinged with disappointment.

"I'm not sure it ever sold in Iceland," I said. In truth, the series had been translated into over forty languages, including Icelandic. I just didn't have the heart to tell her that I was relieved about its absence from the cabin. Seeing my books, especially the last one, was something that I actively avoided, even now, more than three years after its release. I kept thinking it would get easier, but the opposite was true. Without something new to focus on, the voices of real-world critics had space to expand and take over—reviewers, Vanessa, angry fans, my dad . . . their narrative drowned out my own.

Stella turned to face me. "I was going to say that these owners don't seem to have much taste in terms of books since they don't have yours, but actually they've got some good ones. The have all of Eva Björg Ægisdóttir's books, which are incredible. Look, Fredrik Backman's *Anxious People*—I loved that one." She pulled out a worn copy of *Smilla's Sense of Snow* and flipped through it. "And I read this one years ago. It was mind-blowing. Chilling and so atmospheric for a mystery."

"I read that one too," I said. "It's fantastic."

She shelved it carefully. "I meant to ask you, how did your writing go today? Are you feeling inspired at all?"

"I wrote a few pages," I told her. "They're probably only good for fuel for the fireplace." Even though I had been excited to sit and flesh out the ideas that had started germinating when we'd searched that waterfall the other day, the reality of trying to turn them into something on the page had felt a bit like surgically removing my own organs—painful, exhausting, and extremely ill-advised—until it hadn't. It started roughly, but then my fingers were flying across the keyboard. I could barely remember what I'd written.

She slid *Home Before Dark* from the shelf and examined the back. "Really? I bet they're great."

I shook my head. "Nope. Definitely not."

"I find that hard to believe. Are you sure you're not just being too hard on yourself?"

I didn't think I was, but it was my default to critique myself. Despite the time and distance, I still heard lingering echoes of my father's harsh judgments ringing in my ears, the acidic way he'd call me Henry because he knew I hated it, the constant admonishments no matter what I accomplished.

Stella was undeterred by my silence. "I could read them, or you could read them to me, if you want a second opinion. It'd be a good distraction from the fact that we're in this isolated cabin whose owners packed the shelves with crime fiction."

I'd never been one to share my writing with people until I was done, but the idea of reading to Stella on a couch in front of a fire, running my fingers through her hair as she nestled against me, was surprisingly appealing. Maybe I'd find myself surprised and like what I'd written when she was the one whose opinion mattered. Then, I recalled a paragraph that I'd composed in a near fugue state. In it, I'd spent multiple sentences describing the curve of her cupid's bow and still more on the slope of the nape of her neck, the compass rose tattoo, the scent of her skin, the hollow of her clavicle and the Piece of Fight necklace seated in the dip between her collarbones. I cleared my throat. "I don't really share my works in progress." Heat flamed on my neck. I wondered if she could see me flush in the firelight.

"Sorry. I probably overstepped." She turned from me, returning the crime novel to the shelf. "I've been known to get ahead of myself."

"You didn't," I said. This warranted a glance over her shoulder. I wrapped my fingers gently around her wrist; her pulse throbbed beneath my fingertips. "You're not ahead of yourself at all."

She turned and eyed me. "Oh."

"I might be, though."

Her voice was almost a whisper. "I don't think so." She looked down to where my hand still circled her wrist. It was a dare, or something, I couldn't be sure. When she raised her gaze to mine, her hazel eyes were all mischief. She lifted a hand to my chest. Could she feel my heart pounding? Was she breathing fast? I didn't know. There was only the fact that her eyes were still locked on mine. The heat in our gaze was searing.

It had been so long . . . so long since I wanted to be this close to someone, since I was willing to take a risk. I took a step toward her, closing the distance between us, and then another, backing her up into the bookshelf. She smiled at me when some of the books toppled over onto their sides with a thump. God, she was so freaking beautiful when she grinned at me like that. I let her wrist go and laced my fingers through hers, pinning her hand above her head against a shelf. I traced her collarbone softly with my other thumb and she caught the back of my henley in her free hand, pulling me closer until there was no space left between us. I was conscious of each point of contact, wondering if it was too much or not enough. I wanted it to be perfect for her. But then her lips parted slightly, an invitation, like she knew what I was asking and she was answering me. Somehow it was too much, it was not enough, it was perfect all at once. *She* was perfect. I leaned down and she met me halfway, bringing her lips to mine, soft but certain. *Keep cool*, I told myself, but there was a hot hunger rising in me that was hard to control. Her mouth was sweet from the red currant jam, her lips plush against mine. We matched each other, naturally finding the right tilt of our heads, shifting our hands and bodies in response, falling into a rhythm. I couldn't help but think that this was supposed to happen.

I could've written an entire volume without finding the exact words to adequately describe this kiss and yet, it was the kind of kiss that deserved a whole book devoted to it. We were spiraling, twisting our limbs together until it was hard to tell where I ended and she began. I slid my hands beneath the bottom edge of her sweater.

"Okay?" I asked, starting to lift it.

She nodded. "Get it off of me," she said. Everything stopped for an instant. I don't think my heart beat, and I know I didn't breathe. And then I was racing, pushing the sweater up, sweeping my hands over the silk camisole she wore beneath it, flinging the sweater down on the floor beside us. I found her mouth again, hungrily this time. She reached for the button on my jeans.

A horn beeping in the driveway caught our attention. We broke apart, breathless, startled. I'd been so caught up in her, in the feel of her, in her taste, that I'd forgotten where we were. I barely remembered that a world outside of the space we occupied against the bookshelf existed at all.

"What the hell?" Ted stood silhouetted in the doorway by the blinding headlights of a departing car.

"Teddy," Stella said, her tone unreadable. She stooped to pick up her sweater. "You're back."

"Uh, yeah. It's a fuh-king reunion." His voice was singsong.

Not angry, I didn't think, but very drunk. He swayed as he took a step forward.

"How was dinner?" Stella asked, tucking her passion-tousled hair behind her ears.

"Fantastic. I brought home dessert to share"—he held up a small bag with handles—"but I see you two were already partaking in your own version."

"I'm full," Stella said.

Ted took a step toward her and stumbled on the edge of the rug. I reached out to help him get his feet back under him. He smelled unfamiliar, like a drunk pickle. I sniffed again. "Is that dill?"

"Yeah, I had this special drink called Brennivín, aka Black Death, icy cold. Apparently I love Brennivín. Who knew? We had two kinds—caraway and dill—so good guess, Sully. You win the prize. Good old Sully. So smart." He patted my cheek a few times, hard enough that the collective impact stung like a slap. "You guys should try it." I helped lower him to the couch. "It's the national drink of Iceland."

"I'm glad you had fun," Stella told him, gently taking the bag of desserts from his hand and starting on his shoelaces. I got some water from the kitchen.

"Not as much fun as you," he slurred. "Black Death had unintended side effects." He curled his index finger dramatically and glanced down, and I closed my eyes in embarrassment. Stella, to her credit, pretended not to understand.

I handed him the glass. "Take a couple sips, Ted."

Stella pulled a blanket over him. "Time for bed," she said.

"Bossy," he slurred, but closed his eyes.

We walked down the hallway, silent tension between us like a coiled spring. "So . . ." I started, running a hand over my hair.

She stopped and turned toward me in front of the guest room door. Did she want me to invite her into my room? She beckoned me with a subtle curving of her fingers toward her palm, and I leaned across the distance in the small hallway.

"Just tell me one thing," she said, "did you kiss me so you didn't have to tell me what your new book is about?"

I shook my head. If only she knew—she'd asked me to read it to her, and I'd gone ahead and lost my composure and practically acted it out. It would've been so easy to pick up where we left off right here, or in one of our rooms. But I didn't want to push my luck and mess this up before it even began. If we were going to do this, it needed to be right. Not just hooking up in the hall while Ted snored on the couch. I cleared my throat and tried to dismiss the daydream that was quickly burning its way into my memory.

"We just got caught up in a rogue moment of fun, then?" she asked.

"I can only speak for myself, but that was way more than a moment of fun for me. You had me feeling . . . inspired."

ELEVEN

Stella

Huck Sullivan was an amazing kisser. His books had always featured the kind of slow-burning passion that built, and then right before it came to the part where one might be inclined to use a euphemism for an intimate body part or make mention of a condom, the door would swing shut and the chapter would end, leaving readers to use their imaginations regarding whether Clark Casablanca was a considerate yet commanding lover or not.

The past few minutes had been sort of like that. It'd been so unbelievably good as it escalated, his touch on my neck, the way his fingertips skimmed the sensitive skin of my clavicle, how he'd walked me back and trapped me against the bookshelf and pinned my hand above my head exactly how I'd hoped he would. It was without a doubt the sexiest kiss I'd ever had, and now I was pressed up against the bedroom door willing him to come back and finish what we'd started.

Actually, it was good that Teddy had interrupted things.

If the way Huck had kissed me was any indication, no one could've lived up to the legend of Huck Sullivan after this. It would be too easy to get close, too close . . . to get attached.

Still. I spun around. I could just knock on his door. He did say that he'd felt inspired, and wasn't that the whole point of his trip? It wasn't like he admitted he had feelings for me.

"Stella." A low voice through the door sent a startled thrill up my spine.

I rotated to open the door slowly, silently. Huck's hair was more messed up than it had been a few minutes earlier, even after I'd had my hands through it. I'd noticed he had a habit of mussing it when he was deep in thought—why was I cataloging his idiosyncrasies?—but he wasn't doing that now. His hands were in the pockets of his sweatpants. He rocked back and forth on his feet.

"Mind if I come in for a second?" His voice was low; he almost sounded nervous.

I stepped aside, trying to ignore my entire body crackling with electric desire.

"I was thinking . . ."

Was he thinking what I was thinking? That maybe we should just stop thinking because if I let my brain have its way I would talk myself right out of whatever this was quickly turning into, wherever this might go, and I didn't want that. I wanted *him*. His hands on me, his lips, his stories. I waited for him to finish.

"Would it be cool if I stayed with you tonight?"

I hesitated while my body and the last shred of logic in my brain battled it out. "Okay."

"We won't do anything. I just want to be near you."

"Oh." The sound practically fell from my mouth, surprising me. I hadn't expected the mix of happiness and disappointment I felt.

"I don't think we should," he added. There went the hand for the hair again. "Not that I don't want to. I mean, I want— What I mean is, there's something here. At least for me. But I don't want to mess this up or rush the physical part." He was flustered and so was I.

I bit my lip. "I understand what you're saying. So yes, you can stay with me." I reached for his hand to reassure him, and he wove his fingers between mine. "I probably should tell you, I'm kind of a restless sleeper. Wandering hands, all that. Don't say you haven't been warned."

Huck grinned and leaned down to brush his lips over mine. Then he moved on to my forehead, my cheeks, dusting over them with his touch. "What are you doing?" I asked. "Not sure this is the best strategy to prevent us hooking up."

"You have this magical Milky Way of freckles that I can't resist."

"Seriously? I don't like my freckles, actually. I used to get teased about them when I was a kid."

"No. That's not possible. They're the best thing ever. I want to kiss every single one."

"Again, not the best way to avoid being intimate."

"I don't want to give you the wrong idea. I definitely don't want to avoid intimacy with you . . . I just want us to have the chance to make sure we really know each other."

"Okay, in that case, you might want to turn around so I can get into my pajamas."

Huck covered his eyes and swiveled away from me. I'd never been shy, but there was something about this that I liked. "Tell me more about how you met Ted. He said you raided him on a beach?"

I smiled, even though the memory was bittersweet.

"Yeah, well, I grew up in the Outer Banks. I guess fate brought us together. I was having a horrible day when we met. It was the kind of bad day that almost made me hate the beach. But you know how it is— Teddy's the kind of person who makes everything better."

"Very true."

"You can turn around now." I pulled the covers back on the bed and climbed in. Huck gave me a long look before he moved toward the bed. "So you don't hate beaches?"

"Not at all. I love them. Though the beaches back home are completely different than the ones here."

"You know, there's a beach near this cabin. It's a short walk down a path just off the back deck."

"I'd love to see it."

"We should go out there one night. It's no diamond beach, but it is black and it shimmers a bit. The stars are absolutely incredible. Kind of like those freckles of yours." He reached for the bedside lamp.

"That sounds amazing. There's nothing better than a night at the beach or on the sea, underneath trillions of stars, to remind us of our place in this world."

"I'm more of a wisher, myself."

"Why is that?"

"I guess I manage to feel insignificant on my own without infinite points of light flickering down from millions of light-years away to remind me."

"That's a lot to unpack. Not that I'm against wishing, I just think that the sky is sort of the great equalizer . . . we're all underneath it, right?"

"Truthfully? I don't get to see much of the starry night sky at home, living in New York."

"Well, you have lots of other things to do there, I'm sure. Isn't it the city that never sleeps?"

"And I'm the guy that never sleeps in it," he said, and forced out a dry laugh.

"Is that insomnia or you staying up late brainstorming?" I asked, hoping that mentioning writing wasn't a sore subject since he'd struggled so much with it until today.

"Fully insomnia. I can't get out of my head. Honestly, before things went sideways, I spent most of my time writing at night. I've never been a great sleeper."

"And what do you do when you're not writing?"

"Other than jet off to Iceland and tag along on treasure hunts with a charismatic woman I met in a bar and my old boarding school roommate?" He laughed. "Not much. I write. I worry about writing. I worry about not writing."

"Sounds like a lot of worrying."

"Yeah, I guess it does. I never really thought about it. I *do* other things in addition to worrying. I cook—I make a really good lasagna. Some people say it's better than the one at Eataly. I volunteer at a writing project for at-risk youth; that's probably my favorite thing I do. I research. I could spend whole days at a time at the New York Public Library."

I'd seen pictures of those famous lions outside the library but had never been to New York. I had to imagine Huck, head bowed over a book lit by the warm glow of one of those old-fashioned task lamps with the green glass shade.

"Is that why your books always feel so believable? The research?"

Huck lowered his head to the pillow next to me. We both tucked our hands next to our cheeks. "That's right, you've read all seven of my well-researched books."

I buried my face in my pillow for a second before answering. "I swear, Teddy's on some kind of mission to humiliate me. First he spills my dark secret and then earlier when he barged in . . ."

"He can be an agent of chaos, that's for sure. Mostly good chaos, though," Huck said this gently, running his fingers over a tendril of my hair that had fallen out of the messy sleep bun I'd crafted. "Fascinating that you consider reading my books your dark secret."

I used my hands to hide my face from him.

"It's sort of reminiscent of when people call romance novels their guilty pleasure. I read a fascinating essay about how that's rooted in internalized misogyny not long ago, actually, but I still have to ask . . . are my books your guilty pleasure?" I was sure he was just teasing, but his books did feel a bit like a guilty pleasure given the level of crush I'd developed on Clark Casablanca and the man who had written him. I peeked through my fingers and found him still looking at me.

I crumbled beneath the weight of his stare. *"No."*

"I'm sure you have some thoughts about them," he said.

"This is embarrassing."

"I don't think so. I'm honestly desperate to know what you think."

I took a breath. "They're good."

"*Good* is the polite thing that friends say when they don't want to tell you that something is actually the opposite. You hate them, don't you? Did you hate-read my books? You seem like someone who might."

"Are we friends? I know you and Teddy are old pals, but *we* just met. I have no reason to try to spare your feelings. Besides, I didn't hate-read. I didn't even know that was a thing."

"Sorry, was the friend label presumptuous of me? I guess I've been feeling some kind of connection with you. After all, we are in bed together . . . platonically as it were."

I smiled at Huck's words, despite my best efforts.

"I know I shouldn't be using you for validation. Blame the fragile state of my ego; my agent told me not to call him until I had a solid first chapter, and he's usually the one who feeds my need for praise. No thoughts, then? Constructive feedback?"

"If I recall correctly, you made out with me against a bookshelf to avoid reading me your new story."

"That's right. I did, didn't I?" He kissed me lightly, as if reminding both of us what had gone down. "Any feedback on that?"

I shook my head. Did I have feedback? Of course I did. Lips, five stars. Hand placement, five stars. Freaking everything, five stars. Take my clothes off and ravish me. Five stars, a hundred stars, an infinity's worth of stars. It took every ounce of my self-control not to climb on top of him. "I don't have feedback, per se," I began, specifically choosing to misinterpret his question as him still asking me for my thoughts about his books. "It's more of a query."

Huck raised his eyebrows.

I took a breath. "What happens to Clark Casablanca? Does he live, does he end up with Rebecca, or does he die trying to save her family?"

Huck sank a little next to me. I could feel him shift on the mattress as he heaved out a sigh. "Honestly, Stella, I would love to tell you, but I can't answer that."

"Oh. Are you planning to revive the series, so you're not allowed to talk about it or something? I won't tell anyone."

He shook his head. "I can't answer because I don't know."

"Wait, what?"

He was quiet for a few moments. I'd been trying to be light, to steer things away from how close we were to each other under the covers, but clearly, I'd led us straight into a totally different kind of trouble.

"Every writer is different. Some have whole stories come to them in dreams. Others write elaborate outlines and use *Save the*

Cat! Writes a Novel. Me? I am a character man. My characters speak to me, they practically write themselves—I'm just along for the ride. And Clark? He burst into my psyche and took over, for years. Honestly, his voice was louder than my own. Then, one day he stopped talking. He was strolling along the canal in Amsterdam and found that note in his pocket, and then, he just went silent. I tried to work out the ending of the book on my own when he didn't come through. Nothing worked. I couldn't figure out what was next, so I just wrote the first thing that came to mind, the easy ending, the one with no answers, just enough to make it all end. Then I stopped altogether. Everybody said I gave up, and they weren't wrong."

I squinted at Huck in the dim light of the bedroom, processing what he'd just admitted. I could only imagine how hard it was for him to tell me. I'd never heard about this before, and I felt like it must be that he hadn't told anyone else, because if he had, it would've been a story in a gossip column somewhere. I'd have seen it.

I had no idea what to say, or how to comfort him, but I knew I wanted to. I wanted him to feel safe and seen and supported, to understand that I didn't see him as just his books. That's what I would have wanted, but words failed me.

"That really sucks," I blurted. It probably wasn't the right thing to say. Not thoughtful or gentle or at all insightful, but I'd been quiet too long, and I had to say something—that's what came out.

A moment of nervousness followed, where I panicked about how he was going to respond to my super eloquent, empathetic comment, but he surprised me. He kept surprising me, actually. He laughed.

"Yeah, it sucks. It really fucking sucks." It was a whole-body laugh, so hard it shook the bed. I couldn't help but join in. I tried to restrain my own laughter because it felt so wildly inappropriate, like laughing at a funeral, that odd kind of laughter that always seemed to precede some sort of breakdown, but it was a struggle.

"It's funny," he said. "My agent, Jim, sent me to a shrink who was supposed to help me reconnect with my inner child." He snorted. I lost the last shred of composure I had been clinging to. I had to mash my face in my pillow so as not to wake Teddy.

"Inner child," I wailed. "I mean, we probably all need to heal our inner children, but still."

Huck continued sharing in intervals between his breathless bouts of laughter. "We tried hypnotism, but apparently I'm what they call 'hypnosis resistant.' It was back to the drawing board. My editor suggested changing my routine, and I started getting up early and going to SoulCycle. I wore spandex! I've never sweat so much in my life. And the chafing. The chafing was god-awful. When that didn't do anything other than change the way my pants fit on my thighs, I took the recommendation of a literary icon who I met at a party and consumed a tea made of magic mushrooms. Nothing—well, not completely nothing, I guess. I thought I could fly for a few hours and then I was violently ill."

I laughed so hard that full fat tears flooded my cheeks and my core muscles ached. Huck's laughter began winding down and then as quickly as we'd been overcome with the ridiculousness of it all, we both fell silent.

"I sprained both ankles with the flying thing. No Clark, though. The wildest part is that everyone kept giving me these bizarre tasks like that would fix it, fix *me*. No one ever got it. I didn't realize until just now how badly I wanted someone to acknowledge how I might be feeling, or that it was hard or even okay to be broken."

"You mean, no one ever came to you and was super eloquent and nuanced and moving in conveying the suckiness of your situation?"

"Nope. You're the first. Thanks for that. I don't know how you seem to know what I need, but I needed this, Stella. I feel so much lighter. I spent eight years with that guy chatting me up, and then he was gone. It sounds stupid to say it, but I was reeling. I went from this star everyone loved—well almost everyone—to someone people hated or pitied. I felt so alone and I didn't know how to move on and no one really seemed to get it until you, just now. And then I haven't written a worthwhile sentence in years, and again I meet you, and suddenly . . . I didn't write what I planned, but maybe it might actually have been good."

"You wrote some really incredible erotic fan fiction of us, didn't you?" I teased. "Is that why you didn't want me to read it?"

Huck's hand slid over my hip, and he nestled close enough that I could feel the warmth radiating from his skin.

"Truthfully?"

I nodded, stopping the dip of my chin so that my lips were only a fraction of an inch, an instant, away from his. When he spoke, his voice hummed through my entire body. His gaze dipped to my mouth.

"I spent two paragraphs on these lips, and it's the best fucking thing I've ever written."

TWELVE

Huck

Stella snored, that surprised me. It was an adorable little whir, like a kitten purring. I glanced over at her curled up beside me on the bed and mulled over this discovery. Honestly, she could've produced a perfect impression of a human lawnmower and I still would've wanted to spend every night next to her. But the gentle vibrato of her breathing only made her more magnetic. Up until now, I hadn't been able to believe that she was real. She was this magical creature. A treasure hunter, a muse? She even sounded made up. But the snoring confirmed she was not a character I'd invented or a figment of my desperate imagination. She turned a bit, nuzzling herself into me, and I wrapped my arm snugly around her. I wanted to keep her safe and warm. To pore over ancient poems and decipher clues with her. I was ready to hold her metal detector, or her purse, or her hand. Whatever she wanted.

I replayed our conversation from the night before. I was fairly certain that we'd both shared things that we hadn't told anyone else, and while that would've normally left me feeling incredibly exposed and like I was reeling with some sort of verbal hangover, I was relieved somehow. But I hadn't said everything.

I hadn't told her why Clark deserted me.

Dawn came early, too early for my liking, but an energy I hadn't felt in a long time left me unable to sleep. I watched Stella as she slumbered beside me, hands still tucked beneath her cheek, her pink lips parted slightly, a strand of light hair fallen over her cheek. The compass tattoo peeked out and made me wonder how many other hidden treasures she had for me to discover. I could've looked at her like this, so peaceful resting there, knowing that she felt safe enough with me to share, to fall asleep beside me, for hours, days even. I reached down to brush the strand from her face. Years?

I could buy a boat, I thought, learn to sail. It wouldn't matter that I get seasick. I could overcome that. Stella could teach me. She could plot our adventures and I could write them. Sea salt–flavored kisses and making love in the moonlight at anchor. I indulged in these daydreams while she snored away in my arms. We were giving couple interviews on *Good Morning America*—I did those again—telling the hosts about how we both found treasure in hidden depths and each other. She was waving to me from the bow of the boat before diving into some cerulean waters; I plunged in after her.

I wanted to stay like this, in a fantasy future conjured beneath the warm covers with the very real woman who'd made me want to imagine things again. My arm fell asleep and I got a crick in my neck, but I couldn't bring myself to move until she did. After she woke, we stayed close as we went about the morning, smiling slyly while we quietly made breakfast, stole kisses in the kitchen, and snuck outside to sip coffee on the patio.

By late morning, Stella had grown antsy and pounced on a still-sleeping Ted in total disregard for his tendency to wake up swinging, hungover or not. I tried not to delve too deeply into what Stella would know of waking him in the morning; just thinking about it made me feel physically sick, especially after I'd woken up to her in the morning like coming out of a dream I didn't want to end.

"I'm feeling lucky," she announced. "Let's go hunting."

"You're the worst, Stell," Ted groaned, sitting up and stretching. "Did you wake me up just to punish me for getting so very trashed last night?"

"Nope. I woke you up to be my bitch. And you're going to like it."

I bit back a laugh.

Ted rubbed his eyes. "You know me so well. Sullivan, please tell me that you have ibuprofen. The Black Death has me dying."

"I got you, man," I said, holding out a coffee and a couple of pills. Our days back at Monadnock had been a mix of hard-core academics, creative arts training, and clandestine partying, so I knew the routine. No one threw a party better than Ted, and he paid the price for his dedication to a good time. Whether it was somehow managing to get the motherlode from the New Hampshire state liquor store delivered in a trunk labeled *Winter Clothes* or fashioning a bong and filtering system out of any typical household item, Ted held that corner of the market on fun times. He was wild, that's for sure, but he also had this uncanny knack for figuring out what made a person tick and could use it to bring even the most reserved wallflower to life. He'd done that for me when I arrived at Monadnock, depressed and defeated. Ted became half cheerleader, half fun catalyst, the perfect antidote to my father's raging disapproval. This same special attention and energy made it impossible to stay mad at him, even if he had rerouted me last night with Stella.

Ted dragged himself off the couch and took the medicine with the coffee in a single gulp.

"Where are we headed, then, Boss Lady?"

She stabbed the map she'd been annotating during the trip with a finger. "Here."

"Beautiful," Ted said. "Sullivan, you're driving. I am in no condition and Stella's driving is too extreme for the fragile homeostasis my stomach is trying to maintain right now."

I agreed. Ted took his place in the back of the van, and Stella punched the address into the navigation system. The drive to the village of Skógar took several hours. We stopped once for gas and another time for food. Ted managed to keep his meal down and by late afternoon he was back to his normal self, amusing us with his wild stories and making up lyrics to sing along to the Icelandic music that played on the radio. His voice was just a tad off-key.

When we reached the parking lot for the Skógasafn Museum, the sun was nearly set; a few cars remained. We did the tourist thing and scoped out Kvernufoss, wandering the paths, taking pictures of each other in the fading light. I tried to keep my cool when the waning warmth of the gloaming transformed Stella's beauty into something that felt miraculous deep in my chest. Finally, the last of the tourists departed and we headed back to the van to get our gear.

"Aren't we near the other falls we searched?" I asked.

Stella nodded. "We passed it actually. It's a few minutes back the way we came."

"Do you have a good feeling about this one?" I asked Stella.

She eyed me for second. "I think maybe I do," she said, and winked. She turned on her headlamp just in time to see my ridiculous grin. I opened my mouth to speak, to save myself from the dumb look on my face, but she was already in motion, racing toward the falls. I knew she was fast, athletic, from the first outing, but somehow, I was still amazed by how nimbly she navigated the twisting path and odd rock jutting from the mossy ground as we neared the falls. The treasure trove of embarrassing-moment stories she'd claimed at the restaurant last night struck me as entirely implausible now. Ted and I followed with the equipment.

"Is she always like this?" I asked him.

He looked up at her just as she leapt over a rock. "Exhausting?" he asked. I guess he was still a little sour from being awakened.

Wonderful, I thought. "So full of life?"

Ted snorted. "Seriously, dude? Keep it in your pants."

"I didn't say I wanted to sleep with her, just that she has a certain joie de vivre."

"You're never as insufferable as when you start speaking in French, Sully. And I didn't black out last night. When I got home from my date, you fully had your tongue down her throat."

I coughed. "That isn't what—"

"You keep telling yourself that. Listen, bud, Stella is just Stella. More energy than she knows what to do with, doesn't know when to quit, only thinks about one thing."

I didn't even bother with the typical response that his "only thinking about one thing" comment warranted. Because her single-mindedness was on full display and I was soaking it up. Ahead of us, she dragged one hand along the rocky face leading to the falls.

It was a simple thing. Not the way her hair shone in the moonlight, or the curved lines of her in the shadow. Not her finding something or even looking back at me, even though I was desperate for it. It was the way she ran her fingers over the stone, almost mindlessly, caught up in her own world. A totally ordinary moment.

I fell in love with her.

THIRTEEN

Huck

Ted and I scrambled trying to catch up with Stella, who had disappeared behind a curtain of water. In the darkness behind the falls, the beam of light from Stella's headlamp scanned the ground and the craggy rock wall, which glistened with moisture. Stella was still at the center, quiet, while her fingertips glided over what looked like moss.

I drew up beside her, heart pounding. "What is it? Do you think something's here?" I asked, my voice low.

She traced the lines of rock.

"It fits," she said. "That line of text was the constant storm within the slice of earth, like a canyon. It fits." Several meters away from us, Ted had started sweeping an area with his metal detector. Stella was still for a moment, tuning everything out. I did the same: mentally washed away the roar of the falls, the uncertainty, until all I saw was her. She turned to me. "You asked me if I have a good feeling. I do. But it's more than that . . . It's hard to explain. There's something special in the sensation of the rock beneath my hands, the spongy moss, like a faint vibration in my knuckles. I know it sounds bizarre. It just feels like all the clues in the poem and nature are all coming together to lead us here."

"Instinct," I said. In the past few days, I'd learned that Stella goes almost entirely off of instinct. I got that. It was like when I started writing a story. I might have had an idea or a character or even just a question, but more than anything, I had a feeling that if I followed that thread, whatever it was, pulled at it just a bit, somehow things would fall into place. Like I just knew where to go.

"Yeah. Something like that."

The moss must've been anchored in some organic matter. She tightened her fingers around it and yanked.

"Stella," Ted said. "What are you doing? You can't just pull out plants."

Stella didn't respond. She was engrossed in rooting around in what seemed to be a hole of some kind in the rock that'd been filled with dirt.

"I think she feels something," I said.

She scooped out handfuls of dirt, littering the ground with the loose earth. "Help me," she said. Ted and I both stepped in and followed suit, using our hands like shovels to empty the contents.

"What is it?" Ted asked. "What do you feel?"

She shook her head. "I don't know. Might be nothing, but there's space here." She reached deeper. Stella was small and could almost fit her whole upper body in the empty pit. She rose on her tiptoes.

"I can't reach far enough."

I got the message and nodded at Ted. Together we lifted her a bit higher.

"That's good," she said. "Something's here. It's not rock and I don't think it's more soil. It's solid, but there's a give to it. I'm not sure but . . ."

My heartbeat thrummed faster in my ears. *Is this it? Is this fucking it?*

"Do you have something, Stella?" Ted asked, all traces of sleep and irritation gone from his voice.

She didn't answer. Her body twisted and writhed in my hands as she struggled to reach deeper. I lifted her higher, supporting her as she struggled to reach whatever she'd found.

"Stella," Ted said. "Talk. What is it?"

"I'm not sure. It's kind of rough. I don't think it's organic. I'm trying to get a grip on it," she said. "It's stuck."

I pushed my arm in next to hers until I found her hand. I settled mine over hers, just as I had last night before we fell asleep, and locked her grip in place. Together we wrestled the object free and lowered it to the ground.

"Careful," Ted warned as we set it down.

The three of us stood in stunned silence for several seconds, staring. Illuminated by our headlamps was a rudimentary box, roughly two feet by one-and-a-half feet. The wood was rotten, crumbling in some places, with a metal latch in the center of one side that must've been what Stella described earlier. The hardware was rusted and nearly unrecognizable, but still, it looked exactly like what an ancient Viking would hide their treasure in. There was a certain electricity coursing through the group. We were all breathing fast. Awestruck, too nervous to speak, like if we admitted what we were thinking, it wouldn't be real. It couldn't be. Could it?

Finally, Ted broke the silence. "Holy shit, guys! Is this what I think it is?"

We fell to our knees and lifted the lid together, gingerly. Stella had taught me well over the last couple of days, so I wasn't surprised by the reverence her careful movements revealed. She and Ted weren't here to destroy history. Stella's goal was to find lost things and preserve the past. And now that was my goal too. This chest had probably been locked at some point, but over the ages, moisture had compromised the structure enough that even without a key, the lock gave way and we were able to open it easily. The beam of Stella's headlamp hit the contents and the glimmer inside told us everything we needed to know. What Stella had been dreaming of had finally happened. I'd been desperate to be a part of the adventure since the moment I met her, and now it was all coming to fruition. I honestly couldn't believe my luck. The only thing better than your own dreams coming true is witnessing someone you care deeply about experience their own.

She found it. She . . . found treasure. Ted whooped, cantering in circles, dropping back down to dig his hands into the coins. I was strangely overcome that I got to be a part of this. That vicious voice I knew so well told me I didn't belong here. I tried to ignore it, told myself that even though she would've figured out the location without me, she'd given me the chance to help by showing me that poem in the bar and we'd worked it out together. It happened. I deserved to be a part of this. Maybe.

Stella walked back to the spot where she'd first touched treasure with just her fingertips in a dark hollow. I approached her as she tucked her hands back into the space. Maybe if I wrapped my arms around her, I could erase the bad thoughts. I wanted to kiss her so badly that my hands shook.

"What are you doing?" I kept my voice at a whisper.

"Lift me up again," she said. She unzipped her jacket and dropped it to the ground, instantly taking me back to that silk camisole she'd been wearing last night. How she'd felt against my hands, in my arms. How desperately I wanted to feel her again. *It's not about that right now*, I reminded myself while I tried not to notice how good her shampoo smelled. *We're discovering history.* My heart rate picked up again, but I complied wordlessly, reaching my hands around the sides of her waist, hoisting her up into the opening in the wall. She dragged herself deeper, and I shifted my hands instinctively to her thighs. I willed myself to keep it together. The excitement of the discovery and the feel of her body against my palms again created a potent mix of desire and adrenaline that surged through my arteries. I could barely hear Ted's triumphant shouts over the cacophony of my own body, my heartbeat thrumming like a bass drum, my pants growing taut as I went hard.

"I—I got it," she said.

I tightened my grip and pulled her back toward me, out of the pitch black she was in, lowering her down until her feet touched solid ground. She turned to me slowly. I had to kiss her. It was the only thing I could think of. What we'd done, what we'd found, the object she was holding in her hands . . . these things barely registered. Those whisper-chapped lips. My heart's trampoline routine in my chest. She was incredible. Beautiful.

Singular.

I wanted her to be mine, right here under the waterfall. "Stella," I rasped.

"Unbelievable!" Ted shouted, lifting a silver necklace glittering with jewels so that it caught in the moonlight. "Do you know how old this is?"

Stella turned to glance at him for an instant. When she faced me again, that perfect mouth of hers was curled into a smile. It took every ounce of control I had not to press my lips to hers. "Don't you want to see what all that effort was for?" she asked.

I was already looking at it. At her. *A brave man would tell her that*, the voice said. *A man like Clark Casablanca.*

I know, I thought. *I've got it.* It had been drilled into me over the years. I wasn't brave. I wasn't anything of importance. I was a failure.

I broke eye contact first. Together we lowered to a crouch across from one other, staring down at the object she'd extracted from the wall. It was long, slender, bound in tattered cloth. The cold had made our fingers clumsy and we fumbled with the bindings for a few moments before we were able to free the ties. Then we carefully unwrapped the fabric and stared. It wasn't much to look at in its current form, but beneath the patina of time and elements was what must've been a magnificent silver axe back in its day. Stella used the cloth to gently brush some detritus away from its surface and held it up.

"Teddy!" she called. "Look!"

"Holy shit!" Ted yelled back. "It's like Iceland's version of Excalibur! All hail King Stella!"

She looked at us both. Ted and then me. "This is it," she said. "We really found it!"

I pulled out my phone and snapped a picture of her holding the axe in the air triumphantly. The falls had soaked her skin and hair so that she glistened in the light of Ted's headlamp.

"I wish Zoe and Gus were here," Stella said. "They wouldn't believe it. We did it," she said. "We really did it."

Ted pulled her into a tight embrace and kissed the top of her head. "*You* did it," he told her. "You. You're the one who wouldn't let any of us quit, who led us here." There was something intimate about the moment, a certain quality to the placement of his hands, the tone of his voice, the way he spoke to her, their matching Piece of Eight necklaces . . . It made me want to look away and sent envy coursing hot through my veins. I turned my attention to a small pebble on the ground that I pushed with the toe of my boot. I wanted to crumple these thoughts on a page and throw them in the garbage, like the other false starts I'd had these past months toiling on my next book.

"Are you writing this?" Stella asked, snapping me out of my daze. She did a little victory dance.

I shook my head, fixing my gaze on her. I wanted nothing

more than to sweep her up in my arms. To do more than kiss the top of her head and whisper, *You did it*. And I hated myself a little for that.

I shoved my hands into the pockets of my jacket. "You're something, Stella. Really something."

"That's King Stella to you."

FOURTEEN

Stella

It was brutally late when we arrived back at Huck's cabin, though I didn't feel it. I was still basking in the high of what was arguably the best night of my life. The excitement drained out of Teddy an hour into the drive, his hangover cycling into a second phase that seemed worse than the first. He shifted restlessly on the couch in front of the fire that Huck had lit when we'd gotten back to the cabin.

"I'm going to pack it in," he said, stretching his arms over his head. "Somebody woke me up before I was ready earlier. What about you, Stell? Calling it a night?"

The last thing I wanted was for this night to end.

"Actually, I was thinking I'd walk down to the beach Huck mentioned earlier. I'm too happy to sleep."

"Count me in," Huck said. He rose and headed to the coat rack.

"Suit yourselves. Try not to become a polar bear snack."

Huck froze mid-reach for his coat and cast a panicked glance around. "Wait. Are you messing with us, Ted? Are there polar bears in Iceland?"

Teddy nodded gravely. He was taking a bit too much hidden delight in Huck's terror. Slightly evil, our Teddy.

I laughed. "Sometimes." I pulled on a down jacket. "I could bring the axe if you're really worried."

"Nice try, Stell, but methinks it might be a bit dull for self-defense," Teddy said, yawning.

"I'll take my chances," Huck said.

Once Teddy absconded to bed, Huck and I raided the kitchen for crackers and cheese and a bottle of an Icelandic liquor called Björk, like the singer. This signature local beverage was made from the sap of birch trees, and the distillery had really leaned into the branding by including a literal stick floating in the yellow liquid inside the bottle. Huck grabbed a thick wool blanket while I stuffed the Björk and the rest of our night picnic supplies into my backpack.

We headed down the winding path toward the beach. Tall volcanic rock formations erupted around us, forming walls on either side of the path, and the gravel turned fine and black as soot beneath our boots as we neared the beach. Our breath created clouds in the cold night air. In the distance, the ocean waves were a powerful hush that drowned out the sound of our footfalls.

"It almost feels like another planet, doesn't it?" I asked.

"It does. I've never seen anything like it."

When I glanced up, Huck was looking at me, and a tiny swirl of elation filled my chest. Could he have been talking about me? We pressed on, struggling in the deep sand. At some point, Huck reached down and took my hand as we helped each other stay on our feet, like it was the most natural thing in the world . . . and maybe it was. It felt right, just like it had last night. In his arms, I'd slept better than I ever had.

The ocean was midnight blue ahead of us, frothy waves slicking over the shimmering black sand. I was glad I'd had the foresight to grab my sleeping bag from the van when we left, and I laid it on a large rock I found so we could sit, wrapped in the wool blanket to block the wind. Huck opened the Björk while I ate a few slices of cheese. He passed me the bottle and I took a swig before handing it back to him. The liquor's taste was earthy and subtly sweet, like brown sugar toasted over a wood fire. It was surprisingly smooth; each sip left a pleasant warmth.

"Today was perfect; it's hard to believe it really happened," Huck said.

"I know. It's weird, I've been waiting for so long to find something—we've been searching the Atlantic seaboard from Virginia to the Caribbean for years based on this map I inherited, and we've found some small things, but never gotten close to our real goal of finding the Stolen Treasure of the Sea People. This time was so effortless in comparison—it almost feels like it was meant to be."

"I get what you mean." Huck's voice was low and husky. I turned to meet his eyes, and the look he gave me made me unsure whether he was referring to Gunnarsson's treasure, or me.

"I didn't want to come here at first. My agent had to plan the whole thing, but when I landed, something shifted. I had a feeling something big was going to happen here."

I nodded.

"Then I met you, and you showed me that poem. Everything changed." I wondered if he wanted to kiss me. I wanted him to. I'd been thinking about it all day and through the evening, even when we were at the falls. His gaze had drifted down to my lips for a moment. "This place is special. Probably it's all the geothermal energy, or the elves. Maybe it's fate."

"Maybe," I said, trying not to grin. We pushed the volcanic sand with our feet. "It's weird. North Carolina beaches are all white sand, dunes—or what's left of them—grasses waving in the breeze. You probably know that from Teddy. I still can't believe that you've known him so long. I'm a little jealous, actually. Anyway, this is like the opposite of those beaches, and it's the strangest thing; it feels more like home to me in some ways."

"Well, home is an interesting concept."

Most people would've probably found this response odd, but I didn't. It *was* an interesting concept, even though it seemed simple and most people probably took it for granted. In my case, home was fraught. After my family fell apart, I didn't think I'd ever have a home again. And then after that, home meant Teddy, Gus, and Zoe, because they were my people. My family. We'd chosen each other. But it never escaped me that my friends had real families too, unlike me . . . parents and siblings and mortgages and legitimate professions, and I was committed to nothing. Even my lease for my crappy little apartment was month to month. I was not tied to anything and hadn't been for a very long time. In some ways, I was free, but really, I was unmoored. I didn't like thinking about how I'd lost my connections so suddenly, like an anchor rope sliced through by a blade. I didn't even know it was happening until it was too late, and I was on my own. I had an urge to share this with Huck, but I held back.

There was a part of me that I always kept to myself. I wanted to be captivating, not messy. Even though Huck was different than the casual flings I used to keep myself warm and I sensed that he'd be safe to share my story with, I liked him—the last thing I wanted was to send him running by recounting my pathetic past.

"Honestly, sometimes it's not so great," I admitted.

He nodded, chewing on his lip for a moment before he spoke. "Yeah."

I could tell that he understood, even though I'd barely said anything. He got it. I watched him while the hunger to tell him why the statement was true for me became almost irresistible. *My parents left me. One at a time, in short succession.* I could say it, couldn't I, show him who I really was? I cleared my throat. "Do you know something about that?"

"I do. And if I'm not mistaken, maybe you do too?"

"It's not a great story," I said.

"Seems like it never is. The day I got shipped off to boarding school was one of the best days of my life. Teddy would probably say it's because that's the day I met him, but really it's because of what I got away from. Anyway, I don't mean to overshare. I guess what I'm trying to say is that you could tell me . . . if you want to. I may not know what your life has been like, or if this place feels like home, but I can say with complete certainty that I wouldn't want to be anywhere else right now," Huck said, and I melted into him a little bit. "With anyone else."

This was what got me. It's something precious and rare to be chosen. Especially for someone like me, who was so easily taken for granted and forgotten. He leaned down then, and I sucked in one quick breath, drinking the last of the air between us the instant before our lips met and thought, *Finally.* This was what I needed, the perfect end to the perfect day. His mouth was soft and confident, lips first, then more, the taste of Björk like sweet forest dew, the firm pressure of his hand low on my back, the other combed into my hair at the nape of my neck. One incredible, soulful kiss, slow and deep and so full of longing that I never wanted it to end. He pulled back for a moment, smoothing my hair and catching a breath. "Even if I never write another worthwhile thing, this trip will have been worth it."

"There's zero percent chance of that happening," I said.

"I guess I just am not sure I can ever be as good as I was when I had Clark Casablanca narrating in my head. Like I don't know who I am anymore. That probably sounds dumb."

"That doesn't sound dumb at all," I told him. "When someone is important to you and they leave, it changes you. Their absence is a gaping hole shaped just like the thing that occupied it. Sort of like the cavern behind the waterfall. It's not something you just get over by riding stationary bikes and doing some shrooms. The terrain of you as a person will never be the same. Fictional or not. It's hard, and it changes you . . . for better or for worse."

Huck's voice was gentle when he responded. "Sounds like you're speaking from experience. You should have the last of the Björk." Huck held out the bottle and wrapped his arm around my shoulders. There was something immensely comforting about the way he did this. I felt so protected and safe, so cared for. It was wonderful and terrifying at the same time.

"That's very Clark Casablanca of you," I said, turning my gaze toward him. We looked at each other for a long beat and I was dying for him to lean down and kiss me again and shift the course of our conversation, of our night, away from these painful memories toward better things. I needed to lose myself in the depth of his icy blue eyes, trace the line of his sharp jaw, feel his strong hands on my body. I pulled in a breath to calm myself. There was an ethereal sort of glow on his skin, and he must've seen it on me too, because we both turned our gazes skyward when we figured out what it was. The sight of the bands of green and pinkish purple dancing above us overwhelmed me. Huck opened the sleeping bag and spread it on the sand, and we lay on our backs and watched the sky, nestled close out of necessity, for warmth. At least, that's what I told myself as I tried to ignore the anticipation undulating over my skin between each point of connection—a bit of hip, an arm wrapped over a shoulder, my head on his chest.

"How's that for reminding us of our place in the universe?" he said.

"Exactly." I felt like I was precisely where I was supposed to be in the world at that moment. With Huck on the dark sand at the beginning of something monumental.

We twined our fingers together, his thumb slowly stroking mine. We didn't speak, we didn't need to. We watched the beautiful sky and held each other. At some point, he propped himself above me on one elbow. I liked the view of him there, eclipsing just a bit of the splendor in the night sky.

I reached up and brushed the dark hair out of his eyes. "Maybe your next thing will be better than you could've imagined. Maybe Clark Casablanca left the country. Rebecca escaped her captors and fled to Iceland, where they met in a little hole in the wall and then found treasure behind a waterfall," I said, breathless.

Huck brushed a hand over my cheek. "Interesting idea." His voice was gravel, low and rough against my neck, as he brushed his lips over my skin. "But I'm not Clark. And you're not Rebecca." I might have deflated in this moment, but the way Huck looked at me when he pulled back made that impossible. "She'd never crawl into a stone wall in the dark and pull out an ancient axe."

"Smart girl," I said.

He shook his head, a half smile carving a dimple into his cheek. "She's fictional. And you're real. You're the realest person I've ever met, Stella. I've never known anyone like you. You're incredible. Honestly, I don't think I would've been able to write you, even if I tried," he said, his voice raspy.

My chest flooded with anticipation. Huck leaned closer. I focused on the sound of his breathing. The quiet rhythm of the ocean waves. The drumbeat of my heart. "Maybe this is a crazy thing to say, but I feel like you and I were supposed to meet. I was lost here, and you found me." Underneath the wool blanket, he slid one hand around my waist just beneath the edge of my fleece.

The fingertips of his other hand glided around the back of my neck and stopped near my tattoo. At his touch on my bare skin, my nerve endings ignited. I couldn't resist anymore, even if I wanted to.

"We found each other," I said, and then pressed my mouth to his.

The frenetic passion we'd had in the living room came rushing back all at once. Huck's hand drifted beneath my shirt, over the bare skin of my ribs.

"Is this alright?" he asked.

It was so much more than alright. *So much.* But I could only pull my thoughts together enough to nod and sigh into him, and he moved on, discarding my shirt beside us, tracing up over the curves of my breasts, across my collarbones, then down to the rise of my hip in one tantalizingly slow motion. He lowered his lips to my skin, following the path he'd marked with his hands earlier with painstaking attention. Heat pooled in my core; my breath hitched in my chest. He unbuttoned my pants and helped me pull them off. Until now I'd been passive, wound up, caught up in the way he was making me feel, but now I craved him too. I pushed his shirt up over his head and he shucked off his pants, while I ran my hands over his firm torso, marveling at how strong and solid he was. I pulled him against me, bare chest to bare chest, only the thin layer of our underwear between us. There was no denying how our bodies reacted to this closeness. Mine ached for his. We brought our hands down between us, exploring each other tentatively at first, while we learned what the other liked, the places that would make him groan when I gripped, the spot that made me pant when he brushed over it in lazy circles. I thanked our lucky Northern Lights that I always carried protection in my backpack and handed one to him wordlessly.

"I want this so bad," I confessed.

"Me too," Huck said, hovering over me for just a moment. "I need you, Stella."

The exquisite pressure, the way we fit together, matched and anticipated each other, fell into a gorgeous rhythm that built and built, up, and up, and up until *oh my god*—it was so right that I almost thought I created the whole thing in my head, like one beautiful dream remembered for a moment right before waking, before it slipped away.

We caught our breath afterward, still wrapped up in each other, a happy, satisfied tangle of legs and arms, and big feelings that should've scared me. Normally, they would have. Huck smoothed my hair from my forehead and left a gentle kiss on my lips. "I'm falling for you so hard, Stella Moore," he said.

I couldn't help but grin. "Me too." I buried my head against his chest and stifled a delighted groan as he clutched me to him tighter than before.

FIFTEEN

Stella

When I rose in the morning, the beach was empty. Soft sunlight set the fog aglow. Huck was gone. His absence left me unsettled—people's absence often did—but I told myself that the feeling was just my history rearing up against this new connection and the empty vastness of the black beach against the pale gray sky intensifying the sense of desolation. He'd left my clothes folded right next to me in a neat, thoughtful pile. He was falling for me hard, he'd said that. Mind-blowing-sex hard. Sleeping-in-each-other's-arms hard. Folding-clothes-in-neat-stacks hard. I pushed my worry down while I packed up the few things left out from the previous evening: the empty bottle of birch liquor, with its stick leaning against the glass, and the remaining cheese.

I trekked back to the cabin, tracing the footprints we left the night before in the dark sand, and let myself in. I half expected to find Huck in the kitchen making us breakfast. Instead, Teddy stood at the counter, hair still wet from a shower, wearing an apron and humming to himself while he poured steaming coffee into two mugs.

"Morning," I said.

He stopped humming. "Quite a night," he said, a question hanging in the space between us.

I reached for the mug Teddy slid toward me. My mind immediately returned to my night on the beach, but that memory still felt a bit dangerous, so I moved earlier in the evening to safer things. "Sure was, I still can't believe we freaking found it."

"I can. I knew you'd lead us to the treasure. For me it's always been more a matter of time than anything else."

"I'm glad one of us felt that way."

"I could never stop believing in you, Stell."

"We still haven't found the Elephant's Heart," I confessed.

"Not yet, but we will. You brought us to Gunnarsson's Gold, it's only a matter of time before you discover the Stolen Treasure and the Heart."

Even after all the years we'd known each other, Teddy's unwavering faith in me came as a surprise. It shouldn't have. He'd dealt with coral rash, leeches, sunburns, a host of other maladies courtesy of my quests, but none of that ever deterred him. He barely even complained.

"Have you seen Huck?" I asked, trying to sound casual. I listened for the sound of the shower.

Ted tore a sugar packet and dumped it into my coffee, just how I liked it. "I took him into town about an hour ago."

"Oh, when will he be back? Do we need to go get him?"

Teddy retrieved the cream from the refrigerator. "He's not coming back, Stell."

I swallowed. The room suddenly felt off-kilter.

"Look, he's a great friend, don't get me wrong. I love the guy, but he's always been kind of obsessed with his writing. A treasure hunt was enough to hold his attention for a bit, and now he's off looking for more book material, probably, or writing his next novel. You get it. Nothing could deter you from the hunt. Anyway, you know how these creative types can be." He paused and eyed me. "Tell me he didn't get your hopes up for anything more than that."

I avoided the scrutiny of Teddy's gaze. Had I gotten my hopes up? Maybe a little. Getting my hopes up was kind of my personal brand. Pretty hard to hunt treasure if you didn't get your hopes up. But I never risked when it came to my heart. I reminded myself that Huck was some guy I met in a bar, a possibility. Someone I thought could be something. That's all. In the context of my whole life, him not sticking around shouldn't bother me. But last night . . . we, we were falling for each other. We'd said those words. We'd slept together, and it was amazing. More than that though, it *meant* something. It had felt so right, so good. I knew he'd felt that too. I couldn't have been wrong about this.

No. He changed his mind, I told myself. People do that. Hell, I'd pulled this exact move more times than I cared to admit. It was the safe one. Have a little temporary fun and then dip out before anyone gets attached. So maybe it kind of sucked being on the other side, but it was nothing significant compared to the other things I'd endured. Those were so much worse than being deserted by a guy I'd known for a few days. But oh, it was so familiar a feeling, and I didn't like it.

Still, I refused to let this hurt me.

I was fine. I would be fine.

Fine. I took a gulp of the scalding coffee before Teddy added the cream. It was bitter and burned my tongue.

I hated how foolish I felt. I stepped to the window and looked out at the view. The beach was almost visible in the distance, but everything looked different in the light. A little less magical. What was otherworldly and enchanted the night before beneath the Northern Lights seemed alien and unwelcoming today. I stared out for a moment, watching a few birds swoop in the wind.

"He did say that maybe he'd tag along for our next adventure. Though, if his performance on our sophomore year whale-watching trip is any indication, he'll probably spend the entire trip dry heaving over the ship's railing." Teddy chuckled to himself before sucking some rogue sugar crystals from his thumb.

I tried to laugh and picture the scene to make myself feel better. But I just couldn't believe that I'd been so off base. I'd always been able to trust my instincts. They'd led me straight to Gunnarsson's treasure less than twenty-four hours ago. Huck's and my connection seemed so natural and strong and he hadn't even said goodbye; after everything we'd shared last night and the feelings we'd expressed, Huck had actually left me alone on a beach without a word. Maybe he was a good friend, like Teddy said, but my feelings for him were quickly transforming from someone I wanted around to someone I couldn't stand. "Sounds perfect for him," I said, surprised at the bitterness in my voice.

Teddy wrapped his arms around me and nestled his chin over my shoulder. "You're not sad, are you, kid?"

"No way. I just didn't realize he was leaving. It's not like I care." I wanted to mean this. It wasn't a lie, not really. It was truth adjacent. When I really thought about it, the normal me, the before-Huck me wouldn't have cared. In fact, if he were any other guy, I would have done this exact same thing to him. Had my fun and then bailed before it got too real. But he wasn't just some guy. I'd let him in. We'd let each other in, hadn't we? And now I couldn't escape the gnawing in the pit of my stomach, the heaviness in my chest. I wished back the vulnerable words I'd shared the night before, the way my lips yielded to his, how I'd pressed my body against him and marveled at how well we fit together. I'd wanted more. More time, more of him. I'd stupidly pictured a future together and thought this could be the beginning of something special. I needed to get myself together. Teddy knew me, and if I kept thinking about this, he would know. And I couldn't have that. The only thing worse than being broken was breaking in front of people.

"Honestly, Ted, I'm not sure he's invited on our next expedition," I said. "Though two weeks of seasickness would serve him right for being so rude and just taking off. That's my move."

Teddy spun me around for a tight hug. "Forget about it. You should feel like a superhero right now," he said. "People have been searching for Gunnarsson's treasure for centuries, and you, we . . . we found it. And next we're going to find the Stolen Treasure and the Elephant's Heart and then we'll be actual legends. You and me, one adventure at a time, just how it should be."

I bit my lip. I didn't care about being a legend, but I wanted to show the entire world what I was worth. That was why finding the Heart was more important than this, more important than anything. More important than the twinge in my chest and the stinging sensation in my nose. "You're right," I told him.

"Of course I'm right . . . and I've got those donut kleina things you love."

The vibration of Teddy's voice against my cheek and the promise of fried doughy goodness soothed me a little. In the landscape of my life and the things I'd experienced, Huck Sullivan's short appearance barely warranted a footnote. It was just a couple of good conversations. A few fun amorous activities. If I reflected purely on the facts, the whole stupid business had gotten sand in my nether regions in an unpleasant manner. I blamed the Northern Lights and the elation of finding treasure for making me think whatever passed between us was more.

"How many kleinas did you buy?"

"Boatloads of kleinas, mountains of kleinas." He spread his arms wide.

"Mountains?"

"A galaxy of kleinas," he shouted.

I arched an eyebrow. A heartbreak's worth of kleinas? "A universe?"

"Enough, Stella. Enough for a celebration, and we're celebrating today."

"Why is that? Because of Gunnarsson?" I took a bite. It didn't taste as good as I remembered. Apparently, Huck Sullivan had gotten sand in my nether regions *and* ruined my second-favorite Icelandic breakfast treat.

Teddy shook his head. "Nope. I mean, yes, but that's not all." He went and got the ancient axe from the case that we'd placed it in to protect it. Holding it out in front of me, he said, "Look closely at the markings. What do you see?"

I squinted at the handle. Carved into the silver were a series of pictographs. A set of boats, a waterfall, an elephant with a tiny red stone pressed into its heart. I looked at Ted and he nodded.

I swallowed. If this meant what I thought it did, then my hunch had been correct. Gunnarsson had found the fabled Stolen Treasure and the red diamond that the Sea People had robbed ages earlier during their days terrorizing the Mediterranean Sea at the northern tip of Africa. It was the missing piece that tied together a history that stretched from the beginning of civilization . . . to us. The diamond had many names—Hjarta Fílsins, Inhliziyo Yendlovu, Elephant's Heart. Gunnarsson had found it and given it to England or lost it to them . . . I couldn't be sure. Either way, this information, when combined with what I already knew from my years of research, meant that the stone had yet another name, one given to it much later—Heart of England—and I knew where to find it.

Teddy did a series of extremely bad dance moves in his apron.

"Come on, Stell—dance! You were right!"

I shoved the rest of the kleina in my mouth. My own heart

was a little raw this morning. But if I kept pushing, and forgot about Huck Sullivan, I could have a new heart, a priceless one, the one humanity had been seeking from the beginning of time. I would be set for life . . . the most famous treasure hunter ever.

Screw that guy, I thought and shook my ass.

I'm about to make history.

PART TWO

NOW

· · · · ·

The next time I see Huck Sullivan

More than a year has passed

He's taller than real life, made of cardboard.

If the bookseller at Coastal Books only knew

How tempted I am

To grasp the sides of his face

Gaze into his eyes

Ice blue

And familiar

Then rip the head off that cutout

Before trampling it beneath my feet

She would run me out of the store

Remember that wherever your heart is, there you will find your treasure. You've got to find the treasure, so that everything you have learned along the way can make sense.

— PAULO COELHO, *THE ALCHEMIST*

SIXTEEN

Huck

Y ou should be happy, Huck. Or on your way to drunk, or something. Anything. *The Fortune Files* is an instant number one *New York Times* bestseller! Do you know how rare that is?"

I rub my temples. Jim is right; he usually is. I should've already busted open the champagne he sent over to my apartment instead of leaving it on my counter to drip condensation as it grows warm. It was a nice gesture. But as much as I appreciate the thought, champagne is for celebrating and I haven't felt like celebrating since that night a year and a half ago when I witnessed a miracle that changed me forever.

How can I celebrate when I fucked it all up?

I wonder what the temperature's like in Iceland now, if it's warmer than the night I'd first met Stella in that bar or the one we spent on the beach wrapped in each other's arms. I'd felt like we were the only two people in the world then—just me and her and billions of particles of light. I still see her face when I close my eyes, iridescent, awash in the glow of the Northern Lights. Her hair fanned out around her in waves, pale against the black sand. It was the coming together of multiple things that people wait entire lifetimes to experience, and for a brief time, I had it all.

That was before the sun came up and everything changed and I made the choice I have regretted every single moment since.

In the lonely reality of my empty New York apartment, the memory makes it hard for me to breathe. The air seems to turn to salt water in my lungs and I wince at the pain in my chest. I can't describe the sensation exactly; I imagine it's like finding myself trapped within the walls of the Björk liquor bottle like the birch stick. Good visual, I think, me trapped in my own creation. I should use it in my next book . . . if I write another one.

"I'm just looking for a sign of life here, Huck. Give me anything. You've been in a walking coma since you turned the book in, and now you're marking the most epic comeback of all time with an instant bestseller spot . . . and not even a blip."

"I'm alright. *New York Times* is good news."

"It's fucking fantastic news."

"Okay, fucking fantastic news. There. Satisfied?"

"No man, I'm worried. You are not alright. I know your dad and Vanessa both did a number on you, and when you were blocked that we tried some weird stuff, but this feels different. Tilda just found this great therapist, could I give you her number? She's doing amazing things with EMDR."

"I don't want her number," I mumble.

"Maybe it would help to get out there. I had a quick call with your publicist this morning and she said that just about every major talk show is trying to book you. Are you still opposed to doing any kind of publicity? People are loving the book. Could be a good pick-me-up."

I pull in a deep, grounding breath. "I don't know. It still doesn't feel right." And I'm still scared shitless.

"You know I'm not going to push you. And if you absolutely don't want to do it, I'll support you, run interference, whatever you need. Let's just focus on the positive for right now. The team is thrilled with the sales and we've already got a battle royale for the film rights—and television's in play too. *The Fortune Files* is going to be huge, Huck. Massive. The best part? Our least favorite critic, fucking Daisy Hickman, is going to eat her words. Not only did you turn out a masterpiece, you created Lucky Malone, a main character even more universally appealing than Clark Casablanca. The data we're seeing so far shows that you're trending well in all gender buyers. Everyone loves Lucky."

I squeeze my eyes shut, pressing my palm to my chest.

We found each other, she says.

Jim is undeterred by my silence and forges ahead. "Listen, Huck, I don't want to pressure you, but everyone's clamoring for book two. I know we'd talked about next May to have a draft ready, but they're hoping to accelerate—capitalize on the momentum, if you will. When do you think you can have the next one finished? Maybe earlier is doable? You wrote this one like a man on a mission. What was it, six weeks?"

He's not wrong. When I got back to the city, the book just poured out of me.

I'd cracked open and *she* spilled out.

But Jim is wrong about something. There is nothing in this to celebrate. The four-book contract? It's an albatross hanging around my neck. I'd written this book like some kind of fever dream, and now I don't have anything left. The only reason I was able to write was her. And now, without her, I don't think I can write another word, let alone three more books. This isn't like before, not the critical voices in my head drowning out my own imagination no matter what I did. This time, I don't even want to try.

"I don't know, Jim. I think I need a bit of a break before I dig back into it. I'm just exhausted right now," I say. It is a shitty cover . . . one that Jim probably won't fall for. He's known me long enough to tell when I am bullshitting. Back when we'd been talking about a multi-book contract, I was still riding the high of writing something that I believed in, something that inspired me so much I didn't care what anyone thought. I'd written it because I had to, because I felt like I'd implode if I didn't. I wrote it for me, for her. Now that reality has fully settled in, I am sure that I can never re-create that.

"Maybe you need to go back to Iceland," Jim says.

"What?"

"Iceland. You were so focused when you got back, completely invested in your writing. It was incredible. Whatever they have there, I wish I could bottle it and give it to all of my authors. I mean, Huck, you didn't just find your mojo, you found fucking magic."

I don't answer him. I can't. Jim couldn't have known, but he's just buried the metaphorical equivalent of Gunnarsson's axe into my sternum. I look down to check for blood, half expecting to find that one of those precious gemstones near the blade is now embedded in the gaping gash in my chest.

"This book is the best thing you've ever written, no contest. Exciting, taut, emotionally resonant. I cried, and you know me, the only time I've cried in my adult life was when my daughter was born. And you're the only person who knows that, other than Tilda."

Knowing how deep Jim's love for his daughter runs makes this praise impossible to ignore. He's the kind of dad whose sun rises and sets with his child; it's beautiful to watch, and a devastating contrast to my own father, who only ever seemed to harbor disdain for me.

"Seriously, I'll book you the ticket back. Whatever it takes."

It's meant as a joke, but it only buries the hatchet deeper into my already hemorrhaging heart. I need to put an end to the painful trajectory of this conversation.

"Nah. I'm fine. This one took a lot out of me, that's all. And I'm not really sure where I'm going to take Lucky Malone next. Honestly, I don't know what I was thinking with this adventure series. I know fuck all about treasure hunting."

"You love to research, Huck. Do what you do best, then, and dive back into the books."

I'd spent the better part of the last six months in the New York Public Library reading about boats and bounties and ancient legends, but it all feels distant and flat to me. The thrill of uncovering the stories behind the treasure just isn't there the way that it had been when Stella told me about Gunnarsson. She brought an energy and excitement to it that is entirely absent now. And to be fair, I already promised my editor that I would set this book on a tropical island because of the whole beach-read angle. Well, that and I never wanted to return to Iceland, not even in my thoughts.

"Tell me what you need, Huck. Anything. I've got you."

I know that he means this. Jim picked up my pieces when I was a broken mess after my dad died and Vanessa left. He put me back together, but a part of me still wonders when he'll get tired of my complex emotional needs.

"I need to get out of here," I say. It's honest. New York hasn't been the same for me since before the last Casablanca. I find myself longing for elsewhere, someplace new that I've never been and therefore holds no memories to hurt me. Somewhere that I haven't been verbally derided or rejected by the very people who were supposed to love and support me. A location that didn't serve as the setting to the biggest mistake I've ever made in my life.

I need a place that is novel and exciting. Cool if it's brimming with history, as long as it isn't mine. "What I need I can't find in the pages of a reference book or on the internet. I need *real* experience, Jim. Saltwater mist on my face and authentic treasure hunters."

"Then let's get you on a boat," Jim says, as if that's the easiest thing in the world. "I'm sure we could reach out to one of the big operations. I think the Mel Fisher's Treasures crew does some investment thing where you can pay to be a part of the action, and there's a Caribbean group. I can only imagine how thrilled they'd be to have a bestselling novelist tagging along. Talk about good exposure."

"I don't know if that's the kind of experience I'm looking for," I say. What I really need is Stella. But she's not an option. I can't even imagine how much she must hate me after the way I left things in Iceland. The way I left *her* in Iceland. I know I hate myself for it.

"Okay, then. Isn't your friend Ted part of that crew that found the Icelandic treasure? Why not give him a call?"

I close my eyes. This is what I get for not telling Jim everything about my trip. If I had, then maybe he would know that there are several reasons, very *good* reasons, why I don't want to call Ted, why I haven't called him in over a year. They're the same reasons that this is an extremely bad idea, and include the fact that Stella might be inclined to hurl me into the sea at the first opportunity, if I don't beat her to it.

I can't explain this to Jim now any more than I can explain why the thought of Stella shoving me off the deck is becoming more appealing with each passing moment. In fact, for the first time today, I'm smiling. I walk over to the counter and crack open the champagne. Casablanca always called champagne a fancy man's courage.

I'm neither fancy nor brave. I'm just a guy who got real fucking lucky one time and hopes maybe I can again.

"You always have the answer, Jim," I say. "Thanks for sharing the good news. I'll call you later."

"Everything good?"

"Yeah. I just have a call to make."

SEVENTEEN

Stella

Coastal Books sits at the end of one of those idyllic streets lined with brick colonials and cherry trees in an upscale Wilmington neighborhood, the kind I never quite feel at home in. Fallen blossoms litter the sidewalks like confetti after a wedding; there's something a little sad about the way the fragile petals lie there awaiting the inevitable shoe, rainstorm, or decay. I'm moving slower than normal, my body and mind engaged in a tug-of-war.

His new book has been out for exactly twenty-seven days.

I glance at my watch. It took me a bit longer than I expected to get in from where I'm currently living in Wrightsville Beach. The bookstore closes in fifteen minutes, at six p.m., the same time I'm supposed to meet Teddy, Zoe, and Gus at The Pit for our monthly excursion-planning meeting over beer and barbecue. At this rate, I'll miss both deadlines. I pick up my pace and push through the weather-worn wooden door of the bookstore, bell chiming over my head.

"Can I help you find something?" a woman placing new inventory on a shelf marked *Local Authors* asks, her eyes darting to the clock. It's only a few minutes before closing, but I'm not here to take my time. A part of me wants to flee.

I try to smile and open my mouth to speak, but my answer is cut off as I practically plow into the table display full of hardcovers. I spin to avoid the collision and slam into a giant cardboard sign announcing **Sullivan's Bestselling New Series The Fortune Files**. I've spent more time than I care to admit over the last year since Iceland thinking of what it would be like if I ever found myself facing Huck Sullivan again. In most of my daydreams, I walk by, unaffected, leaving him behind to wonder if he'd made a huge mistake by leaving. But occasionally, I look over and he reels me in. I lose myself in his blue lagoon eyes and realize what we'd felt had never left us. Pathetic.

None of my fantasies feature me staring into the face of the cardboard version of Huck, though, gripping his flat shoulders until the staff member clears her throat to keep me from crushing the cutout. I steady myself and fix the sign.

"I get it, doll," she says. "You'd be surprised how many times a day someone tries to get intimate with that cutout. I don't blame them. Those eyes, the hair, the jawline. He's so much sexier without the beard. It's hard to resist." She does a little shimmy and I fight the bile that threatens to rise in my throat. Instead, I glance back at the rendering of Huck's face. It is physically painful to look at him, but it's better than throwing up all over the Trending on BookTok table.

I pick up a copy, my cheeks warm. "Just here for the book. No plans for any, uh, intimacy," I say. I wave the hardcover in the air as evidence to my claim and then make a beeline for the checkout counter.

"Great choice! This one is even better than any of the Casablanca Chronicles. My entire staff loved it and I read it in a single afternoon. I never do that. We're featuring it this month for our store book club, if you're interested in joining. We usually have around ten people come, though I expect it will be triple that this time. It's a good group, though. We call it the Bookish Babes and it's so much fun. We partner with Grapes of Wrath next door and have wine and charcuterie boards for a twenty-dollar cover. Next Friday at eight p.m." She chuckles. "We were hoping to get him in for the event, since the main character is from the Outer Banks, but he's not touring. I've heard he's very private."

"Oh," I manage, preoccupied with turning over the previous revelation like a stone from the black sand beach, trying to understand its history. Huck made the main character from the Outer Banks. I stare at the credit card terminal, which is taking its sweet time processing the payment, and tap my hand impatiently on the counter.

"I can't wait to see the movie," she adds, filling the gap I've left in the conversation. "I've been fan casting it myself but can't decide who should play Lucky Malone. She's so special and unusual. Anyway, that's one of the activities we're planning for the book club event, if you join."

Mercifully, the machine beeps, alerting me that my payment is approved.

"Need a bag?"

"Sure, thanks," I tell her.

Outside, I wrap the bag tightly around the book and tuck the package away at the bottom of my tote, along with my thoughts of the motivations of a certain author for his character choices.

I power walk the several blocks to The Pit, where my friends are undoubtedly already waiting. The hard edges of the book thump against my hip with each step; not that I need a reminder of its presence. As hard as I'm trying, I'm failing just as epically to put Huck Sullivan and his new treasure-hunting North

Carolina–style heroine out of my mind. I'm as intrigued as I am pissed off.

I find Zoe and Gus camped out at a high-top table on the patio. Zoe throws her arms around me. "Hey, baby girl," she says. "It's so good to see your face."

Gus tousles my hair. "How are you, kid?"

"Good," I say, sliding onto a stool. Flummoxed. Guilty. Irate. Still hung up enough on a guy who left me on a beach to be truly humiliated. "Where's Ted?"

"I think he got tired of waiting for you and went off to play cornhole with some people he knows from town," Zoe says. "You know how he is."

"I think you mean he went off to *dominate* at cornhole," Teddy announces. "I won three games in a row."

"Show-off."

Teddy lifts me into a massive squeeze. "You know you love it, Stella. Just like you, I was made to stand out."

"Well, you certainly weren't made to be patient. I'm, what, a whopping seven minutes late and you had to find new friends?"

"I find friends everywhere I go. It's got nothing to do with time, just a zest for life. But since we're on the subject, what kept you, anyway? You're the most punctual person I know."

"Just needed to make a stop."

Teddy narrows his eyes at me. "A stop, huh? The deliberate vagueness is intriguing. What are you hiding? A seven-minute tryst doesn't seem worth keeping to yourself."

"Wouldn't you like to know?" In theory, it's fun to pretend like a hookup is even a remote possibility, and safer than admitting the truth. Before Iceland, there was definitely a time when I enjoyed casual companionship, but not after Iceland. I haven't even been able to bring myself to try a dating app. This is a fact I would never tell my friends, who think I'm fine and swiping right just enough to sustain my basic need for human physical touch. Because admitting that would mean that my time with Huck had meant something to me; it would mean that I'd actually lost a real thing when he walked away and left me on that beach. That he'd hurt me.

"Should we order?" Zoe interjects.

"Please," Gus says. "I'm starving. I need pulled pork stat."

Teddy sets me down and I stumble back, knocking over my purse in the process and spilling its contents all over the patio. The bag with the Coastal Books insignia does little to hide its contents. I consider lunging for it but instead cast a furtive glance at Teddy. We both make a mad dash for the bag at the same time, but his arms are longer and he reaches it first, holding it up like he's snagged a jellyfish on his line. "What do we have here?" he says.

"Nothing."

"Is that so? Because it looks distinctly like you raced out and bought Sully's new novel."

I cringe at the judgment in his voice even though he's mostly teasing. Frankly, I'm judging me too.

He peeks inside. "You did."

"What is it?" Gus asks.

Teddy holds the book out for everyone to see, as if he's revealing an important piece of evidence for admission into a trial. I'd been in too big of a rush at the bookstore to fully absorb Huck's new book, but now that Teddy has thrust it into my eyeline, I study it. The cover is a rich, matte indigo, the kind you find in certain seas a ways down. The lettering of *The Fortune Files* is gilded and bold. Off to one side, there's a figure on a black beach facing out toward a rough ocean; it's all a bit too familiar, the light blond hair lifted off the character's neck by some invisible breeze, the compass freaking rose tattoo barely peeking out in between strands. Holy shit.

The air rushes out of my lungs. I wasn't off base with my wondering if maybe he'd thought of me when he'd made the main character from the Outer Banks. She isn't a vague reference. She is me down to the ink on her . . . *my* skin. I wrestle the book out of Teddy's hands and back into the bag as fast as I can while surveying my friends to check if they've noticed the resemblance as well.

Gus is engrossed in the menu, his stomach ranking higher than my minor relationship drama, which I'm okay with. He'd only spent one evening with me and Huck, so he doesn't really know about our connection or the aftermath. And I've been quietly nursing that wound on my own for some time anyway; I've learned it's better that way. If you want to forget about something, you don't talk about it. You bury it deep beneath the surface, and you don't leave any clues behind. You definitely don't put them on the cover of your book. On my side, I might've let it slip to Zoe during one of her post-trip cross-examinations that what had seemed promising in Iceland had culminated in an epic night together followed by an even more epic letdown the following morning, but that was the extent of my sharing. All of us were more focused on following the clue we'd discovered on Gunnarsson's axe to help us find the Stolen Treasure. That meant scouring archives to figure out what ship was carrying the renamed Heart of England and then finding it on my mother's map. We also were busy dealing with the fact that according to Icelandic law, we had to return the treasure to the government. It's displayed in a museum now. We'd received one-tenth of the current value of the metal, not the find, which wasn't as much as we'd hoped. Our flights were reimbursed and we were a little famous in small treasure-hunting circles and our local paper, but that was it. We were fine with it, except for the fact that we missed the summer search window while we were sorting it out. Riches and fame aren't why we hunt treasure anyway. It's always been about the history, getting one step closer to finding the Elephant's Heart, preserving the past, and discovering answers to age-old questions . . .

Why did he leave me like that?

I'd asked myself that question a thousand times and never thought of a reason that didn't hurt.

Maybe he hadn't cared for me in the first place and my instincts about him had been wrong. Or maybe he left because that's what people do . . . they leave me. I don't know why. Maybe it is because I'm not good enough, or pretty enough, or interesting enough. Huck probably realized that sleeping together was a massive mistake. A search for answers will never bring me peace, I know this, yet I can't help wondering if somewhere on the pages of this book there's an explanation.

"I can like his books without liking him." I shrug. Teddy eyes me as I stuff the book back into my bag. "But actually, I doubt I'll like it. It's probably trash worthy of a public evisceration on Goodreads. I might even do some sort of social media rant about how it's exceptional bullshit and I had to DNF."

Huck's voice is a low whisper in my ear. *Did you hate-read my books? You seem like someone who might.*

Gus lets out a low whistle. "Somebody's pissed."

"What do you expect, babe?" Zoe says. "That man weaseled his way into our good graces and then beat Stella at her own game in the morning."

"Oh, yeah, I forgot about the dine and dash."

"We agreed not to call it that," I say.

"What *did* we agree to call it?" Gus asks. "For the life of me, I can't remember. Was it, like, the dawn and dip?"

"Bang and bail," Teddy says.

They don't know the impact of each word. How could they? I hadn't told them. I'd participated in the fun, offering my own version—the fling and wing—which was rejected because it rhymed instead of starting with the same letter.

I take the beer from Teddy's hand and down a big gulp before dropping into a seat at the table. It's time to forget about the book and the humiliating alliterations we'd crafted to make light of what Huck did, and put the tangled net of emotions and memories aside. We're here to focus on one thing—finally finding the Stolen Treasure and the Elephant's Heart—and Huck Sullivan isn't part of that narrative. Not anymore. Not ever again. "Can we focus on important things, like planning our expedition? Please?"

"Hush puppies first," Gus growls. "Then we can talk about the search and salvage permit application for the site."

"Nope," Zoe says. "We kick things off with a toast. To finding our next big thing, and roasting Huck Sullivan with the most tasty one-star review of all time."

"Hear, hear," Gus says, raising a beer. "Nobody puts baby in the corner."

"Or bang and bails," Zoe says.

Teddy takes his beer back to cheers them, so I lift a glass of ice water. I pretend I'm enjoying this.

"I think I'll call it an utterly *unsatisfying* read," Zoe said, laughing at her own joke.

"While I am loving the energy, maybe don't go *too* hard on him, ladies," Teddy says.

"*Why?*" I ask, narrowing my eyes at him.

"It might make things awkward." Teddy stares at the menu and shrugs with his typical nonchalance. "He's coming with us."

EIGHTEEN

Stella

Teddy honks the horn of his Toyota 4Runner from outside my apartment and I scramble to throw the remaining items into my duffel. One might be surprised that I didn't disown him after he dropped the bombshell that the guy who broke my heart in Iceland was tagging along for an entire month at sea. I am.

In Teddy's defense, I've hidden my emotional devastation well. None of my friends witnessed the tears, the pints of Ben & Jerry's, and the sleepless nights, or the potbellied orange kitten I nearly adopted from the Humane Society on a particularly rough Saturday. That's why they joked so hard at the restaurant about his behavior and the bad reviews—I'd only shown them my wounded ego, not my broken heart.

It's okay. I'm uniquely equipped to handle this kind of hurt on my own. I almost expect it. So yes, Teddy is a massive pain in my ass sometimes and *wow* he could use some lessons on how to read a room, but at least he's loyal. He sticks when other people don't and that makes him easy to forgive, no matter how uncomfortable this little reunion is going to be. It didn't make it easy to pack, though. Apparently my subconscious flatly refused to subject the rest of me to this bunking-on-a-boat-with-Huck-Sullivan scenario, because I am the least prepared I've ever been for a trip. I prepped my apartment earlier this week, but never bothered packing. Now, I rush around grabbing random items, things I probably won't need: a dress, my cowgirl boots, the laundry I'm not even sure is clean from a hamper in the corner of my bedroom, the entire contents of my underwear drawer.

I lock the closet that I use to store all of my personal belongings since, this year, just like the past few summers, I'm renting out the unit while I'm away for June and July. Before I go, I do one last quick survey of the space to make sure that everything is in some semblance of order. The AC is set to the correct temperature for efficiency and mold prevention. The blinds and curtains are closed. The refrigerator is empty. I've put a little welcome basket out that has a bottle of wine from the Duplin Winery, some hot maple pecans from Try My Nuts, and a cool map to the area with stars next to my favorite activities and beaches. Little touches like this get this place good reviews and make sure that I can afford the time away.

My copy of *The Fortune Files* sits on the coffee table, and I debate leaving it for the renters. Every time I pull it out to start it, I can't. It's the cover . . . it always stops me. The character's resemblance to me down to the tattoo on my neck either leaves me swirling with questions or sends me back to that black beach and all the memories I left there, both options that I'm not up for. Because of this, over the past several weeks I've been engaged in this dance of picking the book up only to set it down. I do this again now, but end up shoving it into the tote bag along with a couple of other last-minute items. It can get boring on the boat sometimes, so having something to read wouldn't hurt. Then again, it might.

I'm setting the electronic lock on the door, when Teddy lays on the horn. He is not a patient man. I hope my neighbors are already awake and out of their apartments.

"At this rate," he hollers out the window of his truck, "we'll make it down to Key West by August. Imagine how pissed Zoe and Gus will be when they land there and discover that you're still lollygagging in North Carolina."

"If you're in such a hurry, you could come up here and help me with my bags, Your Majesty," I toss back.

The lock clicks into place, and I sling the strap of my duffel bag over my shoulder. I'm mostly a light packer, but there's research and other gear that I keep in the apartment and need to transport. I'm working out how I can manage it in one trip when Teddy arrives only slightly winded on the fourth-floor landing and grabs the two heaviest bags out of my hands.

"At your royal service," he says. His sun-lightened hair is wild underneath his backward hat. He grins at me as he bows playfully and then bounds back down the stairs.

This day has all the makings of a beautiful one, warm and breezy, with sunshine the color of a ripe lemon against a bright blue sky. In Teddy's truck, there's fresh coffee and Duck Donuts waiting. He must've felt guilty; he hasn't bought me treats in a while. I grab the maple bacon donut—my favorite—and take a big bite while Teddy stows my gear in the trunk.

We already hauled out our boat, a retired Coast Guard vessel renamed the *Lucky Strike*, and tackled the laundry list of repairs during weekends and evenings this past month while we waited for our search permits to be granted. Those came through a few days ago, and just in time since *Lucky Strike* is now sound and ready for our cruise down to Key West, where we'll meet Zoe and Gus.

Teddy settles into the driver's seat and takes a swig of coffee. "Tell me you're not eating the maple bacon, Stell."

"You got it for me, right?" I mumble, mouth full. "These are *I'm sorry I'm a thoughtless dumbass who agreed to let the man you hate come spend a month on our boat* donuts, right?"

"Absolutely not," Teddy says, and takes hold of my wrist to bring the donut I'm clutching within biting distance. "And maple bacon is *my* favorite. The peanut butter and raspberry jam with chocolate drizzle is for you."

"Don't even think about it," I say, just as he rips off a large portion with his teeth.

He navigates out of the apartment complex and turns right, the opposite direction from the marina. "Jeez, take the donut if you need it that badly. You don't have to go back to the store," I say.

"I'm full," he says.

"Then what are you doing? The marina is back that way." I take a sip of my coffee, wincing at how bitter it is without cream.

"Yes, I'm aware. I've only lived here my whole life, friend. The airport is this way."

I pinch the bridge of my nose. "What's at the airport, Teddy?" I ask, though I really don't want to confirm the sneaking suspicion I have.

"I think you mean *who*. And I'm concerned, Stell, that you might be losing your touch. How can you solve ancient mysteries and understand the complexities of storms and sea currents and sediment, but not have the common sense—"

I want to give him a shove, but he's merging into rush hour traffic, so I control myself and interrupt instead.

"It's not a lack of common sense. I know the answer, even though you never bothered to share this information with me—very conveniently, I might add. I just don't want to acknowledge it." And I thought he'd be meeting us in Florida.

"Do I need to remind you that you said it was fine? That's a direct quote."

I grit my teeth. "It *is* fine."

"It's just occurring to me that this might be one of those cases of a person saying something is fine when actually they mean that it's absolutely anything but fine. Is that what is happening here? I mean, I could always just leave him at the airport, but he is one of my oldest friends and he asked for help. Also, I basically can't tell him no. I really did almost drown him in the Monadnock golf cart crash of 2008." Teddy sighs.

"Don't leave him at the airport," I say through my teeth. Though it would be poetic justice. "I can handle a month of Huck; a couple of extra days makes no difference. Like I said, it's fine. It's no big deal. I couldn't care less, really. What's a little water under the bridge when there's treasure to be found?"

"That's my girl," Teddy says, and taps the bill of my hat. "Are you going to eat the last of that donut?"

I pop the remaining bite into his open mouth.

"You made sure that he knew what he was getting into, though, right, Teddy? That it's possible we won't find anything? And that boats and diving can be dangerous, and we work during hurricane season, so we could encounter rough weather and have to head in or potentially capsize or sink? And there are sharks? Huge sharks?"

"Wow, you make it sound so irresistible. If it weren't for your charm, I might want to bow out myself for this season. But yes, I did let him know these things. There was even paperwork for him to sign to the extent of he can't sue us or our insurance company if he experiences demise or dismemberment."

I work hard not to make a poor-taste joke about Huck's potential dismemberment. "And you warned him about seasickness, because, honestly, Ted, I'm willing to let the past be the past but I'm not dealing with puke of any kind on my deck."

"Scopolamine patch—he's already got it. I was very clear about your deep disdain for anyone who vomits onboard."

"Wonderful. Just so we're all clear that he gets no special treatment."

Teddy pulls up in front of arrivals. "No special treatment. You have my solemn oath. My word is my bond and all that shit."

Despite the terminal expansion at the Wilmington airport, it's still not too busy here, especially at this time of day, which makes it impossible *not* to spot Huck when he emerges from the building. Then again, he isn't the sort of guy who blends into a crowd. That tall frame, black hair, and pale electric blue eyes, the jawline so sharp he could cut someone . . . Huck's impossible to miss. He's dressed for the locale, in a pale blue T-shirt and light tan Bermuda shorts with boat shoes, but other than his clothes, he looks the same as he did when I last saw him in Iceland. My mouth goes dry. I've been thinking about this moment for weeks, ever since Teddy announced that Huck would be joining us.

I didn't expect him to look this good.

Never mind that I'd practically fainted at the sight of a cardboard cutout of the man at the bookstore. Seeing Huck in real life—here in North Carolina, getting ready to climb into Teddy's car, was not something I could've prepared for. And I know. I tried. I have rehearsed this moment what feels like a million times.

Teddy hops out to greet Huck and grab his bag. I watch them clap each other on the back in greeting in the side mirror. Then I catch a glimpse of my own reflection. My hair is fine, French braided and tucked beneath a trucker hat. It's the kind of hair that says, *I could not care less about how you think I look*, while also looking cute. Reflective polarized lenses obscure my eyes, and that's a good thing. I have a million more freckles than when we last saw each other, and as usual I'm in desperate need of some lip gloss. I reach into my belt bag for a ChapStick but can't find one. Typical. Why the state of my lips would matter to Huck Sullivan,

I have no idea nor should I care, but that doesn't stop me from rooting around in Teddy's glove compartment in hopes of a hidden stash of Carmex.

The door to the back seat opens and I take a single deep breath. I can do this. The boat, the hunt, that's where I'm comfortable, where I'm in charge. It's my safe place. Nothing and no one can change that, ever. So this is all fine, cool, copacetic, and I am calm, collected, and not nervous in any way. Nope, I am excited. If all my research since I left Iceland is right, I am this close to finding the Stolen Treasure of the Sea People tucked away on a Spanish ship called the *San Miguel* that sank more than three hundred years ago. So Huck's here. You know, I've been thinking about this all wrong. Maybe he's lucky. The first time we found treasure he was with us, so who's to say that lightning won't strike twice? Maybe Huck is our own personal rabbit-foot. Not a man who made me think there was something between us and then left while I was asleep.

Stop it, Stella. Go back to the rabbit-foot thing. That was good. It was helping. Huck, hot pink. Soft fur. Aww, isn't he adorable, the bookseller is saying. A little lucky charm. I just want to pop him into my pocket and buy lottery tickets with the Bookish Babes.

"Hi Stella," he says, and damn if his voice isn't subdued and deep and sultry in a way that completely obliterates my lucky charm tactic and raises goose bumps on my arms beneath my sweatshirt. It makes me furious, at my body for betraying me, but mostly at him. "Thanks for letting me come along. I know that this might be—"

Teddy chooses this exact moment to slam down the accelerator and screech into traffic, causing a near miss with an Uber and forcing Huck and me to grab on to the nearest vehicle fixtures for dear life. "You need some ChapStick, Stells," Teddy says, louder than he needs to, and tosses me a little pot, totally unfazed by the near miss.

While Huck scrambles to put on his seatbelt, I take a moment to send a thanks to the sky for Teddy, his absolutely horrendous driving, and the impeccable sensing of my needs and perfect timing to stop the conversation I'm not ready to have yet, not now, maybe not ever.

NINETEEN

Huck

I thought this would be easier. Yeah, I'm an idiot. I've pictured seeing Stella again so many times, what I would say, how she would look at me, and how I would play it cool and contrite and everything would be fine, and yet now I find myself woefully unprepared. Freaking dumfounded by my stupidity.

Wrecked.

Even though it's been over a year, very little has changed about the way I react to being in the same space as Stella. She can still take my breath away with a single look, but now the weight of the choice I made that morning in Iceland presses on my sternum and makes it hard to breathe.

I study human nature extensively for my books and like to think that over the years, I've cultivated a pretty good understanding of people. And still I manage to clearly underestimate my own human ability to trick myself into thinking I've made peace with my decision.

Seeing Stella again is awkward and surprisingly painful. Fuck that. It's just as painful as I worried it might be when I was honest with myself.

There were obvious signs that should have told me that this

difficulty was a forgone conclusion. Maybe I willfully ignored them. Over the last year, there hasn't been a day when I didn't think of her or wish things could've turned out differently. But it turns out that focusing on writing a novel, perfecting it, so much so that you forget to eat, leave your apartment, see the sun, talk to anyone other than the occasional delivery person and your long-suffering friend and agent, is a very effective diversion for a heart problem. And conjuring a character that is essentially a very close fictionalization of a woman that you could've fallen for . . . did fall for . . . and spending every page with her adds to the mind-bending magic. Now all of that distraction has faded away and Stella is not fictional. She is very much real . . . living, breathing, seething, and within two feet of me, and all I can think is that I better start writing my next book soon because I'm not sure how I'm going to make it through the next four weeks in this type of proximity to her.

It makes my chest ache.

I steal a glance at her in the passenger-side mirror. *Objects in the mirror are closer than they appear.* She seems a million miles away from me and looks a bit like an undercover cop today, with a worn baseball cap pulled low and sunglasses obscuring most of her features; I wonder if it was intentional. A barrier so we don't get too close. She's smart, but I already knew that. She hasn't spoken to me yet and the anticipation of what she'll say and how is a unique form of torture.

You did this to yourself.

"Hungry?" Ted asks, holding out a box of donuts, probably consolation for the fact that his aggressive driving nearly flung me across the back seat a moment ago. "Just don't take the peanut butter and jelly, it's Stella's favorite—"

"Not my favorite," she says. And there it is. That beautiful voice, full of energy, playful but firm. I'm not sure if she's really referring to the donut flavor or if she's reminding me of where I stand.

I think of the jam-and-cheese pizza in Iceland and resist the urge to bring it up in the context of a potential favorite donut flavor combination. I fail at trying to hold back the memory of that red currant–flavored kiss against the bookshelf at the cabin, though. I clear my throat. "So it's a safe choice, then?" I ask instead.

"No. It's my second favorite," she says, reaching around to remove the donut in question before I have a chance to take it. She lifts her finger to her mouth to clean up some peanut butter glaze in a way that seems automatic, as if she has no idea what this does to me, or maybe she knows exactly the effect that this has, and yeah, again, what the actual fuck was I thinking? We're two minutes in and I'm already done for, fantasizing in the back seat of Ted's truck.

I can see the headlines now: "Writer Perishes in Back Seat Before Finishing Book Two of His Blockbuster Series." I'd probably win a prestigious posthumous award. *Best thing you ever did for your writing career, Huck*, Jim would say to my headstone. Stella wouldn't come to the funeral, I imagine. Or maybe she would—it would be the perfect ending given that she likely hates me after what I did. She might want to dance on my grave. They'd put me in the ground next to Dad, so he'd have a front row seat to my downfall. *What did you expect, Henry?* he'd demand for eternity. My very own personalized hell.

I pick out a standard-looking glazed donut, no one's favorite, I surmise, and remind myself silently that I am here to work, to observe, to do research. Not to pine for the past. Not to be affected by seeing Stella lick some glaze off her fingertips.

We drive in silence for a while until a rundown marina comes into view. I suddenly don't know how I feel about boats. Teddy had warned me about all the unpleasantries and risks of being at sea—accidents, nausea, storms, equipment failures, sinking, sharks—when I first asked him about joining the expedition. Perhaps their crew was worried that I wouldn't be able to handle it or I'd get in the way. Maybe Stella had asked him to make me not want to go. He'd nearly succeeded in that.

But I have another book to write, and Jim is a very compelling man.

The truck's barely stopped before Stella is out, heading to the back hatch, grabbing things, shouldering gear. She thrusts a giant duffel bag at me, and then spins on her heel toward the water. The French braids she's fashioned slip to the side and the tattoo on her neck peeks out.

"Not much has changed, I see," I say.

"Time waits for no man, and Stella waits for no one." Ted pulls out the last of the baggage from the back and locks up the car. "Hey, Bubba," he calls to a large man in worn overalls. "Still okay for us to leave the truck here?"

"Sure thing. Long as you leave the keys. I got a hot date this weekend." The man has a strong Southern accent and a warm, hearty laugh. I like the melodic quality of it.

Ted tosses the keys to him. "I filled up the tank so you should be set for all your galivanting."

"Does he really use your car while you're gone?" I ask in a low voice. It seems like a liability, though like a lot of people from New York City, I don't own a car, and I'm not sure of the conventions.

"Nah, he's just messing with us. The keys are in case we get any big weather and he needs to move the truck to high ground. Bubba drives a Porsche."

I glance back over my shoulder at Bubba. He's summiting one of the massive boats with an agility I hadn't expected. I wonder if he might make a good character in the next book. I'd started plotting out ideas based on the loose itinerary that Teddy had shared—a sail down the Intracoastal Waterway and then to Key West, where we'll be searching an area off the coast—but so far nothing is exactly singing to me.

"I take it that big weather means a hurricane?" I ask.

"Yup," Ted says.

"And what's the likelihood of that?"

He shrugs. "Depends a lot on the season. Down here we do get hit from time to time. Over at Oak Island, not far from here, the beach is almost gone from all the storm damage over the years. They do beach nourishment projects all the time, but it's hard to keep up."

I'd read about the disappearing Outer Banks; Rodanthe, where that one Nicholas Sparks book was set, was famous for pictures of the carcasses of abandoned beach houses slipping into the sea. They even had to relocate the one they'd used in the movie before it nearly fell victim to the beach erosion and rising tides and was smashed to bits in the churning waves.

I don't want to think about beaches or how things get destroyed on them. I can't.

"And what about down where we're diving? Planning on bad weather there?" I ask.

"Who knows, man? You want to back out? Storms roll through all the time, but our boat is well equipped to handle it. The bigger problem is that when it's stormy at all, we can't drag the magnetometer and we definitely can't dive, so we better hope for good weather. And we ought to get a move on," Ted says. "Stella's probably ready to shove off already."

I bite back a comment about her wanting to shove me off the deck of the boat, which I couldn't blame her for, not really, but Jim told me to attempt to be positive, and so I try. I break into a run, and Teddy, ever the competitive pal, picks up speed to try to pull ahead. We reach the pier at the same time, huffing. Ted drops the gear he was carrying and raises his arms behind his head while he sucks in air. The boat is bigger than I'd expected, with a smaller craft that looks like a step up from a Zodiac strapped down on the deck. Across the hull, Lucky Strike is scrawled in ornate letters. Stella's walking the deck, checking on things with a clipboard in her hand and a clear air of confidence that would take my breath away if I had any left after the sprint to the boat.

She's left her stuff haphazardly on the wooden planks, as if she couldn't wait to get onboard. I reach down to get a canvas tote and spot my book inside sitting on top of a bunch of things that appear to have been tossed in at random. I suspect that this is her afterthought bag, containing the random objects hastily grabbed at the last minute before she left. It's not an honor for the book to be on top, I remind myself. But it's there.

And that is enough to give me hope.

TWENTY

Stella

We head out of the Intracoastal Waterway and the Cape Fear River between Southport and Bald Head Island. The Bald Head Marina is full of yachts, glistening like new veneers in a giant, rich mouth. Teddy's family has property on the sound side of the island, a mansion so large that we can see it clearly from the deck of our boat as we pass by. I went there once, years ago, in the off season, when most of the restaurants were closed and the hurricane shutters were already set into place on the majority of houses. Zoe and I roamed the island on bikes with baskets, pedaling past streets with names like Edward Teach Wynd and Stede Bonnet Wynd, while Teddy and Gus bought steaks and lobster tails at Maritime Market to grill. We talked of Blackbeard's treasure while we ate; Ted drove the golf cart recklessly around the winding roads to Potato Beach for a bonfire and a dip in the sound. Teddy's mother, a woman who wore pearls unironically, had warned me that the jellyfish were bad before we'd left town, but I hadn't heeded the warning and got stung. Red welts along my arms and thighs were painful reminders of the trip for days after we'd ridden the ferry back to the mainland. I glance down to where Teddy is showing Huck the dredge, a long tube rigged to a pump that helps improve the efficiency of our searches. Huck looks up at me for an instant and it stirs a sensation akin to those jellyfish. Despite the time that has passed, I can almost feel the memory of Huck's hands stinging on my skin.

It would be smart to keep my distance.

Our boat is fifty-two feet long, closer quarters than it sounds, making the prospect of avoiding Huck almost laughable. I return to the safety of work. There's an instrument panel that requires my attention: weather to check; the Gulf Stream, wind speed and direction; the height of the surf; other ship traffic. I smear extra sunscreen on my face.

Teddy takes over at the helm in the late afternoon, and I retire to the galley to eat. Huck's in the kitchen poring over a notebook while he drinks what I suppose must be a coffee from the aroma that fills the space. He glances up, just for an instant, and I avert my gaze.

"We didn't really get a chance to talk on the way here from the airport," he says, collecting his papers into a pile. A lock of dark hair falls over his forehead and he pushes it back. Back in the car, I couldn't see him well. Just a glance here and there in the sideview mirror, where objects are closer than they appear. Now I have to face his full height, the solidness of him, the strong body I know the feel of, even if it's covered with preppy clothes. At least he isn't looking at me. He doesn't see my composure unraveling.

I pull out a jar of peanut butter and slices of bread and start making myself a sandwich while attempting to sound unaffected. "We don't have to talk. This is business, right? I'm here to work, you're here to work. We can just be coworkers." The knife I'm using to smear the peanut butter rips the bread.

"I guess I thought maybe we should clear the air."

I mash the battered bread back together and turn. "Why would we need to do that?" The harshness of my tone surprises me. I don't want him to know how impacted I was . . . am. I soften the edge in my voice. "I just mean that there's no point in dwelling in the past." As soon as I utter the words, I'm aware of how ridiculous my statement is. My whole life is about trying to unearth the past, but there's no treasure between me and Huck Sullivan. There never was. I change the subject and nod at the pile of papers next to Huck. "What were you working on? New story?"

"Kind of. When Ted and I connected about my joining the expedition, he shared a basic background and itinerary for the trip."

"How much did he tell you?"

"He said that you're searching for a Spanish ship called the *San Miguel*." He pauses.

"And?" I ask.

"I was surprised, that's all. I expected you to be searching for the Stolen Treasure and the Elephant's Heart. I guess I was wrong."

I start to smile. I can't help myself . . . He remembers. "You're not wrong. I am still searching for them," I admit. The path of the Stolen Treasure has more twists than all of the Casablanca Chronicles put together. I have to take a minute to think about how I should tell the story to Huck.

"Remember Gunnarsson's axe from Iceland?" I ask, and Huck nods. "How the handle was covered in intricate designs? I didn't really think anything of them at first. But when we examined it more closely, Teddy realized it was a pictograph. That axe was supposedly a gift from the British king, and the engravings depicted what looks like a bunch of boats and a battle and a giant elephant with a red stone in its chest. In theory, it could mean anything, but for me, it confirmed what I'd suspected—England had been in possession of the fabled treasure and the Elephant's Heart during the time that Gunnarsson had been alive." I get out my phone and scroll to a picture of the engraving to show Huck. "Turns out that the red stone on the axe is a diamond. We had it verified."

He shakes his head in amazement. "No fucking way. You're right—it has to be the Elephant's Heart."

"Exactly. I had the same reaction."

"Incredible." Huck's brows furrow.

"What?" I ask.

"It's nothing. I'm just trying to understand how the English having the treasure ties to the *San Miguel*. Isn't it a Spanish ship?"

"Good question. The fact that England had the treasure explained a strange passage I'd found a couple of years ago in a set of Sir Francis Drake's personal letters in the UK's National Archives. The text detailed how he'd taken a horde of precious materials, among them a massive stone the color of blood, east to the New World. Everyone we talked to figured it was a ruby, but Gunnarsson's axe proves it wasn't."

"Okay, so Drake brings it over here." The look on Huck's face is the same one I've seen before when he's really into something and getting inspired. I try not to think about how much I love that look, and instead focus my attention on how pale he appears in the dim light of the galley. We are out on open water now, and even though our boat is large, the seas aren't as calm as they had been. Teddy's previous announcement about Huck's weak stomach on the whale-watching trip comes rushing back. I quash the swell of sympathy. A little seasickness serves him right.

"What then?" he asks, gulping hard. The boat pitches and if I'm not mistaken, Huck's skin goes green right before my eyes.

I turn to the fridge and take out a ginger ale. "Okay, well, years later, after a skirmish between England and Spain"—I hand him the can—"a report went out that the Spanish soldiers had stolen the Heart of England. But it was clear that the heart was something tangible . . . a precious red gemstone."

Huck takes a sip of the soda. "Thank you for this. So that's where the *San Miguel* comes in? I remember reading that it was part of the Spanish Treasure fleet in 1715 . . . but the manifest I found listed sixty-two people on board and no real cargo."

I'd been confused by the same thing at first. "You're right. The official manifest didn't list any cargo. There are reports that it was carrying a massive load of tobacco from Havana. We know of a letter from the Casa de Contratación that basically indicates that they used a thirty-gun ship, which the *San Miguel* was, to pick up 1.5 million pounds of tobacco because it would've delayed the owner of the 1715 treasure fleet, Antonio de Echeverz, to go back and get it. That's part of the reason why no one's really gone after the *San Miguel* hard."

"Because there's no treasure?" Huck sounds perplexed. He takes another sip of ginger ale. "I don't get it."

I smile. I want to savor both his confusion and peeling back the layers of this story. "Well, that's what everyone believes, or they think maybe there's a small amount of silver and a couple of smuggled coins or personal effects. But they're wrong. A correspondence between Echeverz and the ship's captain, Joseph Coyo de Melo, indicated that they were only going to carry ten tons of tobacco because he had more precious cargo to be collected and transported in secret. The cargo is not a full inventory, of course, but he mentions several mines of gold, rubies, and emeralds. There is also reference to a special present for the new queen from King Philip: the Heart of England."

"Unbelievable," Huck says. "No wonder no one has made this connection. It's so complex."

"Definitely. We also think that even if they somehow made the link, which is doubtful, they are looking in the wrong place. There're several documents that seem to indicate that everyone thought that the ship went down around St. Augustine."

"Okay, yeah, I saw some things about that when I was researching. But you don't think it did?"

"Absolutely not."

"You found another letter?"

I shake my head. I'd shared a lot of things with Huck in Iceland, but I never told him about my mom's map. Only Teddy, Zoe, and Gus know. And my dad, wherever he might be. I take a breath to steady myself. Huck's here and because of that, he's in this, whether I like it or not.

"I have something other people searching don't. See, I come from a family of treasure hunters. My mom was part of this group of pilots that searched for wrecks off the coast of Florida and in the Caribbean as a hobby. She met my dad and he got super into it . . . but he was only interested in the legend of the Stolen Treasure and the Elephant's Heart. His obsession drove her away eventually. When she left, she didn't take her research with her. Anyway, I have it all . . . aerial photos of the ocean in Florida and the Caribbean, a coded sea chart. It took me a really long time to figure out her code, but I realized that she'd found evidence of a wreck that could be the *San Miguel* at the coordinates where we are going to search. How she got that information, I don't really know. I vaguely remember my dad saying something once when he was on a bender about her being involved in some kind of reconnaissance aimed at searching for underwater anomalies."

As soon as I say it, I wish I hadn't. Huck stares at me.

"Ted said you stole from him on the beach when you met . . . Were you on your own?"

I close my eyes. "My mom took off when I was fifteen. She

was there one day and the next she was gone. I never heard from her again. My dad had problems before, but he wasn't the same after that. He said maybe she just didn't want to be a wife or a mother anymore, but"—I sigh—"sometimes I wonder if that wasn't the truth. I never understood why she left the maps when the last big fight I remember them having was when he mentioned selling them. I think maybe she wanted to leave her old life behind. It's silly, I suppose, that I keep thinking about it."

"No, it's not. Have you tried looking for her?"

I nod. "Treasure's not the only thing I've been searching for. She did a good job disappearing. A few years back, Teddy paid for this private investigator, who was supposed to be incredible, and even he didn't turn up anything. She must not want to be found."

"What about you and your dad? Are you two close?"

I shake my head. "Not really. He's a complex man."

"What do you mean?"

"I guess you could say he wasn't around much and when he was, I wasn't the focus. We had a lot of debt, and he was always out trying to get people to fund his trips. When he wasn't grinding, he was drinking. When I was sixteen and a half, he got this investor in Corolla and was planning a trip to search for the Heart. That benefactor was even going to pay him a stipend. Enough to rent a nice apartment near the beach and for me to come along. My dad promised me things were going to be better . . . different. He handed me a twenty and dropped me off at the pier for the afternoon so I could explore and grab some ice cream while he signed the paperwork for the rental and squared away things for our expedition. He never came back."

Huck is still, absolutely silent beside me.

"A beach is nice for a while," I say, trying to smile. "Then the summer sand turns scorching, and your skin burns, and twenty dollars doesn't go very far. I didn't even know the address of the apartment he'd rented. I don't know what would've happened if I hadn't met Teddy."

Huck's eyes are wide.

I wait for the exclamation. When I told Teddy this back then, he must've said *holy shit* about forty times. I actually got worried that he was having some sort of short circuit.

Huck does not say *holy shit.*

"Both your parents left you?"

His question catches me so off guard that I don't know how to respond.

"I'm sorry, I just . . . I didn't realize—" The boat pitches a little, throwing us off-balance. Huck grabs for the galley table and knocks over his can of ginger ale. I'm relieved that he has to look away from me to sop up the spill. "Stella, I didn't know."

"That I don't have a family?" I say. It's been true for so long, that I realize this must hit him harder than it hits me, but I'm not totally unscathed. "Yeah, well. Why would you? We don't really know each other that well. And I have Ted, and Zoe and Gus. So, I do fine."

Huck doesn't speak for a long time. His brow is deeply furrowed.

"I'm really sorry, Stella, I—"

"Don't do that," I cut him off. I don't want to be pitied even more than I don't want to hear Huck apologize. The tough exterior I've spent the last ten-plus years crafting—and rebuilding after last year and Iceland—isn't as impervious as I led myself to believe. If we start this conversation, I may not be able to maintain my defenses.

"Got it," he says. "You know, I did find one cool thing that could be related to the treasure . . . There was this old book in the library at Columbia that featured some pictures of different shipping documents from the time period of your wreck. I was able to connect with a translator through my publisher who helped me with some passages. It looks like it could contain some interesting information about the sinking of the *San Miguel*."

I lean over his shoulder to peer at the annotated photocopies. "Actually, I haven't seen this," I admit, lifting the printout to examine it more closely.

"I don't know how relevant it is," Huck says. "I just wanted to contribute if I could. You know I love to research."

"That is one thing I know about you, yes. I also know you didn't put your scopolamine patch on like we told you to."

"It was so calm before; I didn't think I needed it."

"Yeah, well, you might want to find that thing and pop it on before it gets worse. We're getting some decent-sized swells from the feel of it and you'll find yourself reliving that whale-watching trip for the next few days."

"You seem okay," he says.

"Well, I'm me, and you're you. We couldn't be more different."

Huck's expression changes, as if he's hurt by my jab. I turn my attention back to the printout and peer at the translated text while I tame my temper with a couple of deep breaths like Zoe advised before I left. It was her go-to tactic for maintaining her cool in a tense courtroom. That and picturing the opposing counsel in their underwear, which felt counterproductive to say the least.

"This is relevant," I admit. "Super interesting, actually. See, several of the other ships in this fleet have already been found off the coast of Florida, but farther north than where we are headed. They were traveling back to Spain when a massive storm hit, throwing several ships off course to avoid the dangerous weather, and others foundered. After it happened, a recovery effort was launched out of what is now Cuba. There're records of that search, which we've been able to go through, so we know that the *San*

Miguel was not found even though the sea was searched from St. Augustine all the way down south closer to the Cuban coast and the Keys. Based on this, it looks like de Melo chose to head south to avoid the storm. And it makes sense. He would've left a bit late to pick up the secret treasure without being detected, and might not have made it very far before the storm set in. They sent an independent boat to search this area instead, but they only recovered some raw gold dust—probably from the mine. This supports the possibility that the wreck we have on the coded map is the *San Miguel*, and that it wasn't found during the initial search."

I retrieve my mother's map from my bag and lay it out on the table in front of us. Wordlessly, Huck shifts his materials to make room.

"Is this hers?"

I nod. The map shows the Atlantic, with red marks indicating the wrecks that have already been found, other debris fields. The routes the envoy was taking based on our research are marked in pencil. I have to lean close to Huck to reach the map, where I trace a different route, a southerly one, with my finger. He smells clean and woodsy; that familiar citrus and cedar scent fills my nose and stirs up memories I have to push down.

"So, if they went this way, and the storm came in, we might expect that the ship either tried to harbor in this area or it sank. Here's Key West," I say, pointing to the land mass and then moving my hand over to the zone marked aggressively by yellow highlighter, "and here's where we're going to search."

Huck turns to face me. "What do you think the odds are that we'll find something there? High, right? Based on your research and this, it seems like you've found the right spot."

"It's not that simple," I say, rising.

"Why not? It was last time."

I take a long pause before I speak. I need to choose my words carefully. "Well, that wasn't underwater. And honestly, we got really lucky. Here, there are a ton of variables that we can try to account for, but we don't really have a good way to model to ensure that we're in the right spot. Basically, we'll deploy a magnetometer and mark all the hits that we get. We take that information and our research and synthesize it to determine which search areas have the highest odds of being our treasure. We might be in the right spot, but everything could be too deep for us to find with the tools we have. Or we might theoretically be in the spot where the initial sinking occurred, but the currents and other things have made a huge debris field that means we only find a few small things and everything else is spread across a huge zone on the ocean floor. We just don't know. It doesn't help that we're looking for something that isn't metal. That's more challenging. From what I was able to ascertain from records, this area hasn't been searched by professionals, at least not anyone who has applied for a permit. Of course, that doesn't mean that it hasn't been searched at all, but there's no record of any finds big or small."

Huck nods, thoughtful. "Then it's possible that nothing's been discovered even though someone may have looked?"

"Yeah. It happens. Even good treasure hunters can miss what they're searching for."

The amount of eye contact between us is overwhelming and maddening. He doesn't get to look at me like this, not now. I turn my attention to folding the map and tucking it away.

"Well, those treasure hunters didn't have you."

I think the words are meant as a compliment, but there's an undercurrent of sadness in his voice; it chips into my defenses a bit.

"I don't always get it right," I manage to say, my voice quiet. It's honest. I take a deep breath to pull myself together. "You might remember Skógafoss, where I dragged everyone out in the middle of the night and we came up with nothing."

Huck fixes his gaze on me. "I wouldn't call it nothing."

His words, his ice-blue eyes, all of him . . . they're pulling me back in. And I can't let that happen.

Fool me once, shame on you.

Fool me twice . . .

I collect the last of my sandwich. "I should get back on deck."

TWENTY-ONE

Huck

We stop in Beaufort, South Carolina, for the night, which is a freaking godsend honestly because those decent-sized swells that Stella mentioned proved to be too much for that off-brand motion sickness patch I stuck behind my ear as soon as she left the galley. Ted and Stella have a favorite restaurant in Beaufort, one of those hole-in-the-wall places that locals guard with their lives like a state secret. It's supposed to be an easy walk from the marina, though, *easy* is a relative term given that I'm struggling to adjust to dry land after a full day of movement of the boat.

"It's not far, Sully," Ted assures me as I sway on the pier.

"Am I *supposed* to feel like the ground is moving?"

"It happens sometimes."

"It will go away though, right?"

Ted thinks for a moment. "Yeah, definitely. It's rarely permanent."

"*Rarely* permanent? That's not very reassuring, buddy." I try to picture how I'd finish writing my next book after the trip is over if the screen were rocking back and forth, and almost lose my lunch.

"I told you not to try to be a badass and just put the scopol-amine patch on *before* we got on the boat. You made your own bed. Just don't get sick in it," Ted says, nodding at me and then toward Stella. "She'll never forgive you if you puke. Very anti-puke, that one."

I make a mental note to find the emergency bottle of Dram-amine I'd packed just in case, and also to ensure that I don't appear nauseated in sight of Stella again, not that it would make a dif-ference; I am nearly certain that never forgiving me is already a checked box when it comes to her. Especially after she told me about her parents, both of them leaving, and her really having no one. I'd known there was some painful truth beneath the surface, even back in Iceland, but I had no idea that it was that bad.

Which means that me bailing was part of a long pattern of complete shit that she's had to deal with her whole life. I feel like the worst person alive.

It's no consolation that I didn't know about her parents when I made that fucking awful choice. In light of her history, I could be part of her villain origin story. Then again, if there's a villain in this tale, it's me. I could explain it all to her, but why would I? Understanding why I made the decision to leave wouldn't change the fact that I'd left. My explanation would be meaningless in the context of what she's endured. Worse than meaningless . . . it would hurt her, like pouring salt water in a wound healed and opened again just so I can ease my conscience.

I might not be a great guy, or one who made my father proud . . . but I would never intentionally harm someone I care about. And I care about Stella, even if I never have the chance to show her.

We stroll along, somewhat unsteadily in my case, down a dusty avenue lined with massive, moss-adorned ancient oaks. Ted walks beside me and Stella is several paces ahead of us. It's a relief that she can't see me struggling to walk in a straight line, but the space between us is palpable. It's heaven and it's hell. She's barely spoken to me since our time together in the galley. I've seen her around the boat, torturing me in a worn-thin T-shirt and frayed cutoff jeans, while she performs maintenance and billions of freckles appear on her skin like I wished them there. This trip just might break me.

Before we left the marina, she traded her uniform jean shorts and T-shirt for a basic chambray sundress and a pair of broken-in cowboy boots that give her a few extra inches in height. She took out her braids and let her hair down. It's longer than it was last year. Now it falls in waves down to the middle of her back, just above the spot where I'd place my hand if we were walking together. Where I've placed my hand before. The fit of my palm against the curve of her back is burned in my memory.

"You're quiet," Ted says.

"Just trying not to toss my fucking cookies." A half-truth. I'm watching her walk in those boots; every few steps she throws in a skip for fun.

"A hundred bucks says you'll be good as new once you have something to eat. You've got to try the low-country boil. It's incredible. The freshest shellfish you'll ever have, sweet corn, tender potatoes, and that heat . . . Pair that with a cold beer and it's paradise for the palate. Start with the oyster crackers."

"How long have you guys been coming here?"

"At least twice a season for the past seven or so years, except for last year. We got to know the owners, Peg and Billy, a while back; they're great. They both grew up here and the recipes they use have been in their families forever." He reaches up and snags a piece of moss in his fingers. "We found it on the way back during one of our early seasons. Lucky we did too. There was a nasty front coming in—we had a much smaller boat then—and we used Peg's Place as a bailout. We were all so naive then. Stella comes up from a dive with a handful of ancient gold coins. The rest of us were so stoked. In our minds, it was the coolest thing that had ever happened to us, and we figured it was only a matter of time before we'd be hauling out giant rubies and emeralds and gold coins after that, but it was a one-off. We didn't find anything else. And we'd missed a front coming in. Gus and Zoe and I were disappointed that we didn't find more before we had to make a run north, but we were still thrilled about the coins, especially since we'd been searching for a few years by then and hadn't found a thing—not Stella. She was *pissed*. Those coins weren't old enough to have come from the Sea People's Stolen Treasure. I asked her if she wanted to give up. Hunting treasure hadn't worked out well for her family, maybe it was time to walk away for good. She told me she'd never stop, not until she found it. She was convinced that if we didn't quit, eventually we'd find the thing that would make it all worthwhile."

"She never gives up. She's tenacious," I say.

"Exactly. She's a real pain in the ass."

"I heard that, Teddy," Stella says without turning around.

"A tenacious pain in the ass," he shoots back.

"Just for that, you're buying dinner," she says, slowing her pace before she veers off the road to the left onto a path that looks like a narrow driveway in between trees.

"When do I *not* buy dinner?" Ted says and casts a glance in my direction.

Ahead of us, there's an unassuming squat building, older but freshly painted, situated in front of a long expanse of marsh grass, black against the peach glow of the setting sun. If we hadn't turned, I wouldn't have known it was here.

"Anyway, as I was saying, we were dealing with bad weather and Stella's angry as hell. Only one thing got us through it."

"Crabmeat," Stella chimes in.

"I was going to say friendship," Ted says.

"Bullshit. You love good crabmeat more than I do."

I reach to pull the door open for her, but she beats me to it. Ted passes through first and she follows behind him.

"What can I say, seafood is my love language." He pulls off his hat and is instantly in his element—hugging the staff, winking at the bartender, heading to a table tucked in a bay window with a perfect view of the sunset. It's almost as if it's been saved for us.

Stella and Ted sit together, leaving me with a side to myself, and Ted orders for everyone—the magic meal, biscuits, low-country boil, and a round of bottled beers. I'm thankful for this, since it's difficult to read the menu in my current condition. It's also a challenge not to compare this to the night that Stella and I went out for Icelandic pizza. But soon, our meal is served and we've all had enough to drink that our sharp edges are softening. I'd hoped that the food and drink would cure my problem that a quick Google search on my phone says is vestibular, but so far, no luck. Thankfully, there's no shortage of conversation thanks to Ted. I don't need my list of thought-provoking questions or even to be particularly witty. He has enough to keep us going late into the evening, through dessert—a cobbler that I might dream about later, it was that good.

"Seems like your new book's doing well," Ted says.

Stella stabs a peach with her fork.

I wipe my mouth with a napkin and swallow. "Yeah, it's been good."

"Dude, they talked about you on *Good Morning America*. I'd say it's been great."

I lift my shoulders. "I'll have to take your word for it. I didn't see it." I have no desire to dwell on the show. A similar TV appearance had set my father off in the weeks before he'd died. He's been gone for years, but I still remember the shade of purple he'd turned, how he threw the remote across the room, the vicious things he'd said. They'd asked me how I came up with Clark Casablanca, and I'd told them about my boarding school days, how I'd loved it there and had all my best ideas up late on the dormitory roof spinning tales with my roommate at the time. It was the wrong thing to say. A slap in my father's face. *They're all going to see through you*, he'd said. *You wait. They'll see what you really are, what I see so clearly, Henry.* Should I have dedicated my success to him, was I forged in the flames of his anger and resentment? I'd been honest. I'd done well in spite of him, and if anything, most of my success was really owed to Ted. Without him, I'd have given up.

Stella flags down a waitress for another beer.

Ted forges ahead. "You were on that big screen in Times Square—instant *New York Times* bestseller. That's huge, right?" It's even worse.

"I'm very grateful," I say. Even though I am, this line is rehearsed. Talking about my books isn't exciting or easy, it's awkward and nerve-racking. Jim had told me about *GMA* the day before it happened, sent along another bottle of champagne that I wouldn't drink. It would be too easy to let the book and the press send me into a spiral . . . because I knew it was only a matter of time until they'd realize that my work was terrible. *I* was terrible, untalented, nothing on my own, and then I'd be a failure again just like Dad said I would. In those moments where I worry, I'm back in that room with him, ducking the remote he'd fired like a missile in my direction. The details are sharp: his crimson cheeks, broken bits of plastic remote, batteries rolling across the Moroccan rug, the boom of his voice rattling the glasses on the bar cart.

"You must be doing pretty well in the royalty department.

Maybe I should let you buy dinner. It's a business write-off, right?" Ted laughs. "I'm going to hit the bathroom."

Stella's quiet, peeling the label from her bottle.

"You didn't like it," I say.

Her brow furrows. "The food was great. Might be the best I've had here."

"I meant the book."

"Haven't read it." She gives a small wince. "Sorry."

"I forgot, you don't do hate-reads, right?" It's a joke. A poor one. My own insecurity rearing up and showing itself like a clam in the sand as a wave washes out.

The corner of her mouth quirks. She shakes her head. "It's not that."

"That's a relief." My face flushes. I hadn't meant to say that out loud.

"I couldn't really bring myself to read it."

"Oh." Thinking about the implications of this admission brings on a fresh round of guilt, and the rotation of the room picks up speed. "Well, I hope you do, at some point. I always appreciate your thoughts on my work."

"Maybe." She downs the rest of her beer. "I'm going to take a walk on the pier."

"What about Ted?"

"He's making the rounds. Anyway, he's really not going to let you pay, and he knows where to find me."

I don't correct her as I follow her out a back door to a small boardwalk that runs along the edge of the property. The wooden walk stretches out a long way. In the distance, the moon is rising against the darkening sky; its reflection on the surface of the high tide is silver and massive.

"I love the salt marsh even more than the beach," Stella says, stopping to stare out. "It's always changing, showing you something new. The tide rolls in and out and the birds go away and come back. It's like a beautiful cycle, departing and then returning."

I stand beside her.

"It's reliable."

She nods.

"Beautiful." I don't mean to say this either. It just comes out of my fucking traitor mouth, honest and raw, which was and is still an effect that Stella has on me. Even so, I don't want to take it back, not until she rotates her head to look at me in a way that vaguely resembles a character from the movie *The Exorcist*. Luckily, a crane swoops by us at the perfect moment, and I lift my arm. "The bird," I clarify awkwardly. "I like birds. That one's beautiful. What is it? Pelican?" I cling to each idea, rambling, desperate to cover my slipup.

I sound possessed myself.

"How are you feeling?" Stella asks. For a second, I think she's riffing after my chaotic scrambling bird explanation, but then I realize she means the land-sickness. I'm not sure if she's being kind or cruel or just moving on to safer topics. I make the mistake of looking down at the wooden slats beneath my feet where a handful of tiny fiddler crabs scurry and almost lose my balance. "That good, huh?" Any lingering anger is absent from her voice now.

I ball my hands into fists, fully annoyed with myself—of course Stella wouldn't be cruel. That was *my* department. "At the risk of being incredibly vulnerable, I was prepared for a lot of things on this trip. Not this, though." She looks right through me, and I quickly add, "The feeling like I'm moving when I'm on dry land was not on my bingo card."

"It takes some people longer to get their land legs back," she says. She reaches down and picks up a white oyster shell, turning it over in her hands before she tosses it into the water. "I think I know exactly how to fix it, though."

"Yeah?"

She nods. "Are you okay to walk down a bit farther?"

"I think so, just as long as I don't look down again. My balance is way off."

"We can take care of that."

"That's great news."

"This should work . . . as long as you trust me," she says.

We reach the end of the walkway. I had trusted her from the moment we'd met, and I still did. "Of course. I do. I trust you. Just please, make this—"

It happens in an instant. She's reaching for me. My mind races. Maybe there's a chance that she still feels something between us like what we had in Iceland, maybe I want that too. I could tell her the truth and we could move past this. Start again. It's probably a huge mistake, but isn't that what living is? And I don't know what to do or how to feel, but if she wants me, she can have me. She never stopped having me. And then, there's a surprising impact on my torso; I'm sailing through the air, my arms flailing, and I hit the water.

I sputter to the surface just in time to see an entire flock of egrets take to the sky, startled by my splash or the rich sound of Stella's hysterical laughter. "What the fuck—"

"If you still have your sea legs, the only way to feel better is to go back to the water," she calls from the boardwalk.

"You could've warned me," I call. "What if I were a bad swimmer?"

"You seem to be doing fine."

There's not one iota of my body that can be mad at her. She's unabashed, delighted with herself. That triumphant smile, and the way she's casually reaching for the hem of her dress, has me in a total freaking choke hold. I feel light-headed and lighter, like maybe I've overestimated the damage I caused her. Because she's laughing, shimmying that sundress over her head, stepping out of her boots, standing above me in her underwear. I only have an instant to admire her figure, the gently curving silhouette I still long to run my hands over in languid strokes and that lacy lingerie that forces me to sink deep into my memory. She doesn't give me a chance to go further. In two steps, she's airborne, knees tucked, arcing over me in a perfect cannonball that sends a jet of water into my face when she lands. She swims back to me in smooth strokes until we're only inches away from each other. Beneath the surface, our hands accidentally graze as we tread water. This could be the Blue Lagoon.

"Feel better?" she asks. She slicks her wet hair back with her hands.

"Not quite," I say. I put my hands on her head and give her one massive dunk. When she comes up for air, she flashes a dramatic angry face and sends a wall of water into my laughing mouth and eyes with a single graceful swoop of her arm. She's laughing too, squealing as we splash each other. I bob gently, warring with her, and forget that the world was moving earlier when it was supposed to stand still. I forget that I'm not happy. I forget that we didn't work out because I did what I always do and ruined everything.

In this moment, with Stella, I forget everything.

I even fail to recall that the salt water down here this time of year can be teeming with jellyfish.

TWENTY-TWO

Stella

This is what I get for letting my guard down. One moment, Huck and I are laughing in the water, enjoying each other as if there isn't a history of hurt between us, and the next, well, I'm thinking of the warning Teddy's mom gave me that year on Bald Head. They're called sea nettles . . . the name sounds mild, but they sting like a mother, and somehow Huck and I managed to do our synchronized swimming-slash-water-polo-style brawl right in the middle of a school of them. I don't even hear Teddy's rapid footfalls on the walkway over Huck's yelps and my own Pterodactyl-esque screeching.

I spot Teddy right before he's about to launch himself into the water.

"Don't!" I squeal. "There's jellies in here. A lot of jellies."

"Shit," Ted says. "That was a close one."

"We've got to swim for it," I tell Huck. I know this may mean additional stings, but we don't have a choice. The options are *fuck it and go fast* or *try to be careful*, which takes longer. It's a lose-lose situation. I choose fast because I know soaking in hot water and applying some antihistamine lotion as soon as possible will ease the pain that's searing my skin. Huck seems to go with careful, but given the expletive he just shouted, that approach doesn't appear to be turning out so well for him. He zooms up next to me. Teddy helps us both out clumsily and manages to knock my clothes in the water in the process.

"What's going on here?" Teddy asks, as he fishes out my sopping sundress.

"We fell," Huck says.

"I shoved him in," I confess, leaning down to examine my torso, where a long slash of fire is welting up on my skin. I stick my feet back into my boots.

"Okay," Teddy says slowly. He hands my dripping dress to me while he processes. "Okay, let me get this straight. You dunk-tanked our unsuspecting guest and then decided to join him?" His speech is slow, sticky like the cobbler we'd eaten.

"I never claimed to be the logical one," I say, shrugging and wringing the water out of the dress. I turn to Huck. "How're the sea legs?"

Huck takes off a shoe and dumps out the water that's filled it.

"Covered in stings," he says. "But I believe my vestibular issue is more or less resolved, so I thank you for that."

"Well, you're both in luck," Ted says. "I got sidetracked at the bar on my way to the bathroom, and I was just about to finish my journey when I heard you both howling out here, so I'm all stocked up to treat your injuries."

"Huh?" Huck looks confused. "What does he mean?"

"He's offering to pee on us," I explain.

Huck shakes his head, grimacing. "Is that necessary?"

I step closer to him, hiding my own discomfort. Huck has quite a few stings, and I'm sure that they hurt as much as mine do, and I feel bad about that, considering I'm responsible for flinging him in. His white polo shirt is stuck to his chest, and his Bermuda shorts cling to his thighs, so he's safe there. Unlike me, who decided to strip down and provide the vicious little creatures with quite a canvas of sensitive skin to attack. But I can't help but have a little fun at Huck's expense.

"You've got *extensive* stings," I say dramatically. "It could be serious, so we need to neutralize the venom quickly. Otherwise . . ."

"Otherwise *what*?"

Teddy, who I'm realizing now is quite drunk and has been holding a highball this whole time, sways as he reaches for his zipper. "I got you, man. Friends for forever. I almost did you in when we were kids, now I pay my debt."

"What about you, Stella?" Huck exclaims. "Ted, listen, take care of her first. I'm okay. I'm bigger than her so the venom will probably take longer . . ."

Teddy turns to me. "Anything for my grill . . . girl."

"Keep it in your pants there, cowboy," I say to him.

He looks at me, incredulous. "I got enough for you too, honey. Or were you going to help him yourself?"

Huck is frozen, his face awash in sheer terror. He closes his eyes and holds out his arms. "Go ahead, then, I'm ready."

I stifle my laughter. "No one is peeing on anyone, Huck, okay? We were messing with you."

"I wasn't!"

"It's an old wives' tale. We need to get back to the boat and wash off. There's some liquid Benadryl in the first-aid kit."

"Oh, thank god!" Huck says.

"In that case, I'll just relieve myself over here." Teddy winks at me and stumbles toward a bush. I take the opportunity to put my dress back on.

P eg, resident saint and proprietor extraordinaire, mixes up a concoction of seawater and baking soda to rinse our stings.

According to her, it's supposed to stop any remaining stingers from continuing to cause damage. Then she gives us a ride back to the boat in her station wagon. It's a good thing she takes pity on us, because my wounds are throbbing and Teddy can't walk in a straight line and has launched into an ear-splitting rendition of "Satisfied" from *Hamilton* complete with Eliza's rap, which he manages to get through several times with increasing volume despite the fact that his speech is slurred. I haven't seen Teddy this drunk in a while, not since the night at Huck's cabin in Iceland. I love him, I do, but I'm not a fan of him when he's like this. He's sloppy. And reminds me of all the times I slid half-full cans of stale beer from my dad's hand while he slept before he left. Ted accidentally whacks me in the face when he tries to throw an arm around my shoulders in the car. Sober Teddy would be managing this situation, making sure that Huck and I were okay via legitimate means instead of urination, and he certainly wouldn't have peed in our friend's shrubbery.

In the marina parking lot, Huck and I thank Peg, and Teddy does a weird military salute before he's back to *Hamilton* with a very pitchy version of "Aaron Burr, Sir," which I assume must've popped into his mind when he clicked his heels together and sent Peg on her way like George Washington. Huck and I flank him on the way back to the boat, making sure he doesn't fall in—we don't need any more emergencies tonight.

"Look, it's my boat! Hercules Mulligan!"

"Let's get you to bed, Ted," Huck says, crossing the deck toward the stairs.

Teddy wobbles and stops inches from Huck's face. He scrunches his nose. "I want Stella to do it."

I hand him a water bottle and steer him toward his bunk. "Go a little easier next time maybe," I say. "The first mate isn't supposed to get trashed at dinner."

Teddy lets out a vicious puff of air that is so rank with alcohol that I come dangerously close to violating my own no-puking-on-the-boat policy. "Me? Drunk? That's ridaclous. Ridiclesuos."

"Yup. Totally ridiculous." I gesture toward the bed. "Get in, friend. Your nice comfy bed awaits."

Teddy complies, and Huck and I work together to take off his shoes and pull the blankets over him.

"We should make sure he's on his side," Huck says, "to be safe."

"Good idea."

Teddy is already snoring loudly by the time we tiptoe out of his room.

"Does he drink like that often?" Huck asks when we're out in the hallway.

"Sometimes." I shrug. "Not for a while."

Huck hesitates. "There was that time at the cabin."

The passageways on the ship are narrow, which forces Huck and me into a proximity that is only made more uncomfortable by the nostalgia. He's referring to the night we first kissed, when Teddy had gotten blitzed and had to come home early from his date. "That was a one-off, I think. We should head to the galley. First, we need to use hot water to destroy the bad proteins in the venom. And the med kit's in there anyway. I think it has Benadryl or cortisone cream at least."

I lead the way, trying desperately to push the recollection of that night, that kiss against the bookshelf, the closeness in my bed afterward, out of my mind. There's not much left to focus on except the lingering pain of the welts that have sprung up across my torso and thighs.

"It's probably nothing," Huck says. "Ted used to be the life of the party in school . . . I guess that part of him hasn't changed. Maybe it has a little." He heats some water and wets a kitchen towel for me.

"How so?" I press the hot towel to my worst sting.

"He didn't sing then." He laughs but it's short-lived. "He loved to showboat, though, and was constantly causing some sort of chaos with his antics."

"Like the golf cart–stealing incident?"

"Exactly. He was always up to something, like streaking large events, sneaking into the headmaster's house to raid his pantry. One time he borrowed a wig and costume from the theater department and pretended to be a substitute teacher for a whole week. I guess I expected him to have grown out of that phase."

I follow his lead and soak another towel with the hot water for him. "Are *you* that different from when you were younger? Sometimes I think I should be more like an official grown-up and know how to navigate things, but I don't."

He lets out a hiss when the towel meets his skin. After a minute he says, "I know what you mean. I feel like a bit of an imposter at times. My dad loved to give me shit about the myriad ways I didn't measure up. I was actually relieved when he decided to send me off to boarding school since it was an escape from his incessant verbal assaults. But he could still call. I guess I expected at some point his words wouldn't have an impact on me anymore, like I'd outgrow caring? Not so much. He died years ago, but his voice is still the one I hear when things go wrong. He's my mean inner critic anytime I fuck up."

"Shit," I say. "What an asshole. I mean, my dad had his own issues and left me to fend for myself, but he didn't tear me down any chance he got."

"Yeah, we both sort of didn't make out too well in the father department, did we? It's almost like some people really weren't cut out to be parents, but who knows why they are the way they are? Take my dad. He was hard on me *and* himself. I hated what he did, but then I remember that we're all doing this life for the first time, and I don't know what he went through before he had me, and that helps. Makes it hurt a little less, maybe."

"I guess. But what if we aren't?" I ask, trying to lighten the mood. "I think I might believe in reincarnation."

"I suppose if that's the case then we're not doing a very good job. By now we probably should know to look out for jellyfish. But to answer your question, I am different than when I was young."

"How so?"

"I hope in the important ways—I'm more empathetic and responsible, less impulsive. I think more about other people now. I eat vegetables." Huck looks thoughtful for a moment.

I pull the med kit from its holder and set it on the counter. "This might sting, but it should help," I say, getting out the antihistamine lotion. I smooth some on the red welt on his arm.

Huck gives me a sad smile. "You don't have to do this, Stella. I can manage." He nods toward his arm.

I pause. Helping him and talking like this had felt so natural, but that was just the magnetism of old rhythms and too much chemistry, I realize. I could learn something from his reserve. I set down the bottle and step back.

"I just meant that you don't have to take care of me. You're hurt too."

I don't know how to respond to this. The accuracy of his words sends a strange sensation down my spine.

Huck's voice is low when he speaks again. "If anything, I should help you. It looked like you got a pretty bad sting on your stomach."

So he *had* been looking. Was that what I wanted when I'd peeled off my dress to jump in with him, or when I'd put on the dress in the first place? No. I was notorious for flinging off my clothes and any shred of caution and jumping into water every chance I got, and before that I'd been dying to wear something other than my jean shorts and T-shirt, which had both been getting a little ripe in the sun all day while cruising. All of that has nothing to do with Huck.

I don't like him, and I don't care what he thinks about me.

Actually, I don't feel *anything* for him anymore.

Except he picks up the ointment, and now he's closing the gap between us, and my breath quickens. "Do you want me to put some of this on your stings?" He's practically whispering, his voice deep and sultry.

I swallow hard. Do I want his hands to trace over my bare skin while he applies the gel? Stand so close that I can feel the heat of his sunburn radiating from him? My pulse turns insistent and thunderous in my ears. I'll have to take off my dress. I have welts on my abdomen, my ribs, the backs of my thighs. They're smarting beneath my clothes, calling out for his touch, for relief. The anticipation of the feeling of his fingertips traveling over the sensitive skin is too much. Would it be like I remembered? He knew then exactly how to touch me.

I squeeze my eyes shut and swallow. *Don't forget what it was like when you woke up happy for a second and then he wasn't there.* That pain, the memory of it is here to keep me safe.

The stings, they were a warning. Nature's way of reminding me that when I get too close to Huck Sullivan—or anyone really—I get hurt.

"No thanks," I say, more shrilly than I would've liked. I snatch the medicine bottle from his hand, and race out of the room before he can follow.

TWENTY-THREE

Huck

Ted's monstrous hangover costs us an extra day. We make it into Key West a day late, just as the sun is setting into the sea, fiery red and massive.

"Red sky at night," Teddy hollers, hopping onto the pier to catch the line.

"Sailor's delight," Stella calls back. I try not to think about how close she and I were in the kitchen and how gently she pressed the hot towel to my jellyfish sting. She kills the ship's engine, and I launch into action tossing the rope to Ted. Over the last few days, I've kind of been getting the hang of being at sea. I picked up the lingo quickly, helped Stella and Ted with maintenance and navigation, and even took a shift at the helm. I'm nowhere near the level that they are, where being at sea feels natural, but I'm not a liability anymore.

My scopolamine patch is doing its thing, the jellyfish stings are healing up nicely, and Stella and I haven't had another moment like the one in the galley, which is for the best. I'm okay with being tolerated by her; anything more than that would only make my heart hurt, I suspect. We've settled into a kind of semi-comfortable cordiality that is only a little awkward and mostly pain-free, except when the wind lifts her hair off her neck, or she walks by in her bare feet and her baseball hat, or I think about any one of the things on the list that reminds me of what could've been, what was then and isn't now . . . the sound of the ocean waves, stars in the dark sky, pizza, waterfalls, notes written on maps, sleeping bags, Amelia Earhart, silk camisoles, Vikings, poppy seeds, and sheep, and now ointment and hot towels and galley kitchens, cowgirl boots and lacy underwear. The list is long, and the situation is as imperfect as I am, but I think it would be fair to say this is progress.

Once everything is squared away at the docks, we head over to the crew's favorite Key West restaurant, where we're supposed to meet Zoe and Gus. El Meson de Pepe is in Mallory Square and apparently is famous for its amazing Cuban food. I've had Cuban cuisine in New York that was pretty fantastic, but this place has been here forever and we're so close to Cuba that I imagine it's super authentic.

Mallory Square is brimming with people, some walking on stilts, others juggling illuminated bowling pins, and the odd illusionist drawing a crowd. "What is this?" I ask.

"Sunset Celebration!" Ted cheers, and zips off into the throng.

"They have this every night," Stella fills in. "Lots of performers come and do stunts and magic or tell stories. It's such a cool event."

"Where did Teddy run off to in all that chaos?" I ask.

"Probably to see if he can find the cats that jump through the flaming hoops. We saw it once several years ago and he was hooked."

I grin. "Are you pulling my leg?"

"Why would I do that?"

"That doesn't sound like a thing. Cats and flaming hoops? What if their tails catch on fire?"

"I don't think any felines are harmed in the Sunset Celebration. Besides, where's your sense of adventure? It's a once-in-a-lifetime experience." Stella jogs after Teddy, and I sprint to catch up with her. We weave in and out of the crowds watching sword swallowers, acrobats, and other acts, and pass by the guy on a super tall unicycle silhouetted against the darkening sky, while snippets of songs sung and played on guitars and steel drums fill my senses. It's magical here. I can't deny it. Stella has come alive, her light hair streaming out behind her. My chest squeezes a little. We find Ted watching an acrobat act.

"No cats?" I ask him.

"Apparently, Dominique the Catman retired, and, get this, they don't even allow fire anymore at the Sunset Celebration. No more flying housecats or flaming hoops. I'm devastated, guys, I really am."

"That's too bad. But it means we can go to dinner now, right?" Stella asks. "And—"

"Let me guess, the picadillo habanero is calling your name," Ted says.

"Oh, good choice! But no, I was going to say that Zoe and Gus are probably wondering where we are. I texted them before we docked, and they were already at the restaurant."

Luckily, the warehouse-like building that houses El Meson de Pepe is only a couple of minutes' walk from the celebration. There's a live salsa band playing, a healthy crowd milling around the patio bar, and a few brave chickens wandering about looking to get lucky with some dropped food. We manage to find Gus and Zoe, lounging at a round table on the patio. Zoe is wearing a flowy maxi dress made of bright coral linen and Gus is in full Tommy Bahama wear; they have the easy happiness of contentment. Stella tackles Zoe, envelopes her in a hug that is halfway to a mixed-martial-arts takedown. Beside them Gus and Ted do an elaborate handshake that has more steps than I've ever seen. I lift my chin at Gus in greeting and he reaches out to shake my hand.

"Nice to see you again," I say.

"Glad to see you made it down here in one piece," he says, handing me a glass of beer.

"Was there ever any doubt?" Ted chimes in.

"With Stella?" Gus grimaces for effect. "A little bit, yeah. Honestly, Zoe was kind of worried that she might send Huck here into the drink and keep going."

I sputter on the sip of beer I've just taken.

"Are you starting some shit over there, babe?" Zoe calls. She steps around her chair to embrace Teddy. "You promised me that you were going to be on your best behavior."

"That was pillow talk, it's inadmissible."

"Don't try to ply me with court lingo. You know what that does to me."

"Here we go," Stella says and groans, but she's smiling.

"Don't listen to a word Gus says," Zoe tells me. "My actual wording was that I wouldn't be surprised if she fed you to the sharks. Less drawn out."

"Thanks for that," I say. "Very generous. I would appreciate avoiding any sort of protracted torture." I don't add that this past year has been its own kind of torture. "Glad to see that your sharp wit is the same as it was in Iceland, and that your hair recovered from the Lagoon incident."

"Now, Huck, we don't speak of that tiny unfortunate event. Though maybe we should—I won the shit out of that case. Maybe the extra minerals soaked into my scalp."

"Your hair looks gorgeous, Z," Ted says. "And you were partially right. Stella did knock him into the salt marsh when we were over at Peg's Place."

I glance over at Stella to see if she's heard Ted's announcement, but she's stepped away to get an extra chair.

"It does, doesn't it?" Zoe does a little twirl before she settles back into her seat. "I need to know more about this alleged Salt Marshing, but first let's sit. I'm beat from a full day of exploring while you three dillydallied your way down to us." We grab menus from the center of the table. The offerings all look mouthwatering. "We already ordered a pitcher of beer and some apps," Zoe tells us. "Conch fritters and coconut shrimp."

"I was thinking it's a good night for mojitos," Ted says.

"Count me in for mojitos," Stella says.

"Those starters should be coming right out," a server says as she passes by.

"Tell us about the trip down. How'd it go?" Gus asks. "No one got fed to a shark, I see, so already we're in a better place than we expected."

Stella casts a glance at me, and I take another sip of my beer. Is she thinking of our hands brushing against each other in the water before the jellyfish had given us a stark reminder of the dangers of getting too close, or maybe of later in the galley when she'd smoothed the ointment on my vulnerable skin and we were so near I worried she'd hear my pounding heart?

"Teddy got shit-faced and sang the entire fucking soundtrack to *Hamilton*," Stella says, directing the conversation away from me and her.

Gus clinks his glass against Teddy's. "Respect."

"And Huck and I got stung by a bunch of jellyfish in South Carolina. Otherwise, totally uneventful. What about you guys? What'd you do today?"

"We went to Hemingway House, of course," Gus tells us.

"Are you guys Hemingway fans?" I ask.

"You'd think that would be the driver for these two intellectuals," Stella says, "but you'd be wrong. They go for the cats."

I'm embarrassed to admit that I don't know anything about Hemingway and cats, so I nod. But Zoe, who I'm learning quickly is amazingly adept at reading people, seems to recognize my ignorance. She generously gives me the history. "The story goes that some old ship captain gave Hemingway a white six-toed cat. The house now is a home to all its descendants. Apparently, they all carry the trait. It's a really neat place. They have these special fences so that cats are safe to roam free on the grounds."

"Very cool," I say.

"There's sixty of them," Zoe adds. "It's beyond cool."

"Zoe loves cats even more than Teddy does," Stella explains.

"Speaking of, did you know the Catman isn't doing shows anymore?!" Teddy asks.

"Yes, we were at a café and someone there knows Dominique. They said he's retired. I'm so disappointed. It's truly the end of an era," Zoe says.

The server drops off the heaping plates of fritters and shrimp. We order our main dishes and a round of mojitos, and then we all dig into the food while it's still hot. The conversation shifts to everyone's favorite local delicacies—the ladies and Ted favor the Key lime pie at Kermit's, while Gus can't decide between the lobster pizza at Seaside Cafe or the Papa Dobles cocktail at Sloppy Joe's—before we move on to the treasure hunt, which will officially start tomorrow at sunrise. Between mouthfuls, Stella shares the link between the text I'd found detailing the fruitless recovery operation and their planned search-and-salvage site. I can't help but grin at everyone's reaction, but mostly I'm happy that she seems to think I've made a valuable contribution to their expedition. Even though it's killing me that I can't change what happened and I can't go back and fix what I did, I still am going to make the best of this opportunity and do whatever I can to help Stella reach her goal and find the Heart, especially now that I know what this means to her.

Ted raises his glass. "To an amazing adventure with the best people I know," he toasts.

"To treasuring this time together," Gus says, and gives Zoe a squeeze.

"I see what you did there," Stella says with a grin.

"Hear, hear," Ted says.

"My turn?" Zoe lifts her water glass a little higher. "To fair weather, fantastic friends, and finding what we came here for."

It's down to me and Stella.

"Can't do better than that," I say. Everyone nods in agreement.

Stella smiles and pulls in a breath before she makes her own toast. "I'll just add to holding history in the palms of our hand and becoming legends in our own right. To finding the *San Miguel* with the best people I know. I love you guys."

I know that last part isn't meant for me and I don't deserve it in any way—not then and not now—but it still fills me with a helium feeling. I float through the rest of dinner and barely sleep that night.

TWENTY-FOUR

Stella

As predicted, the morning dawns clear and cerulean skied. Being in Key West where my mom had lived and flown and found her own silver coins as a young woman always fills me with a sense of happiness and optimism, and this time is no different, even if this trip isn't like any of the other ones thanks to the presence of—I don't even know how to label him—the famous author I hooked up with in Iceland, Teddy's old friend who happens to be an amazing kisser but sucks at mornings, the man who bashed my heart into a billion bits?

Because Zoe is an angel, she went out early and is now back with coffees and Cuban bread with guava and cream cheese from Cuban Coffee Queen on the waterfront for all of us. Gus and I finish a final gear check and then we enjoy our breakfast while the sun grows strong in the cloudless sky. Teddy's sleeping in, a habit he's started on this trip, but Huck's up studying the PADI Open Water Diver training book I'd given him back in South Carolina.

"It's the perfect day to head out," Zoe says, tapping her takeout coffee cup against mine.

I nod, tucking my arms around my legs. There's a slight breeze and the sun is warm and golden, like honey butter.

"How's work been?" I ask her. "Was it hard to get the time off?"

Zoe takes a long sip of her coffee. "It's been good. Busy. I'm glad to have a break, actually. I just finished a challenging trial last month that had me and a bunch of associates working around the clock. My sleep bank is pretty depleted."

"Did it turn out well?"

"It did, thankfully, or I wouldn't have been able to come. It's kind of hard to say no to a winner. For a while there during the trial I wasn't confident that the outcome would be in our favor."

"You're probably being modest," I say. "You're such a rock star."

Zoe shakes her head. "I'm serious. It could've gone either way, and the jury deliberated for a long time. Sometimes being a rock star isn't enough. I know the firm believes in me . . . Cagney said if my next case turns out well, then they'll consider making me partner."

"Zoe! Talk about burying that lede. Partner? That's a huge deal, right?"

"Yeah, it is. It's always been the goal. But enough about work stuff, my whole life the past couple of months has been consumed with work stuff. I want to hear more about how things are going with the author, and how the heck the two of you ended up getting attacked by jellyfish." She eyes me, and I remember why she's so successful—we're not even in a courtroom and I'm ready to crumble under her cross-examination.

I shrug. "It's going fine. I guess it would be fair to say that the magnitude of my loathing is less than it was last month. He's trying. He did all this research before he came, which was a nice gesture. It feels like his interest in the expedition is genuine. I appreciate that. And he's just been curious and helpful—you know, all the kinds of things that make it hard to hate a person.

Plus, he got land-sickness in South Carolina so I couldn't help but feel a tiny bit sorry for him when he was struggling to stay upright."

"And the jellyfish?"

"A side effect of a totally innocent evening swim over at Peg's."

"*Totally* innocent? I might've believed you if you hadn't added the adjective." She scrutinizes me while she takes a long sip of her coffee. I shift uncomfortably under her gaze. "You went skinny dipping, didn't you?"

I shake my head. "No. He even had shoes on."

"And what about you? I know you didn't ruin your shoes in the salt marsh."

My eyes snap shut. I walked right into that. "Teddy blabbed, didn't he?"

"He wasn't too clear on the details, but he was very forthcoming about you wearing only your fancy underwear when he found you both out there. He went on and on about it. Apparently, he had no idea you owned sexy lingerie. I never doubted that you had some good stuff, but I was a little surprised you packed it for our expedition when we're spending ninety-nine percent of our time on the boat or in the water. Didn't you once tell me that the only thing you needed other than your scuba gear and your metal detector were a bikini, instincts, and sunscreen?"

Heat rises in my cheeks, and I pull my hat down farther on my forehead. Of course I own nice underwear. I just save it for special occasions, which generally do not include our expeditions, as Zoe has so graciously pointed out. The fact that I'd packed my special-occasion lingerie for this trip fills me with flaming-hot shame.

Zoe lowers herself so I can't avoid looking at her. "What gives, Stella? I feel like you undersold what happened in Iceland with Huck. You told me that you guys had very casually hooked up one

time and then he'd bailed on both you guys . . . but I'm starting
to get the feeling that the hookup was anything but casual and
you feel like he deserted only you."

I'm quiet for what feels like hours. "Did Teddy blab that too?"
I ask, trying to keep the defensive edge out of my voice.

"No. He didn't say anything about it, but you've never been
one to care about casual connections, and you seem extremely
bothered and are packing your nice undies. Evidence doesn't lie."

"It doesn't matter," I say. "That ship has sailed."

"Maybe it has for you, which I would get . . . honestly, if he
bailed on you, I have half a mind to punch his face myself . . .
except I saw the way that man was looking at you last night at the
restaurant."

"So?" I take a large bite of my Cuban bread and chew.

The pause doesn't have the desired effect of making Zoe give
up this line of discussion. She continues to watch me, eyebrows
lifted.

"Okay, fine. I give up. How did he look at me?"

"Like a puppy staring at its favorite shoe. You know, the one
it wants to chew on so bad but knows it shouldn't?"

"I'm leather now? Jeez. Great. I'm a shoe."

"Look, I'd happily be a Manolo Blahnik. Stylish and sharp.
No one said you had to be a worn clog or something, touchy. I
feel like I hit a nerve. Tell me, then. Am I right? 'Cause I also
noticed that you were trying real hard not to look at him." She
pokes me.

I sigh. "I don't know. Maybe the hookup wasn't all that casual." Maybe I'd thought I could fall for him and felt that he'd
seen me and saw the same potential that I did. Maybe I'd stupidly
thought it was fate running into him in that bar. Maybe I'd let
my guard down and gotten bitten by that puppy and his stupid
New York Times conversation-starter questions. What was I sup-

posed to do? He wrote moving stories and asked me about who
I'd most want to have dinner with and if I knew how I was going
to die. Huck Sullivan did not play fair.

"I knew it." Zoe isn't the kind of person who gloats, even
though she is a winner through and through. She wraps her arm
around my shoulders. "Look, I don't know exactly what transpired last year between the two of you, but I can tell that there is
something that hasn't quite been resolved, so I suggest that you
resolve it so we don't have any more jellyfish stings, or broken
hearts, or anything else that could wreak havoc on this trip.
You're too important, and I know how much this trip means to
you. Sort it out."

I hold up my hand in a Scout's honor pledge. Seemingly satisfied, Zoe tilts her head to the sky, and I take the opportunity to
sneak a quick glance across the deck toward Huck, who is scribbling a note in the margin of his diving book several feet away. I
lean back on my elbows, soaking up the sun.

"Look at this day, Zoe, it's perfect. What could possibly go
wrong?"

"Did you just say *what could possibly go wrong*?" Gus asks. He's
brought Huck with him, and they both drop down beside us.
"The number one rule is that as soon as you say that every freaking thing that could go wrong will. Why'd you feel the need to
jinx us, Stella? God, I probably should go check all the systems
and gear again just to be safe."

"I love your pessimistic nature," Zoe says.

"I'm a realist, baby."

"Paranoid," I say. "Teddy still sleeping?"

Gus nods. "I don't know what's up with that guy. Normally,
first day out, he'd be the first one ready to shove off and get out
to our site. Remember last time we were here, and he woke us all
up with steel drum music blaring from that old boom box? Should

we just go? And more importantly, can I eat his treat? I love that guava."

"Don't eat his breakfast, Gus," Zoe says. "You know how possessive Ted can be over his snacks . . . and Stella's already tempted fate this morning with her nothing-can-go-wrong speech."

"Wise woman," Gus says, and leans in to kiss Zoe on the mouth.

"On that note," I say, awkwardly scrambling to my feet. Huck, who's been silent so far in this exchange, stands as well. "I'm going to get us underway. Huck, can you give me a hand?"

"Definitely," he says. "What's the plan this morning?"

"We're going to head southwest, toward Dry Tortugas. The site's not too far from there, but that will be a good place for you to practice diving before we go out in the open water. Can you cast off the lines and pull in the fenders for me?"

"Sure thing."

Huck assists with the undocking like a seasoned pro, and I practice an exemplary level of self-control and barely register the way his muscles flex and contract with the effort. He rejoins me at the helm, and I set the course west. "Have you ever seen anything about Dry Tortugas?" I ask.

He shakes his head. "Nope."

"It's cool. The fort has kind of a moat surrounding it. A bunch of coral has built up on the walls of it over the years so there's plenty of wildlife to see, but it's also shallow and well protected. It'll be a good chance for you to practice clearing your mask and get a feel for your regulator and BC."

"Buoyancy compensator? Did I get that?"

"Yup, you got it. You brought your own fins, right?"

"Yeah. And sorry that I wasn't able to do the open water training class before I got here. I tried but by the time this all came together and I called, it was too late and all the classes were full. Teddy said that he'd teach me."

"I'll do it."

"I definitely don't want to trouble you. I'm sure you have much better things to do than supervise me."

"Well, I run things, so I do the training. Anyway, Teddy has some bad diving habits. He's experienced and we've all dived together so many times that it doesn't cause problems for us, but I don't want a beginner like you picking them up and causing a safety issue."

"Right. I wouldn't want that either. I value not drowning."

Do you ever get a feeling that you know how you're going to die? I can almost hear his voice and remember the way he looked across the restaurant table. I give him a tight-lipped smile but say nothing.

"I guess I'll make sure that I'm ready to go," Huck says, and then heads toward the stairs below deck.

Zoe sidles over to me.

"You want to take over?" I ask.

"Nah. I just came over to inquire why exactly you're so adamant about teaching our esteemed guest how to dive when we all know that Gus is the most experienced dive master here and has zero tolerance for bad habits."

"I don't know, Zoe, you keep talking but all I hear is that you want to navigate."

"Fine, whatever, evade my questions. I have a picnic to pack anyway."

TWENTY-FIVE

Huck

Today I vow to keep my cool. I can't have any more of those moments when Stella is so close to me that I can make out the unique shape of every pinpricked freckle on her face and count every fleck of gold in her eyes. Because I know that if I'm near her again, like I was in the galley, I might not be able to stop myself from cupping her cheek or leaning in to kiss her. Or worse, I might start confessing everything, letting the words I've been holding in since the moment I walked away from that beach in Iceland flow like lava from my mouth, searing away any chance I have at making this trip work. So far, I'm doing a decent job.

She hasn't read the book yet, I can tell.

I don't let my gaze linger on her when she steps on deck in a blue metallic bikini that by some trick of nature manages to pull every last atom of oxygen from my lungs. I don't do anything embarrassing with the scuba equipment. I manage to not trip over my fins as I follow her to the water. She shows me the full-face masks we'll be using, which means that I don't have to manage a regulator and can breathe out of my mouth or my nose. It's all going so well at first.

I say at first, because it turns out that I am claustrophobic. I never realized this about myself since my uniquely embarrassing form of claustrophobia apparently only manifests underwater with a mask over my face that is for some inexplicable reason filling with water. The entire hour-long trip over to Dry Tortugas I'd been anticipating a morning passed at Stella's side, leisurely frolicking in crystal-clear waters, repairing what I'd broken while millions of fish passed by. I was envisioning peace. The quiet sound of my own breathing. Weightlessness. But no. What I get is panic and water in my mouth.

I start off okay on the surface. The mask covering my face is weird and feels awkward, but I'm fine. I get the hang of the buoyancy compensator and after giving Stella the okay sign, we start to descend. That's where it all goes to shit. The noise underwater is loud, and then my ears hurt and I'm trying to clear them when, out of nowhere, water starts to fill my mask. I wish I could say that I stay calm and composed and manage to clear the mask and get it back on like Stella had me practice several times. Instead, I thrash around like a fucking octopus on coke and manage to get a mouthful of water and a view of my imminent demise. My heart is racing. And all I can think is that I deserve this. This is what I get . . . death by freak-out while Sebastian the Crab and a bunch of snorkeling tourists watch. Well, we can't all be heroes. This is just like me.

"Huck, what's happening?" Stella's voice comes through the built-in comms system. I want to answer her, but I can't. I don't know what to do. Then I look up, and even through stinging eyes, I can see Stella's right there with me. Her hand squeezes mine and I stop writhing. She maintains eye contact as she shuts the ambient breathing valve I'd forgotten to close and helps me clear the water out of my mask.

"Slow down your breathing. You're okay," she says. "Follow me, nice and even." She's still holding my hand, but with the other, she sets the pace for me to regulate my breathing with her free hand moving in a leisurely up and down motion. My body can't help but obey this woman, totally unfazed and in charge. When I'm calm, she signals for us to surface.

I almost don't want to go back up there to face her after this. I'm humiliated, humbled. I thought I'd be good at diving. Like with the research and learning how to do all the jobs on the boat, I want to be useful on this trip. I want to be useful to her. But I'm not. Of course I'm not. I'm no good to anyone. We bob at the surface, and I sputter.

"You okay?" she asks me.

I nod, but I'm honestly still too shaken up to speak. Part of it is the fear about what happened underwater, the other piece is that harsh voice being back again when I've tried so hard to shut it up. We start to swim toward the beach.

"Look, it's alright, Huck. Anybody can panic under the water. Let's just take a breather and then you can try again."

I shake my head. "I think I have ocean claustrophobia. A severe and incurable case."

"I freaked out the first time I dived, if it helps," she tells me, as we reach the sand. "I was going along fine, and then I got snagged on something. I had plenty of air left in my tanks, but I flailed around until I was even more caught up and I was fully convinced that I wasn't going to make it. Luckily Teddy was with me and used his dive knife to cut me free. I'd gotten tangled in a discarded fishing line; it was barely visible."

"Okay, but that's legitimate. I basically sabotaged my own breathing apparatus and drowned myself trying to pop my ears."

"Look, Huck, I'm trying very hard not to laugh at you, and you're not cooperating."

"You think this is funny?" I want to be mad at this, maybe

mad at her, but that would just be my stupid pride, and must be that it's taken the day off because somehow, I already feel lighter and better. "Go ahead and have your laugh at my expense. Enjoy my mortification." I pick up a handful of wet sand and let it slip through my fingers.

"I think I deserve to get a little enjoyment out of your very suave scuba moment. Given everything that's transpired between us. Don't you?"

Her hair is slicked back and her freckles are taunting me. I only nod. It's all I can muster. She squints at me in the strong sunlight. "I was pretty humiliated when I woke up alone in Iceland," she says. I almost miss this; her voice is so subdued compared to normal.

I deflate like the buoyancy compensator that I'd barely used. "I'm beyond sorry for that," I say. There's so much more that I want to tell her, but I can't. I don't even know how to begin, what words to use, how to show her just how sorry I am. I have no right to be forgiven. At first, I'd hoped that I hadn't hurt her, hadn't caused her anywhere near the level of pain that I'd inflicted on myself. But now it's clear to me—from the way she's holding herself, her arms wrapped around her torso, the way she won't look at me anymore—I did hurt her. Maybe we're the same in that way; that morning on the beach had damaged us both, but she's stronger than me, better, more resilient. She pulls in a deep breath, her shoulders lift.

"Let's move on and put the past behind us."

I nod. "Yeah. I can do that." I'm not sure I can.

"Good. Step one, time for you to get back in the water."

I shake my head in protest. "I'm good here, thanks. I'll just be a dedicated deck hand."

"You want to hunt for treasure at sea, you've got to learn how to scuba dive. There is no alternative here. You won't know what it's like down below if you let fear trap you up there. Now let's review so we don't have a repeat of the bad experience."

I follow her back into the water while she goes over the procedure again. "This time you're going to remember to close that ABV, okay, so that you don't get any water inside of it. Let me see your mask?" She turns it over and points to a wedge shape. "This is your equalizing block. I want you to test it and make sure that when you push up on the regulator, it blocks off your nose so that you can do the Valsalva maneuver to clear your ears easily. Basically, it is taking the place of pinching your nose like you would in a regular mask while you blow out. You can also try swallowing instead. Do it a little earlier, before the pressure starts to build up. Both of those work pretty well for me. It takes a bit of practice, but the most important thing is to take your time and clear your ears often. And if it doesn't work or you have a problem, just stay calm and call out to me on your comms system. That last part is super important when we're diving for targets. We want to be able to let each other know if we see something. It's easy once you get into it. Don't sell yourself short and give up. I promise, I'll stay right next to you the entire time."

This last bit feels too generous. That's why, even though every fiber of my rational being is screaming at me that I am a land creature, meant to breathe atmospheric oxygen, and that the ocean clearly agrees since it seems to have it out for me based on the panic and the prior jellyfish stings that still smart on my skin and it's only a matter of time until Zoe's prediction comes to fruition and I end up snapped up by a shark for upsetting the balance of the universe, I pull my stupid mask on and follow Stella into the waves. It's not because I'm afraid of failure. I've already failed. My dad made sure I knew that right up until his last breath. It's not because I never give up. I have proven myself to be a quitter, just ask anyone who read the last Casablanca book. And it definitely isn't because I'm brave. I'm terrified right now. This scuba thing terrifies me. Stella terrifies me. My unresolved feelings terrify me. But I don't want to disappoint her, not now, not again.

My Eustachian tubes open easily now that I know how to block my nose with the mask. I get used to the sound of my breathing and the weird underwater noises that surround me, and Stella and I keep talking to each other.

"How are you feeling?" she asks.

"Honestly? I think I'm okay."

"See, I knew you could do it. You're doing great. Let's head north along the moat."

When we reach a comfortable depth, I forget all about my freak-out. I'm too taken by the sights—schools of bright tropical fish, coral plastering the aged stone walls, completely calm water so clear that I can make out a fish ahead of us that I hope is actually a fish and not a shark. It's beautiful here. I start translating it all into a scene for the new book in my mind. Stella moves through the water, so efficiently, so naturally, that I can't help but study her like she's a new species of underwater mammal, precious and rare.

"Look to your right, Huck. Isn't that gorgeous?" She points to a cobalt-colored fish. "It's a blue tang. My favorite."

They're my favorite now too, and I add them to the list of things that I can't think about without bruising my heart a little further.

After that, she draws my attention to different sights—an octopus hiding, a spotted fish called a red hind, and a tarpon that I'd thought for a second was a shark when I first saw it. Time bends, turning in on itself—and after what feels like only a few moments, it's time to head up. We take it slow, stopping periodically to make sure I control my ascent, even though we didn't go deep enough to require a real stop. I recall Stella's first experience of the terror of being caught up and think that must be why she's such a stickler for safety, and why she didn't want Ted to teach me.

The more I learn about Stella, the more I respect and admire her.

And the more I regret the choice I made to walk away.

TWENTY-SIX

Stella

The spread that Zoe has put together is pretty impressive for a casual beach picnic. Huck and I square away our equipment and settle in on the edge of the blanket where individual bags of chips, croissants stuffed with herbed chicken salad, and individual slices of Key lime pie are laid out in the center.

"How'd the lesson go?" Zoe asks.

Huck and I exchange a glance. "Once he got into it, he did well," I say.

"I think you're being kind, Stella," Huck says.

"Did she berate you for safety violations?" Teddy asks, and takes a large bite of his sandwich. "She's always on me about safety stops and tank levels."

I shake my head. Teddy's exaggerating. I gave up on nagging him a long time ago when I realized that trying to change him was an exercise in futility.

Gus grins. "Someone has to keep you under control. And who better than Stella? After all, she is the mom of the group."

"I don't know if I love that," I interject, going straight for the Key lime pie. "I'm still too young for motherhood. Especially for such a *giant* baby." I laugh, and Teddy points his soda at me.

"Who are you calling giant baby? I am perfectly proportioned."

Zoe tosses a small bag of chips at him. "You know we can tell that you're mewing now, right, Tedders? For someone so well put together physically you're really trying to show off that jawline."

Teddy pops open the bag and tosses a chip into his mouth, completely unbothered while he smiles at her.

"Actually, Stella was very professional," Huck answers, finally finding a space in the conversation. "Incredibly patient."

"Funny. She's usually just bossy. She must've felt bad for you and given you special treatment." Teddy bumps me with his shoulder. "You've never been patient with me." He says this last part low, meant only for me to hear, and the playfulness drops along with the volume.

"That's because you're constantly testing my patience with your antics," I tease. I wait for Teddy to say something back—after our years of friendship he has more than enough material to ridicule me with—but he stays quiet. He sets down the bag of chips.

Zoe and Gus start cleaning up the picnic items while Huck and I finish our sandwiches and desserts. I'm in the middle of a perfect bite of pie, where the ratio of whipped cream to graham cracker crust and tart Key lime filling is just right, when Teddy pulls off his T-shirt and wanders off into the waves.

"What's that all about?" Gus asks.

I shrug. "Maybe he's heading out for a swim?"

"So much for not swimming on a full stomach," Zoe says. "He does know we're getting ready to leave, right?"

Gus holds his hands out in a hell-if-I-know gesture. "We can always pick him up as we motor by I s'pose."

Huck holds out a paper bag, and I drop some used napkins

and my empty chip bag into it. "You think Teddy seems okay?" he asks.

"He's just in a mood. He'll be better once we get to work. Fortunately, it's a short trip to our real dive site and the weather's perfect, so we can get the magnetometer straight out there."

Huck nods.

With sand shaken from the blankets and all our trash packed up, we head back to the boat. On our way, I can't help but scan the water for Teddy. I'd told Huck that I thought he was just in a mood of some sort, but I can't shake the feeling that there's something else going on with Ted. He's been quieter than usual. And yes, he often does disappear when we are out and ventures off to do his own thing, but all of that has always had an air of fun to it, like he's this young golden retriever running around to investigate every exciting thing he sees without thinking because it just might be the best thing. His pursuits are light and hedonistic and funny, not wandering off alone. Whatever this is that he's doing is different. My mind eases when I see him on the deck of our boat, feet up, hat pulled low over his face. He's still wet from his swim; his skin, already deeply tanned, glistens like the scales of a fish in the sun.

"At least he's not nude sunbathing this time," Zoe says with a chuckle.

"There is a god," Gus says, and throws an arm around her.

"He still does that?" Huck asks. We all turn to look at him. He adds, "The roof of our dormitory was an unsafe space most spring weekends, or a popular spot, I guess, depending on who you were."

A pair of pelicans coast on the wind ahead of us, and Huck stops to watch them for a moment before stepping on the boat. "He also streaked all the final exams."

"That tracks," Gus says. "Then again, if I had Ted's build, I might be inclined to show off my stuff too."

"Excuse me?" Zoe fixes him with a look. "Who exactly would you be showing your stuff to in this hypothetical scenario?"

He clears his throat and forces his body into a stretch. "Man, I am so ready to get this search started. Treasure, oh yeah. Shall we weigh anchor?"

"Sounds like you're volunteering to pilot us over there, Gus?" I ask.

"Well, I was thinking of dipping Ted's hand into some warm water and seeing what happens, but if you want me to take over as captain, Stella, then yes, ma'am."

Huck and Zoe take care of the lines and bumpers while I perch next to Gus at the helm double-checking our coordinates.

"He's not doing too bad," Gus says lifting his chin to gesture at Huck.

"He's making an effort," I say.

"Is it terrible that I'm sort of surprised? I really liked the guy for the short time we overlapped in Iceland, but I'd sort of pegged him as one of those hands-off fancy boys who sits around scribbling in overpriced notebooks and pecking away on their gold MacBook Pros given his prep school background and fame. You know him better, Stell. Was I wrong?"

"His MacBook was gray, but who knows. I don't think we need to toss him overboard just yet, but there's still time." It's glib, but honesty wouldn't fly.

Truthfully, I don't really know Huck. I mean, I thought I knew him, but how much can you learn about someone in just a few days? I'd been fooling myself. I say nothing of this to Gus. I'd kept most of what happened between me and Huck on the last trip out of the headlines, but I wasn't sure if Zoe had shared our conversation from this morning with Gus. They seemed even closer than when I'd seen them back in March at The Pit. I can't imagine that they keep many secrets from each other.

Once we reach our general search area, we double-check the gear and make sure it's all ready to go and functioning properly. The *Lucky Strike* is outfitted with sonar equipment, the magnetometer or "mag," and underwater and aerial cameras. The first step is to drag the mag and identify target sites, or narrower search windows where we know there's metal. The mag doesn't pick up precious metals, but it can help find other parts of the shipwreck, like cannons, anchors, and ballasts . . . and where those are, treasure—including the Elephant's Heart—may be nearby.

"Okay," I call to Zoe, "deploy the mag."

"Mag deployed."

I head over to Gus, who is stationed by the monitors showing Huck how to interpret the readings. "See this? That's a hit, so we'll mark it with a buoy and then keep going. We drag the entire space and then go back on the same line spaced out thirty feet apart from the last swath. See, there's another one."

I peek at the screen. "That's definitely something."

"Could be a big one," Gus says. "What do you think, Stella, you want to dive on this one now?"

"Yeah, let's go ahead and check it out since the weather's calm at the moment. It would be nice to see if we can find our target from this hit. You want to come, Huck?"

He looks nervous, and I wonder if he's thinking about the earlier scuba incident. I was glad he'd given himself another chance, I wasn't sure if he would.

"You don't have to dive with us if you don't want to. Someone should stay on the boat anyway."

"I'm okay either way. I think I'm alright with diving again. It ended up being really good, once I forgot that I was underwater and totally dependent on an oxygen tank strapped to my back and everything going right for my own survival. Thanks for pushing me to try again. I'm not sure if I would've been able to do it if I'd stopped and tried again later. I probably would've talked myself out of it."

This makes me curious about what other things Huck has managed to talk himself out of. Was I one of those conversations he'd had with himself where he weighed the risks and decided, nah, not worth it?

"Just remember not to think so much, and you'll be fine," I say, conscious of the bite that I'm not able to keep out of my voice.

Teddy finishes his nap and, thankfully, wakes up refreshed and in a much better mood. As I expected, the promise of the hunt has energized him. He races around, squeezes everyone's shoulders, amping us all up while he pulls on his wetsuit.

Zoe volunteers to stay on board while the rest of us dive a couple of hits that are all laid out relatively close to each other.

"I'm not feeling my best," she says. "I'm happy to just stay on the comms."

The seas are calm, and Zoe usually doesn't struggle with seasickness anyway, except for that one time in Key West apparently. I search her face. She does look a bit wan, but it's entirely possible that this is a ploy because she wants me and Huck to start resolving things. This all feels a bit too *Parent Trap* adjacent.

"Are you sick?" I ask.

She shakes her head. "Nothing like that. Just a little piqued, I think."

"Huck, Zoe's out so it's you, bud. Let's do this," Teddy says. He starts grabbing gear, tosses his fins overboard, slings on a tank, and jumps into the water.

Huck looks at me, worry in his expression. "Was that the lack of safety you were talking about?"

"That's nothing."

Gus and I suit up and check each other's equipment before he steps off the boat to try to catch up with Ted. I hand Huck the underwater metal detector he'll use and start checking his gear.

"You're going to be fine," I tell him. "And we'll stay in sight of each other, just scanning with the metal detector."

"What do I do if the detector indicates something?"

"In that case, call me over. But we'll essentially clear the sand by waving our hands to wash it away. Then we'll see what it is. Sometimes it's easy to recognize, other times we need Gus. Our permit allows us to bring some small things up for identification and verification. Make sense?"

"Yeah, okay. I think I got it."

We step to the edge of the boat. I give Zoe a wave. Huck pulls on his mask. I can tell by his shoulders that he's breathing a bit fast. If he keeps this up underwater, he'll burn through his air way too fast, and even though the bottom here isn't very deep, maxing out around thirty feet, we want to be able to search as much as we can before we have to surface. I give his hand a squeeze like I had in the water. "Try to regulate your breathing," I tell him. "You're searching for treasure. That feeling? It's nervous excitement, not fear, okay? I'm feeling it too."

Huck nods again, but this time, it's a single sharp drop of his chin, confident and resolute. He pulls his face mask on and picks up his metal detector.

"Go for diver one," Zoe says. "Go for diver two."

"Clear diver one," I say and together Huck and I step off into the sea below.

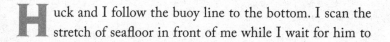

uck and I follow the buoy line to the bottom. I scan the stretch of seafloor in front of me while I wait for him to clear his ears again. Then we swim along the sand, listening for hits. I look for familiar shapes: round ballasts, long cylinders that could indicate cannons or an anchor, grappling hooks, even the metal rings that would've formed barrels that could have been storing some of the contraband gems and gold we're expecting.

"Radio check topside," Zoe's voice comes over the radio. "See anything yet?"

"I got nothing," I say.

"Teddy, Gus—you have any hits so far?"

"We have a whole lot of nada over here."

"What about you, Huck?" I ask.

"I think I have a signal. Yeah, I definitely do. It's right over here."

"Okay, I'm on my way," I say. I chalk the school of fish swirling in my stomach up to the first hit of the season. It always generates excitement. It has nothing to do with him.

Huck is hovering over something, moving his metal detector back and forth, when I arrive.

"I'm going to fan the area to see if I can expose anything," I say. I show him how to move his hand gently to displace the sand without force. There's something there, I can feel it. My heart rate picks up. Is this it? Something comes into view, but I can tell almost immediately that it's modern-era construction.

"What is it?" Huck asks, still excited.

"Modern trash," I say. "Let's move on."

We keep looking until the light starts to fade. Teddy and Gus find something that could be a ballast, but we don't turn up anything that indicates we're in a debris field or that we're near the wreck.

"Guys," Zoe calls over the radio. "It's sundown up here. I'm calling it."

I meet up with Huck, trying not to think about the disappointment I'm feeling that we've come up empty today. This is part of treasure hunting. Some days are amazing and others suck, and a lot of the time, frustration runs high.

"Time to head for the surface," I tell him.

We rise slowly, cresting above the surface just as the sun is settling into the horizon. "Really sorry about that false alarm," he says.

"It happens. We'll get a lot of signals that may not be what we're looking for. You'll get used to it."

"I really thought we had something for a second."

I lean back on the water's surface and float. I thought so too.

TWENTY-SEVEN

Stella

I don't know why I pick up Huck's book. It's been sitting on the small desk in the corner of my quarters since we left North Carolina, collecting dust. I could certainly use the distraction right about now, so maybe it's that. We searched for hours today, covering roughly five percent of our search area, and turned up absolutely nothing. It's only day one, but I'm frustrated. The fact that the last time I went on a hunt with Huck we found Gunnarsson's treasure is at the forefront of my mind. I did not enjoy the feeling of going out and coming back empty-handed at the end of the day—I never have. But I also acknowledge the amount of pressure I feel to show him what I'm capable of. Even if he didn't think I was good enough then and lost the right to have me care what he thinks about me now . . . I still do. I have no intention of letting Huck get close to me again, but that doesn't mean that I don't want to prove that I was something special—not to win him over, but to show him that he was wrong. To tell him that leaving me was a mistake. He's become yet another reason why I have to find the Stolen Treasure.

It's only the first day, I remind myself, and treasure hunting is about persistence.

But how long have I been searching . . . how long have I been trying to prove myself? Too long.

I open the book and read the inscription.

To everyone who's searching for something . . .

Interesting. I don't hate it. Maybe it's even good?
I turn the page and test the waters with the opening lines.

CHAPTER ONE

The first time Finn McCool saw Lucky Malone she was knocking back a beer at a bar on the island after a long day of hunting treasure with her crew. He'd said, you look like a woman who I'll upend my whole life for. She'd smiled and shaken her head, bought him a drink, and said only if you're lucky. They were both right.

I read late into the night. My eyes grow tired and dry and my hands start to hurt from the physical strain of holding the book for hours. As suspected based on the cover, Lucky Malone is a treasure hunter and Finn McCool is a drifting adventurer. They are diametrically opposed—she craves the history, the thrill of the search, righting wrongs, and returning artifacts and riches to the groups that they belonged to, while he is sort of a morally gray Indiana Jones–type character—hotter, maybe, but not smarter—who only cares about getting his payday. I screech when I discover that he was at that bar trying to meet her so that he could leech on to her crew and steal the treasure. The twist came out of nowhere. Was it surprising that he fell in love with her even though she was basically his mark? No, but that didn't mean that I wasn't eating up those pages where he waged an all-out war of ambivalence on himself like my Key lime pie slice at lunch.

Now I've reached the part of the book where Finn has just tried to confess his transgressions and his love to Lucky, but he gets interrupted by the henchmen of a furious collector who funded his expedition. He and Lucky are on the run and take refuge in a hidden cavern under a waterfall.

We were behind a waterfall once, me and Huck, icy spray coating our faces. He'd wrapped his hands around me and lifted me up so that I could realize my dreams of pulling history from hidden depths. It had been one of the most pivotal moments of my life.

And now I'm reading about two fictional characters who are sort of like us, but not exactly, in a made-up place that's reminiscent of where we were but isn't the same, and I can't bring myself to put it down. I don't want it to end.

While I scan the pages, I catalog the ways Finn and Lucky are imbued with us. There's the obvious stuff: Lucky has my tattoo and some of my physical characteristics—my freckles, lips with a shocking propensity for getting chapped. But she's different . . . braver, bolder, captivating . . . things I'm not really. If I am, I don't see it. In that way, it's like viewing myself through someone else's eyes. There are hints of Huck in Finn, but if he's fictionalized himself, he hasn't been generous. Yes, Finn is dashing and daring, and sexy as hell. All the things that you want in a hero, but he is a disaster emotionally; he does the stupidest stuff. And so far, he's not someone anyone could ever rely on. Alright, maybe that part of the characterization is exactly like him. I have the feeling that Huck was working out some deep-seated self-loathing with this character, and maybe that makes me love the book more, almost as much as it makes me sad. One thing is clear about Finn—he's in pain. He hides it well, covers it with mistakes, but there's a tragic backstory peeking out between the lines, just waiting to be revealed. I have no idea what it could be. All I know is that whoever Lucky and Finn are and whomever they were based off of, I am completely invested in them. They don't want to trust each other; they shouldn't. But they can't stay apart . . . and I am all in on the ride with them.

I take a break around one a.m. when I can't stand the gnawing feeling in my stomach any longer and sneak down to the galley to make myself a snack. I need sustenance if I'm going to finish this book tonight, and I plan to. I have to know if Finn and Lucky survive the latest attack by the gangs of criminal financiers and the impending natural disaster. I'm pretty sure that Finn is finally about to profess his undying devotion to Lucky even if it means he has to leave his entire life behind, and I picture how he's going to do it and the precise words Huck chose for him to say. I don't expect to find Zoe and Teddy rooting around in the refrigerator for leftovers.

"Fancy meeting you here," I say to them.

"Couldn't sleep," Zoe says. "Figured snacking was the next best thing."

"Good call," Ted replies. "I sleep fine, I just had the munchies. Stell, did you eat all that pie from lunch?"

"No. I restrained myself. Though I was kind of hoping that there was some left as well."

"I guess we'll just have to fight for it."

Zoe leans into the fridge and emerges moments later with a totally uncut pie in a box. "I'd say keep your shirt on, Tedders, but too late, I guess. Anyway, there's no need for you hooligans to brawl in the galley. I bought two and hid this one," she tells us triumphantly. "Gus can't control himself around sweetened citrus."

"Is that what you guys call it?" Teddy says and bites his lip flirtatiously. "I'm not familiar with that particular sexual act."

"Nasty," Zoe says, whipping him lightly with a dish towel. "That's because it *isn't* one. You would know them all by now."

I hold back a snort of laughter.

"Thank you for the compliment," Ted says.

"Was it a compliment?" I ask. "It kind of sounded like something else. Zoe, tell me you weren't slut-shaming our dearest friend here."

"Not at all! I was just acknowledging the extensive library of carnal *knowledge* he's amassed over all these years of promiscuous research."

"Now, that's not fair. He didn't go out once on our way down here or in Key West. Maybe he's turned over a new leaf."

"Yeah," Teddy says, grabbing a fork and preparing to attack the pie. "Listen to Stella. I'm a changed man . . . with a very impressive repertoire."

"And why are you changed exactly?" Zoe asks. She's trying to stay out of lawyer mode, keeping her voice soft, but that doesn't stop Teddy from crossing his arms over his chest and avoiding eye contact with her. He shrugs.

"Just trying something new. No reason."

She makes a face. "What about you, Stella? You and Mr. Writer get all those unresolved whatevers resolved while you were diving today?"

"What?" Ted says. "What does *unresolved whatevers* mean?"

I roll my eyes and turn my attention to cutting a large slice of pie for myself. I don't go straight in with a fork like Ted, because I'm not a Neanderthal.

"Figure it out, Tedders. You're slick."

"It's nothing," I interject. "There's nothing to resolve. He's here to get writing inspiration for his next book, we're here to find *San Miguel* and the Heart and that's all there is to it."

"Sure," Zoe says. She takes a sip of ginger ale.

"Still not feeling great?" I ask, gesturing at her drink.

"Don't try to change the subject," she teases.

"I'm completely fucking lost. I'm going to take a slice to go and leave you gals to it," Teddy says. "I wish you the sweetest of citrusy dreams, ladies." He saunters out of the room, waving over his head.

"That guy," Zoe says, chuckling. "He's a goddamn delight." She takes a bite of a cracker.

"That's not a very exciting snack, ma'am," I say. "Are you sure you don't want some of this delectable pie?"

Zoe wrinkles her nose.

"It's seen better days since Teddy massacred it with his fork, but it still tastes good."

"Maybe. I'm not feeling great," Zoe admits. "But I know how you feel about people getting sick, so I'm going to continue managing it prophylactically with ginger ale and saltines."

"Look, that's just emetophobia. I'm not heartless. You don't have to hide not feeling good from me, ever, especially by asking a bunch of totally off-base probing questions about me and Huck. We've barely talked about anything else. Pretty sure we wouldn't pass the Bechdel test."

"Valid, but counterpoint. Are my questions off base, though? Because it's obvious to me that there's something between you guys. Maybe it's just lingering from before, but that man clearly has feelings for you."

I shake my head. "No."

"Agree to disagree."

"Maybe I'm just his muse," I say, thinking aloud.

"His *what*, now?"

I scrunch up my face. "Muse? I only say that because I started

reading his book and, um, well, let's just say that the main character might kind of bear a strong resemblance to me and the guy
kind of seems a lot like him."

Zoe shuts her eyes for a moment and shakes her head. "Oh,
come on. He fan-fic'd your relationship? Really?" Her shoulders
start to shake. "Yeah, no, he's definitely *not* into you. He only
wrote a book featuring you and him hunting treasure together.
Oh my god. Are these characters in love? Don't tell me. They are,
I can see it on your face. You're redder than the exit sign."

"It's not like that."

She leans over the steel counter and props her chin in her
hands. "How's the spice level? Where does it land on the Scoville
scale? Are we talking Italian Sweet or Scotch bonnet . . . Wait,
not Carolina Reaper hot, coming in at a whopping 2.2 million
Scoville heat units— You know what? I'm ordering it." She picks
up her phone and starts tapping away on the screen.

I toss a dishrag at her. "You are not a nice person." I'd tried to
say it lightly, but it doesn't come out that way.

Ever the perceptive one, Zoe eyes me. "Oh jeez, you really do
have some unresolved whatevers, don't you?"

I sigh.

"Stella?" she presses gently.

I wish I could say no.

"Stella?" It isn't Zoe this time, though, saying my name like
it's a question and an answer. It's Huck, tall, dark, and enigmatic,
standing in the doorway. "You're reading my book?"

Zoe looks at us both in quick succession. "Uh, I'm going to
go see if Gus and I can invent 'sweetened citrus.' I'll leave you two
to whatever this is."

I try to signal to her that I would very much like her to stay
in this room, but she and her sleep caftan are already on the move.

"What's sweet citrus?" Huck asks.

"You don't want to know."

"Okay, then." He steps closer to me. The tiny galley amplifies his presence, and the scent of his soap fills my nose. I can almost feel the heat coming off his sunbaked skin. He's near now, looking intently at me. "What do you think of the book? Or do I not want to know that either?"

I pause. How can I answer this? I have so many questions and thoughts, but they all seem like they would lead to conversations and truths that are better left undisturbed. They also seem like they could lead to him pressing me up against the counter and doing things to me until I'm calling out his name.

Both are more than I can handle, so I choose silence, but I make a critical mistake in this moment. I meet Huck's eyes.

They're the same in some ways as they were in Iceland, that unusual pale blue, like the lagoon we floated in, legs accidentally touching beneath the surface. His gaze is so intense, it makes me feel exposed, undressed, seen. But in his eyes, there's something new, a sadness at the corners; I hadn't noticed it before. I recognize the look because it's the same exact one I've been seeing in the mirror for the past year and a half.

And if I'm right, it's heartbreak.

I take a deep breath. I can't do this. I need to get out of this kitchen and away from Huck, and from the memories, from these feelings that I don't want to have.

"Stella . . ."

Why do I want him to reel me into him? I force my lips into a smile. "It's infuriatingly good," I say.

He looks surprised for an instant before his expression breaks into a wide grin. "I'll take that. So, you've read it all?"

"Not yet. I'm on chapter fourteen."

He nods, slowly processing the information. "They're hiding at the waterfall, right?"

"Yup. Good memory."

"For the important things, I guess. Other stuff, not so much. I can't even remember why I came to the kitchen."

"The rest of us came for pie," I tell him, holding up a clean fork. "You can have the rest if you want. I should get back to bed. Tomorrow'll be another long day."

He shifts his attention to the dessert but doesn't take a bite. I view this as my opportunity to go and head toward the door. "Listen, Stella, when you get to the end of the book, maybe we can talk? You could let me know what you think."

I pause in the doorway. "Why do you care what I think, Huck? Everyone loves it. It's a bestseller. It's not like my opinion matters anyway."

He's silent for a moment and I step over the threshold. Then he speaks.

"You're the only one who matters to me."

TWENTY-EIGHT

Huck

The day starts early, and I am wrecked with exhaustion and the unique kind of hangover that comes after one has opened their big and extremely moronic mouth and said the worst possible thing ever.

Did I haul ass back to my bunk just to lay in bed with a pillow over my face contemplating smothering myself to end my imminent misery as soon as Stella left the kitchen? Maybe. Did I pray that our kitchen interaction was some kind of scopolamine-induced hallucination, and I did not just fucking say *you're the only one who matters to me*? Yes. Yes, I did.

Unfortunately, I mentally checked the tape about a thousand times last night and every time the replay was identical. Stella says her bit and then I basically ask her to marry me. Well, maybe it wasn't that bad, but it was in the fucking neighborhood. She knew it. And I knew it. And she didn't say anything back to me, of course she didn't. Stella's smart. She understands that we have a history and we're on a boat in very tight quarters for a month and that dredging all of that up is the definition of asking for it.

Still, I wouldn't be surprised if she spent the night plotting my murder.

But she's reading the book. That can't be nothing. At least now I can die with hope.

That hope is why I force myself to get up, get dressed, have a cup of coffee and a croissant, and prepare to face the day. Now I glance across the deck to where Stella is organizing the gear along the bow. She's wearing those frayed cutoff jeans that have become my obsession over the last week and a neon pink string bikini top that it would be unwise for me to delve into further detail about. Dwelling on the contrast between her creamy skin and the bright fabric does things to me that I can't explain. She looks so fucking good.

Teddy is working next to her, shirtless. His skin is already golden brown. He looks like he belongs beside her. Arranging oxygen tanks, stopping to double knot the bows on her back and at her neck, smoothing reef-safe sunscreen on her shoulders. They're laughing about something. At one point, she glances back in my direction, but her baseball hat's too low over her eyes. I can't tell if she was looking at me.

I find Zoe and Gus engaged in their own morning preparations, eating cinnamon toast and dancing to calypso music played on an old boombox.

"You want to dive today?" I ask Zoe. "I don't mind staying out of the water." Space could be good. Necessary even after the kitchen confession and that fucking bikini.

"Nope, it's all you, Huckleberry Finn." There's an edge to her voice. Gus must pick up on it too because he kisses her on the cheek and says, "As much as I love an awkward moment, I'm going to take this energy as my cue to get another cup of coffee before we start the dive."

We both watch as he shimmies across the deck, stopping midway to yell over to Ted about prepping some heliox tanks.

"Turn that shit up," Ted calls, before he does a move that can only be described as something between the most glorious and most pathetic attempt at twerking that has ever occurred on land or sea. It makes me forget about the kitchen and the pink bikini with its sunscreen-smeared edges for just a moment.

I turn back to Zoe. "I'm happy to go out again."

"Well, good, because I don't plan on diving at all."

I frown. "Sorry, I'm confused. Stella said that you all dive. She called you, specifically, a fish, said you love sea life and protect everyone from sharks?"

Zoe places a hand on her abdomen and taps her index finger one-two-three. "That's true. It's also a fact that you and I both have a secret. So how about a trade? I'll tell you mine and then you're going to tell me everything that happened with Stella in Iceland and all about that thinly veiled love letter you wrote her that people are currently snagging from the front tables of Barnes & Noble and their local independent bookstores."

I choke on my coffee. Zoe smiles saccharine sweet at me while I wipe a drip from my chin. I glance around to see if anyone's heard, but Stella and Teddy are far from us, still totally engrossed in checking tanks and smearing zinc on each other.

I feel physically ill.

"I'm pregnant," Zoe says. "I literally cannot dive. And before you ask, no, Stella and Teddy don't have any idea, and they're not going to. I'll tell them when I'm ready, and I'm not yet."

"And Gus?"

"He knows. He was there when it happened." She smiles and the tension breaks. My nausea subsides a little.

"Congratulations to you both, then. That's big news. Not sure why you're telling me, though."

She takes a bite of cinnamon toast and shrugs.

"I don't mean to sound like an asshole, but I am under the impression that you'd never do anything just because. Stella's told me how brilliant and strategic you are. This feels like a play."

"Guilty as charged. Let's just say that I need an ally. This baby is a miracle, honestly, but it will change everything, and Stella doesn't really do change. I mean, look at her. She's been searching for the same treasure her parents were hunting for the last ten years. She's always been someone who needs stability more than anything else, and I'm really worried about the shift in the dynamic and how not being able to take these trips, at least not in the way we do now, will impact her. And I don't know what the heck is up with Teddy. Maybe it's nothing, but I feel like he is about two drinks and a revelation away from a full-fledged nervous breakdown."

"I get it, sort of. And as much as you may not believe this, I don't want to upset Stella and I don't want my friend to snap. I'll volunteer to dive every time so you don't have to reveal your news. I don't think anyone would see through it . . . I could use the experience for research anyway. But you might want to lay off the saltines. They kind of scream *morning sickness*."

"Cool, but you're not getting off that easy, Huck. Tit for tat, remember? I want to know why you're really here."

I don't even know how to respond to this. For one thing, I am not used to people being so direct with me, at least not in recent years. That's what happens when they start to think you're fragile. Zoe's not the only one concerned about Ted. I've been the guy who was nervous-breakdown adjacent. It's brutal. There's struggling alone, which is awful. And there's people finding out and changing the way they act around you. After growing up with brutality, gentility doesn't feel like something you can trust. At home, my agent and editor treat me like a bomb that might go off at any time if they move the wrong way. Not that I blame them; I'd worry too if the roles were reversed.

I let my mind drift for a moment before answering. If only I'd just dropped everything back in Iceland and followed my whim of becoming a sheep farmer. I could be drinking Björk and being booped by wooly creatures all day long, and I wouldn't have to answer these questions or feel this way. I wouldn't have to wake up each morning with the knowledge that I'd met the woman who filled in all my gaps, who understood the way that I was broken and made me want to piece myself back together so I could stand by her side . . . only to ruin it. Now she's laughing with my old friend and I'm jealous. I should be sick with regret and shame over my transgressions—I am, but I'm also neon green with envy and freaking disgusted with myself over it. Across from me, Zoe starts tapping her foot on the deck.

I clear my throat. "For research."

Her brow furrows. "*Research.*" She over-articulates this so that I can't miss the you-have-to-be-fucking-kidding-me in her tone.

I nod.

We're in a face-off. I realize within a few seconds that trying to lie to Zoe was a massive error. She knows every possible tell, and she's about to call me on it. "You sure you want to go with that?"

I can't bring myself to speak.

"Okay, let's talk about the book, then. Not sure if you knew this about me, but I happen to be a voracious reader myself."

I swallow, hard. "You are?" She had called it a thinly veiled love letter earlier, hadn't she?

"Mmm. Quite a fast reader too—a very helpful attribute for an attorney, as you can probably imagine. When I heard Stella was reading your book, I grabbed a copy on my e-reader and read it from cover to cover last night. Imagine my surprise when I realized that the main character in it is a very lightly fictionalized version of my best friend. And the hunky criminal love interest with a troubled heart of gold bears a striking resemblance to you. *Finn?* I mean it's so obvious it's almost painful."

Zoe's on a roll now, a train barreling down the track aimed directly at me. I can only watch her close in. It's not mean-spirited, I don't think. Just direct.

"She's never said what went down. Only that you two were getting close and it just didn't work out. But that's not what I read between those lines."

"It's just a book, Zoe. It's not real. It's fiction."

"Were you in love with her?"

Direct? Fucking hell. This is an inquisition. *Just say no.*

You're the only one who matters to me.

"Was she in love with you?"

"I can't answer that."

"Why?"

"Because I don't know. I really don't. I would say that I wish I knew, but it wouldn't make this easier. It might even make it worse. You have to see that. At the end of the day, it changes nothing. I know I blew it."

"I think we both know that's not exactly the whole truth."

I don't respond. It's not like I forgot what I wrote, it's more that I haven't completely cataloged all the ways everything from Iceland permeated my story or the impact it would have for everyone who had lived it.

"You should tell her all of it."

Zoe's right. "I want to . . . but I can't. Even if I could, I just don't know how to do it. I think about it every day, even now, and wish I could go back and change it but I can't, and I'm not sure that telling her everything will help."

"So that's not why you're here?"

"I don't know. I don't know *why* I came. Maybe I thought I could fix it. Or maybe I was just being selfish. Maybe . . . I can't write without her."

"You need your muse in order to write your next book? Are

you serious? That better not be your real answer because if it is, I'll turn you into chum— Oh, hi, Ted!" She grins at Ted, who slides an arm around her waist and joins our conversation, but her eyes are fixed on me like two murder orbs. I actually get the chills. Zoe is kind of amazing . . . She's going to be a fantastic mom.

"Gear's set," Ted says. "Think Gus will be up soon?"

"Yeah, he's just grabbing a coffee below deck. I'll go get him," Zoe says.

"Fantastic!" Ted takes a deep breath and spreads his arms wide. His hair's gotten lighter. He looks like when we were in school, the golden boy who let us all bask in his glow. "Gotta love that salt air, right, Huck? Smells like treasure."

TWENTY-NINE

Stella

I decide to dive with Teddy today. We haven't really spent the same kind of quality time together as we usually do. I'm not sure why that is, but regardless it will be good to remedy that. Gus can teach Huck how to be a better diver and spot artifacts that are covered in coral and other detritus. He'll keep him focused. My switching dive partners is purely practical; it is in no way because of what Huck said in the galley last night, or what I read in his book before that. And it definitely isn't because I feel like spending hours beside him is too big a risk to take with my waning resolve, with the heart I put back together with glue and string and sheer will.

Teddy is on his best behavior this morning. He got up early, inspected all our gear, even made sure I didn't miss any spots with my sunscreen. He's all fun memories and inside jokes and thoughtful gestures. This is the lovable Teddy who makes life better just by being around, who dances while he works.

"You're in a good mood today," I say.

"Must be the company." He smiles.

"The company hasn't changed."

He glances over in Huck's direction. "You think he's getting the material he needs for his next book?"

"Not sure." I'd almost forgotten that this was a work trip for Huck. "He's learned a lot about the boat, navigation, and diving. Maybe that's useful? I'm hoping that today we at least turn up some interesting finds."

"What's it Mel Fisher used to say? 'Today's the day'?"

"I think so, but I'm not sure. It would be great if today *was* the day, though, wouldn't it?"

Teddy glances down at the chart and the marked search zones where we detected hits with the magnetometer. "Well, the good news is we have about twenty solid hits to check today, so the odds are at least one of them should be something. Personally, I'm betting that the *San Miguel* disintegrated in the ocean and all these hits are a massive debris field of gold and other precious artifacts. We'll be pulling treasure up all day long."

"Wouldn't that be amazing for Huck's new book?" I ask.

"I guess. To be honest, I'm more interested in things that are real."

I don't stop to try and decipher his meaning while I get into my wetsuit. Teddy zips me up and I sling on my BC and my air. We check each other's tanks.

"Good to go," I tell him. "Let's get to it."

I turn to Gus and Huck, who are looking at a notebook together and talking thoughtfully. "I numbered the mag hits on the chart. Ted and I will take the odd-numbered ones, you guys take even, okay?"

"Right on," Gus said. "We'll be right after you."

"If you're not first, you're last," Ted calls, and flings himself off the boat in a spin move that probably dislodges his face mask. But he doesn't miss a beat. An instant later he disappears under the surface. I chase after him as he powers down to the ocean floor. Fortunately, it's not too deep here. We follow the buoy line we dropped to orient ourselves, scanning the ocean floor with our metal detectors as we go.

Teddy is hard to keep up with. He zigs and zags wildly and has to circle back when I get a hit.

"Are you getting the Gunnarsson vibes, Stell?" Ted asks as we wave the sand away with our hands and focus our attention on the object that's starting to emerge from the sandy floor.

"I don't know. Can you see what it is? I think it might be a bronze pin from the ship."

"It's the right size," he agrees. I take out my underwater camera and document the find while Teddy places a black-and-white marker. "I'll let everyone know."

He radios up to the boat. "We got something. Can Gus check out the site one once he's down? I'm moving the buoy so he can just follow the line."

"Roger that," Zoe says. "He's on his way."

Gus verifies that what we've found is likely a brass pin. While it's not the most exciting find of all time, it is absolutely a good sign. These pins were used to nail the decking boards down on ships like the *San Miguel*. Since wood tends to break down over time in warm waters like those off the Keys, we might not see the actual shipwreck and find only the metal components that were left behind. Gus and Huck stay to take additional pictures before moving on to site two. Teddy and I head toward the next hit on our list. It's not too far to swim, but I am conscious of the time it takes to get within range of it, and how much air we've used so far.

"How's it going down there?" Zoe's voice comes in from the boat. "Getting anything else?"

"All good, but nothing yet," I say. "How close was number three from that trench? I don't see the line yet."

Zoe is quiet for a minute while she checks the map. "Pretty close. Watch that. If you get over there, you'll want to stick to the ledge. Teddy, are you hearing me? No going rogue today."

"When do I go rogue? Concrete examples, please," Ted says.

"Rogue is practically your middle name."

"Please. My middle name is Danger. Besides, Stella likes my unpredictability."

"Ha, it certainly keeps things interesting," I say.

"Sorry to interrupt." It's Huck. His voice sounds so good, even through the radio. "We got a hit! It's big."

"Looks like a grappling hook," Gus adds.

"It's freaking amazing."

"Seriously?" I say. "You guys aren't messing with me?"

"I wouldn't do that," Huck says.

Gus's voice comes through, "Hell yeah, it's for real!"

"Woohoo!" Zoe whoops.

"You guys have to see this," Huck says.

"Are you meeting us here or have you got something too?" Gus asks.

I'd passed the line for the target a few meters back and didn't get any signal from my metal detector. It couldn't have been a bottom strike of the mag that caused the reading—we're too deep here for that and the ocean floor is still sloping down at a sharp angle. We're already at almost eighty feet.

"Ted, let's head back to site two," I say.

"No. Not yet. I think we should keep going."

"Did you grab a trimix air tank?" I ask. Depending on how deep this goes, the helium in trimix can help stave off the nitrogen narcosis that sets in around one hundred feet.

"Just checking the ledge, Stell, no need to alert the media."

"I'm taking that as a no, and here I was thinking you were on your good behavior today."

"When am I ever on my good behavior, gorgeous?" He propels past me over the edge, following the angle of the wall that descends deeper into darkness. I check my air—still doing okay—and follow him down. As I scan the ledge, I calculate the amount of air we'll need for our ascent and the safety stop. I can stay down for another fifteen minutes or so, but Teddy's cutting it close. Because men typically have larger lung capacity, they burn through their air at a faster rate than women. I remind him of this, but he makes a flippant comment about ladies being the stronger sex and keeps going. My mind flashes back to Huck's lesson and how I'd told him that I was used to Teddy's underwater shenanigans. That was true, but it didn't stop me from worrying now.

If Teddy goes much deeper, his three-minute safety stop turns into a ten-minute decompression stop to let the nitrogen out of his system. I check my dive computer again. We're past one hundred twenty feet. "Ted, you need to go up."

"Just a little bit further, Stell," he says. "Hang in there with me. A little bit more. I think it's here."

"Teddy," I say. "Stop fucking around." He's dropping out of sight.

"Stella, Ted, you both good?" Zoe says.

Teddy doesn't answer either of us.

"I'm going silent to save air," I tell her, and then I head down to get Teddy.

THIRTY

Huck

Something is very wrong.

Gus and I are hanging out at a depth of thirty feet, searching around the grappling hook to see if we pick up any other signals. I've been hoping that Stella would get here so I could share this with her. Finding the relic was an incredible experience, but I wanted her next to me when I found it. And maybe a stupid part of me hoped in that moment that she would see that I'd done something worthwhile to help her to her goal and it would make up for my past mistakes a little. I would give anything for her to like me even a tiny bit again. But it's been a while since our last contact and she and Ted have not appeared. There's been patchy conversation over the radio that I struggle to decipher. Talk of depths and deco stops—terms I vaguely remember from the training manual she made me study, but it's a shorthand and I'm not even sure I'm translating it right. I'm not allowed past sixty feet.

I switch to the channel that lets me and Gus talk to each other. I remember Stella telling me that Ted had bad safety habits when it came to diving. Is that what this is?

"What's going on?" I ask.

Gus doesn't answer right away, and while I'm waiting, my stomach swirls with growing unease. I don't like this anymore.

"Their next site was near some deep water," Gus says. "I think Ted's gone too far. He could be narc'd since they're just diving on air. It's not smart."

"Shit." I worry for Ted. Even though Gus is using terms I don't fully grasp, I recall something about nitrogen narcosis from my studying and that different gases need to be added to the mix for deeper dives. Even without this knowledge, I've been aware that something has been bubbling under the surface with Ted this last week or so. He's been distant since South Carolina. I've tried to broach the issue with him, but he hasn't wanted to talk. And now he's putting himself at risk.

"She's going after him."

This hits me hard, right in the chest. I nearly choke on the air. Teddy's recklessness has always been a one-man-band situation where he thinks he's invincible, except for the golf-cart-versus-pond incident. I know personally just how quickly his grand schemes can go awry.

It was one thing when he was jeopardizing me. Now he's putting Stella at risk.

"You should head back to the boat," Gus tells me.

"Where are you going?"

"I'm going to meet them and make sure they make it up top."

I don't want to but I do as Gus says, and slowly ascend following the mooring line, stopping for a few minutes at fifteen feet before making my way to the surface. I want to crawl out of my skin, I'm so worried, and I can't help. I can't fucking do *anything*. I climb onto the boat and start stowing my gear. Then I walk over to Zoe to see if there's some action I can take. Her entire face screams stress. I think of her confession earlier; this is the last thing she needs right now.

"Those three are on a list. I swear to god." She rakes her hands through her hair. "I shouldn't have said that."

"It's okay, I totally get it. This is freaking stressful and scary. But they're experienced, right? They know how to handle the situation. It'll be okay."

Zoe bites her lip and nods. "Gus was a technical diver in the Navy before he went back to school for archaeology. He's solid and smart. Out here, he always dives with two tanks, including a trimix if he needs it to go beyond recreational limits, and he's not hotheaded, so he'll make sure those two fools make it back."

There was anger in her voice at the end, which was understandable. Stella had drilled it into me about how not being careful when you are diving could endanger everyone who's with you. Teddy's fixation on finding something down there today wasn't just bad for him. I swallow hard. *Let her be okay. They all have to be okay.*

"Is this something that's happened before?" I ask.

"I don't know. No. I mean, Teddy's cavalier as shit and Stella maybe takes the hunting a bit too far, but they're not stupid. It's just that this time, it feels like they both have something to prove and that makes me really fucking nervous."

"What do you mean?" I pick at the skin at the edge of my thumb.

"She told you about the Heart, right? It's all she's got left of her family. I think she feels like she needs to find it so she doesn't lose them completely . . . I don't know. I can't even imagine what it would be like to have both your parents leave you like that. She's never said that maybe if she found something huge they'd come back, but I sometimes wonder if that's what drives her to chase so hard. She lives and breathes this treasure hunting stuff even though it's basically what broke her family. And you know, Gus and I love her and Teddy, and we like to dive and it's kind of fun, but we don't have the same obsession. I could just as easily have gone on a Disney cruise. In fact, maybe I'd rather be on a cruise. Just *Frozen* live shows and warm pretzels all day. Or maybe I'm just saying that because I'm not out there in the water and I'm on a saltine diet."

I think back to Zoe who, according to Stella, is as adept at redirecting sharks as she is at courtroom questioning. It must be so brutal for her to be stuck up here with me when everyone she cares about is down there. All I can do is nod. I don't know how long it's been since they've checked in. "Should we radio down to them?"

Zoe gets on the radio and hails them. There's a stretch of silence. Gus checks in; he can't find them. My lungs are burning. I squeeze my hands into fists.

And then finally, finally, Stella's voice, distant but real, comes through the radio. I strain to hear her, my next breath depending on each word. "We're heading up. Ted and I need a deco stop."

She's alright—I can breathe again.

"I see you," Gus says. "How's your air?"

"I'm good. Ted might need to borrow your phase two. He's low."

The time for the rest of their ascent and the decompression stop feels like an eternity. Zoe and I pace the deck together. I bite my nails down to the quick.

"Should we talk more to make this go faster?" I ask.

"Yeah, that would be good. I could use the distraction. Let's talk about something totally different, something other than history and shipwrecks. Tell me about your life in New York. What's your favorite bagel place?"

"Sure, good plan. I love Court Street Bagels in Brooklyn. I could eat this sandwich called the Prospect Park every single day. It's got mesquite turkey, sun-dried tomato, and honey mustard. I get a slice of Gouda on it."

"I miss cold cuts so much."

"Sorry. They have great breakfast sandwiches too. Eggs are safe, right?"

"Yeah, they are. Continue. I might be turning a corner with this morning sickness thing, because those sandwiches sound surprisingly appealing."

"It's so good. The breakfast bagel is fried in butter so it's got a crunch. The guy who manages it, Gigi, treats everybody like family. I don't even have to order when I go in. It sounds ridiculous, but that place is one of the reasons that I stayed."

Zoe's brow wrinkles. "What do you mean, stayed? Were you thinking of leaving? Teddy said that you were so New York apple juice ran through your veins."

I scoff. That was something Ted used to tease me with whenever we'd go out in high school and I didn't drink. "I went through a rough patch a few years back. Didn't really want to be there anymore."

"With the book?"

"Before that. It's probably the reason why the book went off the rails."

She gives me one of those *okay, tell me more* looks that she is so good at.

"I don't really like to talk about it."

"It's interesting. You'd be amazed how often clients don't want to talk about it, especially when something's gone really wrong.

But most of the time they feel better once they do. Even if it was their fault. What's your story?"

"Nope. We were supposed to be talking about lighter stuff, distracting things, like bagels. I don't need to scar you with my secret trauma."

I say this lightly, but I really don't want to talk about what happened . . . because it *was* traumatic. That last fight that I had with my dad before he died, the vicious disappointment he'd shared in front of everyone in the signing line at the convention, the way I'd finally stood up for myself and told him how I hated him for making me hate myself. I didn't know that he'd pass two hours later, on the red line subway. That Clark would be gone too. I'd tank my book after that and prove everything awful my father thought about me was right. That within a month, my fiancée would realize I wasn't fun or successful anymore and not even bother with a Dear Huck letter when she left. The idea of coming close to it at all, let alone sharing it with someone, feels risky. Thankfully, Gus, Ted, and Stella appear on the surface of the water a few yards away and I don't have to say anything. Gus gives us the all-clear signal, and then they swim toward the boat. I help Ted out first, and Gus hops up and ushers him over to a bench to lie down. I lower an arm to take Stella's fins from her.

Everyone is quiet.

Gus wraps Zoe in his arms and holds her. "We're fine," he tells her, smoothing the hair she'd worried up into a mess. "It's all good, babe. All good."

I glance at Stella. She's watching them too, biting her lip. She still hasn't taken off her tank. She's just standing there, dazed and dripping.

"Can I help you with this?" I ask, gesturing at her tank.

She shakes her head, like she's emerging from a dream. "Oh, I got it." She pulls off the tank and her BC and sets them on the deck. The boat pitches on a wave, and I reach out to steady her as she stumbles, struggling to stay upright.

"I must've left my sea legs in the ocean," she says, and tries to smile.

The boat rocks again. "I got you," I tell her.

"You don't have to. I'm okay."

I swallow with effort. "I wasn't sure you were going to be . . . okay . . . for a bit there."

She squints up at me and then turns her attention to Teddy. Gus is handing him a mask connected to a small tank of oxygen. "We're alright," Stella tells me. "The pure oxygen will help." She still hasn't looked back at me.

"Feels like a close call."

"Yeah, well, that's Teddy. King of the close calls." She finally turns around, and I try to erase the worry from my face. "Tell me about the find you guys had. I can't wait to see it for myself."

THIRTY-ONE

Stella

In my opinion, among the few things that feel appropriate after a day like the one we've just had, getting extremely drunk tops the list. Okay, maybe not everyone's list. Zoe and Gus, for instance, seem to be interested in a different way to celebrate life, and after dinner they head down to the room where they're bunking while the rest of us stay behind. Zoe presses her forehead to mine, and then she does the same to Teddy.

"No funny business," she says. "I'm already going gray early. I don't need any help from your shenanigans."

Teddy flashes a grin. "Scout's honor, madam. We'll leave the funny business to you guys and we'll stay here and be very, very responsible."

"See, it's the two *verys* that I find concerning."

"You're off-duty now, mama," Gus says, kissing her hair and pulling her away. "Let the large children take care of themselves." She smiles up at him. But then he glares back at us. "Stay away from the deck rails, capisce?"

"Aye, aye," Ted says.

"You don't have to tell me twice," Huck says. "I'm fully invested in safety."

Teddy waits for them to leave and then crosses the galley. He pulls out a bottle of rum and three cups. "I'm fully invested in getting smashed," he says. He pours the rum into two cups and hands one to me and one to Huck before filling his own to the brim.

I raise my glass. "To living, so we can search another day."

Huck hesitates but clinks his cup against mine. Teddy does a cursory lift and then swigs down half his rum. Huck and I sip while we look at the pictures of the grappling hook that he and Gus found and talk about what it means. It is a match for some other similar finds from the time period of the 1715 treasure fleet, which is a good sign that it might be from our ship. It occurs to me that based on discovering a brass pin and a grappling hook, tomorrow could be the day that we find the motherlode. It doesn't feel real. I know how close we were to not making it out today, but I try to force it out of my mind.

Across from us, Ted fills his cup again.

"Let's play a game," he says.

"Sure, what should we play?" Huck asks.

"Two truths and a lie?" I suggest.

"Why not?" Ted says. "Ladies first. If we guess correctly, you have to drink. If one of us guesses wrong, that person drinks."

"This feels like it could go very badly for me," Huck says. "You guys know everything about each other. My information is either out of date or . . ."

"I'll try to be fair," I interrupt, not wanting to hear what he has to say about me. I think of what I should pick. It's an easy enough task. Two things about me that are true and one that isn't. Of course, the statements that come to mind are things I will never admit to anyone.

Huck Sullivan broke my heart. Truth.

Even though he's a heartbreaker, he still looks really good right now. Truth.

If he were to reach over and pull me in for a kiss, I would stop him.

Lie.

I shake my head and take a long pull of rum. My cheeks warm.

"Go, Stella," Ted says impatiently. "Otherwise I'm calling delay of game and you have to drink."

I pick things from my childhood to even the playing field. My first word was cat. True. I once stole a Jesus figurine from a souvenir shop when I was a toddler. True. I learned how to read ocean maps when I was four. Lie. I was six, but I learned fast.

Teddy guessed my first word was the lie. I'd used his knowledge of me against him. Mom took Skipper the orange tabby with her when she left, so for years, I've avoided feline reminders. My friends just assume I don't like them. Skipper used to curl up in a ball next to my face when I was little. His soft fur tickled my nose, just like the little kitten I'd almost adopted after Iceland.

Huck got the lie.

Teddy and I toast and take our punishment.

"Weren't you just bitching and moaning about how the odds were against you? How'd you get that?" Ted says. "And why do you look so smug? You only know the stealing thing was true because I told you she was a little thief."

"Teddy," I say, growing irritated, "stop giving Huck a hard time. It's your turn."

"Alright, then. It's on. You guys will never get these. I secretly want a penguin as a pet, I cried after losing the second-grade spelling bee, I've never been in love."

"Penguin's the lie," Huck says immediately. "You don't like the way they waddle; you told me that once when we watched *Happy Feet* while you were high."

"Maybe I got past that, dude?" Ted says. "Stell, is that your vote?"

I turn my glass, weighing everything I know about Ted. "All

of these could be true. I seem to remember you spending extra time by the penguins that last time we were at the zoo. And of course, I buy that you've never been in love . . . in lust, maybe. Definitely, but not sure about love. I guess that you wouldn't have given a shit about the spelling bee, not even in second grade. That or you did something obnoxious and won it."

"Smart girl," Ted tells me, but his voice is flat. He takes a long drink and then tops off his cup.

Huck takes his shot since he lost. "I guess it's my turn now." I watch his Adam's apple bob. "This is harder than I thought."

"It doesn't matter," I say. "Just pick random things."

Do I want him to say something about me, about us? No. I've already been fooled by that lie.

"Or don't," Teddy says.

Huck nods. "Okay. I have a pet snail. I did Irish dancing from ages four till twelve. I don't ride the subway."

"It's the subway," Ted says immediately. "New York equals subways. It's not even hard. And of course, we know that you owe us an official Riverdance across this kitchen now in addition to having to drink."

I watch Huck's expression twist and then go back to normal. He turns to me, waiting for my answer.

"Is it the snail?" I ask.

Huck smiles tightly; his nod is almost imperceptible. Across from us, Teddy empties the rest of the contents of the rum bottle into his cup and then does some kind of jig across the galley for a fresh bottle. He seems to have forgotten the rules of when he needs to drink.

"How did you know?" Huck asks quietly.

I shrug. The rum has me feeling warm, with softened edges. "You seem like a man that wouldn't have a pet. Too much responsibility."

"Ouch," he says. "Actually, I have two cats—Lord Whisker-pants and Mewowzer. My agent is watching them while I'm away."

"Glad to hear you didn't just leave them behind."

Huck winces a little and I immediately regret the statement. I'm not supposed to care about this anymore, not after all this time. Besides, I am the one who said we should leave the past in the past, and I don't get anything from his displeasure.

Teddy slams his mug down. "Are you guys cheating over there? I'm over this game. It's dull. We should do something fun. Like strip poker. No, I know—truth or dare," Ted says.

"No," Huck and I chorus. At least we agree on this.

"I pick dare," Teddy says, ignoring us.

"I think you've had enough dares for today, pal," Huck says. "In fact, I think you've had enough altogether." He reaches out for the rum bottle, but Teddy snatches it away. Even drunk, his reflexes are intact. He narrows his eyes and locks them on Huck as he shifts back and forth, evading him, and I can't tell if this is all in fun or if they're about to tear each other apart like sharks.

"What about your conversation questions?" I shout. "The ones from Iceland."

It takes a moment for Huck to understand. "Yeah, okay. We still have, like, thirty left."

"What conversation questions?" Teddy asks. He doesn't like being on the outside.

"I guess you could call it a game, it's just a bunch of random questions," Huck says.

"If you could have dinner with anyone in the world, Ted, who would it be?" I ask, borrowing the first question that Huck asked me at the pizza place.

"We just had dinner, Stella. I'm good." Teddy's sounding more like he did in South Carolina when Huck and I had to tuck him into bed; he talks like his mouth is full of gauze.

"Have some water," I say.

"I'm not thirsty, I'm fabulous."

"How about this, Ted?" Huck interjects. "If you were going to live until you were ninety and could either keep your mind at age thirty or your body, which would it be?"

"Ha, easy. My body." Teddy whips off his shirt as evidence and whirls it around his head. He goes back to his jig, then does a jump turn and shakes his ass at us. I'm fifty-fifty on whether he's about to flash it at us. "You'd want to keep your mind, right, Sully? I get it. That beautiful mind of yours. Everybody loves it. They pay thirty bucks for hardcover copies. Stella did and she's broke. But she bought it and hid it in her purse. And why? It's not like you can do this." Teddy initiates a motion that can only be described as wild gyrations. I have to put a hand over my mouth to stifle my laughter. It would only encourage him, and at this point he is very close to muscle-pulling territory.

"You win, bud," Huck says. "My body can't do that."

Why this makes me think of the multitudes of other amazing things Huck's body can do, I'm not sure. He catches my eye. "I guess I should stick with my mind and let my body succumb to the relentless march of time."

"Look at him getting all literary and shit," Ted says. "He knows he can't compete. Holy shit, guys, you know what we need right now?"

"A nap?" I say.

"Music, Stella. We need some jams." He finds a playlist on his phone and drops the device into an empty mug so the sound of steel drums fills the galley. Huck and I watch as Teddy puts on a one-man show, head down, feeling the beat, shifting between merengue and extremely bad popping and locking around the small space. Halfway through the second song, Ted snags me around the waist.

"Dancing, like treasure hunting, is not a spectator sport, Stella Moore. Since when have you ever watched from the sidelines?" he shouts in my ear. "Let's salsa."

He's uncoordinated and handsy, but the exuberant grin on his face is hard to resist—it always is. I give in. It is more fun to dance.

"If we both live until we're ninety, we definitely both need our bodies. We can dive and dance until we die."

I think of earlier today and how far Teddy pushed it. How close it came to having to make a choice, save myself and leave him behind or sink together. The thought, or maybe the combination of Ted's chaotic dancing and rum and too much sun, makes my head swirl.

"You're an idiot," I say, smiling. My voice is warm, of course it is. Teddy's my oldest, closest friend. But I'm also angry at him. His breath is hot and reeks of rum, his bare chest is sweaty and close, that hand of his is sloppy, too low on my waist. He's still holding his cup of rum, and some spills down the back of my shirt. Huck is not dancing; I can feel him watching us.

"I need some air," I say, and push away from Teddy.

He stumbles back, but barely misses a beat. "Suit yourself," he says, takes a big swig of his drink, and goes harder with his dance.

I head up to the deck and face the sea, gripping the handrails. I desperately need to clear my head. The stars are brilliant, infinite points of light against a squid-ink sky. I take a deep breath, trying to pull in the fresh scent of ocean air, but instead all I smell is the spilled rum soaking my shirt.

"You okay?"

I don't turn around. I'd felt Huck's presence even before he spoke. His footsteps on the deck are different than everyone else's, like gravity acts in some unique way on him.

"Not sure it was a great idea to leave Ted unsupervised," I say.

"I did try to keep him entertained, but he gets a little frisky when he's dancing. I wasn't a fan of his wandering hands."

I rotate to see if he's joking. He is not.

"That's valid. Did he spill rum on your shirt too?"

"That honor he saved for you, I guess. Though I suspect his cup was empty by the time I got to him."

I nod.

"You don't have to worry. He started to wind down on his own and went back to his bunk. It was a pretty eventful day. I imagine he's going to sleep hard."

"*Eventful*'s one way of putting it," I say, trying not to scoff.

"Well, *eventful* sounds a little less bad than *terrifying*. I'm trying to be a breezy guy here."

"*Were* you terrified?" I ask.

He dips his head. "Were you?"

"Maybe a little. I kept thinking about that time in Iceland when you asked me if I had some notion of how I was going to die. It felt like maybe I'd jinxed myself."

"Yeah." He runs a hand through his hair. "I thought about that. It scared me too."

"Seems like Teddy's theme for this trip is scaring his friends."

"Yup." He twists his hands around the deck rails. "I was really worried about you."

I can't help myself, I do scoff at this.

"I'm serious."

"I can't imagine why. We hardly know each other. I'm nothing to you."

"C'mon, Stella, you can't actually believe that's true."

I close my eyes. "I didn't want to talk about this. I was fine with a truce, but you keep bringing it up. It's like I can't be in a kitchen with you without you muttering something or other about my opinion or my personal safety and how they matter to you. And what about the book?"

"Have you finished it yet?" His expression almost looks hopeful, which makes me more exasperated.

"No, and I'm not going to. I guess that makes us even. Both of us don't finish the things we start."

"You're talking about Iceland."

"Forget it. I'm talking about nothing." I sigh. I'd vowed not to bring this up again.

"You've never been nothing, Stella, not to me. And Iceland wasn't nothing."

I won't look at him. I can't. I focus on the water sloshing against the stern.

"I know I still owe you a real explanation about that."

I turn to him. "You really don't. It's like I said, we're both here for treasure and work. That hasn't changed."

"I still think about it," Huck says.

I don't know if it's the rum or the motion of the boat on the waves, but I suddenly feel off-kilter.

"I still think about you. About us."

I shake my head. "I don't think we should talk—"

Huck turns to me. "I'm so sorry, Stella. I can't even find the right words to explain how much I regret what I did. It seemed like I was doing the right thing at the time. I thought I was only hurting myself. I would never want to hurt you. I need you to know that. I don't expect you to forgive me, I don't deserve forgiveness, and I won't even ask for it. I just need you to know where I stand. You will always be important to me."

I try to muster up some kind of response. One that makes me seem tough and not wounded, one that slices to his core . . . except, I make the mistake of looking at him. Of seeing him. His normally pale eyes are dark, soft. He looks, I don't know, re-morseful, broken? His brows knit together.

"Okay," I say.

"Okay?" He reaches out and tucks a windblown strand of hair behind my ear, and I sigh.

"Let's just leave it at that. We have better things from the past to focus on. We found a grappling hook today." I bite my lip.

For a second, Huck looks like he wants to kiss me, and I think back to two truths and a lie. If he were to pull me in . . . I don't want to push away. He hurt me before. He said he didn't mean to, he only meant to hurt himself. I can't understand this, but I know he's being honest.

"That means we could have found it, right? The *San Miguel*, the Stolen Treasure . . . what you've been looking for? So the Heart must be somewhere nearby?"

I swallow. Unsteady. I feel unsteady. The way Huck is looking at me, like us finding treasure is the best thing that's ever hap-pened in his whole life. It makes me want to let him break my heart all over again. A strong breeze kicks up and the boat bobs awkwardly in the surf. I trip forward against Huck, and my hands land on his chest. His hands catch the small of my back, steady and sure. Inside me something that I thought was lost glimmers. I believe in one-in-a-billion odds and never giving up. Maybe that's why I think just for an instant that this time could be dif-ferent.

No.

I stumble back from him. It can't. I can't.

I cling to the railing tighter and face into the wind again.

"It means we're close."

THIRTY-TWO

Huck

I want to stay with Stella in the dark, beneath this gorgeous expanse of stars all night. Fuck it. I want to stay right here with her forever. I know it can't happen, but my hand still fits in the curve of her back like it was made to go there, a lock and key, exactly like last year. It is taking every ounce of freaking control I have not to pull her in and make her mouth mine, make *her* mine, and let her brand me as hers with her lips.

The universe brought us together once, but now it seems to have other plans. That zephyr from a few minutes earlier is quickly becoming something more akin to a gale, and the gentle rocking motion of the ship turns chaotic. Sea sprays into our faces and my scopolamine patch waves a white flag and now my self-control shifts from Stella purely to the prevention of me hurling the contents of my stomach over the railing.

"This doesn't seem normal," I call over the wind.

She squints as rain comes at us sideways. "It's just a little squall."

She and I seem to have very different definitions of *little*. "Cool, cool, cool," I mutter, eyeing the door to below deck, which is farther away than I remember.

"You look like you are about to freak out. Are you working up to a scuba moment?" Stella asks.

"Kinda, yeah." I don't even have the energy to lie. My stomach is a tornado and the railing I'm death-gripping is getting wet and slippery and the boat is thrashing. Stella is calm, of course; she's a badass. She slicks her hair out of her face and goes to double-check on all the gear, confirming it's secured. Then she starts making her way toward the door.

"Coming?" she asks.

I will not vomit in front of her. I will not. "We don't have to stay up here? Make sure we don't sink?"

"The bilge is on auto with a high-water alarm, and we've got plenty of chain on the anchor. We'll be fine. Let's get out of this weather. You're soaked." She extends a hand, and I grip it, and just like that, my scopolamine patch is back in freaking business. I know we'll be safe. Stella is in control.

We make it through the door and stand, chests heaving, hands still intertwined for a moment in the refuge of the landing. The urge to kiss her is back, and so fucking overwhelming that I have to untangle my hand from hers.

"Thanks," I say. "I guess I'm not good in a crisis."

"Did you think that was a crisis?" she teases. "It was just a bit of weather. It's probably already over."

"Now you're just rubbing it in."

She smooths a hand over her soaked hair and wrings out her ponytail, smiling. "Maybe a little. Fair play, in my opinion."

It seems like maybe she's right. The motion of the boat has slowed. But then it pitches in a motion so sudden and violent that it catches us both off guard and flings Stella past me toward the stairs. Without thinking, I reach out and pull her back, spinning us away from the steps and we collide against the door. I have to catch myself with my hands so my chest doesn't crush her, but this also manages to trap our faces close together, which I did not intend. My heart jackhammers around in my rib cage and the air squeezes out of my lungs. What if I hadn't caught her? Man, my chest feels tight. For a second I think this is just a weird physical effect that the combined stress of little squalls and Stella in a stairwell has on me, but then I look down and realize that she has the fabric of my shirt in her fist and is twisting it. She notices it at the same time and releases her grip.

I clear my throat and take a step back.

"Not bad for someone who isn't good in a crisis," she admits, peering up at me.

"Nah."

"You saved me from the steel stairs. I'm calling that slightly heroic, and this is the only time I'm going to be that generous, so take the damn compliment, Sullivan." She grips my shirt again, and oh shit, does *she* want to kiss *me*? Yeah, okay, I'm still freaking out a little and I did just embarrass myself on deck and almost toss my cookies, but now she thinks I'm a hero, and heroes kiss the girl. Even if they completely fumbled a year ago. As long as we both want this. God, I freaking want this . . .

I press myself against her and start to lean in. "Slightly heroic, eh?"

"Maybe just a smidgen." She's still. Her gaze drops to my mouth.

I'm a millisecond away from her lips. "I'll take it."

"Well, well, well," a deep voice booms from below.

Stella peeks around my shoulder. I can't see her expression, but I can imagine that it's something like mine. A mix of shock, guilt, and absolute *for the love of everything holy, could you not have just waited thirty seconds . . . forty-five seconds . . . who the hell am I kidding—twenty minutes . . . so we could finish this kiss, dude?*

"Everything good, Gus?" she asks.

"I would ask you the same thing, but your situation is looking, ah, pretty good." He snickers.

"No, it's not. She's still mad at him." Zoe. She bellows the last part, just to make sure we both hear it. I have to give it to her, she's masterful. This move would bring me back down to earth under different circumstances. However, Stella's still holding on to my shirt.

And to be totally honest, the presence of Gus and Zoe judging us from below doesn't really compete with Stella's small hand hanging on to me. Her expression is positively defiant. I marvel at the fact that her friends interjecting themselves into this situation doesn't matter to her. It certainly hasn't really dulled my, ah, enthusiasm.

She blinks up at me and catches the parched skin of her bottom lip with her teeth in what is arguably the sexiest thing I've ever seen. I wonder if our kiss will taste of salt. I'm just getting started with this mental exploration when she releases my shirt and ducks under my arm in one swift motion.

She pauses at the top of the stairs. "Probably time for bed," she tells me, and then jogs down as if nothing ever happened.

"What the hell was that?" Zoe says.

Maybe she doesn't realize the way her voice carries in the hollow stairwell and her previous announcement was only incredulity and not gamesmanship.

"Just a little squall," Stella answers.

"Squall my ass."

THIRTY-THREE

Stella

We wake after the storm to clear skies and mild seas. I'm more tired than I'd like to be for a day of searching, but I'm not about to waste these perfect conditions just because I couldn't sleep last night. Zoe spent nearly twenty minutes cross-examining me about the events in the stairwell with Huck before she finally acquiesced and left me alone. I didn't have to lie. I honestly couldn't tell her what that was between me and him, because I had no clue.

It was just the rain and the wind and his hands and a bunch of memories; rum and the way he pulled me back from a fall and drifted into my space, making me feel safe and dangerous at the same time; how he smelled like the beach and forest simultaneously, like lime and cedar; his wet shirt clinging to his chest and abs; those eyes so blue and soft as they looked at me.

I'd known the way he felt once.

I could almost remember his skin under my fingertips.

In that moment, *want* didn't fully capture my state. I needed Huck.

Now, I need coffee. An entire pot, guzzled black while standing at the counter. It's a biological requirement. I shuffle into the galley. Huck and Teddy clutch tin mugs of coffee in silence. Teddy's wearing sunglasses in the kitchen and only acknowledges my presence with a lift of his chin.

"We had to brew a second pot," Huck says.

"Oh."

"It should be almost ready."

Teddy shushes us both.

I ignore him. "What's for breakfast?" I ask.

"Stella, for the love of god. Stop torturing me with your talking," Teddy says. "My head feels like a grenade with a pulled pin."

"Theodore, you are a full-grown adult," I retort. "If you're going to mainline cheap rum until your boarding school roommate has to cut you off and put you to bed, then you've got to be prepared to face the consequences of your decisions. I'm not going to tiptoe around all day in honor of your hangover."

"You are cruel," Ted says. "I can't take all the blame. Whose idea was it to play a drinking game?"

"Yours," Huck and I say at the same time.

"Fine. I'm going up where it's quiet to get ready for the dive."

"No, you're not," I tell him.

He groans and lifts his sunglasses up to squint at me. "How many times have I dived hungover?"

"You know that's not why I'm benching you. Yesterday was a full-blown shit show, Ted. You're on the boat."

Huck fills a coffee mug and slides it over to me wordlessly, along with a breakfast bagel sandwich that he's just assembled. He's staying out of it.

"I'm on the boat," Ted says, like he's mulling it over.

"You heard me." I take a bite of the sandwich. It's delicious. Huck's toasted the bread in the frying pan with butter, giving it the perfect crunch.

"I paid for this boat."

"All the more reason for you to enjoy it, then." I hold out the sandwich for him. He gives in and takes a bite.

"I made one for you too, bud," Huck says. He hands Teddy his own sandwich.

Teddy examines it. "You didn't toast mine. Why does Stella get a toasty one and I get a limp bagel? Actually, never mind. This probably is not going to stay down long enough for it to matter."

"On that note," I say.

"I'm going to bring the rest of the breakfast up to Gus and Zoe," Huck says. "Want to join me?"

I nod and follow him.

"I'm going back to bed for a bit," Ted says, walking in the opposite direction. "Wake me up when you're ready to dive." He waves his bagel over his shoulder and a piece of egg falls out. He stoops to pick it up and pops it into his mouth. "Five-second rule."

"That's truly nasty," I say.

"I heard that! Don't fault me for my conservation efforts, grump."

"Did you really not toast his bagel?" I ask Huck when Teddy is out of earshot.

"Of course I toasted it. I'm not a monster."

"That's a relief. He'd never let it go if he truly believed you gave my food special treatment."

Huck laughs. "Really? The guy just ate off the floor, or did you forget?"

"Oh, he's gross. I didn't forget. But he also has a big thing about fairness."

We start up the stairs. "To be honest, I'm surprised how good of a cook you are. I guess I shouldn't be. You told me as much before. Lasagna, right?"

Huck looks back over his shoulder. "I told you I was a good cook? That's embarrassing. I should've said that I *like* to cook. Who says that?"

"I think your exact words were 'better than Eataly.'" I grimace.

"So it gets worse. I must've blocked that out. Forgive me for that mortifying braggadocio? In my defense I was probably trying very hard to impress you."

"You didn't have to try."

He stops abruptly to turn to me, and I nearly crash into him. "Really?"

"Oh, come on. You're Huck Sullivan. It's like Teddy told you, I'd read all your books."

"I thought he was being ironic, or trying to embarrass you."

"He does love to do that. No, I wish. I waited in line for the last Casablanca."

He manages somehow to look absolutely flummoxed and charming, juggling the breakfast sandwiches and this new piece of information. His dark hair has fallen over his forehead, and I resist the urge to smooth it back for him. "No way."

"I don't know why I'm admitting this to you, but I'm a fan," I confess. The corner of Huck's mouth lifts, and I feel the need to correct myself. "I was a fan."

He nods, smile receding, and I wish I hadn't added the caveat. "That's fair."

"I shouldn't have said that."

"It's fine, Stella. You don't owe me anything, especially feeding my ego. Anyway, being a fan isn't the same thing as knowing someone. A lot of the time it's an artificial relationship, not genuine closeness."

"Well, I'm sure you have so many that one doesn't make a difference."

"You'd be surprised." I thought he might be flirting, especially after last night, but he isn't. He's retreated from me.

"What does that mean?" I ask, pushing open the door to the deck as he walks through with the breakfast delivery.

"It's nothing. I guess I appreciate the support of my fans so much and know how lucky I am to have it, but also, it's a lot of pressure. Constantly being subjected to attention and opinions and judgment starts to wear on you. Or maybe not on everyone, but it did on me. I was primed for that. I just wanted to write books, but people would get irate about different plot lines or something a character said. Some of them conflated my characters' thoughts and actions with mine. They only loved me when I wrote what they wanted. When I didn't, they hated me. I tried not to let it bother me. All the DMs and emails, I ignored or shrugged off. But I couldn't avoid all my critics. Some were much closer." He's staring at the deck. The breakfast sandwiches are probably getting cold.

I want to ask him if he's talking about his dad, but before I get a chance, he adds, "But hey, that's why therapy exists, right?"

I nod. We're both silent for a long beat. "Thank you for the coffee and breakfast. You have no idea how much I needed it. I didn't really sleep last night," I say.

He looks at me. "Me either."

Zoe comes over to us, her bright caftan billowing around her. "Tell me those are bagel sandwiches," she says, "and I might fall in love with you."

"I think that position is already occupied," Gus says, snatching one of the bagels up. "Freaking delicious, man. Thank you."

My face feels like it might melt off and slide down to the deck in a bubbling puddle of goo. I gape at Gus.

"*What?* I meant she's in love with *me*. But valid interpretation, Stell." He laughs and takes a bite of his sandwich. "Weren't you two getting it on in the stairwell last night?"

"Absolutely not," I say.

"Noooo," Huck adds, a faint flush peeking out from the neck of his polo shirt.

"There was some definite leaning." He flattens his hand and then tips it at an angle to demonstrate. "Don't you think, babe? There was means, opportunity, intent."

Zoe doesn't look up from her food.

"Honey?"

She stops chewing. "Don't you dare ruin this bagelwich for me."

"My god, I love this woman. She's practically feral."

"Don't forget how glorious she looks in the caftans she's rocking this season," I say.

Zoe glances up at me. "The salesgirl called it a sophisticated muumuu. Very chic, very in."

"You look gorgeous and *very* sophisticated in your muumuus," Gus says, and presses a kiss to the top of her head.

"Gus, hurry up and eat. I want to get out there while the weather's still mild. Teddy's on deck duty, so, Zoe, you ready to get wet?"

She casts a glance over at Gus. He smiles broadly. "We're going back to the grappling hook site, right? Why don't just you, Huck, and I go? Someone should probably keep an eye on Teddy anyway, and we can easily make do with three in this smaller search grid. As long as Zoe doesn't mind supervising our friend."

"He is very hungover," Huck says.

"And cheeky," I add.

"Oh, all my favorite things." Zoe grins. "You better find some good stuff today, guys."

Gus finishes off his sandwich in a few bites and we start prepping for the dive. I shuck off my cutoffs and T-shirt and drop them into a pile. Huck pulls his polo over his head. His skin has darkened from a wintry parchment-color to a light tan, like that buttery bagel I just devoured. Even in this short time, working on the boat has brought out the muscles of his back and abs. He looks good. Not irresistible. Not like I want to run my tongue from neck to navel, or whatever. This is entirely innocent appreciation of his physical form and nothing more except maybe a bit of mild amusement as he struggles to apply sunscreen to his upper back. He twists and flails like a fish flopping around on a deck but with octopus arms. Except hot. A hot-ass fish.

Who made breakfast. And who I matter to . . . maybe. I sigh.

"Give it here," I say, holding out my hand for the sunscreen. "You look ridiculous and you're going to have burnt stripes all over you."

"Was I really doing that bad?" he asks.

"Yes. The streaks look like the Northern Lights on your back." I smooth the lotion onto his shoulders and lat muscles, trying to be businesslike about my application. It's difficult; I shouldn't have mentioned the Northern Lights.

Huck clears his throat gently. "Thanks."

My hands glide over his back, down his spine. I love the way he feels, the way I feel touching him.

"I stand by my comment about the leaning," Gus says, and I jump back.

"All set," I announce too loudly. "Someone's not getting sunburned today."

Gus grins and pulls on his mask before stepping over the side and splashing in the water below. I take the excess sunscreen left on my hands and smear it on my face.

"Did you need me to get you?" Huck asks.

I shake my head. "I'm wearing a wetsuit today. Thanks, though."

"Of course. Do you mind checking my tank?"

"Getting a little high maintenance, aren't we?" I tease. "Anything else you need? Bonbons, a massage?"

Huck doesn't laugh.

"Everything okay?" I ask. "I was kidding, by the way."

He pushes a fin that's lying on the deck with his toe. "Yeah, I know. I guess I'm feeling a little nervous after yesterday."

"Totally understandable—that never should've happened. That's why Teddy's staying out of the water today. We shouldn't have to be worried about preventable mishaps and he needs to fully grasp that he can never pull that shit again." He nods. I give his arm a light squeeze. His entire body is tense. "We aren't going anywhere near deep water today. I promise. Gus and I will take good care of you."

"I believe you." He doesn't sound particularly convinced.

"Buck up, you," I say, giving him a gentle shove. "You never know . . . we just might strike it lucky today."

THIRTY-FOUR

Huck

You'd think that being meters beneath the ocean's surface, with the chance to find the wreckage of a centuries-old treasure ship and a priceless red diamond, would take my mind off the feel of Stella's hands smearing sunscreen on my back. You'd be wrong. I barely notice when my metal detector alerts at first because I'm too freaking preoccupied with the eroticism of UV protection. The beeping grows more persistent, and I move closer to see what's setting it off.

When we first started hunting together on this trip, I spent a lot of time on the comms calling the others over to see what each hit was, but this time I'm playing it cool. Stella and Gus are doing their own sweeps around the zone where we found the grappling hook yesterday, and I don't want to bring them over here if it turns out to be nothing exciting.

In the sand, I make out a dark circular shape near a rocky mound. It almost looks like the metal hoop of a barrel. I take out a marker and place it, documenting the find with my camera as Stella and Gus have taught me. I let them know about what I see and then start to move on. A shaft of sunlight appears ahead of me, near a collection of rocks and kelp, and a glint of something catches my eye. I blink and look again. I can't tell what it is, but there's definitely a glimmer there. I swim closer and wave my hand gently through the water to clear away the sand.

I stare at the ocean floor for a long moment in complete disbelief. A shadow passes in the corner of my vision, and I don't turn away to see what it is. It could be a shark sizing me up and I wouldn't even know. I'm completely rapt. *So this is what it feels like,* I think.

"You are never going to believe this." It's Gus's voice in my ear. "Guys, I found a cannon! It's unbelievable. It's, like, twelve feet long and totally intact. You've got to get over here."

Cheers fill my ears through the comms. I'm speechless, completely awestruck, staring at the gold that peeks out like liquid sunshine from the bottom of the ocean. I've written things like this. In *Fortune Files*, Lucky and Finn discover a hidden cavern where there's an entire trove of gemstones and ancient golden statues, but somehow my imagination failed to capture the full thrill of it. There's so much adrenaline coursing through my body that my heart beats recklessly and my vision sharpens. I can hear every tiny sound, even my pulse.

"That's amazing, Gus," Stella says. "But I think you're going to want to come over by me and Huck."

I turn to my right where I'd seen a shadow passing earlier to face Stella, floating up beside me. She's staring straight ahead at the treasure.

"Seriously?" Gus asks. "You've got something more exciting than a cannon? Is it the ship's bell? Holy shit."

Stella rolls slightly in the water and now she's looking at me, a broad, bright smile on her face.

"It's not a bell," Stella says. She's staring straight at me and the excitement of seeing her so happy while she looks at me makes my heart feel like it might sprout a motor, fly through the wall of my chest, and zip away with a wake behind it. "It's better."

"Gold," I blurt.

"Wait, what'd you just say?" It's Ted over the ship's radio. "Zoe and I are having a hard time reading you guys."

"Gold," Stella yells.

Ted crackles through. "Say it again!"

"Gold," she and I shout.

"Say it again!" he hollers in delight.

They can hear us just fine—the demand is a celebratory one. A joyous call-and-response. My last shred of composure gives way. There's only one thing that would make this better and she's floating a foot away from me. I fling my arms around her. The hug is awkward, a tangle of tubes and bulky air tanks, my bare skin and her wetsuit and face masks that bump.

"Gold," Stella says one last time.

"We found the fucking gold!"

THIRTY-FIVE

Stella

The salt breeze has turned my hair curly and wild, and the freckles form a dense network on my face. I like myself more like this, in my natural state from the sun and sea. We're going out to celebrate tonight, so I add a little mascara and lip gloss, fluff my hair, and head up top. Even though I rinsed my dress, it's a little crunchy from the dip in the sea water. I make do since it's all I have, but Zoe shakes her head at me.

"No," she says. "That's not going to work."

"Is it the hair?"

"Definitely not the hair. The hair works. It's giving wild lion mane and I'm here for it. What I am referring to is your dress. It's a disaster that looks like you pulled it up with the gold today and it hasn't aged nearly as well in the elements."

"To be fair, gold doesn't oxidize in the ocean, so it will look pristine forever, but I get your point. The problem is that this dress is all I have, unless you're going to lend me one of your sophisticated muumuus?"

"You wish. Stella, I love you and you're glorious, but you're too petite to pull off this look. It works better on a fuller figure. Not to worry, I'm going to take you shopping. Gus and the guys are going to take care of securing the gold at the safe deposit box, and we are on a mission to get you a new outfit. My treat."

I know enough not to argue with Zoe. When we dock in Key West, she and I head off in one direction and the men head in the other. We try not to show our excitement too much. Treasure salvage is not without risk, and even though Key West is a fun and casual community, there are people around who would love nothing more than to figure out what we found and where we found it so they can beat us to the rest. And there is more. I'm sure of it. Based on the research that we've done over the past several years, we are envisioning millions of dollars' worth of treasure. Not just gold, but the Elephant's Heart Diamond and massive quantities of other uncut gems. We have to be careful and hold our secret close.

Zoe and I stroll through a few boutiques before finding an upscale secondhand store that has a cool mix of unique clothes ranging from casual daily wear to gorgeous special occasion dresses. I run my fingers over dresses in a kaleidoscope of colors until I find the perfect one. It's a short, pleated A-line dress with a tight bodice and sweetheart neckline, made of a soft, glistening gold fabric.

I hold it up.

"Zoe, what do you think of this one?"

She nods. "Wholehearted yes. You must try it on, it's perfect."

I slip into a dressing room and put the dress on. The top is snug to the point that I'm not sure that I will be able to zip it, but once it's on, it's light and comfortable. I do a little twirl and it flares out. Zoe's face says it all when I step out of the dressing room.

"The top's not too small?" I ask.

She shakes her head. "It's just the right amount of tight to make your boobs look amazing. Huck's going to choke."

I scoff. "I doubt it. And I don't care."

"Uh-huh. Sure. You don't care and he's not going to wish that he'd found you instead of those coins earlier today. His gorgeous golden treasure."

"I'm getting it," I tell her. "But only because *I* love it, not because of what Huck will think when he sees me wearing it."

"I love it too." She rubs her hands over my bare arms affectionately. "Stell, I'm going to tell you something and you might not like it but at least hear me out. I know Gus and I have both been teasing you during this trip and saying there is something brewing between you and Huck, but I'm positive that he has real feelings. You both do. And you are good together. I feel like he brings out something different in you—"

"Annoyance?"

"And *you* definitely bring something out in him. I'm not saying you should run off to city hall or anything, but maybe you can talk or finish up whatever you were starting in that stairwell. Don't give me that look. You know you two were kicking something off during that storm."

"I don't think so." I shake my head. "I will admit that I've been tempted on this trip. Huck's very pretty and smart and there is this weird magnetic pull between us. And I guess I *am* tired of being on my own and having nothing more than occasional casual hookups. I want something more. I think maybe I'm ready for it finally. Just not with Huck, no matter how attracted we are to each other. Things ended so badly before and whatever's left— it's not enough. I want someone I can count on who won't bail on me. Someone who is loyal above everything else."

"I don't know. I think he's pretty loyal."

"Yeah, maybe to Teddy." I laugh half-heartedly.

"Maybe." She turns to a saleswoman. "Can she wear this out?"

"Sure. I can cut off the tags at the counter when you pay."

We're quiet as we follow the staff member to the cash register, where she removes the tags and Zoe refuses my money and plops down her credit card. "Next time, you can buy me something fancy," she says. "Since you're going to be rich."

"Even split, remember?" I say.

Outside, Zoe uses her phone to locate the restaurant where we'd made reservations on a map. "It's this way," she says. We start off together.

"I take it you're not going to finish reading the book either?"

I shrug. "I thought about it, but I don't think so. It was too hard reading about this couple that felt like us but wasn't. I loved reading it, but it hurt too much."

"I can understand that. And I know you don't need advice. You've always walked your own path and I love that about you. But if you can, try to keep an open mind."

"About the book or the author?"

"Both.

We have some time before we need to meet the guys, so we stop at the Key West Butterfly and Nature Conservatory, where we watch the two flamingos standing on single legs in a shallow lagoon while hundreds of multicolored butterflies float through the air around us. Zoe must look like a flower in her bright fuchsia-and-orange gown because several butterflies land on her. I snap pictures and text them to Gus and Ted. Gus texts back something about his glorious queen, and Teddy sends a set of tilted action shots and selfies of him, Gus, and Huck touring Truman Annex on rented bicycles and one picture of them posing outside of the Mel Fisher Maritime Museum, captioned Look, it's us! Zoe and I get lemonades and drink them by the ocean while we watch the sun set, and then we head over to First Flight for dinner.

Despite a day spent biking around in the humidity, the guys look clean and fresh when they arrive at the restaurant. I realize they've all bought new shirts. Teddy's wearing a straw fedora with a black band that matches the fine embroidery on his shirt. Gus has on an orange shirt that perfectly complements Zoe's dress. Huck is dressed plainly, in a white linen shirt with the sleeves rolled up. The cream color against his tan skin looks surprisingly good. Teddy goes to talk to the hostess, and Huck and I stand facing each other while Gus twirls Zoe around.

"You look beautiful," Huck says to me, his voice low. "New dress?"

"Oh." The comment catches me off guard. "Yeah, thanks. Well, new to me. My other dress got kind of ruined in a salt marsh, so . . ."

He nods slowly. "I see. I also ruined an outfit in a salt marsh. What are the chances?"

There's that smile. It's gentle, inquisitive. Like he wants to know how I'll respond before he lets himself be completely happy.

"I'm probably a little overdressed."

"I don't think so. I think you're perfect."

And there it is, that soul-crushing ache in my chest and butterfly wings fluttering in my belly.

"Our table's ready," Teddy calls, and then disappears into the garden. The daylight is waning and the lights hanging in the patio flicker on. Huck and I catch up with Teddy while Gus and Zoe lag behind, walking hand in hand.

"I like your hat," I tell Teddy.

"Huck bought it for me," he says. "I'm the only one who can pull a hat of this nature off."

"You know, you and Zoe are very confident in your fashion. She told me that I couldn't rock one of her caftans earlier."

"Good thing she did," Ted says. "Then we wouldn't have been able to enjoy you in this magnificent gold dress. Very apropos. I dig it."

"Solid pun," Huck says.

I do a delighted twirl. "It felt like the right choice under the circumstances."

Teddy pulls out my chair for me and I sit. Huck takes his place on my left, Ted on my right, and the lovebirds sit across from us.

"This place is paradise," Zoe says, settling into her seat. We all agree, admiring the tropical foliage, the trees that feel ancient.

Gus rests his arm gently on the back of Zoe's chair while we all exchange tales of our expeditions and our friendships like war stories. I like watching them together. There's that easy understanding we all have with each other, but the warmth in their expressions, the volume of their laughter at each other's jokes? It's special. It makes me wish I had that too. Teddy orders for everyone, champagne, appetizers, and main courses to share. He even arranges a special dessert that will be brought out before the night is over. I eat so much and laugh so hard that I worry my dress might split. We savor our delicious food beneath a canopy of palms and the glow of soft white globe lights hanging from the trees.

At some point, soft music starts playing and Gus rises and holds out a hand for Zoe.

"It's a perfect night," she says, as she stands and heads with him to an open space to dance.

"We found gold today, and all those two want to do is slow dance," Teddy says, and I'm not sure if he's marveling or complaining. Huck and I turn to watch them.

"I don't know," Huck says. "I think it's nice."

"To each their own, I guess," Teddy replies. "Different strokes for different folks . . . unless you want me to whirl you around the dance floor, Stella?"

The temperature has dropped, and I shiver in the soft breeze. "Maybe in a minute," I say. "I think I'm going to ask the waitress for a hot tea to warm up."

"Have more champagne," Ted says. "That will help."

"I can get the tea for you," Huck says. "I was going to find the restroom anyway. What kind of tea do you like?"

"Mint, any kind."

"Sure thing."

I watch Huck wander across the patio. His walk is smooth and easy; as he moves, he looks around at the trees and the lights with a kind of wonderment. Someone stops him for a picture, and he obliges, smiling. Up until this moment, I'd almost forgotten that he's famous, that at one point, I might've stopped him at a restaurant to ask him for a picture. The group at the adjacent table swarms him, engaging him in an animated conversation. He's nodding along.

"Should we go rescue him?" I ask.

Teddy looks up from his shrimp. "Probably. Sully hates crowds. That's why he doesn't do events."

"He doesn't like being the center of attention?"

Teddy picks up a shrimp and bites it down to the tail. "No. Honestly, I don't think he likes being perceived. His dad was an absolute asshole and never missed an opportunity to tear Sully down. He had this way of saying Huck's real name . . . Henry . . . with such disgust, it even made *my* skin crawl. Anyway, before Sully finished the last Casablanca, his father accosted him at a signing to tell him how ashamed he was of him because of something he'd done. I don't know all of the details, but Sully didn't do any events after that."

I thought about what the lady in the bookstore in Wilmington had said about trying to get Huck to come for an event and how his publisher had declined. But now that I thought of it, I hadn't seen anything about him being on tour. His cardboard likeness was everywhere but he was not.

"I'll go over there in a minute," Teddy says. "I'm just going to finish my food first."

I glance over at Huck. The volume of the group has risen and more people have joined in the circle that surrounds him.

"When's the next book coming out?" a woman wearing a flashy hot pink jumpsuit that leaves very little to the imagination practically shouts. "Not as long in between this new series and the last one I hope, though I suppose it's good that you took your time. The last Casablanca was so awful; this one is so much better." It's at this point that Huck casts a furtive glance over at me. I recognize the slight furrow in his brow, his hand on the back of his neck, the way he's shifting his weight on his feet. Now he's running his hands through his hair.

Teddy's stuffs another shrimp in his mouth. "Last one," he says, mouth full. He starts to stand.

I propel myself out of my seat. "I got it."

The breeze lifts my hair and my gold skirt flutters as I stride toward Huck. When I arrive, I insert myself into the circle. I stand slightly in front of Huck and slide my arm through his, my version of a territorial girlfriend. He stills, the tension in his body uncoiling.

"Sorry to interrupt, babe," I say. "I was just wondering about that tea. The waitress never came back."

He blinks at me. "Of course, ah, sweetheart. Why don't we go check on that together?" He unwinds my arm from his and takes my hand as we start toward the restaurant. "Forgive us," Huck says to the group. "Have a lovely evening."

"Has anyone ever told you that you look just like Lucky Malone?" Pink Jumpsuit says.

"I *am* Lucky Malone," I call over my shoulder.

Inside, Huck and I duck into a quiet back hallway. We both lean back against a wall, decompressing. He's still holding on to my hand. After several moments of quiet, Huck breaks the silence. "'I *am* Lucky Malone.'" We both burst out laughing.

"*What*?" I say when I catch my breath. "That lady was really rude about your last book. I saw the opportunity to get under her skin and I took it. It's a bold person to critique another person's art while rocking that degree of camel toe."

Huck shakes his head. "It was fucking amazing." After a few moments, his laughter winds down.

I tilt my head and look up at him. "Are you okay? Teddy told me you don't like crowds."

He nods. "I'm okay now. Thanks to you for rescuing me. You really are a hero."

"That's Lucky Fucking Malone to you, mister."

Huck still hasn't broken eye contact. We haven't looked at each other like this, not since Iceland. His pale blue eyes are like memories trapped in the ice, thawing out with each second that passes, with us standing so close to each other. It seems strange after such a short time together last year that I missed him as much as I do. He's right here now and I still miss him. His warm hand is holding mine and I miss him. I pull in a deep breath. One of us has to look away. It should be me. I need to call *uncle* before this barely healed wound I have from him opens and all of our memories spill out.

One hard swallow. One deep breath to steady myself and then I will look away.

"What did Ted say exactly?"

"Pretty much what you told me . . . your dad was pretty tough on you."

Huck's laugh is tight, miserable.

"Yeah, that's one way of putting it. Sometimes I think his goal in life was making sure I never forgot just how big of a disappointment I was. And man, did he love an audience."

Even though I promised I wouldn't, I hold his gaze. I wait for him to go on.

"Just now, I wanted to tell those people that I had somewhere to be, but I couldn't move. This time it's nothing, just some pictures and a bit of criticism, and I can handle it. I should be able to handle it . . . but . . ." He looks down at the floor. I step around in front of him and fill his line of sight with me. And I'm patient while he finds the right words to tell me his story.

THIRTY-SIX

Huck

I tell Stella about my past in the hallway while she smooths her thumb over my palm, gentle and predictable, like ocean waves across a beach on a calm day.

"It was a big con right after the sixth Casablanca came out. I'd been signing for hours. I had a planned break so I could eat, go to the bathroom, rest my hand before the second four-hour session. I was talking to my agent and there was my dad, livid that I hadn't sent him a check when I made the *New York Times* bestseller list. He went on and on about how I was an ungrateful and talentless hack and that Clark Casablanca was so clearly him that he should be the one being paid, not me. The room was still full and noisy, but everyone stopped and they all heard him. I wrote this guy, and everyone loved him. The quintessential hero. And all those people stood in line for hours for a signed copy of the books he was in. They heard my father say that *he* was Clark—the guy who thought I was worthless—he made them believe that I was a thief, that Clark was his. It wasn't true, but that didn't matter. I was so furious. I snapped and yelled at him and he shoved me. My agent got security and they escorted him out."

When I stop talking, my hands are shaking. Stella takes them and holds them steady for a moment.

"That's awful," she says. "You did the right thing to stand up for yourself. I know it must've been so hard." Then she leads me toward the front door, wordlessly. I stop at the hostess stand to leave my credit card for the table, explaining that I'll be back tomorrow to pick it up. The hostess looks from my face to the name on the card, and nods.

"Of course, Mr. Sullivan. That will be fine. Thank you for your patronage."

Outside, Stella turns to me. "Why did you do that? You didn't have to pay for everyone. Teddy usually takes care of the trips."

I mull over my response for a moment. "You all were so generous to let me come along and have this experience. Today was one of the most exciting days of my life, and I wouldn't have had it were it not for you guys. Buying dinner is the least I can do." There's more I could say, but I'm not ready.

She seems to accept this answer.

"So where are you taking me?" I ask.

"You'll see." I follow her down streets brimming with music and tipsy visitors until the noise dissipates and the path grows darker. We feel like we're the only people in the world.

"This feels a little ominous," I say, as she stops in front of a gated entrance. She looks around and then starts to scale the fence.

"Stella," I hiss. "What are you doing? Are we going to get in trouble for this?"

She lands on the other side, and I stand debating whether I'll have to follow her over this gate or if I should run. I don't think my publicist would appreciate having to spin me getting arrested for trespassing in Key West while on a research trip.

"You know what your problem is, Huck? You care too much what other people think," she says. I'm about to explain that my publicist is a lovely woman who just had a baby and doesn't need this kind of extra stress, when the gate swings open.

"Don't you want to see Judy Blume's house?"

"We did not just break into Judy Blume's house!"

Stella grins. "No. This is my friend Amber's Airbnb. It's actually unoccupied at the moment. I have the code, I just thought it would be fun to mess with you a little."

"After I poured my heart out to you? You have a mean streak I wasn't aware of," I tell her. "Even after you threw me in a salt marsh as jellyfish bait."

"Consider it inspiration for your next book as a thank-you for buying dinner."

"I'm relieved to know that we're not disturbing the peace of Judy Blume, but what exactly are we doing at this Airbnb?" My mind is racing with possibilities, not all of which are entirely PG. Especially not after she climbed a fence in that little dress that is so tight up top some people might call it scandalous—not me; it's fucking sheer tantalizing perfection, the way it hugs and squeezes and flares, in my opinion—and set every atom in my body ablaze with desire.

"I thought we could take a night swim, without the risk of jellyfish this time. Amber has a nice pool in the backyard." Good idea. I'm practically self-combusting here.

We walk down a short stone path and Stella enters a code on a keypad, which unlocks the pool gate. She turns on a strand of twinkle lights, illuminating the patio. Amber does have a nice pool. It's one of those natural-looking ones with a little grotto and a short waterfall.

Stella does a little spin in front of me. "Can you get my zipper please?"

I slide the zipper down, and fuck me if I have to stare up at the sky to avoid getting aroused by the sight of her back. The brush of my knuckles against the skin over her spine practically does me in. The dress flutters to the ground, and she turns to me. I'm good. I'm staring over her shoulder at that grotto. Does she have the fancy underwear on? I have no freaking clue. That's an interesting arrangement of succulents over there in the corner. Look sharp. I swallow hard.

This strategy of distraction is why I don't notice her reaching for me. She undoes one of the buttons on my shirt, and then another before I glance down.

She's wearing the nice underwear.

Dammit.

She's another button closer to my waistband, and looking up at the sky isn't going to cut it anymore. My self-control is like that poor little button she's wresting free. A goner.

"Cool, thanks, got it," I say and fling my shirt off and onto a lounge chair. I kick my feet out of my deck shoes and jump into the water without another word. I need to put distance between us, so I swim toward the grotto.

Stella slides into the pool and skims under the surface toward me. I can see her in the pool lights. She looks like a beautiful impressionist painting and then she rises and rolls to float next to me.

It's not the attraction that's the problem. I mean, it is. The heat inside of me could boil this pool dry in an instant if I don't hold back. But the thing is . . . I can't.

I'm in burning agony.

I loved her last year. And I love her now. Not one bit less. Not the same.

I love her more.

And there's nothing I can do. I look at her, with her wet hair and her bare shoulders. Beaded pool water on her skin.

I don't care about the gold anymore. Or my books. Just a chemical element and words on a page.

Nothing compared to Stella.

"I need to ask you something," she says, skimming her fingers across the water's surface. I stare at her, unable to move or speak. "Zoe told me earlier that you still have feelings for me. Why would she think that?"

I close my eyes for a second and take a breath. "Because it's the truth."

"Did you leave me behind in Iceland because of what you told me earlier . . . with your dad? Did you think I wouldn't want you?"

I don't even know the answer to that. In some way she's right, but that's not all of it. She still hasn't finished the book. "Does it matter? I can't imagine any ending in which I didn't ruin everything, regardless of my motivation."

She's quiet for a long time, too kind to admit that I'm right. Then she moves a little closer. "You did have writer's block for years. Maybe your imagination isn't what it used to be."

True, but my imagination is intact now, spinning into overdrive; the stories it's telling me drown out every other thing that matters, things I shouldn't forget but which I bury for the moment, because she's looking at me, breaking me down. Her movements make tiny waves that brush against my skin.

"Is that so?" I manage to choke out.

She nods. "Here's the thing about treasure hunters. We're tough people . . . with wild imaginations and unlimited reserves of hope." She's getting closer, and I cannot move. I almost can't believe this is happening. But all my dreams of her have either been nightmares of leaving her again and my teeth tumbling out onto the beach and being washed away, or wild X-rated reunion-sex dreams where she finds tantalizing ways to punish me for my bad behavior. This is neither of those things. My heart smashes against the wall of my chest as she closes in and loops her arms around my neck.

"I really wanted to hate you," she says.

Fair point, but I'm loving the past tense.

"But I can't. I don't. And I'm tired of trying, when all I want to do is this."

It's not right. I shouldn't. *I'm not.* Stella is. She's choosing this. She's choosing *me.* Her lips find mine. The warm lights glisten on the surface of the pool, and then I close my eyes and forget everything but her. She told me what she wants, and I want it too, and that's all that matters. Her mouth is soft, and she presses her entire body into me, and I hold on to her, maybe too tight, maybe just tight enough. I slip a hand up the nape of her neck into her wet hair to protect her from the edge of the pool when I push her up against the concrete coping. Is the water boiling now? I pull away for a second to look at her before I lean in to nip at her neck. She's so fucking beautiful, I might break into a million pieces in this pool. Her friend will have to drain the water to find all the shards, like a shattered champagne flute. Stella digs her nails into my back, pulling me close, closer. I know she can feel my erection, and I don't care. I want her to know what she does to me and how fucking crazy she's making me as she grinds herself against my body. I undo the clasp to her bra and toss it on the pool deck before dipping my head to her breasts. She tips her head back, moaning as I take a taut nipple into my mouth, encircle it with my tongue, suck on it for one moment, and then move on to the other.

The noise she makes does something to me, wrecks my last shred of restraint. I slide one hand to her lower back and slip the other into her underwear. God, she's so soft. She's breathing hard in my ear while I bite her neck and stroke her into a frenzy. I hold her firm while she squirms against my hand, the sounds of pleasure from her lips almost sending me over the edge, and then she tenses against me, emits the sexiest little gasp of all time, and reaches for me.

I want her so fucking bad. I need her.

You're in her friend's pool, I remind myself.

"We're in my friend's pool," she says, her voice breathless in my ear, as if she's reading my thoughts.

"We should move," I agree. "Where should we move?" I look around wildly.

She bites her lip but doesn't answer. Is her expression contrite?

"I'm sorry. Did I get carried away?" I say, reality setting in. I can delay this gratification. I should. It's enough for me that I made her feel good.

"I think *I* did, actually." She slides over a little, putting some distance between us.

"We don't need to rush this," I tell her, and I mean it.

"Exactly. We both, ah, said what we needed to say. Cleared the air, right?" She passes her hand under the water. She's not looking at me. She reaches for her bra.

"Stella." I move over to her, wrap her in my arms, and kiss her gently. "To be clear, I just don't want this to turn into a quickie in your friend's Airbnb. I'm not going anywhere."

She softens. I help her put her bra back on, kissing my way over each shoulder to the clasp at the back.

"Let's just float for a bit," I say. "We can talk and swim, and then later we'll go back to the boat and go to bed."

We lay back on the water, our fingertips touching. "Just float and talk?" she says.

"I've missed so many conversations with you this past year."

"Are you going to break out your question list?" she teases.

"I only did that because I was nervous. You're this larger-than-life adventurer and I was just a boring failed writer."

"That's ridiculous. You weren't a failure."

"I felt like one . . . and then I met you."

"Yeah, well to be honest, I felt like a failed treasure hunter before we met. You're not the only one whose parents fucked them up and made them believe they were worthless. Now back to the list. I like the list. Ask me one."

"Alright." I think over the questions for just the right one. "What's your perfect day?"

She turns her head toward me in the water, and I know her answer is the same as mine.

"Today."

THIRTY-SEVEN

Stella

We walk back to the boat in a dreamy haze. Huck drapes an arm over my shoulder and we weave our fingers together.

"Do you know what your next book is going to be?" I ask.

When he doesn't answer, I peer up at him. He has a playful expression on his face.

"You better not write about the pool," I say, and bump him with my shoulder.

"I would never." He smiles at me, a real smile, with crinkly eyes. "They get it on in a salt marsh and get stung by jellyfish."

"Cute."

"Adorable," he says and plants a kiss on my hair. "Actually, I was thinking about turning our search for the *San Miguel* into a hunt for Blackbeard's treasure—but I don't know."

"No way," I say. "Teddy and I are obsessed with Blackbeard. We've done so much research over the years. All our material is back in North Carolina, but you're welcome to use it. You know, that first summer when we met, we found a Piece of Eight and we were convinced that it was part of a larger buried treasure belonging to Blackbeard on Corolla beach."

"It's not on your map?"

I shake my head. "No. Or maybe it is and I just haven't figured out the code. But the map is only Florida and some of the Caribbean."

"How'd you end up in Iceland searching for Gunnarsson's treasure, then?"

"I like to do my own research too. I guess I don't really know how to do anything other than search. I can't even take a real vacation."

"Me either."

"Seriously?"

"I was either on tour or doing research. I went to Amsterdam and spent the whole time scribbling in a notebook."

"Okay, well, if you could go somewhere, just to go—where would it be?"

"Bali maybe? No, wait—I know. But it's kind of embarrassing."

"I love embarrassing. Go."

"I'd like to go to Switzerland."

"I'm not getting how that's embarrassing," I say. "That seems very legit. Are you planning on some kind of *Sound of Music* tour or something? Do you want to wear lederhosen?"

"I want to see Iseltwald. It's where part of *Crash Landing on You* was filmed."

I stop walking and turn to him. "You watch K-dramas?"

"Some of them have phenomenal storytelling. Sometimes when I would get in my head about Casablanca and wasn't sure about how Clark and Rebecca would be, I'd watch a few episodes and bam, inspiration would hit."

"I'll admit *Crash Landing* was a really good show. Zoe and I cried our eyes out."

"When was that? I can't really picture her binge-watching something on Netflix."

"It was a while ago. She and I don't hang out the way we used to. She's either busy with work or Gus."

"Do you miss that?"

"It's fine, just different. We're all growing up. That's how it works, right?"

"I guess. A reviewer said that *Fortune Files* was the most mature thing I'd written."

I nod. I could see that. There was something different about the newest book, a quality that had nothing to do with me or the plot. It felt more authentic, maybe.

"I guess if I'm being honest," I say, "I sometimes feel a little left behind. Everyone's moving forward. Zoe's making partner and Gus is getting tenure and they'll probably get married. I'm still eating microwave dinners."

"You're fancier than me. I eat cereal dry and love peanut butter and jelly. I also put jelly on pizza since someone taught me that it was delicious."

"Oh really? Well, I can't afford jam. I can barely pay the rent for my shitty apartment."

"Isn't that changing too?" Huck asks. "I don't know how much what we found is worth, but it seems like it could definitely help you with the paycheck situation."

"Yeah."

"Do you think there's more? The Elephant's Heart? I know it's really important to you."

I nod. He pays attention to the things I tell him, even the things I don't fully say. "To be honest, I've imagined what it would be like to find the Heart so many times. My dad was so obsessed. He'd tell me stories about it when I was a kid, and he dedicated everything to it. It became the most important thing in his life. I guess I always thought that if I found it, I'd show him that I did what he and my mom couldn't do. It would force them to see that even though they didn't think I was worth sticking around for, they were wrong."

Huck stops walking. "They *were* wrong. They must know that, whether you find the Heart or not."

"Maybe." I lean into him. "I only know I really hope we find it. It should be there . . . the Heart and more. So much more if all of the Stolen Treasure was on the ship."

"But like, how much? Enough to fund a charity for a year, or like enough to do something really gross like buy an island and name it something obnoxious like Hulla . . . ?"

"Hulla?"

"Yeah, it's our couple name. The other combination is Stuck, which doesn't have the same vibe, for an island at least, unless we were going for a creepy-island vibe. Which, you know, I could be down. Maybe I'll switch genres and write horror. I might finally make it on the bookshelf at the cabin in Iceland. But first, I just want to know what amount of treasure we're talking about."

"I don't know if it's island money. Good thing, because those names are terrible. Anyway, the diamond's out there . . . it's just a matter of finding it."

"Well, we both know how good you are at finding things. You're also talented at climbing fences. That was new, and very much appreciated."

"You looked up my dress, didn't you?"

"I wish I could say I was a gentleman."

"That's a good line. You should use it in your next book."

"Really?"

"Definitely. It goes with the pirate theme you mentioned. And if anyone gives you a hard time about it—"

"I can just tell them that *the* Lucky Malone said to kindly fuck off?" The deck lights are lit on the *Lucky Strike* in the harbor and faint music emanates across the water toward the lane where Huck and I stand. I'm not ready to go back, not yet. Our friends will have questions.

"Ready to face the music?" Huck asks, reading my thoughts.

I shake my head. "I don't want to."

"Me either. I'm good right here."

"Yeah?"

"I'm really happy. What about you?"

"I'm happy too. Ask me another question," I tell him.

"What's the memory you hold closest in your heart? The one you treasure?"

I think back to the Northern Lights on the beach after finding Gunnarsson's treasure. The first time my mom showed me the map. My father's bedtime stories about the Heart. My Piece of Eight necklace on my eighth birthday. When Teddy and Zoe and Gus invited me to join them in Corolla. The first time I read the Casablanca Chronicles. Finding gold today with Huck.

I think of the moment we met in that bar.

"There's too many to choose," I admit. "What about you?"

He takes my hand. "Can I show you?"

We stroll back to the boat and wait nearby until the music stops and the lights go off, and our friends filter off to their rooms to sleep. Then we sneak back to Huck's bunk.

"Was this a ploy to get me alone in your room?" I ask him.

"I mean, the thought had crossed my mind," he says, grinning at me, "but actually I wanted to give you something."

I raise an eyebrow. His room is tidy and spartan. His laptop and papers are set on a small table. His bunk is made neatly, with tightly tucked hospital corners. I sit on it while he pulls something out of his messenger bag.

"My most treasured memory was meeting you in Iceland. I'd

gone to the Westman Islands that day, and we'd talked about the sheep? I had this. I meant to give it to you." He lifts his hand to show me the small sheep figurine.

My insides feel like cotton candy, sweet particles turning to clouds, spinning and spooling within me. He sets the sheep in my palm and sits next to me.

I stare at it for a moment. It's small and precious, made of tiny twigs and real wool that's soft against my skin.

"When we met, I was convinced the universe had sent me exactly what I needed. I knew my life would never be the same, and it isn't. To this day, it's still the best thing that's ever happened . . . meeting you. *You're* the best thing that's ever happened to me."

"Really?" I say, smoothing a finger over the sheep and setting it down on the trunk next to his bed.

"I was lost there, you know, utterly lost. And you found me."

I smile. "I am very good at finding lost things."

He leans down and kisses my neck gently, his hands finding the zipper of my dress. I hope we're going to finish what we started at the pool.

"We have to be quiet," I whisper.

Huck's fingertips trace over the bare skin of my back. "Whatever you want," he says. Together, we lay back, losing ourselves in the memories of what we once were, of what we could be again.

We lose and find each other over and over in the darkness of night until the sun crests over the horizon and I sneak back to my bunk.

THIRTY-EIGHT

Stella

It's one p.m., during a brief window before some weather I've been tracking to the southeast is likely going to hit us, when we discover the treasure debris field. I find a coin first, and then an uncut emerald the size of a child's fist. By three, Teddy pulls up what looks like several large uncut rubies and a full-size bar of gold, Gus's count is up to almost thirty coins, Huck has found another emerald and two coins, and my mesh bag is nearly full. No Heart yet. We are racing the clock before the squall line comes.

We'd been careful that the others didn't see us sneak back on deck, holding hands; they missed us kissing on the deck; they weren't there to witness Huck leading me back to his room and securing the door behind us, or me racing back to my bunk in the early morning, clutching the tiny sheep he'd given me in one hand and my gold dress in the other. Now everyone's too focused on salvaging as much as we possibly can before the storm to notice me and Huck. It's nice to enjoy stolen moments with each other while our friends focus on other happy things. This feels like something that belongs solely to me and him.

It almost feels too good to be true, pulling up priceless finds beside someone that I'm falling for . . . again.

Almost.

Gus calls me over the radio. "Ted and I are heading up."

"Everything okay?"

"Yeah, I'm going to need a fresh tank in a few," Ted says. "Perfect time for some water and a protein bar."

"I'm going to start cataloging what we've found so far," Gus says.

"Can you set up the dredge?" I ask. "It might speed things up given we don't have a ton of time before the storm gets here."

"Sure thing. Zoe already had the compressor out, so I just need to make a few connections and then I can send the dredge pipe down to you."

"Awesome. Huck, how's your air? Do you need to change out your tank too?"

"Nope, I'm good for a while longer. How about you?"

"I'm set, so I guess we'll continue to search down here."

Teddy and Gus slowly ascend, and I turn to Huck. I point to my face mask and then hold up three fingers, telling him to switch to channel three so we can talk in private.

"Hey," he says.

"Hi."

"Pretty slick with the hand signals," he tells me.

"If this treasure thing doesn't work out, I might have a future as a spy."

"Just a hunch, but I think the treasure thing might work out for you. Based on today."

I grin. "Do you know how a dredge works?"

"No, this will be my first time."

I laugh. "Interesting . . . So, basically the dredge is just a giant hose. Honestly, it's easy once you get the hang of controlling the hose. It will do most of the work. Just make sure to get a good grip."

"Stella. I'm trying extremely hard to take this seriously and be on my good behavior, but if I'm going to be able to do that, I'm going to need you to stop saying the word *hose* so provocatively."

"You're shameless," I say.

Gus lets me know that he's sending the dredge down. I show Huck how to wrangle it. "You're pretty good with that, ah, hose."

"Later," I tell him, giving him a playful tap on his wetsuit. "For now, get to work."

We continue until sundown, surfacing only once to change out our tanks and have a quick make-out session against the hull where we are pretty sure no one will see us. We are back into this so naturally. I don't stop to worry—I only obsess over the next time I can kiss him, the next opportunity for him to put his hands on me, the next question he'll ask.

The winds pick up late afternoon, and the weather for the next day doesn't look promising. We make the decision to head back to the harbor before the storm comes in. Huck finds a hotel with vacancies and books a set of rooms for us, and Teddy guides us into the mooring.

"I'll square us away here," Ted says. "Where are we booked?"

"Pier House," Huck says. "It's at number one Duval Street."

"Posh," Zoe says. "I like it."

It's a short walk to the resort, and I can tell before we even step inside to check in that this is the fanciest place I've ever stayed.

"They have room service and glass balconies," Zoe says. "Well done, Huck. Fully support your choice. This is *the* way to handle weather."

Gus turns in a circle in the lobby. "Riding out the weather in style." He holds out an arm to Zoe. "Shall we, my dear?"

"We shall." She turns back to us. "Enjoy! I'm going to go and have a nice hot shower and then order an embarrassing number of dishes from that room service menu."

The woman at the front desk slides two room keys to me and

Huck. He slides one back to her. "Actually, we still have one more member of our party coming. We're together."

We're together. Why do I love the sound of this?

"Got it," the woman said, giving us a sly smile. "Can I assist you with anything else?"

"Could we get a bottle of champagne sent up to us?" Huck asks.

"Of course."

I grin at her and weave my fingers between Huck's. "We're celebrating."

H uck's gotten us the penthouse. From the chairs on the balcony, there's a perfect view of the sun dipping into the sea and the moon rising into the sky before it's occluded by cloud cover of the impending storm. Teddy texts that all's well with the boat and he's all checked in. Do we want to go out and hit some of the bars down on Duval with him? We don't.

Instead, I nestle into Huck on the bed and we drink champagne and watch television.

"What are you going to do with your share?" he asks.

"Actually, I have no idea. I guess I never really thought it would happen."

"Never mentally spent the money?"

"Nope. It was never really about money for me, but you know that."

He nods and kisses me gently on the crown of my head. "I do. What about the next treasure? Do you have another one? Blackbeard, maybe?"

"I hadn't thought that far either. Right now I'm just trying to live in the moment."

"Me too," he admits. "I guess I also don't want to think about what happens after this when we both go home."

I turn my head from its resting place on his chest to face him. We've only just gotten back to a good place. I'm not ready to leave it. "Let's not think about that right now."

"How do you suggest that we shift our focus?" He bites his lip mischievously.

"Well, I could always start talking about dredge hoses again," I say, undoing the belt on his hotel robe.

He slides his hand under my matching robe, gliding his fingertips along the backs of my thighs to cup the curve of my ass, and drags me on top of him. I smile down at him, my hair falling over my shoulders, and we lock eyes. No matter how many times I've looked at him, I can never really get over the color of his eyes. I've never seen anyone else with eyes like Huck's. Actually, I've never met anyone else like him full stop. He carefully tucks the loose strands behind my ears and then I lower my face to his and our lips meet.

This isn't the first time that we've slept together. We had sex on the beach in Iceland, and that was magical before it ended. This is different. I wouldn't call it magic. I'm not under Huck's spell. There's a realism to it. Teeth that occasionally bump when we kiss because we're smiling or we get too carried away. We're not performing or trying to be perfect. We're learning each other, mapping each other's bodies, what we like, and what we *really* like, the sounds we make, the way a little adjustment changes everything. We don't rush this. I take him in my hands, study the way he responds, how he gets even harder when I hold on to him; he groans and his muscles tense when I bring him to me.

"You don't have to," he says, barely holding himself together.

I glance up at him, and then at his hand where it's gripping the duvet cover like he's hanging on for his life. "I'm in charge," I say.

"I totally support that," he manages.

Then I keep going. Afterward, he does the same for me, kissing his way southward from my neck to navel, tracing the soft skin where he'd used his fingers last night to push me over the edge.

"I love that sound you make," he says, "the little gasp. I want to make you do that again and again." I close my eyes.

When he produces a condom, he says, "I hope you don't think I was being presumptuous."

"I like a man who thinks ahead," I say, taking it from him.

He lets me run things, lowering myself down on him, finding the right rhythm, but then somehow even though I'm above him, he takes control when I want him to, pushing deeper, gripping my hips, matching me with long powerful strokes. His thumb slips between my legs and increases the sensation until I can barely think, barely exist. It feels so good like this, so good with him, and I . . . Oh my god.

Oh my god.

The fingertips of his other hand press into my ass, grinding me into him, and it's rough and exquisite and freaking amazing. His skin grows slick with sweat and we kiss, messily, our tongues tangling together as we both rocket higher and higher and then, well, when we finish together, I nearly black out. My vision goes sparkly and I let out a loud moan, and he groans against my skin before wrapping me tightly against him.

It has never been this good for me.

Ever.

He kisses me slowly, running his fingertips over my back, while we let our breathing slow and match each other. I curl in beside him, fitting my head in the crook of his arm, watching his chest rise and fall.

"Wow," he says.

I smile. "The author is speechless," I say. "Must've been pretty great for you too."

He laughs. "That's the understatement of the century."

THIRTY-NINE

Huck

The storm passes through during the night. Stella sleeps with her head against my chest, one leg thrown over mine, and I run my fingertips over her soft hair and skin. The gesture probably seems absentminded, but I was starved of her so much over the last year that I'm intentionally trying to satisfy my desperate need for contact with her. All of this feels right, good . . . It can't be wrong. I make a decision . . . maybe I'd already made it back when I decided to come on this trip, or even before that when I'd written *The Fortune Files*. I'm not going to let anything come between us again. It doesn't matter what happens. I'm in this, fully and for real.

Once I admit this to myself, I fall asleep instantly despite the howling wind and the rain whipping against the glass door to the balcony and the whir of Stella's gentle snoring.

In the early morning light, the storm damage appears to be minor. The streets are scattered with palm fronds and other detritus and there's some minor flooding on some of the low-lying areas, but other than that, everything is pretty much unscathed. The *Lucky Strike* is right where we left her in the harbor, a little messy but no worse for wear. Stella and the rest of the crew take care of the more critical checks of systems and drains, and then she and Zoe head to the market for some provisions while I clear the debris from the deck. Teddy joins me where I'm neatening some gear. He's still wearing the clothes he had on yesterday on the boat and his hair is greasy even though all the rooms at the resort had luxurious showers. Deep purple shadows beneath his eyes suggest he hasn't slept. Maybe it was the partying on Duval, or potentially something else that I don't want to consider . . . it seems not everything came through the storm unscathed.

"How's the research going?" he asks sharply.

The antagonism in his tone catches me off guard even though I should've been expecting it. I decide to play it cool.

"It's going alright," I say. I've filled two spiral-bound notebooks with notes for my new Blackbeard-inspired book, ideas for the plot and various scenes, technical lingo, snips of dialogue, but I don't want to tell him this.

The muscles in his jaw tense. He nods. "Did we give you enough material?"

"It's been an incredible experience so far," I say.

"But you're probably just about ready to go back and start writing now, right? I mean, it's only going to get stormier in the season, and how much tagging along do you really need to do to write a book? That's what Google is for, am I right?" He laughs, but I know Ted, and this isn't his real laugh. It's tight and hostile . . . practically a warning shot across the bow.

I play dumb. "Sure, but I thought I was staying the full month with you guys? That's what we agreed, right?"

"Okay, but we found the *San Miguel* so . . ."

"Exactly, why would I want to go now? It's so exciting discovering new relics each time we dive. Did you see that emerald? And Stella still needs to find the Heart diamond."

"Yeah, totally. I'm just thinking of how much we have to get done in the remaining time. We really don't have room for a rookie on our dives when we need to move quickly and the weather's all over the place. Low visibility, strong currents, those things require a certain experience level, and you'll slow us down. Plus, you're taking someone's spot when you go because somebody has to stay up top for safety. Zoe hasn't even gone out once."

"Well . . ." I run a hand through my hair, trying to think how to respond. I don't want to give Zoe's secret away. "I'd be glad to make myself useful in a different way."

"I bet."

I sigh. This comment is less shot-across-the-bow and more like a direct hit. We're not talking about me slowing down the treasure salvage or not being a skilled diver anymore. I really didn't want to do this.

"Look, bud, if you have something you want to say to me, just go ahead and fucking say it. I can handle it, I assure you."

"Can you, though? Handling criticism's never really been your forte, *Henry*."

This is a low blow and Ted knows it. Better than most people. That doesn't stop him from forging ahead; in fact, it's probably the reason why he said it. "You're in the way here. I don't know what more I can say on the subject."

And there it is. I'm in the way. I'm in *his* way.

I'm not sure why he says this. Maybe knowing me and my history makes him think I'll just bend to this. I'll give in. I'm not even nothing, I'm an obstacle, worse than nothing. I hate this feeling. But he knows that, and he's using that knowledge to try and control me, which pisses me off.

I narrow my eyes at him. "The way I see it, you're more of a liability than I am."

"Are you fucking for real, man? I'm a liability? I'm not the one who had a panic attack when I went snorkeling in five feet of water."

"No. You're the one that put both Stella and Gus in danger because you ignored all safety precautions, went way too deep, got yourself narc'd, and then ran out of air. But sure, think whatever you want about me."

"That kind of thing happens in our line of work—we have to push limits. If you had any experience, other than sitting behind a screen trying not to get your feelings hurt, you'd know that."

"Nope. Sorry, Ted. You were reckless. It shouldn't have happened and we all know it."

"Jesus, I never should've let you come. And I wouldn't have if I didn't feel sorry for you about your dad dying after you unleashed on him and your fiancée leaving you, and yeah, I still felt bad about what happened in high school, which you knew. But I think I've paid my debt, don't you? I mean, you did get the idea of Clark Casablanca from me."

It's a half-truth—we'd created Clark together one night on the roof when we were teens. A vague idea of a man who was everything we hoped we'd be someday.

"Ted, c'mon. We both know that's not why you let me come, and my debt is paid too."

"Yeah, fine. At least now I know my mistake and am in a position to fix it. We found the treasure, so we don't need your money anymore. You can just pack up your little notebooks and your laptop and go."

"I don't want to."

Teddy looks at me, incredulous. "Why? Because you figured out a way to weasel back into everyone's good graces, or is the sex with Stella just that good that you don't want to give it up? Don't look at me like that. You think we're all idiots, like it wasn't totally obvious that you booked the honeymoon suite for the two of you last night just so you could get laid."

"You're out of line, Ted. I honestly can't believe you're acting like this. You know what's between me and her isn't like that—it never was. You and I haven't been tight in a long time, that's true, but we were good friends once. And Stella? You guys are practically family, but you're talking about her with such fucking disrespect. You make this about money—you can't just buy your way out of things and treat your friends like they're your employees. You don't get to fire me because you suddenly are back in the black. Grow up."

"We were never friends. You were just some guy who I had to drag around because you couldn't make any friends of your own. If I didn't feel bad about the pond, I never would've let you come along."

"Did you even tell your friends that you made a bunch of bad investments and burned through your entire trust fund?" Ted doesn't answer, but his entire body goes rigid. It's enough to tell me that he must not have known that I knew. "The thing I don't understand is how the four of you proclaim to be so close and yet none of you tell each other the truth."

"Fuck you, Sullivan. You act so superior, like I should be freaking grateful to the magnanimous *New York Times* bestseller who funded the trip when I had a rough patch. It wasn't that long ago when you were the loser who had to hide from the entire world so you didn't have to hear how big of a failure you actually are, but yeah, sure, I'm so lucky that I have such a generous old pal who deigned to help me out."

It takes all of my energy to control my volume. "You know, I was happy to help and it felt good to be able to give something in return for this opportunity. But I didn't do it for you. I did it for her."

"You know what? Your dad and Vanessa were right about you. You are nothing. You think Stella won't realize it too?"

Ted's cruelty would've taken me out before. But he's wrong. Stella knows exactly who I am.

"All of this, the book, the trip, everything . . . it's all for her. Because I love her . . . I love her, Ted, and it doesn't matter to me if you hate me. I only care what she thinks, and I think she loves me too—"

That's when Ted hits me.

I don't remember him being much of a fighter in our school days, but he's older now and has packed on some muscle and a lot of rage, which he fully channels in my direction. Maybe that's why when his right fist connects with my jaw, I'm positive that I see the aurora borealis before I pitch over the edge of the boat into the harbor.

When I first pictured this trip, I'd smiled about the thought of Stella hurling me into the sea. I'd been amused. It felt like poetic justice that she'd send me flying, and a part of me hoped that if the score was even, maybe we might be able to have a fresh start. Being catapulted off a boat the size of the *Lucky Strike* is nothing to smile about I now know. Especially if you are propelled by the fist of a longtime friend who now seems very likely to be a *former* friend or maybe even an enemy. It hurts. My jaw, the rest of my body, all of it. I feel like an absolute freaking idiot. Gus throws one of those orange lifesaver rings at me and even though it's humiliating, I cling to that foam donut like my life depends on it while Gus pulls me toward the ladder by the attached rope. I'm just glad that Stella and Zoe are still in town picking up fresh supplies and lunch and aren't here to see this. Stella loves pie, and we were out, and for that, I will forever be grateful. I might recover from the embarrassment of getting my ass kicked by Ted, but I wouldn't be able to overcome her hearing that conversation, seeing me lose my cool and act like an asshole, and in case that wasn't enough, learning that I've been keeping things from her.

This is not new, keeping Ted's secrets. It started in high school, when he'd gotten hammered, stolen and crashed that golf cart, pinning me underneath it in the pond, and then there was what went down with him last year in Iceland. But the bankruptcy thing, I get it. Stella's always relied on him, and being the benefactor has, in a lot of ways, become his identity. Without money, he's just a good-looking guy with a fancy family who makes a lot of impulsive decisions, sleeps around, and drinks too much. Sure, he's fun, but he has the privilege and protection to not give a shit about anything and to just fucking frolic through life. It's amazing how once someone starts acting like a jackass their charisma doesn't seem so positive anymore, even if they're one of your favorite people.

"Get him out of here," Ted rages at Gus when I step back on the deck sopping wet.

"Teddy, man, calm down," Gus says. "Catch me up at least. All I know is you guys were having a heated discussion and Huck went for an unplanned swim."

I stretch my jaw. It's sore, but it doesn't feel broken. Gus catches this movement, and I watch understanding appear in his expression.

"Did you hit him?" he asks. "We don't fight on the *Lucky Strike*. Those are the rules. Other crews fight, but not us. We're a team."

Ted shakes his head. "*We* are a team," he says, pointing a finger back and forth between himself and Gus. Then he points to me. "He's not on our team."

"What? Why? This season's been great. He's been picking up stuff really quick, helping out—"

"What world are you living in, Gus? You're on another planet.

This guy goes and takes Zoe's spot diving every single time, and you don't even seem to give a shit."

Gus looks at me, lips pressed together. He tilts his head back. "Yeah, maybe I am distracted, but I'm not pissed at Huck. Zoe's not going out because she's pregnant; the doctor told us she's not supposed to do any scuba diving."

Ted's face goes slack. "I didn't know that. Why didn't you tell me?"

"Well, we were keeping it to ourselves for now, but it wasn't like it was a mystery. She's been wandering around in those caftans when you know normally my girl likes sporting as little clothes as possible. That should've told you something. She's also been scarfing down saltines and guzzling ginger ale this whole trip. I'm not shocked you didn't pick up on it, to be honest. You haven't exactly been yourself this time around, Ted. You've been preoccupied and drinking more than any of us would consider healthy and borderline obnoxious. So yeah, we didn't feel like the timing was right to share our news. You and Stella aren't into change, something's up with you, clearly, and this is a big change."

"Okay, but you told *him*?"

"Zoe did," I say. "I don't think it was intentional. Anyway, it was probably easier to tell someone who wasn't a core member of your crew. I don't really matter."

"True," Ted says, and I hate that it stings worse than my jaw. "I guess it's good that you filled in for Zoe, but that doesn't change anything. I want you off my boat."

Gus's brow furrows.

I'd been avoiding Ted's eyes up until this exact moment. I freaking hate confrontation. Because of my dad, it makes me feel sick and threatened, and usually I just shut down and stare at the floor because that feels safer than seeing yourself reflected in the eyes of someone who thinks you're terrible or worthless, or someone who was your friend and now they really just want to punch you in the face . . . again. But I don't see any of that when I look at Ted.

His eyes are glassy and red. His expression looks like a deflated soufflé I tried to make while baking my way through my writer's block era—defeated and sad.

Broken.

I have no idea what to do.

FORTY

Stella

I beat Zoe back to the harbor after finishing my half of the shopping list in record time. I'm so invested in planning the best spot to wait for her arrival and launch my full gloating campaign, I almost miss Huck heading toward me. I beam at him for a second before I spot the suitcase he's rolling behind him down the dock. I can barely process what I'm seeing. My reusable grocery bag slips out of my hands, spilling the items I'd bought for the next few days of meals on the wooden slats. An orange rolls past me off the pier and drops into the water. I watch it bob and float away before I turn to him.

"I don't understand," I say. "You're leaving?"

"It's not what it looks like."

"It looks like you're packed."

"I know, but I'm just moving off the boat."

My mind is racing, and I realize I've started pacing. "We just started salvaging. You remember, right? The bars of gold and massive emeralds? The Elephant's Heart Diamond? And we're working together so well. It's like we've all been diving together for years. Everyone loves having you here. I just don't get it."

"Stella, I promise, I'm not leaving." He reaches out and cups my face with his hand. "Yes, I think for everyone's sake, it would be better if I didn't go out on the *Lucky Strike* anymore. But I'm not going back to New York, I'm staying in Key West. I've rented a little bungalow in Truman Annex for the whole summer. You can stay with me whenever you want."

I shake my head. I'd barely gotten over the pain of what happened in Iceland, and even though I hear his words and see the earnestness in his expression, I don't trust them.

I don't trust him. I thought I did. I thought I *could* . . . but I was wrong. What could have made him want to walk away from me again?

My life is maps and instincts and people I love choosing to walk away from me toward something more important every single time. My throat tightens.

"I feel so stupid," I say.

"Please don't. You're not. I'm not getting this right. I know what I'm telling you doesn't make a lot of sense right now. I don't know what to say."

"I don't feel this way because I can't understand you. I should've known you would do this, that's it. But the timing. God. I just let you close again, and this feels like history repeating itself. You don't know what to tell me?" My voice crescendos. "Tell me *something*. Explain. You owe me that. Because all I see is that you're leaving, and asking for my blessing or something, but really it just feels like this is you breaking my heart again."

He stares at his feet and that's almost the worst part of this. "Meeting you, searching for treasure with you . . . it's been one of the greatest adventures of my life. I've been incredibly lucky . . . I know that. I didn't want to break your heart then and that's not what I'm doing now. I swear."

"That's not an explanation."

"I know it isn't. I just can't yet. But listen, you'd like the house

I rented. It's a two-story house on Admirals Lane, white with a bright blue door and shutters. You can't miss it. There's an old-fashioned light on the front porch; I'll leave it on for you. Come whenever you want."

I shake my head. It sounds so promising, but it isn't real. It's like one of his books. I'm trying not to say the words that I know will break things so badly that they'll never be fixed. But I can't stop myself. The hurt and disappointment are too strong, fusing into fury in my chest. I found the Stolen Treasure. I am this close to finding the Heart. And nothing has changed. I'm still the one everyone leaves.

"I can't. I can't do this again. If you go, it's for good," I say.

"No, don't say that. You want the truth? Okay. Let's go talk to Ted—"

"I don't care what he says. He's not going to win me over for you. It won't work. I tried to give this another chance. I don't think it's too much to ask that I could have someone who wants to stay by me, who can give me a little stability, who won't always leave me waiting for the other shoe to drop."

"I still want to be that for you."

"Leaving a porch light on isn't enough."

He nods. I want him to stop looking at me with that sad expression, the one that makes me believe that there's something left to fight for here, that I wasn't wrong twice, but I know better. There's nothing. Maybe there never was. Tears fill my eyes.

I don't know. I don't know anything anymore.

The only thing I'm sure of is that Huck Sullivan is a good storyteller. Better than anyone knows.

He made me believe.

Even now, he looks just as broken as I feel . . . another story he's spinning for me.

I wipe my tears and pick up the groceries I'd dropped on the pier and head back toward the boat. I can't be near him anymore, trying to hold myself together before I break apart like a ship on a reef in a hurricane. Years from now, someone might salvage the relics of my heart from this very spot, but in this moment, I walk away from him.

"Stella," Huck calls. "It's not what you think. Please, let me find the right words to explain."

The distance stretches between us and I want to stop and end the painful tearing that comes with the separation, but I won't. I can't. I don't look back.

I walk down to my quarters and shut the door behind me. My hands are trembling. A tide of emotion and hurt swells inside of me, and I shake with the effort to hold it in. I spot my copy of *The Fortune Files* on the little table next to my cot. In one swift motion, I pick it up and launch it across the room. It smacks against the wall and clatters to the floor along with the tiny Icelandic sheep Huck gave me, which it knocked off the shelf.

I crouch down to look at the carnage. The figurine's head has broken off and I'm immediately furious at myself for breaking it. The book landed open beside it, and I pick it up to throw it in the trash along with the dismembered sheep. I don't even want them in my room. I need every trace of him gone.

I thought he'd written me our love story.

I got it wrong. I sit on the floor and lean against the wall while I cry.

He made me believe that he loved me . . . that this time was different.

I let him make a fool out of me. Again.

I glance down at the page the book is open to. Ripping it apart page by page won't change the truth but it might be cathartic. A tear drops on the paper and the words come through blurry, but still there.

I have this urge to take care of Lucky, to greet her with coffee and those pastries she likes with poppyseeds and the moon in the name. While we eat, I'll confess my feelings. Tell her what I want—to be with her no matter the cost. She has upended my life, irrevocably, in the very best way. I unwrap my arm from her, carefully, and rise from the blanket we share. It's fast, I know that. And even though it surprises me, I'm sure of my feelings. The fact that I feel this way again is a miracle in itself; the purity with which I recognize it and don't question it is another thing altogether.

I used to think of myself as a lucky man, but that stopped a while ago when my dad died, and Veronique left me and I lost myself. I lost everything. But I feel lucky today. I know now that losing the people who don't care about you leaves space for the ones who will change your life. Their absence left space for her.

The sound of crunching gravel startles me out of my thoughts. Timothy stands a few yards away, shrouded in a black peacoat, thermos in his hand. Steam rises from it. He lifts his chin to acknowledge me and I step away from my spot next to Lucky to meet him.

"Hey, man," I say.

"You guys stayed out here on the beach all night?" he asks.

"Wasn't intentional. We got talking and just kept talking." I wonder if he can tell that I love her. Does emotion radiate from me like the sun on the waterfall's mist?

Tim's eyes drift over to where Lucky still slumbers, her bare shoulder just visible in the sleeping bag. "Must've been quite a conversation." The weight of his gaze presses on me.

I lift my shoulders a fraction. "You know Lucky," I say.

"I do." There's a sharpness in his voice that's new.

He stares out at the beach long enough for me to wonder if he's going to speak again.

"You've been spending a lot of time with her," Tim says finally. "Have you forgotten why you're here?"

"She's incredible." I can't stop myself from grinning. "When I'm with her, I can see a whole new life for myself. It doesn't matter who I've been or where or the things I've done."

"That's great. But you shouldn't put her on a pedestal. Things put on pedestals tend to fall and break."

"I won't let that happen."

"I think we all know that that's exactly what you're going to do." The menace in his tone is impossible to miss. Still, I almost don't recognize it at first. And maybe I understand a little. I'm flawed. I've done bad things. Unforgivable things. Tim knows this. But I've tried to make things right, be a better man. Lucky made me want to change.

"You're not right for her."

"What makes you say that? We've been having a good time together."

"This is a trip, man. It's a rush being around her, right? She's 100 percent committed to what she's doing, to the hunt. I get it. Her enthusiasm is contagious, inspiring. You're probably already planning on joining her next expedition, only without her crew, just the two of you and the open sea."

I shift as his words hit a little too on the nose.

"How long before you do exactly what you always do?"

My body turns cold.

"At the end of the day, you'll always be the guy who messes up and disappoints people and leaves them holding the bag."

"I'm different. I'll be different for her."

"You're not different. You're the same old guy you've always been. Finding that treasure was a rush. But you got lucky, Finn. We've been hunting for years and never come close. And you spend a few days tagging along and suddenly you're the one helping her extract a trove from behind a waterfall? It's a onetime thing. Beginner's luck. And when that's over and it's the off season or you keep coming up empty, this feeling, it won't be the same. You'll find out that she's just a regular girl, not some magical creature. What then?"

"Then we live happily ever after," I say, glancing back at her. Her face is still peaceful in sleep.

"What, you're planning a future with her? Long-term plans?" Tim's laugh is acid. "You think you love her?"

I want to argue, I don't think, I know . . . I know, don't I? That's why I feel more alive than I have in years, why my heart beats fast when she's near me. The reason I shared those things I haven't told anyone. Why else would I be figuring out how to walk away from the life I've always known, ready to risk it all for a future with her? These feelings aren't fiction.

Realization washes over me like the rough waves behind us. Tim and Lucky, a collection of moments, of long glances and touches on the shoulder, the waist, the back; of knowing smiles, inside jokes, and borrowed clothes, come together to play on a reel. There's no denying it.

Tim is in love with Lucky. My oldest friend and the woman of my dreams.

From the look on his face and the sad rage in his voice when he speaks to me, he has been for a very long time. I should've known. That's why he never mentioned her to me. She was only for him.

He must sense my understanding, because his face, the tone of his voice, every single aspect of him changes. The heat and color, even the air, seem to drain out of him. He takes a tentative step toward me. "You know I've never asked you for anything, Finn. And after everything that happened, I really do want you to be happy, but not like this, not with her. Please."

I feel like an asshole.

My heart falters as I realize that not only is my oldest friend head over heels in love with Lucky, but it's possible that this woman who has captivated my body and soul and made me believe in a future might just be in love with him too. And why wouldn't she be? He's been the one by her side. He's never tried to steal from her or told her lies. He's a good man. One who has never left her. And will make sure that she's never alone or in need. He would even betray his best friend to protect her.

And I, well, he's right that I don't deserve her. I'm the guy who always lets people down.

I'm nobody's hero.

"You're not good enough for her, Finn."

I look back at her one more time. Memorizing the way she looks, the exact placement of each freckle on her nose, the precise location of the tattoo on her neck, the movement of her pale hair in the ocean breeze. I gently pull the sleeping bag up so that her shoulder is covered, and then I do the only thing I can do, because I love her, I love them both.

"It's for the best," Tim says to me as I pass by him. "We both know it."

And I believe he's right in that moment. It's only that knowledge that allows me to keep breathing as I walk away.

I shed a tear with each step. One for every year we might have passed by each other's side if I had been a better man, a stronger man, a braver man. If I had been different, or good, or right . . . but I'm not. So I let her go.

I know she'll find happiness, even if I'm not there to witness it, now that she's free.

She's free. This is what I tell myself as the distance between us grows.

She is free . . . And me? I'll carry her, and what could've been, with me for the rest of my days.

Oh my god.

FORTY-ONE

Stella

In all the years I have known Teddy, I've never been truly furious with him. He's made me mad a million times probably, with his carelessness or his antics. Nothing like this. He's never hurt me before. But this betrayal rips me in two and fills me with such anger, I feel like imploding.

I find Teddy sunning himself on the deck, hat covering his face. I knock it off with a swift flick of my hand.

He jumps to his feet. "What gives, Stell? Gus said I had an hour to nap before we get back to the salvage site."

"You said he was fickle and wanted to find his next adventure. That he didn't care about me. But you lied. You told him to go, didn't you?" I choke out.

"What are you talking about?" Teddy asks. "What did Huck say?"

"He didn't say anything! I figured it out . . . it's all in the book. I'm Lucky, and he's Finn . . . You're Tim. And you're the reason he left me behind, admit it." Even as I speak the words, I can't fully fathom them.

Teddy hangs his head, but he doesn't say anything. He doesn't have to. The guilt in his body language says it all. But I still don't understand. How much of what Huck wrote was true?

"Why?" It comes out as a wail.

Teddy still doesn't answer, and rage swells up in me again, lava hot and liquid. It threatens to spew out.

"Tell me why. You owe me that, Ted. Because I've been going around and around in circles, and I can't figure it out."

Teddy fixes his hat on his head. His face is splotched with red, and his eyes are glassy. I can't tell if he's been drinking again or if this is emotion.

I push him. Not hard, just one sharp shove, to snap him out of it. "Tell me!" I yell.

"I was losing you," he says, voice strained.

The boat pitches slightly beneath us and I have to grab the rail to keep my footing. No. This makes no sense. I think back to the scene from Huck's book. The confession between the two men. It couldn't be true. I stare at him.

"Don't you understand, Stella? I was going to lose you to him, and I couldn't, I couldn't."

Confusion softens me. "You're my best friend," I say, "you could never lose—"

"I don't want to be your friend," he shouts.

I recoil, and his face twists at my reaction.

He tries to pull back, regaining control of his voice. "All these years, I've tried to let friend be enough for me. I wanted to be content just being your pal and going on our trips. Why do you think I bankrolled everything? Then we went to Iceland and Zoe and Gus got together and I thought, why not, all these years those two were right next to each other, being just friends, like us, and then they were so much more. It seemed so easy. I thought maybe you and I could have that too. That Iceland was my chance, I'd tell you how I feel and that would be that. I went to the bathroom to give myself a mirror pep talk and I send you to the bar to buy the drinks and in comes fucking Sully. Of all the people who could have been there at that moment, it had to be him. My friend. You never want to be with anyone, and then you go and fall for him."

I wince.

"I swear I tried so hard to be satisfied with just being beside you, and it nearly destroyed me. I wanted . . . I want to be more than that. I want to be the guy who lights you up from the inside out. That you want to spend the night on the beach with. When we get back from trips I want you to come home with me. And in one day I could see it on your face; you were already gone."

"Why should I believe you? You were always with a new girl."

"Yeah, and every time I wished it was you. Every time. But I knew you weren't ready for a relationship. Only I knew that. I understood what your family stuff did to you, and I was patient, and I waited. I was biding my time until you were ready. And then Huck appears and everything changes. Suddenly he's the thing that makes you believe that love isn't trash."

"None of this makes sense. Maybe before, but if things changed in Iceland, *you* didn't! You hooked up with our diving guide."

"Why do you think I got hammered and came home early? Nothing happened."

I turn from him, letting the wind carry his words away. "And that's supposed to change things? You lied to me."

"I've loved you as long as I have known you," Teddy says, closing the distance between us. "I've loved you since you snatched my wallet and thought I didn't see. I've loved you since you showed up on that beach."

I swallow as Teddy takes my hand in his. I think about how quiet he's been this trip, the stupid risks, the excessive drinking. I knew something wasn't right, but I never would have thought that it would be this. I feel sick. How could I have missed it all this time? I turn to peer at his face. He looks the same, but he feels like a stranger, someone I don't know or understand. "I've always loved you, Stella," he says.

For an instant, I let myself wonder if there was ever a moment that I loved Teddy like that too. It's impossible now. Maybe it always was. I do love him, but not in the same way, not in the way that he's talking about, and I can't get past the lies. He loved me while he paid for these trips I wasn't even sure he wanted to go on; while he watched me go off with strangers for a night of fun; stood by as I fell in love with Huck and then told Huck to leave?

I wrestle my hand out of his grip. "You don't love me. Maybe you love the idea of me, Ted. But you couldn't. If you did, you would have never asked someone to wound me in the worst way possible."

"C'mon, Stella, I didn't—"

"Do you know what I felt like on that beach? As if someone took me up to the top of the world and showed me everything beautiful, everything I could have, everything I've wanted, and then pulled the ladder from beneath my feet. I plummeted. I haven't felt so alone since my dad abandoned me."

The color drains out of Teddy's face. "I didn't think of it like that."

"Of course you didn't. You've never been left behind. You've never had to face the world entirely alone. When my dad left, I didn't know where I was going to sleep or if I could find food or if I was safe. I didn't know what would happen. I was so afraid. And devastated. The whole world was going on with their stupid volleyball and their splashing in the surf like nothing happened, while I lost the only person I had left who cared about me at all. Or who I *thought* cared about me. You have a family. You never have had to worry about food or money. Your entire life has been this privileged protected existence. The first time you think you're not going to get what you want, you blow it all up. If you can't have me, no one can, is that it? That's not love, Teddy. Not even close."

"Stella. That's not true. I lost it."

"What?"

"My money. I lost it all. That's why Huck was here—I couldn't fund the trip. He reached out and he was focused on his book and he had all this cash, and I didn't want to let you down. I didn't want to risk having him here, but I didn't want to disappoint you. I know how much these trips mean to you."

"No," I say. "You don't get to act like you made some noble sacrifice because of your feelings for me. I don't want any more of your lies. I've heard enough."

"I'm sorry, Stella. I never meant to hurt you, I swear. I would never do that. I was just desperate."

"Maybe that's true. But you *did* hurt me, Teddy." I swipe at a tear that is sliding down my cheek. "When my dad disappeared, I couldn't figure out what I'd done. All I knew was that for some reason I wasn't even worth saying goodbye to. Then I met Huck and I felt like I'd met someone who saw me, who knew the dark stuff inside, my doubts and fears, and he still wanted me. I thought, maybe I was wrong. Maybe I am enough for the right person, that the sun could rise and set with me for him, and likewise. Then he left me too. It confirmed my worst fears—that I am not someone worth sticking around for. And then, he came back and we had another chance and I was so close to happiness, I was, it was right there in my hands. You have no idea what it took for me to risk my heart again. Now he's gone. It hurts more than the first time."

Teddy's expression is pained. "I didn't know that."

"You're the reason why he left this time too, right? You kicked him off the boat." I shake my head, swallowing my anger. "I hated Huck for leaving me, and it was so hard to forgive him. He's not innocent here and he was stuck between you and the person he fell for. But you, what you did was worse. You made him go. You forced his hand. You used your connection with him to break my heart. Every moment of heartache, of blaming myself for not being worthy of sticking around . . . was because of you." I pull in a deep breath.

"But we finally found what we were searching for, Stella! What we've been seeking all of these years. We found it."

"No. I still haven't found the Heart. Even without it I thought I'd found what I was looking for, but now . . . I don't believe anything. We should've left it all at the bottom of the ocean. Better yet, I wish I'd never started searching."

"You don't mean that. Not now. Not when it's within our reach!" He turns to gesture at the sea around us.

The boat pitches and Teddy struggles to absorb the motion.

I clench the deck rail tight in my fist. "Actually, I do. When this trip is over, so is all of this. So are we. I never want to see you again."

FORTY-TWO

Huck

"O h man, you are a real dumbass." Zoe, truth-teller, lawyer, and future awesome mother, has my cell number. I don't remember giving it to her, but I'm glad when she calls even if she starts off strong with a string of insults.

"Fuck. I know."

"A quaint little house with a blue door and a porch light you'll leave on for her? This isn't *Pete's Dragon* and you singing "Candle on the Water" to your lost ship's captain. You broke her heart last year, and now you're doing it again for a really stupid reason."

"It's not that simple. There's nuance."

"Yeah, if nuance has developed a drinking problem recently and has a long history with you. You could've told her about Teddy. Better yet, you could've stayed and fought for her."

"I don't think so. I didn't want to ruin their friendship."

"You think that they're coming out of this unscathed? You're an even bigger dumbass than I thought. What exactly, may I ask, was your plan?"

"I didn't have one. I guess I thought maybe she'd read the whole book and understand about Iceland. And honestly, when Ted agreed to let me come, I hoped he might have moved on.

Though it became pretty apparent pretty fast that he hadn't. I tried to stay away from her, keep things professional, but I couldn't. I can't explain Stella. She's like a force of nature that's impossible to try to overcome, like gravity or magnetism. If I'm being really honest with myself, I don't want to overcome her. I don't feel very good about myself most of the time. I'm either failing or waiting for things to fall apart as they inevitably do when I'm involved. She makes me brave enough to try anyway, even if I might not succeed. And if I don't, it doesn't matter. At least not to her."

Zoe sighs loud enough for it to register through the phone line. "Look, maybe it's not a completely lost cause. Come back, Huck. Tell the truth. Stand up for what you want and let her choose."

"What if she doesn't choose me?"

"Then at least you'll know that it was her letting you go, not you making the decision for her."

FORTY-THREE

Stella

Teddy is a seasoned diver. He knows not to dive alone, not to dive when his senses are dull and he's tired, to stay out of the water when the winds are strong and the seas are rough and visibility is low. But he's already tested his limits once this trip. And then we fought.

And now . . . his gear is gone.

My words from earlier echo in my head above the howl of the wind. *I never want to see you again.*

Gus and I look at each other for a single beat, one squeeze of my heart, and launch into action. Buoyancy compensators are pulled on, feet shoved into fins, masks grabbed. We check each other's tanks and then we step off the boat and plunge into the churning waves below to find him. We don't hesitate. We don't think about the risk.

We are seasoned divers too. We know it's not safe to go, but what we are is so much more than that. We are Teddy's people. His friends, his family. The people he loves. The people who love him. Even if he hurt me, even if *I* hurt him.

It's all going to be fine because it has to be.

We head straight to the site—it's the only place he'd go.

The visibility is shit; clouds of sand make it hard to see my own hands in front of me. Gus and I work to stay in sight of each other, but we can barely manage that. I pull out my flashlight, hoping it will help. The rhythmic sound of my breathing does little to drown out my panicked thoughts.

I never should have said those things to Teddy. Teddy, who has been taking care of me for years. Bringing me into his family. Supporting my dreams. Struggling in silence. He loves me and I was vicious.

FORTY-FOUR

Stella

I always say I've made a life out of finding lost things. People think what I do is all about adventure and the thrill of holding something precious and valuable in your hands.

This isn't like that.

When I finally locate Teddy, he's almost out of air. His body is limp, kelp-like as it undulates in the invisible currents. It's dark down here. I need to work quickly, but my hands are shaking and my mind is chaos. I press my secondary to his mouth and wrap my arms around him. This is why we train, because in situations like this you don't have time to think or make a decision. I need to act. I deflate my BC and inflate his to start our controlled ascent. My training tells me I can't help him if I'm not okay, but I can't be okay if he's not. I need to get him to the surface.

"Gus, Zoe," I yell into the radio. "I found him! He's unconscious and almost out of air. I've put him on my secondary and have started an emergency ascent."

"Roger, I'll meet you up there," Gus says. "Zoe, make sure you've got the one-hundred-percent oxygen ready, and radio the Coast Guard."

We still don't know how bad off Teddy is, but I can't fool

myself. I found him unconscious, even if I'm not able to admit it yet because admitting it would make me panic in the dark water or want to stay down here where nothing is real because what if I can't help him now? What if I was too late?

What if he's already gone?

The sound of my controlled breathing reverberates in my ears. I still need to slow down. I squeeze my eyes shut. *What have I done?*

"I already made the call," Zoe says, her voice thick.

I'll take them back, those words I said. My anger. My pain. I'll bury them all at sea along with what's left of the *San Miguel*. None of it matters anymore. I don't even care about the Heart diamond or the *San Miguel* or my mother's map. I'd give them all up if it just means I have my friend back, safe and sound; if we get up on deck, and he sputters some water and takes a few minutes of oxygen and then comes around; if he's his normal self within a couple of hours, and tomorrow he's back to playing steel drum music and shaking his butt on deck and ruffling my hair like he used to. The Teddy who has always been there.

He tried to warn me.

Diving too deep, drinking too much. Thinking back, there were signs that Teddy wasn't okay. Were there signs that he loved me too? I don't know. I can't think about it now because it hurts too much.

I never want to see you again.

The memory thunders in my mind, but it's lighter here closer to the surface, and I see Gus and I push the thoughts away and focus on what we need to do. He's waiting to guide Ted the rest of the way to the boat. I want to hang on to Teddy, but I let Gus take hold of him and can only watch as he powers toward the boat on his back with Ted tucked under his arm. In the distance, Zoe's red caftan billows in the breeze like a warning sign.

I take a couple of seconds to collect my breath and then I swim after them. Moments later, I pull myself up onto the deck, chest heaving, face slick with tears. It's hard to see what's happening with Ted. Gus and Zoe crouch down next to him on the deck. I fling off my mask and gear and drop down next to them.

"Is he breathing?" I ask.

Gus nods and I let out a relieved breath. "He's alive." He wipes roughly at the tears spilling from his eyes with the back of his fist.

Alive but not awake. We don't have any idea what kind of shape he's in.

Zoe relays everything Gus says to the rescue chopper that's on its way from Trauma Star in Key West. Teddy's pulse, respiration rate, the log from his dive computer. I hear the approaching helicopter, its rotors sounding like a racing heart and then thunder as it gets closer. They lower a basket stretcher down for Gus to load Teddy into, lift it up, and then they fly away. None of this seems real. It can't be.

We pull up anchor and Gus sets the *Lucky Strike* at full throttle on a heading toward shore. No one speaks on the trip back to Key West harbor.

Our dive gear is strewn across the deck. The oxygen tanks and tubing and masks mark the spot where Teddy lay. I sit in the center of this chaos, unable to move, unable to think. The sun dips down into the sea, and I start to shiver in my wet clothes. Zoe wraps a towel around my shoulders and leaves her hands there a little longer than she normally would. By the time we reach land, it's dark even though Gus pushed the boat as hard as he could.

Zoe emerges from below deck with a duffel bag, just as Gus and I finish tying up the boat.

"I got you a change of clothes, babe, and your wallet, toothbrush. And I grabbed a couple of things for Ted."

Did she just say something to me about my things? I don't know. I'm not thinking straight.

"They're taking him to Mariners Hospital in Tavernier. They've got a hyperbaric chamber there if he needs it." She turns to me. "Stella, you coming?"

I almost don't hear her from my daze. I shake my head.

Zoe sighs. "Come on, I know you guys had an argument, but that doesn't negate over a decade of friendship, does it?"

No. It does not. But we didn't just argue, we blew our friendship apart. I did. I wounded him, and he made me question everything I've known over the last ten years. If he's up, he won't want to see me. And if he's not . . .

"I should stay with the boat," I say.

She gives a short nod.

"Call me and let me know how he is?"

"We will," Gus says when Zoe doesn't answer me.

I can hear her as they walk by on the dock. "She should be with us, Gus."

"It was a lot, finding him. She's just having a hard time. You know Stella. She'll come when she can."

"I know. I just don't want to leave her alone."

"Then don't."

I close my eyes. I can't hear her response; they're too far away. *I am alone, Zoe*, I think. *I always am.* Maybe it's better that way and everyone knows it but me?

I sink back down to the deck and wrap myself in the damp wool blanket we'd used to keep Teddy warm while we waited for the helicopter. The night sky is black and cloudless, dotted with trillions of stars. I feel so small and insignificant. So many stars to wish on for my friend before exhaustion finally drags me into a fitful sleep.

FORTY-FIVE

Huck

When Zoe calls me a second time, I think it's just to yell at me again and I answer right away to let her. I am not expecting her words.

"There was an accident." She speaks at a pace that is almost unintelligible, but I manage to catch enough that I'm fully aware of just how serious this situation is. Ted lost consciousness while he was diving. Stella found him. He's being airlifted to a bigger hospital in the northern Keys and Stella's by herself on the boat. They'd had a fight. It isn't good. Even though my mind races, the world seems to slow down. I text Jim and within minutes he sends the information for a hired car that will take Zoe and Gus north of Marathon to the hospital.

I'm already sliding my feet into my shoes and halfway to the front door before I end the call with Zoe. I'd go with them, I say, but I have another place I need to be.

"Take care of our girl," Zoe says.

"I will." I burst through the front door of the rental and race down the lamplit streets, past palm trees and shadows of matching historic houses, through Truman Annex toward the wharf. I'm not used to running; my lungs burn and I get a stitch halfway;

or is it the sensation of my soul wrenching that I'm feeling instead? I'm not sure. I can barely think as I sprint toward the harbor.

This is exactly what I wanted to avoid. Exactly why I chose to leave, why I carried the troubling truth alone instead of sharing it.

I never wanted to come between Stella and Ted, or strain their friendship, or cause anyone pain. They are both so important to me—I couldn't stand the thought of causing them any harm. Sometimes speaking up, even if it feels right, has heart-wrenching consequences . . . I'd learned that lesson the hard way. I didn't know how to navigate the situation and thought it was better just to put some distance between us all. Like that was a solution. I'd been running away, trying to prevent the damage. Somehow, I'd managed to make it worse.

None of that matters now.

They fought. She found him.

She's alone.

I want to wrap her in my arms and keep her safe, make sure she doesn't blame herself, take away the pain she must feel—let her know that everything will be alright, but will it? I shouldn't make promises I can't keep. That's what my dad always used to say. *Under promise and over deliver, Henry. You always seem to do the opposite and disappoint.* Even his voice in my head, the words he used to belittle and control me, don't matter now. He's gone, but Stella is not. She's here, and she may not want me, but she needs *someone.*

When I reach the *Lucky Strike*, I'm winded and drenched in sweat. I almost don't see Stella at first. She's wrapped in a wool blanket, curled into herself on the deck, fast asleep in the center of the fallout. Her hair is a mass of wild pale waves that remind me of how she looked that morning before sunrise on the Iceland beach. Even then, I'd been trying to prevent something like this from happening. I was fortune's fool, I guess. Was this always going to end with Stella, Ted, and me smashed to bits? If I'd known it then, would I have still talked to her in the bar, followed her around Iceland, come to Key West?

Yes. I would choose her a million times, more than that, more than the collection of freckles on her skin, all the stars in the sky.

I stoop down and even in the dim light, I can see her eyes are swollen from crying, her lashes crusted with salt. My hand trembles as I reach out and smooth the hair away from her face with my fingertips.

She slowly wakes and stares at me, bleary-eyed.

"You're here."

"Hi, sweetheart," I say, my voice low and gentle. She blinks at me, and then her entire face crumples. I drag her into my arms. "I'm here," I whisper. "I'm not going anywhere."

It's hard to see her like this—Stella, the strongest person I know. She carries a deep hurt from her family, and she never gives up searching. I'm not completely certain why, but I have a feeling that if she stopped, she'd have to face that they're really gone. She blames herself for it; she blames herself for a lot of things she shouldn't. And Stella is tough and brave and brilliant and relentless, but she's vulnerable too. She's been broken apart and had to piece herself back together, and sometimes things happen and she takes on water and feels alone. Ted, Zoe, and Gus have been her whole world for so long.

I wanted to be a part of it. To orbit around her.

I settle for holding her tight while she sobs. This is what I can give her, arms wrapped tightly, quiet comfort, being present. After a long time, she sits up.

"I couldn't go with them to the hospital," she tells me. She lifts her shoulders and lets them fall. "What if he dies?"

I shake my head. "I don't know, Stella."

"I should've known something terrible would happen. You

know, my mom used to say that the Elephant's Heart was cursed. That's the real reason why no one has found it. They were smart enough not to look. Am I like them, like my parents . . . putting myself, putting treasure, before everyone else?"

"No."

"This is *my* fault. I don't know what Ted was thinking when he went out on his own, but I do know that he was upset when he left and that's on me. Whether what happened was intentional, or he was trying to prove something to me by finding the Heart, it's still *because* of me. None of this would've ever happened if I hadn't brought us here, if I hadn't forced everyone to go on these stupid treasure hunts year after year."

"You didn't force anyone, Stella. We all wanted to be here. And sometimes things go very wrong and it's not under our control."

"You don't get it. How am I supposed to be okay if he's not? If I'm responsible for this?"

"I don't have an answer, but I actually understand. I know it's not the same, but that fight with my dad that I told you about, the one at the conference where I told him off and had security kick him out . . ." I swallow. I can do this. I can admit to her what I've done. I run my hands through my hair. "He died on the subway ride home from the convention center. I couldn't even protect myself without doing damage."

"Huck . . ."

"And this situation . . . I am more to blame than you are. I should've just been honest and stayed away. But I couldn't. My weakness set this in motion."

She hugs her knees to her chest and shakes her head. "Why did you come back?"

"Because I love you. I love you more than anything or anyone I've ever known. I could go, be sent away, leave a hundred times over and I would never not go back to you. I would follow you anywhere. They all would follow you anywhere, even if you didn't ask."

She turns to me. "And that makes it better?"

"You don't see. *You* make it better. You made my life better just by appearing, by being in it, and I know the others feel that way too."

She sniffs and nods sadly. "He said he loves me. But you knew that."

I look down. "Yeah, I did . . ."

"You knew in Iceland. Like you wrote in the book."

She finally read it, but this isn't how I'd wanted it to go when I wrote it. I hadn't thought it through. I wanted to confess how much I loved her, how I wished I'd stayed. My eyes are starting to sting and I squeeze them shut, willing myself to keep it together. I'm worried about Ted—even though we argued and fought, I still care about him. He's my friend. But I'm also afraid for Stella . . . she's already been through so much.

"I didn't want to leave you," I tell her. "I just . . . I could tell how much Ted cared about you, and I owe him so much. I spent my whole life being told how stupid I was, how everything I did was wrong or not good enough. Ted was the first person who didn't believe that. He's never given a fuck what anyone thinks, other than you, honestly. The day I told my dad I wanted to be a writer, he laughed in my face. That night, Ted and I went up to the roof at school and came up with the character of Clark. He was the guy we thought we'd be when we grew up, not like my dad, somebody brave and special. I didn't write him then, not for years. I kept trying and failing, and Ted cheered me on. He pushed me. He encouraged me to write what I knew . . . Clark. So you see, he's the reason why I'm an author. Everything good in my life—even you—is because of Ted. How could I get in the way of his happiness? I couldn't. I had to step aside for him, even though it meant sacrificing my own happiness. That's the thing; he's wild and reckless, but he will do absolutely anything for the people that he loves, and I owed him the same."

Stella nods. "That's true."

"There's really no one like him. He makes me so fucking angry sometimes; you know he clocked me in the jaw and knocked me clear off the boat earlier? Doesn't matter. I love that guy." My voice breaks a little at the end. A tear rolls down Stella's cheek. "Maybe if I'm being totally honest, a piece of me believed that if you had to choose between me and him, I wouldn't stand a chance."

"What made it different this time? *Is* it different? You really meant to stay in Key West?" Her voice is quiet.

"Yes, I stayed. I ran here. You're like gravity, Stella, impossible to resist."

"Yeah, well, gravity is also what makes planes fall out of the sky."

"No one said I was good at analogies." I give her a wry smile and take her hand in mine.

She leans her head on my shoulder.

"You asked me if this time is different. Do you think it is? Now that you know everything . . . does it change things?"

Stella is quiet for a long time. A gentle breeze lifts her hair from her neck. "I don't know."

My heart gives a squeeze in my chest.

"I don't know if I want to keep searching or walk away from this thing I've shaped my life around. If I'm completely honest with myself, I think maybe I was always searching for the Heart because I thought if I found it, they'd have to see, and they'd come back for me. If I stopped searching, I'd lose them too, for good. It seems so ridiculous now after everything that's happened. I want to fix things with Ted."

I nod. I don't know what to say.

"It doesn't change things between us."

"I understand." I breathe a sigh.

She reaches up and cups my face with her hand. "I think I loved you even before we met, Huck Sullivan, and I still do, with my whole heart. I'm not sure that there's anything that could ever change that. I may be afraid, and lash out or push you away, because I don't know how to do this, but I know that I love you."

I press my lips to her forehead, her lips.

"What's going to happen now?"

"We wait until you're ready," I tell her, "and then we get in a car and go to the hospital."

Stella looks over at me.

"I know you're scared, but we're going to face this together." I wasn't sure what I could say before and wanted to avoid promises I couldn't keep, but now I'm feeling hopeful for the first time. Against all odds, she loves me. I just know. "He's going to be okay," I say.

"How do you know that? I'm not sure, and I'm the optimist between us."

"Oh, I'm a realist. Teddy is too full of spitfire and sass to die on us. He's going to outlive us all, irritating us with his antics until we go before him. He's going to live just to give us a hard time about this next season."

"I don't think I'm ready yet."

"Then I'll just sit here beside you until you are."

FORTY-SIX

Stella

"I look good in a hospital gown; don't you think, Nurse Roberta?"

"You look like someone who needs to calm down."

"That's a yes."

"Get back in that bed."

"Seriously," Gus says, "get back in bed, man. You're flashing your bare ass to all of us, including poor Nurse Roberta."

Teddy climbs back under the covers obediently. I stand in the doorway watching this scene unfold.

"It's a very nice ass, okay?" Gus adds. "Happy now?"

"Delighted."

"Are you going to eat that pudding?" Zoe asks.

It feels like old times, but everything is different. I register the moment that Teddy sees me, the way his expression changes. Zoe and Gus turn around and spot me, then they act weird and slink out of the room with some sort of made-up excuse about needing oyster crackers to go with the pudding and really needing to find some deodorant.

Zoe catches my eye on her way out and gives my hand an encouraging squeeze.

The inertia is difficult to overcome. I stand, fixed in the doorway, for what feels like a long time.

"Well, this is awkward," Nurse Roberta says. "I think I have a few urine collection bags that need to be emptied." She brushes past me, and the movement jars me into motion. I step into the room.

"I'm sorry," I say.

Teddy pulls his blanket up. "Don't do that, Stell."

"I really am. I was just angry and upset. I didn't mean what I said, and I definitely didn't mean for you to go out and get hurt."

Teddy looks at me. "I know you didn't. You are a kindhearted softie underneath it all. Look, I deserved what you said. I messed things up massively. With me and you and Huck and you. I never should've gotten involved."

"I get it."

"I'm an adult, Stell. I need to start acting like it. I could've told you I had feelings for you at any time and left it up to you to make your choice. Instead, I tried to manipulate the situation, and you, so that I was the only choice. You were right, a friend wouldn't do that. That sucked."

"Kind of," I admit, perching on the edge of his hospital bed. "But I'm still your friend. And I'm really glad that you're okay."

"Actually, I'm not." He looks down at the covers, and I bite my lip, braced for bad news. "The doctors say that I am . . . a giant asshole."

"Jesus, Ted!" I whack him on the arm.

"Fair. Sorry. I'm just a little heartbroken, and semi-traumatized by this experience. I need humor to cope. Besides, I'm pretty sure Nurse Roberta put something in my IV line. And I did not like being alone with my thoughts in that hyperbaric chamber. I don't do alone, and I don't do thoughts. Especially of the contrite nature." He smooths his blanket.

We're quiet for a stretch.

"I really wanted you to love me back, Stell." He sighs.

"I know."

"To be clear, what happened . . . that was an accident. Zoe's already given me the cry-for-help lecture. It was nothing like that, I promise. I just thought I'd go out and try to find the Heart, that maybe if I did, you'd forgive me. I wasn't feeling good and I started to head up when I blacked out. I guess Huck's right that I take stupid risks sometimes. I mean, I risked my friendship with you, with him, and myself all in a span of twenty-four hours."

"That's pretty impressive, even for you." I smile at Ted and lean close to kiss his cheek.

"I heard someone had their pudding stolen by a pregnant lady and could use a replacement." Huck's standing in the doorway holding out a pudding cup. Teddy looks at him and that pudding like he's offering up a $500 million rare red diamond heart.

"You look like you lost a fight," Ted says.

"You should see the other guy."

"I hear that guy is really sorry about the things he said, and for putting you in such a shitty position. He'd get it if you didn't let this one go."

Huck shakes his head, then walks over and wraps his arms around Teddy. "I'm just glad you're alive, man. If you can get past it, then I definitely can."

"Hell yeah. It would take more than a fight over some girl to break up our lifelong bromance."

"Wait a second!" I gasp.

"*Some girl* was a poor choice of words," Ted says. "One amazing woman?"

"That's not it . . . Huck said a pregnant lady stole your pudding cup."

"I did say that." Huck's mouth curls into a grin.

"Zoe's pregnant?!" I cover my face with my hand. "That's why she never dived, and was mainlining saltines and wearing those caftans the whole time? How did I miss that?"

"I mean, you kind of missed a lot of really obvious stuff," Ted says. Then he laughs, a full, deep, mischievous Teddy laugh that is so glorious I want to cry. He's going to be fine, and we are going to be okay. "No wonder you dragged us around looking for the same treasure for so many years . . . so much of my youth and my bank account squandered by your obliviousness . . ."

"Hey!"

"I wouldn't change a thing," he says. "Except, you know, like a couple of minor details."

I lean over and squeeze his face in my hands.

"I take it by this affectionate gesture that you forgive me."

"I hope you don't mind me saying this, Ted, but I hear Clark Casablanca was half your idea and I know you love this line so it seems only fitting to tell you that"—I lean close and whisper—"'you're a devil, who often deserves to have some sense delivered by the smack of a delicate hand. But I'll forgive you every time.'"

"Now, now," Ted says. "While I'm over the freaking moon to know that you forgive my past and any future indiscretions, and I did indeed cocreate the famous Clark so I'm quite fond of him, I'm still a little raw here for you to be quoting Sully's books at me. Frankly, I don't know that mean suits you, Stella. And you don't want to upset Nurse Roberta. I think she's got a little crush on me."

"Smart lady," I say.

"Should we call her in so you two can be alone?" Huck asks.

"Now don't get sassy there, Sully. I've keenly observed Nurse Roberta when she gave me my sponge bath and I'm fairly certain that she's got a better right hook than I do based on her forearms."

Huck grins and holds up his hands in surrender. "Point taken. I'm glad you're alright, Theodore. You had us really worried there."

"*Us?* C'mon, guys. Give me a little time to get used to this before you start pet-naming each other. I promise, by next season, I will be fully on board with whatever this is. Who knows, maybe I'll bring my own guest star on the next search. Huck, didn't you say you knew Scarlett Johansson? What do you say, guys? Next summer—Blackbeard?"

I turn to Huck and bite my lip. "Actually, I think I might be done searching for a while. I'm ready to find my own thing."

"You?" Teddy exclaims in total disbelief.

Huck steps over and threads his fingers between mine. "I was just thinking the same thing. You know what might be nice? Spending some time getting booped on the leg by Icelandic sheep."

"Life-changing, even."

EPILOGUE

Huck

"We've got a real treat for you this morning, folks," the host says. "He's the bestselling author of *The Fortune Files*, and she's the world's most famous modern treasure hunter. Huck Sullivan and Stella Moore."

The audience applause is thunderous, and I swallow hard. I glance over at Stella. She must sense the panic that's rising like the tide inside of me, because she squeezes my hand gently and smiles. *You've got this*, she mouths.

I shake my head. But she only kisses me. "Listen, if you want to run, I'm wearing sneakers under this dress."

This calms me instantly, and we stride onto the stage together and take our seats.

"This is so exciting," the host says. "Huck, I'm told that this is your first interview in years."

"It is."

"Well, we're delighted that you are joining us here on *Good Morning America* to talk about your newest book, *The Diamond Heart*. And you've brought your subject-matter expert, Stella Moore, who is a legend in her own right after finding the *San Miguel* treasure ship last year. Now, we're told that this book features our two favorite heartthrobs, Lucky and Finn, on another adventure to find a fabled red diamond that's bigger than an elephant's heart. I'm dying to know if this is based on a true story."

Stella laughs.

"There's some element of truth in all of my books. I have been lucky enough to go on a couple of searches with Stella and her crew and learned so much from them; not just technical terms, but about history and tenacity and the spirit of treasure hunting. I pull all of it into my writing."

"Are you saying that you *didn't* find the Elephant's Heart?"

Stella and I glance at each other. I clear my throat. "*The Diamond Heart* is absolutely a work of fiction."

"What about your relationship? We recently heard a rumor that you two bought a sheep ranch on an island together."

"Our relationship is anything but fictional. We're very happy," Stella says.

I don't know if she knows what I have planned as soon as the show is over and our plane takes us back home when she says this, but she must know it's coming. We've been on this course since the moment we met. Ted should already be there with his girlfriend, Molly. He met her a few months ago at a cookie shop down the street from the church where he's been attending AA meetings once a week for the last year and a half. They bonded over a shared love of dance and the sea and have been inseparable since. She's good for him.

Zoe and Gus might be a little late since they are now wrangling Miguel, who started walking a few weeks ago and is already zooming everywhere at top speed. The kid is magnificent. Strong, with a booming voice and fantastic laugh like his dad, and bright-eyed and brilliant like his mom. I've spent the past few weeks shut up in my office at my desk planning the whole thing with all of them on the phone and via email, the row of sheep figurines across my desk, all shapes and sizes (including the one whose head we had to glue back on) watching, overseeing everything.

Before we'd left for this interview, taking a boat and a plane to get to the city, I'd gotten up at sunrise while Stella, Lord Whiskerpants, Mewowzer, and our newest tabby kitten, Sam, purred away in the darkness. I snuck down to the beach and buried the treasure in a hidden spot that matched the one on the map an illustrator friend of mine and Jim's had drawn just for the occasion. It's a quintessential ancient treasure map, with aged edges, beautiful calligraphy, and a heart marking the spot instead of an X.

"I have to ask you, Huck," the host says, "where do you get your inspiration for these stories and these characters?"

I turn to Stella and take her hand, my smile deepening. "The very first idea I ever had came to me and my best friend, Ted, when we were teenagers at school together. That was Clark Casablanca. I didn't have another good idea for a long time after that. I'd honestly given up on writing or ever being inspired again. And then *she* walked up to me at a bar in Iceland, and the rest is history."

"By *she*, I'm assuming you mean Stella?"

"Absolutely."

"And do you plan to write more?"

"I think so. Time will tell. We're actually working on a secret project together that might keep us both pretty occupied for a while."

"How about you, Stella? You became the most famous treasure hunter in recent history after you found the *San Miguel*. The gold and uncut gems were worth substantially more than the *Atocha* and the rest of the 1715 treasure fleet. Do you plan to keep searching for new treasures?"

"I think I've found what I was looking for," Stella says. "I wouldn't rule it out completely, but for now my search has ended. It had always been my parents' dream, and I'm finally ready to find my own dream. Whether that's treasure or something else—"

"Sheep farming, maybe?"

"Maybe." She smiles, and my heart flips in my chest.

When the interview is over, we head home, resting in each other's arms during the journey back to the island. "You did so well," Stella says to me as she plays with my hair.

"I didn't think she'd come right out and ask about the Heart."

"Me either. I think we struck a very nice balance of bullshit." Her laugh sparkles, and I can't help but press my lips to her freckles.

After Ted recovered and we returned to the *Lucky Strike* to finish the salvage, Zoe and Gus and Ted went back to their normal lives. Stella and I stayed in that little house in Truman Annex and dedicated our days to relearning each other, writing our story, and finishing the search. It took us eight months to find the Heart diamond. Hundreds of strolls from our front porch to the wharf, where we got on a smaller boat, zipped up each other's wetsuits, and navigated out to the *San Miguel* treasure field to dive. We marveled at the blue tangs and learned how to redirect sharks to keep each other safe. Sometimes we'd find another bit of the ancient Stolen Treasure that we'd missed during the original salvage and we'd call Gus to give him an update about the discovery that he could add to the museum display. We'd return to the boat to watch the sunset while we enjoyed a slice of Key lime pie. And then one day after a late spring storm, Stella got that tingling sensation in her hands and the Elephant's Heart revealed itself to us. We vowed not to tell anyone outside our group until we found its rightful home.

"You're a real trooper for making the trip, Stella. Jim's going to be elated. I told him he could send Key lime pie as a thank-you."

Our home comes into view and Stella and I buckle our seatbelts for the landing. She sequeezes my hand. "I'll take the pie, but it's not necessary. I never would've sent you on an interview alone. You're stuck with me."

It turns out we didn't need the Heart for the island and the sheep. Between the books, movie, and our finders' fees, we had more than enough. Enough to buy Hulla and start our little ranch. We wake most mornings and stroll the fields, checking on our little charges, picking wildflowers that Stella pushes into their wool before booping her nose to theirs. We eat fresh fruit and take the boat out and dive and make love on secluded beaches.

I couldn't have imagined a better ending to our story, and this is only the beginning. The one-of-a-kind engagement ring I had made might look similar to the massive red diamond we tucked away for safekeeping, but it definitely isn't cursed. It's waiting on the beach in front of our home, buried in a replica of Gunnarsson's treasure box for her to find. Then I'll promise her forever in front of our best friends, the people we love, the family we found and cherish, who cherish us too, who never leave, who know our flaws and love us anyway.

The island jasmine is blooming, perfuming the ocean air with its scent. Ted, Zoe, and Gus have lit the candles for us on the beach, and when Stella and I wander out there and I hand her the map, she already knows. Of course she does. This is Stella. When she's about to find something important, she feels it in her hands. She humors me, racing around, figuring out the clues, using her fingers to dig the box out of the soft white sand.

After she says yes, our friends come out to join us. Ted surprises everyone with a live steel drum band and we dance beneath the stars.

"Well done," Zoe says to me. She throws her arms around us

and Gus bops over with Miguel on his hip. "I'm so happy for you both."

A few feet away, Molly and Teddy are breaking it down with all their worst moves. "Do we need to worry that she might pull a muscle?" Stella asks.

"God, they really are a perfect match," I say, and twirl the love of my life around in the moonlight. Stella grins at me. She's never looked so beautiful or so happy.

Zoe stops and stares at us. "Um, hold up just a moment, you two. How many secrets are you keeping right now? Because if I'm not mistaken, Ms. Stella Moore soon-to-be Sullivan . . . are you rocking a sophisticated muumuu right now?"

ACKNOWLEDGMENTS

I want to start off by asking for your forgiveness. Treasure hunting is a brutal business that often skirts the law and operates in gray areas, and I've taken more than a few liberties for the sake of the story. The poems of Gunnarsson were inspired by Egil's Saga, which tells the tale of Egil Skallagrímsson, a Viking who came to Iceland and may have hidden a trove of silver somewhere in the country. I should make it clear that even though Stella and her crew use metal detectors, they aren't allowed in many places, including Iceland. So please don't get any ideas, and mind the foliage. The Elephant's Heart is fictional of course, but many of the details of the ships that sunk off the coast of Florida were based on the 1715 Treasure Fleet. I would be remiss if I didn't acknowledge the many indigenous people who suffered for the spoils of greed and imperialism that now rest at the bottom of the ocean, and for the things that are found, which modern nations engage in legal battles over. Like treasure hunting, writing a book is often a rather messy act of faith. I'm sure there may be some things that I haven't gotten perfect, but I hope at least that you're entertained.

Thank you to . . .

The readers. It's all for you.

Sharon Pelletier, my literary agent, voice of reason, and constant advocate. Also Lauren Abramo, Nataly Gruender, Michaela Whatnall.

At Berkley, my wonderful editor Kerry Donovan, Chelsea Pascoe, Elisha Katz, Genni Eccles, Mary Baker, and the art, marketing, and sales teams.

My writer friends, who keep me encouraged and inspired: Elizabeth Everett, Ali Hazelwood, Mazey Eddings, Serena Kaylor, Sarah Grunder Ruiz.

My parents for instilling in me creativity and grit.

My family, my strength, my reason for everything—Tom, Greta, Elliot—this only happens because of you.

HEART
MARKS
the
SPOT

LIBBY HUBSCHER

READERS GUIDE

DISCUSSION QUESTIONS

1. Stella and Huck meet by chance on the other side of the world, and both wonder at times if fate brought them together. Do you believe in fate?

2. Stella chases the treasure that drove her family apart. Why do you think she does that? Have you ever focused on a goal to prove something to yourself or others?

3. Huck hurt Stella and hid the truth from her about why he left. Do you think what he did was understandable, and he deserves forgiveness? Have you ever kept a secret to protect someone else, even at great cost to yourself?

4. *Heart Marks the Spot* is told in two distinct parts—a past and a present. Why do you think the author chose to structure the story this way, and what did you think about this choice?

5. Stella, Zoe, Teddy, and Gus keep taking their summer trips even though they haven't found a major treasure. Why do you think they stick together and keep trying after all these years? What do you think makes friendships last?

6. Huck's latest book was clearly inspired by Stella and used as a way to express his feelings and explain why he left. How do you feel about Huck's approach, and why?

7. Teddy and Stella have a special but complex relationship. What do you think about their dynamic? Have you ever had a friendship where the lines were blurred?

8. Huck struggles with feelings of inadequacy and failure, both in his personal and his professional life. How do you think they influenced his relationship with Stella and the choices he made during both phases of their relationship?

9. Zoe and Gus have their own roles and relationship happening in the story. Do you think they were good role models for Stella and Huck? Why or why not?

10. At its core, *Heart Marks the Spot* is about hope even in the face of heartache and disappointment. Were you able to relate to elements of Stella's story? Do you believe that happy endings are possible?

Continue reading for a preview of

PLAY FOR ME

Available now!

I lost everything I loved in the span of twenty-four hours. Well, nearly everything, since Dad was still safely tucked away in Sommerset Meadows, but that's a different story. Heartbreak comes in all forms.

For me, baseball went first.

My home in Boston and cannoli from Vitales in the North End quickly followed.

I was eating my feelings in the form of a chocolate chip cannoli when a man holding a sheet cake paused to look me over, and upon recognizing me, he promptly spit in my face. He was wearing an autographed Big Papi jersey and an expression that can only be described as murderous. They say hell hath no fury like a woman scorned . . . well, a woman scorned has nothing on a Red Sox fan who just stumbled upon the trainer responsible for ruining the team's World Series run stuffing her face with pastry.

"That's for benching Iwasaki!" he hollered. "You cost us the series!"

The rabid fan couldn't have known that only two hours earlier I'd been forced to resign in front of a room full of middle-aged men in ill-fitting polo shirts. He wouldn't have seen me sitting on the T next to a cardboard box full of my things, willing myself not to cry. And he definitely had no earthly notion that I'd arrived home to find the rest of my worldly possessions packed away in a matching luggage set my boyfriend, Patrick, had originally bought for me to use on our trip to Zurich in January. As the team doctor, he hadn't taken kindly to me calling his medical judgment into question. He'd carved me out of our shared brownstone and his life with speed and surgical precision.

I didn't fault any of them for being angry, even this guy. I was a Red Sox fan, after all, one who grew up watching every home game while my dad worked as a custodian in Fenway; the agony of defeat had rocked me to my core more than once. But I wasn't at my best, and my cheek was damp with spittle, which is probably why I exploded out of my chair, knocked the cake box out of the man's hand, and smashed my half-eaten cannoli into his face.

"I'd do it again!" I yelled. Cake splattered on the floor around us. It was completely out of character—the aggression, I mean, not the thing that had brought me to that moment; still, I meant what I said. At only twenty-two, Iwasaki was already the kind of pitcher that comes along once every hundred years. He'd had an ulnar collateral ligament sprain that the medical team had been treating with stem cells and plasma injections, but his body wasn't ready. I could see it in his face, the way he grimaced and guarded his arm when no one else was looking. Just hours before the game, he'd been drenched with sweat after throwing a couple of easy pitches.

"How bad is it?" I'd asked him.

He'd shaken his head. "Not bad," he'd said. "Just nerves." As if the league's best pitcher had ever been that nervous a day in his life. I gave him a look. "I'm good," he lied.

What ensued was a series of fights with what felt like everyone in the organization from Patrick to the GM, but in the end Iwasaki went back on the injured list, and I went on a list too—one that started with "black" and ended with "balled."

"It'll be fine," I'd assured everyone. "Morano is one hundred percent and he's looking great."

The backup pitcher, Morano, was solid. The pitching coach agreed, and everyone conceded; no problem, I thought. I am an optimist.

Morano choked. Epically.

The Phillies hadn't just beaten us; they'd humiliated us in Fenway Park.

The man who'd been on the receiving end of my cannoli was screaming, a strangled animal sound. Espresso cups stilled. Around us, the bakery patrons fell silent. There were no shouting spectators here egging us on. A woman with a small child cowered, shielding the toddler with her body. The worker behind the counter who had winked at me when he handed over my food now picked up a phone to make a call. I retreated, accidentally placing my shoe directly in the middle of a chunk of cake. I slipped on the mass of buttercream and nearly fell. Frantically, my arms windmilled, and I grabbed for anything to keep myself upright. I caught the man's shirt; a button popped off and thwacked against my forehead.

I looked up. The man's screaming ceased. He reached up and wiped the cream from his face. A glop of frosting landed in my hair—pale white against my deep red waves. I had a sudden, sickening realization that there was no team behind me, ready to get in the mix, and there never would be again. I was on my own, and my life in baseball—and at my favorite bakery—was over.

There's no bullpen in the North End, no dugout to cool off in, and since, as I learned later, the delectable flaky pastry scratched the man's cornea, I spent the better part of the afternoon in a holding cell in the Boston district A-1 police station.

I was braiding my hair and trying to figure out how I was going to tell my dad about my fall from grace when my best friend, Astrid, appeared, looking like a cross between a blonde bombshell with a foul mouth and a glorious angel. She was wearing oversized black sunglasses, ripped high-waisted jeans, and a tube top with puffed sleeves that revealed her pale midriff. She might have been the only person over the age of thirty who could pull a look like that off. Astrid was warm and disarming, and at the sight of her, relief pooled in me and that feeling of utter loneliness dissipated.

She tossed her blonde waves over her shoulder and removed her sunglasses.

"Sophie, in all of our years of friendship, I never once envisioned having to bail you out of jail," she said, tucking the glasses into her purse. "I feel like we've reached a whole new level of closeness."

"Thank you for coming." I smiled; I couldn't help it.

A cop unlocked the door and gestured for me to get out with a quick jerk of her head.

"It better be a good story," Astrid said, folding me in her long arms. "Was it a pervert? I love it when a perv gets what's coming to him."

I grimaced. "I *was* defending my honor. Sort of." I eyed the room. From the glares I was getting, the police were also Red Sox fans. It was Dunkin' Donuts with a side of dirty looks in there. "I didn't mean to hurt him."

"Let's get you out of here," Astrid said. "I know everyone loves Iwasaki, but geez." She raised her voice. "It's just a game."

"Astrid, shhh. Don't antagonize them." She slung one arm

around my shoulders and together we speed-walked toward the exit.

"So, where to?" Astrid asked once we were outside beneath the old blue station sign, standing in the shadow of the brick behemoth. "Home?"

"About that . . . Patrick's pretty mad." I glanced up at the brick building. The architect must've had a mandate to put in as few windows as possible.

Astrid's eyes narrowed. "How mad?"

"'I can't be with someone who would question me at work. It's over' mad. At least that's what he wrote in his note."

"Wait, you haven't talked to him? He left a note?"

"It was taped to my suitcase."

"You've been together for what . . . four years? I know you said things had kind of cooled off a bit, but that's beyond cold. Okay, well . . . I never liked him anyway. His nurse was an extra with me on *ShadowWorld* back in March and she said he's a dick to all the office staff."

"You're just telling me this now?"

"Yeah, game night's been wicked awkward."

Astrid was trying to cheer me up, so I obliged her, but the laugh I managed to conjure was paper-thin. My stomach swirled. I wasn't sure whether I was going to burst into tears or throw up, but some kind of dramatic emotion was threatening to surface.

"Could I stay with you for a bit?" I asked.

"I would love to be your roommate again, Soph, but I'm headed to Toronto in two days for that film I told you about. Since I'll be gone for a while, I sublet the place to a family of four. You should see the baby. Cheeks for days. Anyway, you can crash until they arrive on Thursday, but after that, you'll have to figure something else out."

"Okay, no problem. Two days is fine. It's great, actually. I'm sure I can figure out something. How hard could it be to find a new place and a new job, right? I mean, this is Boston, the land of opportunity."

Astrid wrinkled her nose. "Especially now that you've been fired and charged with assault."

"I don't think I was actually charged. It's all kind of a blur."

"I think I know exactly what this situation calls for," Astrid said.

I peeked up at her. "You do?"

"Yup, I do. I'm going to feed you and get you really drunk."

"Seriously? I don't think that's the best idea."

"Good thing I'm in charge now, because you need to drown your sorrows, and I do my most optimal thinking when I'm hammered."

I opened my mouth to argue, but Astrid's legs were longer than mine, and she was already several steps ahead of me. "Let's go, Cannoli Kid," she called over her shoulder. "I promise you, by the time I leave for Toronto, we'll have this sorted out."

Astrid's ideas for sorting things out were generally questionable, even in the best of times. But lobster rolls from Neptune Oyster and unlimited Sam Adams Porch Rocker in Astrid's rooftop garden with a view of the Charles River felt like an inspired choice, even if she'd claimed to have selected lobster rolls because they were soft, in case my temper flared again. It was a beautiful evening: we couldn't see the stars, but the lights of our beloved city twinkled and the air turned cooler. The beer and the buttery lobster smoothed out the rough edges of my horrible day.

Astrid leaned forward in her lounge chair. "What about another team?" she said. "The Lowell Spinners, maybe?"

I shook my head. "The Spinners have Ricky Phillips as their trainer and he's fantastic. Besides, there's no point deluding myself; I'm tainted goods right now. A job in pro baseball isn't going to happen. At least not until everyone forgets about this—*if* they forget—or some kind of miracle takes place."

"It's such bullshit," Astrid said, slamming her beer down. "You said if he pitched he probably would have blown out his elbow completely. You were just doing your job. It's not your fault Morano had a bad night. Did they fire *him*?"

"I see the point you're trying to make and I love you for it, but I'm sure Morano's getting his fair share of abuse right now. And it happens. The pressure he was under was immense. Everyone forgets that, at the end of the day, athletes are people too." I pulled at the label on my bottle.

"I know! Morano is *definitely* a person. A fine person. I enjoyed watching him wind up for every terrible pitch he threw last night," Astrid said, mischief twinkling in her gaze. "How about this? Maybe you could come to Toronto with me. I could be your sugar mommy."

I squinted at Astrid and took a long draw from my beer. "You are an angel, but you're not really my type."

She tossed her hair over her shoulder and batted her eyelashes. "I thought I was everyone's type."

"You're too beautiful."

"That's fair."

We opened new bottles and clinked them together, then fell into the kind of comfortable silence that only longtime friends can have.

"Besides, I can't leave Dad without a visitor for that long. But I do think you're onto something. It might be nice to get out of the city for a bit," I said. "A girl can only be spit on so many times before she needs a change of scene . . . and a new bakery. And by so many, I mean one. Once was one time too many. Plus, I'm pretty sure I'm banned from Vitales until the end of time. And the idea of running into Patrick at Trader Joe's is not appealing."

Astrid grabbed another lobster roll and took a bite.

"I've got it," she said, her mouth still half-full. I waited for her to swallow. "Where's the perfect place to hide away and reinvent yourself?"

"Is that supposed to mean something to me?"

Astrid narrowed her eyes.

I held my hands up. "Okay. I don't know, Vegas?"

"That's ridiculous. Vegas is where you go to see a Britney Spears concert and somehow wake up married and broke. No. The place you go to hide is New Hampshire."

"How many beers have you had?" I asked. "You go to New Hampshire to hike and buy stuff without sales tax. It's not exactly transformative."

"Not true. And also, not enough beers. But that's beside the point." She pulled out another bottle and used the side of the farmhouse table to thwack the cap off in one smooth and slightly vicious motion. "Remember how I got into some trouble junior year?"

"Yeah?" How could I forget? Astrid's parents went through a brutal divorce when she was sixteen, and her coping strategy had been her mother's painkillers and a pretty bad shoplifting habit, culminating in an actual chase through Faneuil Hall, of all places. Her parents had shipped her off to boarding school in New Hampshire for the rest of high school. At the time, I'd been devastated and braced myself for what were sure to be the loneliest two years of my life. About a month after she'd left, Dad let me borrow his car to meet her in Concord at Bread & Chocolate, and sitting across from her, I could see that she was happier and more herself than she'd been in a long time. So I was thankful, and content to count down the days until we could be roommates at college together.

While I'd been lost in memory, Astrid had fiddled with her phone. She thrust it in front of my face.

I squinted at the bright screen until the words *The Monadnock School* and a mountain scene came into focus. "The boarding school you went to? I'm not following."

"I donate a boatload of money every year to the theater department, so I get all the emails. I remember seeing one recently that said they had a position open for a trainer for the school year that's already underway."

"Isn't it an arts school?"

"They have sports teams. They're just not very good."

"'Not very good'? What does that mean?"

"They suck, okay, but that's not important. This is your answer."

"I feel like I'm missing something. How does a training job at a school in New Hampshire solve my problems?"

"Boarding school," Astrid corrected.

"And?"

"And everyone on staff at a boarding school gets housing, smart-ass." Astrid leaned back in the chair she was sitting in, a smug smile spreading across her face.

It took a few more beers before I was convinced. Astrid waxed poetic about how much she'd loved it there. The nature, the community, the fresh mountain air, the hours of therapy with the school's psychologist. It had changed her life, she said. She'd gotten clean, made a handful of lifelong friendships, and fostered her love of the arts, which had led her to her career. A really good career. The kind of career that got you a rooftop garden with the view we were currently enjoying. Acting was what Astrid was put on this earth to do. Kind of like me and working for the Red Sox.

God, Astrid was compelling. No wonder people loved seeing her on-screen. The way she spoke about the school, I started to wonder whether it might change my off-course life too. Also, truth be told, the beers were going down a little too easily, and since I'm not a big drinker to begin with, they were hitting pretty hard.

"I'm a distinguished alumna," Astrid said. Energized by the drinks, she had started dancing around her roof and was doing something that looked like a cross between a runway pose and an arabesque. "With me as a reference, you'd be a shoo-in."

"Okay," I replied, trying not to slur.

"Really?"

I nodded. "I'll do it. How do I apply?"

"I can just email them from my phone. They'll probably want your CV or something later."

I thought maybe that should wait until morning, but Astrid was already pecking away.

"I told you I could solve the problem!" she said, triumphant.

"I never doubted you for a minute."

I woke in the morning, sore from sleeping on a small love seat and sticky hot from the sun blazing over the edge of the rooftop, forcing me to to shield my eyes. The evening had been exactly what I needed to feel better about the state of things, save for the severe hangover I was going to have to nurse.

Across from me, Astrid was splayed out on a sectional, her hair fanned out around her like a halo, a single pool of drool at the corner of her mouth. My stomach grumbled.

"Hey, Astrid," I whispered. "Want a bagel sandwich? I can go get us Dunkin's."

She sat up. "Best roommate ever," she said. "I need an iced coffee. Extra cream, extra sugar. And I want bacon on my sandwich."

Her phone pinged and she looked at the screen. "Guess what, buttercup," she said, stifling a yawn. "The job is yours if you want it."

Did I want it? I didn't know. In the car, I pulled up the school's website on my phone. A glance at the athletic program page was enough to make me question what on earth I'd been thinking letting Astrid even plant this seed. But by the time I'd finished my breakfast, I was pretty sure I was going to take it despite my ambivalence. Things usually worked themselves out—maybe I could turn their lackluster athletic program into something special or take the opportunity to do some cool research that would put me back in the big leagues. Plus, there weren't any other viable options, unless I wanted to crash on the recliner in Dad's room at Sommerset Meadows. There was nothing left for me here. At least not now, not until I could stage some sort of comeback. I'd figure it out. I always did. In the meantime, fresh mountain air and a free apartment couldn't hurt, *and*—you gotta love a good silver lining—I was already packed.

Photo by Thomas Hubscher

Libby Hubscher is an author and scientist. She studied biology at Bowdoin College in Brunswick, Maine, and holds a doctorate of philosophy in molecular toxicology from North Carolina State University. Her work has appeared online and in textbooks, scientific journals, and literary journals. Her short story "The Unwelcome Guest" was long-listed for the Wigleaf Top 50 in 2018. She lives in North Carolina with her husband, two young children, and a menagerie of pets.

VISIT LIBBY HUBSCHER ONLINE

LibbyHubscher.com

🦋 LibbyHubscher

📷 LibbyHubscher

f LibbyHubscher